As New

Books by Jennifer Dawson

As Good As New

The Name of the Game

The Winner Takes It All

Take a Chance on Me

Published by Kensington Publishing Corporation

As Good As New

JENNIFER DAWSON

WITHDRAWN

ZEBRA BOOKS
KENSINGTON PUBLISHING CORP.

http://www.kensingtonbooks.com

ZEBRA BOOKS are published by

Kensington Publishing Corp.
119 West 40th Street
New York, NY 10018

All Kensington titles, imprints and distributed lines are available at special quantity discounts for bulk purchases for sales promotion, premiums, fund-raising, educational or institutional use.

Special book excerpts or customized printings can also be created to fit specific needs. For details, write or phone the office of the Kensington Sales Manager. Attn.: Sales Department. Kensington Publishing Corp., 119 West 40th Street, New York, NY 10018. Phone: 1-800-221-2647.

Zebra and the Z logo Reg. U.S. Pat. & TM Off.

First Printing: April 2016
ISBN-13: 978-1-4201-4013-2
ISBN-10: 1-4201-4013-2

eISBN-13: 978-1-4201-4014-9
eISBN-10: 1-4201-4014-0

10 9 8 7 6 5 4 3 2 1

Printed in the United States of America

*To my two favorite people in the whole world,
my kids Jake and Jordyn.
Thank you for being the best kids
a mom could ever ask for.
I love you.*

Chapter One

Feet sore, mind weary, Penelope Watkins surveyed the crowded dance floor as one of her best friends tugged her hand and whined, "Please, come dance with me."

Penelope turned her attention to Sophie Kincaid with a heavy sigh. Sophie looked like a rogue Disney princess in a powder-blue, spaghetti-strapped dress that set off her blond hair and big, brown, doe eyes.

Was she the only person ready for the wedding of the century to end? She scanned the room, still crowded with guests. After midnight, the music had been cranked up to concert decibels and the dance floor was packed. Apparently, she was.

Despite the three Advils she'd taken, her head still ached. Unfortunately, she had two hours and fifteen minutes until she could take another dose, at which time she hoped to be in bed, asleep. At the thought of her fluffy comforter and pillow-top mattress, she groaned. All she wanted was to slip in under the soft down, the crisp white sheets, and close her eyes. But, as a bridesmaid at Shane and Cecilia Donovan's wedding, she had to stay until the bitter end. Not that she wasn't ecstatic for the couple, because, of course, she was. Shane wasn't only her boss, but one of her closest friends and the big brother she, as an only child, had never had. Penelope had also grown quite close to his new wife, Cecilia, and couldn't be happier Shane had finally met his match. She loved them and wished them nothing but happiness. She just wanted their wedding to be over so she could go home.

Penelope shook her head, glaring at Sophie's four-inch heels. "Aren't your feet killing you?"

"Hell no, come on. I need you to do a slutty little dance with me. I'm trying to drive Logan mad with lust." Sophie gripped Penelope's hand a little tighter and peered over her shoulder at the man in question, sighing.

Penelope couldn't blame her. Logan Buchanan was fantasy worthy. With sharp, watchful blue eyes, dark hair, and a commanding presence that filled a room, he was the kind of man a woman was supposed to get excited about.

Unfortunately, he had no effect on Penelope.

Nope, she had to be stubborn and pine away for the first boy she'd fallen in puppy love with at the age of six. If she'd had any brains at all, she would have befriended Tiffany White, who had all sisters, the first day of kindergarten. But no, she had to sit next to Maddie Donovan-Riley.

If Penelope had picked Tiffany, she'd probably be involved with a nice accountant who liked order and comfort as much as she did. She could almost picture that life where she and her fictitious significant other would discuss spreadsheets and the best task apps for their iPads over dinner. Unlike most people, she wasn't interested in excitement.

In her opinion boring was highly underrated.

But she wasn't involved with a nice accountant because, like the rest of the female population, she'd taken one look at Maddie's wild, reckless, completely unsuitable youngest brother and become instantly infatuated.

Up until then, she'd had the good sense to think boys were icky.

Unable to help herself, she scanned the room for the man in question. At six-five, Evan Donovan, pro football player and womanizing scoundrel, wasn't hard to pick out of a crowd, but he was nowhere to be found.

She took a drink of water. Good. At least she didn't have to look at the Barbie doll he'd brought to his brother's wedding. Penelope was still cringing at the girl with her minuscule dress, blond-mermaid-extensioned hair, and flotation-device breasts. Some football groupie, wannabe model, if Penelope had to guess.

Aka, his normal type. Otherwise known as Penelope's exact opposite.

She shook her head. No. She would not start down that road.

She turned back to Sophie, standing there expectantly, and smiled. "If you want to drive Logan crazy, I'm not your girl. We are strictly in the friend zone."

Besides, she wasn't really the type to drive men mad with lust. Sure, she was attractive enough with classic bone structure and well-formed features. Tired of wearing glasses, she'd treated herself to Lasik surgery six months ago and she'd been told by numerous dates that her blue eyes were startling against her rich, dark hair. At five-seven she had a nice, trim figure she kept in shape with workouts at the gym, yoga, and running along the lake-shore. Overall, she was a pretty woman and had nothing to complain about.

Sophie puffed out her lip in a pout that would sway most people but had little effect on Penelope. "Isn't this just my luck? Since I really wanted to cause a scene, I tried to coerce Gracie, but stupid James said no." Sophie released her grip on Penelope's wrist and threw her hands up in frustration. "And she listened! I mean, really, what is that? The whole world must be mad if the great Gracie Roberts has started listening to a mere man."

Since the woman in question might be one of the sexiest people on the planet, it was a smart choice on Sophie's part to rope her into her quest to seduce Logan. After all, Gracie had been known to bring grown men to their knees. Only Sophie hadn't factored the middle Donovan brother's hold on Gracie. A pairing that Penelope had never seen coming, but damned if it didn't seem to be working. James, a mild-mannered professor of forensic anthropology, hadn't tamed the sex goddess per se, but when he spoke, Gracie paid attention.

In sympathy, Penelope clucked her tongue. "What are you going to do? That's new love for you."

"Well, it's annoying." Sophie grabbed her hand again. "Now come dance."

"I've got a headache."

Sophie rolled her eyes. "I don't expect you to put out after."

Penelope laughed. God, she loved her friends. Needed them as a reminder to do something other than work. Remember how to have fun. It wasn't that she didn't like fun, she did.

It was only that so many other things required her attention. With her demanding work schedule and workaholic proclivities, fun wasn't a priority. And that's where Sophie and Maddie came in, to reset her priorities. Why, if it weren't for the two of them, Penelope would have spent her childhood getting into no trouble at all.

Well, except for that one thing Penelope refused to think about.

As if Maddie sensed her thoughts, she ran over to them, her heavy, auburn hair spilling from the topknot after the long night of dancing. The long skirts of the deep, jeweled purple bridesmaid dress that matched Penelope's, flounced as she came to a stop. Being the groom's sister and bride's sister-in-law, she'd had just as long a day as Penelope, only she seemed full of energy and not at all impatient for the wedding to wind down. She grinned. "What's up?"

Sophie huffed, jerking her thumb toward the dance floor. "Penelope won't dance with me so I can seduce Logan."

Maddie threw an arm around her and squeezed. "I'll dance with you. We'll give everyone a show."

Sophie's face lit with excitement. "Mitch will be jealous."

At the mention of her husband, Mitch Riley, Maddie laughed, and said in a sly voice, "I know. I'm in the mood for dirty sex, and this is just the kind of thing that sets him off." Maddie gave a little shudder, obviously thinking about the dirty things Mitch had apparently already done to her.

Penelope smiled at her two best friends. Okay, she needed to shake off this mood, put her headache aside, and go party it up with her girlfriends. With Maddie living in Revival, a small town hundreds of miles south of Chicago, they didn't get this chance very often, and Penelope refused to waste it.

Headache be damned. She'd just gulp a couple cups of coffee and dance.

She looked at her friends, wearing twin expressions filled with the same reckless, excited anticipation that had convinced her to ditch seventh period and hang out at the forest preserve with a bunch of bad boys from the public school. She smiled. "You guys go. I need to run to the ladies' room and then I'll come find you on the dance floor."

Maddie rocked on her heels. "Promise?"

"Yep. Cross my heart." Repeating the sacred promise of their youth.

Sophie winked and skipped off with Maddie, the two of them holding hands and laughing. A surefire sign they were up to no good, and Penelope had no doubt she'd return to find them gyrating on the dance floor causing quite the scene. If Logan would notice was anyone's guess, but Maddie's husband was bound to enjoy himself.

Penelope weaved through the crowd, pausing a few times to talk to a coworker, before she finally reached the hallway. Instead of heading to the bathroom, she veered right and headed toward the balcony, needing to clear her head.

She pushed open the door and the cool spring air brushed her cheeks and ruffled the tendrils of hair that had fallen from her twist. She breathed in deep, her pounding temples instantly easing with the music now only a distant, muffled beat. Small clusters of people filled the expanse of the balcony, enjoying the first hints of warm weather after a long, frigid Chicago winter.

Penelope searched the area for a secluded spot where she could be alone. She didn't want to talk. She wanted quiet. To stand by herself and let the night air and skyline soothe her aching mind. It took some searching, but she finally found what she was looking for: tucked into the corner, a concrete structure partially obstructed the view, which left it deserted. She walked over to it and slipped into the tiny alcove, resting her elbows on the rails. She closed her eyes, and as a breeze blew over her skin, sighed in relief. Finally, some quiet.

And *that's* when she heard a female giggle, followed by a distinct male chuckle.

Oh God, please don't let it be him. Anyone but him. Penelope's shoulders stiffened and she craned her neck, dread already pooling in the pit of her stomach. When her gaze locked with Evan's, she wasn't the least bit surprised.

Even in the dim glow of the lights, she could see his vivid green eyes boring into hers. His tux jacket was undone, along with his shirt, exposing the cords of his neck and barest hint of his strong chest. With dark hair and strong, chiseled features he was so sinfully gorgeous it was nauseating. He was also wild and reckless. He didn't care about anything but football and screwing as many women as possible. Not her type at all.

The girl he'd brought was on her knees, working at his belt buckle. She peered over at Penelope and smiled with glossy, over-collagened lips. "Oops, busted."

Evan's attention didn't leave Penelope's and his lips curled into something that resembled a half sneer. "Hey, little Penny."

She wanted to scream. She hated when he called her that. She clenched her hands and thought about committing acts of violence. She wanted to kick him, throw a drink in his face, or maybe grab the girl hovering at his crotch by the hair and scalp her.

But that wasn't the role she played. No, she was a calm, rational, logical person. She swallowed her emotions and turned, keeping her expression cool and impassive. She flicked a dismissive glance at the woman who didn't have the decency to get off her knees, and smirked. "Evan. I see your girlfriend's mom let her out past curfew."

This wasn't the first time this had happened, and it wouldn't be the last. Sometimes Penelope wondered if he did it on purpose. Just to hurt her. Although, in fairness, that probably gave him too much credit. Penelope doubted he thought that deeply.

The girl rose and plastered her hands on spandex-encased hips. "I'm twenty-two."

Penelope laughed, and let her eyes go wide. "Wow, twenty-two, you're practically ancient."

"Who is this woman?" the girl asked, her voice filled with scorn.

Penelope shifted her attention back to Evan. "I'm nobody."

"Evan?" his date asked, before slithering alongside him.

His expression flickered. "She's my sister's best friend."

"Nobody you need to concern yourself with," Penelope said.

"I didn't think so." The girl flipped her hair, but her eyes were wary behind her overly mascaraed lashes. The girl might be young, but she was no fool, and she sensed the undercurrents lacing the air. She looked at Evan, who still watched Penelope as though searching for something. The girl's lips curled. "You're hardly his type."

True. Since his current age cutoff for dating seemed to be around twenty-five, she was long past her prime. Penelope gave the child her sweetest smile. "Of course not, I'm an adult."

The girl opened her mouth to say something, but Evan shook his head and encircled her wrist. "Go wait for me inside, babe."

Penelope stifled the gasp and resisted the urge to react. What was he doing? They were never alone together. Those were the rules.

The girl pouted. "But, Evan."

"Go. I'll be there in a minute."

Penelope didn't know what he was up to, but she wouldn't stand for it. She held up her hands. "No, don't let me bother you. I'm leaving."

He looked like he was about to say something, but then he stopped, and shrugged. "Suit yourself."

The girl curled into Evan, draping her perfect, Playboy body all over him, and giving Penelope a smug smile. "You didn't forget your walker, did you?"

Evan's jaw tightened, and for a fraction of a second Penelope thought he'd be decent and put the girl in her place, but then his expression smoothed into impassive.

His refusal to defend her stuck like a thorn in her side, reminding her just how much she didn't like him. She shifted her attention back to the twenty-two-year-old. "By the way, he doesn't know your name."

The girl's smugness fell away. "Um, yeah, he does."

Penelope shook her head. "Nope. Sorry. He always calls you girls 'babe' when he doesn't remember." She flicked a glance at Evan. "Have fun."

Then, before she could get caught up in any more of his crap, she turned and walked away.

Last thing she heard was "babe" asking Evan what her name was, but Penelope didn't have to stick around to wait for the answer. She knew Evan and he had no idea.

Of course, as a famous, bad-boy football player who was notoriously reported as insatiable and wild, Penelope knew it wouldn't matter. Evan would get his blow job, and probably a hundred other things, before the night was through.

Little things like names didn't matter in the NFL.

Penelope slipped inside and hurried down the hallway, searching for a place to collect herself. When she found a tiny recess at the end of a corridor, she rested against the wall, squeezing her lids tight.

For a smart woman, she sure was stupid.

She had everything she could want from life. A great home, respect, friends, and a family who loved her. She had an MBA from Northwestern, and was admired by her colleagues for her logical, analytical brain that could solve even the toughest of problems. Shane had recently promoted her to chief operating officer of the Donovan Corporation, with a huge salary and even bigger bonus.

She'd done everything right. She'd walked the straight and narrow. Made no big mistakes. She'd achieved success beyond her wildest imagination.

And what was she doing with all these brains of hers? Still pining for Evan Donovan.

It was so ridiculous and frustrating. Crushes that began at six were supposed to end. They weren't supposed to plague her at thirty-one.

She rubbed at her temples. She'd tried countless times over the years to talk herself out of him, but it hadn't worked. Ironically, her heart seemed to be the only impetuous, self-destructive thing about her.

And she'd tried. God knew how hard she'd tried. She'd dated plenty of men. Good men who appreciated her and treated her the way she deserved. And still she couldn't forget Evan, or the past that meant more to her than to him. He lingered in the back of her mind, always present.

She didn't even like the man he'd become. He wasn't a real man by her definition. More like an overgrown frat boy. The grown-up version of Evan, she could get over.

Only her memories wouldn't allow that.

No matter how many times she'd told herself that boy was a figment of her imagination, her heart refused to believe. And thus, like every bad country song ever written, she pined for a man who would never love her in return.

She hated it, but didn't know how to stop it from being true.

The one saving grace was that nobody knew. Not her friends. Not her parents. Not even a stranger on the street. No one. She refused to even write his name in her journal for fear someone would discover the truth.

She hid her feelings well. She never reacted. Always played it cool. And no one had ever guessed. In the long list of humiliations she'd suffered at the hands of Evan Donovan, this wouldn't be one of them.

This secret would follow her to the grave.

Chapter Two

Six months later

The expansive, messy desk separated Penelope from her boss and friend, and as he talked on the phone, she sat and tapped her high heel on the carpet, her one concession to fidgeting when what she really wanted was to pace around his office like a madwoman. Her brow creased in concern as she listened to Shane talk to his mom.

Things were bad. These conversations were becoming a daily occurrence.

While he talked, Penelope carried on a mental conversation to remind herself that this crisis was none of her business. That it had nothing to do with her. That, despite her closeness to the Donovans, she was not, in fact, family.

"I've tried," Shane said, tone beyond frustrated as he pinched the bridge of his nose. "I don't know what else to do, Mom."

Penelope fiddled with the cover of her iPad and tried to distance herself, but it was impossible. Not when the subject matter was the man she couldn't forget. Or the deep depression that seemed to have taken ahold of Evan, and wouldn't let go.

Four months ago, he'd taken a hard hit that ended in a severe concussion.

It had been a home game against Minnesota. Penelope had watched, horrified, as he'd gone down. It happened so quickly. One second his body had arched, stretched gracefully into the air as he caught the ball for the winning touchdown, the next he'd been tackled midair by an overzealous rookie. When the play had been called, Evan hadn't gotten up. An unnatural hush fell over the stadium as the team doctors attempted to revive him. Penelope had sat glued to her screen, her heart in her throat, as he'd been wheeled off the field unconscious.

When he'd come to, he'd been told his days of playing football were over. That he couldn't risk one more bad hit.

Those first couple of nights had been rough, for everyone. While Penelope fought the urge to sneak into the hospital to see him, she'd soothed her need to take action by caring for the rest of the Donovans the best she could.

She'd handled everything for Shane, managing and rearranging his schedule, talking to clients, and handing out tasks to the executive team so he could focus on his family. She'd offered Maddie a shoulder to cry on and told her everything was going to be all right. She'd made Mrs. Donovan chicken noodle soup, and had a service go clean her house. Privately, though, she'd been distressed right along with them as Evan sank deeper and deeper into his depression.

"Okay, I'll try again," Shane said, pulling Penelope from her thoughts. "I will." Pause. "I'll do my best." Longer pause. "He's an adult, Mom, I can't force him."

Penelope had overheard many of these conversations between Shane and members of his family and she felt horrible for all of them, but Shane in particular. This was one problem he couldn't fix and it was eating him up inside.

"Yeah, Mom, I know." Shane looked at her with pleading eyes, but there was nothing Penelope could do. "I've got to go. I'll talk to him again and let you know."

Shane hung up the phone and blew out a breath. "Fuck."

Penelope stood, walking over to the cabinet to pull out the emergency bottle of Advil, she made sure his admin kept stocked in his office. She shook out three, poured a glass of water, and returned to Shane with an outstretched palm. "Here, take these."

He didn't argue, popping the pills and downing them with a large gulp.

When she'd graduated from college she'd known she wanted to work at the Donovan Corporation, which, at the time, was a fledgling company. Shane wouldn't hear of it, but she'd hounded him until he finally relented, attempting to scare her off by giving her the job as his assistant.

It hadn't worked.

She'd labored tirelessly to prove herself until her position had grown in both scope and responsibility. Now as COO she truly was his right-hand man. She ran all the operations of the company, but she'd never gotten out of the habit of looking after him. After all these years together, he trusted her more than anyone else, and they were more friends than boss and employee. He took care of everyone, and she took care of him.

He put down the water glass. "Thanks."

Penelope sat back down. *Don't ask.* She asked anyway. She needed information. "Evan?"

Shane nodded, his green eyes bloodshot after the long day. "I don't know what they want me to do, Pen."

In sympathy, Penelope frowned. "You saved them once, they want you to save them again."

After his father's death, Shane had worked his ass off to make ends meet and save his family from financial ruin. He'd worked tirelessly until he'd built his company into one of the largest commercial real-estate firms in Chicago. Now he was rich and powerful, with a connected wife and influence all over the city, but he was powerless to help his brother.

And Shane didn't do well with powerless.

"I've tried everything I can think of." Shane shook his head. "I've tried being nice, tried kicking his ass, brought therapists to him, but nothing penetrates."

"How long has it been since he's left his apartment?" Penelope understood what the game meant to Evan. Once upon a time they'd talked extensively, and she knew football was the only thing in this world he cared about. It was his one true love.

And now that it was over, he couldn't handle it.

"Don't know," Shane said. "A while. Last three times I saw him he was dead drunk. I don't know what to do. It's killing my mom."

Penelope nodded. "It's tearing up Maddie too. She hoped to make progress when she came down last weekend, but it didn't work."

"James has tried too, and you know if anyone can take care of business it's him, but it fell on deaf ears." Shane sighed. "I'm at a loss. When my dad died Evan was still underage. I had some control over what he did. Although he sure as shit doesn't act like it, he's a grown adult, and it's out of my hands." He pointed at the phone. "But they won't accept that."

"You can't save Evan," she said, stating what he already

knew, but it was important for him to understand. "You can only hope he sees the light."

Shane swiveled in his chair. "I could handle rage. But he's just despondent and unresponsive. When you talk to him, it's like he's staring right through you. It's scary as hell."

"I'm sure he'll come through this." The words rang as hollow as she felt. The truth was, she didn't know. If he chose to give up, there wasn't anything anyone could do. He had money and resources, so there was no reason he couldn't hole up in his condo and refuse to come out. He didn't have to worry about paying his bills or putting food on the table to propel him out of bed in the morning.

Penelope understood him well enough to know that was part of the problem. Evan needed purpose; he just believed football was the only way he could achieve that.

The intercom rang and Shane glared at it. "My five o'clock. You take off. Enjoy the sunshine. And that's an order."

Penelope smiled, and jumped up. "You don't have to ask me twice."

Shane laughed and she returned to her office, at least partially appeased that she'd lightened his mood, if only for a brief minute. She sat down at her desk and opened her e-mail to return any messages that couldn't wait until tomorrow, but her eyes glazed over as soon as she started reading, unable to stop thinking about Evan.

Something had to push him out of his apathy. It was killing his family. And it was killing him.

Penelope nibbled on her bottom lip, an impossible idea stirring in her mind.

He needed a push, and she knew him, in some ways better than anyone. Could she help? Once she would have been certain of her power to persuade him, but that had been a long time ago.

It wasn't her business. He wouldn't welcome the intrusion. Hell, he'd probably throw her out.

But the Donovans needed a long shot and maybe she was it.

Evan Donovan punched the end button on his phone and wished for the old days when he could slam the receiver into the cradle.

It had been his mom. Crying. Again.

God, he was such an asshole. He didn't want to make her cry, but they wouldn't stop calling. And all he wanted was for them to fucking stop. His so-called friends had gotten the hint and left him alone; why couldn't they do the same? It was the downfall of having a close-knit family; they were relentless in their attempts to pull him from a depression he only wanted to sink into.

Having given up drinking from a glass a couple of days ago, he took a long pull off his bottle of whiskey.

They didn't understand. Nobody understood. To them, it was just a game. If he couldn't play, nobody died. Nobody got hurt. In fact, he'd already been replaced by the rookie who had nipped at his heels all season. His career was over and the game had gone on without him.

The world hadn't come to an end for anyone *but* him.

He had no idea what to do now. Football was all he'd ever been good at.

He wasn't smart like James. Didn't have killer instincts like Shane. He wasn't a survivor like Maddie. The only thing he did in life was play ball. It had defined him for so long he had no clue who he was without it.

When his dad died, football had been the grounding force of his life. It had become his distraction. His drug of choice. It was how he'd medicated through his father's death, his sister's coma, and his family's desperation. It was how he'd numbed the pain and fixed everything that was fucked up and broken about him. The game had been his salvation, his religion.

And now it was gone.

The worst part was, he'd known the hit would be a bad one. Had seen the blood in the overzealous player's eyes, as he'd come barreling toward him. Evan had a choice, and he'd chosen the touchdown.

It had been a mistake. And now his entire life had been fucked because of it. So, like any good addict, he'd turned to a new drug. Whiskey.

His new religion.

He sat in his apartment, got drunk, played video games and passed out. It kept him numb and mean, and pushed everyone away, which was exactly what he wanted.

Only his family refused to leave him be. They just kept coming, forcing him to deal with the outside world and his lack of a place in it.

The door buzzer rang and he growled. He hit the button on his phone to quell the insistent noise, too shrill in his head. "I don't want visitors, Carl."

A refined, disembodied voice came over the line. The doorman's inflection never changed, no matter how surly Evan became. "It's a delivery, sir. From Mr. Shane Donovan."

He snarled. His oldest brother had appointed himself as Evan's father figure when their dad died, and had been riding his ass ever since. "They can leave it at the desk, I'll get it later."

Shane—or maybe his wife, Cecilia—had taken to sending over food for fear he'd starve.

There was a long pause before Carl came back over the line. "The woman says you have to sign for it."

"Sign my name," Evan said and hung up.

A second later the phone rang again. "Apologies, Mr. Donovan, but the signature must be yours."

Evan sighed. If he didn't live in a high-rise penthouse he wouldn't have to deal with a doorman. Maybe he should move someplace nobody knew him. "Send them up, the door's open."

He grumbled, shifting in the chair that now had a permanent imprint of his ass and taking a swig from the bottle. Maybe he'd disappear for a while to some remote place in upper Wisconsin or Michigan, where no one would bother him. While he contemplated his options as a recluse, the door pushed open and Penelope Watkins stood in front of him.

Fucking hell.

His worst nightmare come to life.

Framed in his doorway, her dark, glossy hair curved over her shoulders in a gentle wave as those killer blue eyes of hers zeroed in on him, her mouth pursed in disapproval. In a black pencil skirt with a wide black belt, high heels, and a white button-down, she managed to look both proper and lethal.

As a teenager she'd been sweet and adorable, but with age she'd grown into her looks. There was no longer anything cute about her. In fact, she was quite beautiful. A fact she seemed oblivious to. Or maybe she, unlike the women he dated, didn't care about those kinds of superficialities.

Since the day she'd started high school, when he'd been a junior, she'd been making his cock hard, and despite the alcohol numbing his system, he stirred to life.

She was the last person on earth he wanted to see and he had no qualms about letting her know it. He pointed the bottle at the door. "Get out."

"Hello to you too," she said in that no-nonsense voice of hers that held the barest hint of rasp.

A rasp he knew just how to coax out.

She stepped in and closed the door.

He went from stirring to hard, and he wanted to punch a hole in the wall. Figured. His cock always had a mind of its own when it came to her. It was what had gotten him into trouble with her in the first place all those years ago.

He needed her gone. Yesterday. She was the last person he wanted in his house, witnessing the wreck he'd become. "I mean it, Penelope. Fuck. Off."

She entered the living room and crossed her arms over her chest. "Nice language."

Why the hell did she have to look so damn perfect?

He took a sip from the bottle and swallowed with a hiss. He was drunk as hell, and twice as mean, so he didn't think twice about breaking the unspoken rules they'd established long ago. In his muddled brain she'd crossed the boundary, now she had to pay. "You didn't mind my language when I was making you come."

She hit him with that dead-on stare of hers. "Really? You're going to go there? Not even a hello first?"

It was wrong that she looked so perfect while he sat here wrecked. He needed to ruffle all that damn composure of hers. He smirked. "I still remember the way my knuckles moved under those white cotton panties of yours while I got you off."

Her expression didn't even flicker as she kicked aside a bottle on the floor, before reaching down and picking up a shirt and tossing it on the couch. "Are you trying to shock me?"

He'd fired his cleaning service and the place had gone to hell. He didn't want to be around people, and he sure as hell didn't want to be around Penelope, who'd never had a disorganized day in her life. He sneered. "After all the things I've done to you, can you still get shocked?"

"That was a long time ago, Evan."

Not so long he didn't remember every detail. She might talk a good game, and she was very convincing in her indifference, but she didn't fool him. She remembered. It had been too good between them. So good, all the supermodels in the world couldn't erase the imprint she had left behind. He'd screwed some of the most beautiful women in the world in an effort to forget her, but late at night, alone, Penelope was the woman he thought of.

She picked up a pile of magazines and put them on the table next to the glass.

"Stop fucking cleaning!" he yelled. Why, after all this time, was she here?

His booming voice didn't rattle her, and with her customary poise she came to stand in front of him. "Are you done with your temper tantrum?"

He leveled her with his meanest, trash-talking sneer. "You haven't even begun to see my temper, little Penny."

She scoffed, shaking her head. "There's not much you can do to me, is there?"

A subtle reminder he'd already inflicted enough damage, not that he'd ever forget. It's why he stayed as far away from her as possible. And why she stayed away from him. Unspoken rules they'd agreed to long ago. If he was smart, he'd let her have her say so she'd leave, but right now common sense had no effect on him. He raised a brow. "You ever tell anyone, Pen? About all the dirty things I used to do to you?"

"Nope," she said, her voice flippant. "Hardly seemed worth the mention."

"Liar." He shifted in his seat, adjusting his balls that now felt full and heavy.

Her gaze dipped, lingering where his hand rested,

before flicking back up to look into his eyes. As usual, her sharp, direct gaze cut right through him, reminding him he'd never lived up to the expectations she'd set. And how the fuck could he? Once she'd acted like he was a god, when in reality he was a mere mortal. A flawed mortal who couldn't even take a proper hit to the head without it sidelining him for good.

She crossed her arms over her chest. "I didn't come here to discuss the past."

He took another drink, his eyes making their way leisurely over her body, remembering all too clearly how she'd felt under his hands. Way back when he was supposed to leave her alone. He'd managed to keep his hands to himself until she was sixteen. She'd been good and pure and all wrong for him, and in the end he hadn't been able to help himself. Now, his palms practically itched to touch her again. Which was why he needed to get rid of her. "I don't care why you're here, I just want you to get out."

"I'm not leaving until I've said my piece."

That had always been her downfall; she had no sense of self-preservation when it came to him. "And what's that?"

"We need to talk about your life." Her voice calm and steady, at complete odds with his inner chaos.

"My life," he said, anger and defensiveness fighting their way through the numbness of his brain, "is none of your concern."

She shrugged. "True, but you're going to listen to me anyway."

"And why should I?"

As she walked toward him, he opened his legs. To his surprise, she stepped between them. "Because you owe me."

Desire roared inside him, mixing with the alcohol and making him stupid. She was so close. She felt like everything he needed. She made him remember what it felt like to feel human. Invincible. And he needed that right now.

Unable to resist, he did something he'd sworn he'd never do again, and reached for her. His hands splayed wide over her hips and he tugged her forward, running his hands along the curve of her body. She felt achingly familiar and so good he leaned his head against her stomach and closed his eyes.

A second later her fingers threaded in his hair. She didn't push him away. Why, he didn't know, but he was grateful.

They'd been teenagers. She'd been his sister's best friend. He'd been the star of the school and she'd been nobody. She hadn't been flashy, or popular, or a cheerleader, like the girls he'd dated, but whenever she'd come over he couldn't help noticing her. She hadn't been someone the guys he hung out with talked about. At school Evan pretended like she wasn't even alive, but secretly, he couldn't stop looking at her in her neatly pressed, Catholic school uniform. He'd been strangely fascinated by her prim and proper demeanor, but he'd never planned on seducing her.

That had just sort of happened.

One night when she'd slept over and been unable to sleep, and not wanting to disturb Maddie, she made her way down to the basement rec room to watch TV. He'd been there, watching game tapes. She'd tried to leave, but he'd insisted she stay. He'd wanted her alone, to be with her even though he'd convinced himself he thought of her platonically.

That night they'd ended up talking for hours.

Somehow their late-night meetings had become ritual, and whenever she'd slept over they'd meet downstairs. They'd never discussed or planned it, but as soon as his sister went to sleep that's where they'd be.

The more they talked, the more he found himself telling her things he'd never told anyone. She didn't seem impressed with his football stats. He didn't have to play a role. With her, he hadn't had to be anything but who he really was.

It hadn't taken him long to figure out she liked him, which hadn't surprised him. Lots of girls liked him; what surprised him was how much he liked her. Not just the stirring of hormones he experienced when watching her, but *her*. Soon he had more fun sitting on that old couch than he had hanging out with his buddies.

When he'd started canceling plans for a chance to be with her, it made him nervous. When he started fantasizing about corrupting her, he'd promised himself he'd never touch her.

A vow he'd kept for six long months before he'd finally given in to temptation and kissed her.

At the time he'd been going out with Kim Rossi, a girl who would let him do anything he wanted. But the sex hadn't compared to what he'd been doing with Penelope, who held nothing back when he touched her. She'd been so sweet he couldn't resist. Having broken his own rules, he'd revised his vow, making a new promise to leave her virginity intact. Anything else was fair game as long as he didn't seduce her into sex. They'd spent endless hours fooling around. Evan could still recall every moment of sheer madness.

The feel of her questing hands and hot, hungry mouth.

Now she was here, and it seemed imperative he remind her how it had been between them. He ran his hands over her back, and kissed her flat stomach.

She sucked in a breath and her body shuddered. "Evan."

He bit at the button on her blouse, tugging it with his teeth. "Do you remember, Penelope? How hot it used to be?"

Her fingers tightened in his hair.

"You made me so damn crazy." He gripped her waist,

and when he found an opening between the buttons, he licked her bare skin. She tasted even better than he remembered.

She gasped, a tiny moan escaping a mouth he needed to possess.

He popped the button, exposing a tiny strip of flesh, and he pressed a hot, openmouthed kiss to her belly. "How many times did you ride my cock with nothing but thin cotton separating us?"

Hard, insatiable lust roared inside him, blocking out the buzz in his head, reminding him how powerful she'd made him feel. He ran his tongue over her belly button. "How many times?"

"Countless." Her voice breathless, that turned-on rasp of hers undeniable.

He raised his head to take in the blaze of her blue eyes, the soft, wet pout of her lips. "Do you remember the first time we kissed?"

Her nails dug into his neck. "I remember."

His lips on her stomach, his tongue trailing over her skin was like coming home. She didn't know why she let him touch her. Maybe it had been too long. Maybe it was because she wanted to feel his mouth on her skin and big hands on her body.

Or maybe he was drunk and she gambled he wouldn't remember, so she indulged herself.

Regardless of her messed-up reasons, she needed to stop.

This wasn't why she'd come. But, as it had always been, the second she was alone with him, common sense eluded her. He'd always been her Achilles' heel. He'd been the one person who could make her take wild, reckless actions.

It's why she stayed far away from him.

And why she didn't push him away now.

His hands slid down her legs and under the hem of her skirt.

She should stop him.

She put her hands on his shoulders with the intention of pushing him away, but then his hands moved up her thighs, and her knees weakened. Somehow, through sheer will, she found the words she needed to say. "You need to stop this."

He lifted his chin and his green eyes bore into her. "Do you remember how you were always so damn greedy? Like you were going to crawl into me."

She gritted her teeth. She remembered. Everything. In vivid Technicolor.

His fingers climbed higher on her thigh.

Hot breath across her skin. Another lick across her belly.

Her mind went fuzzy with the desire she'd suppressed for years.

"God, you used to drive me so crazy." The words whispered in that same sinful voice of both her fantasies and nightmares.

She needed to get this back under control or she'd do something she'd regret.

She steeled her spine. "Let's get back on topic."

"What's the topic?" His mouth brushed over her abdomen, making the muscles there quiver.

"Your life. You need to pull it together, Evan." Good, her voice sounded reasonably calm. Like she was in complete control and not affected by him. "You need to sober up, take a shower, and stop making your mom cry."

He gripped her legs and pulled her forward. "Come sit on my lap."

"No." Her tone was certain, but she hadn't stepped back to a safe distance. She'd always been a glutton for punishment where he was concerned.

"I miss you in my lap." His fingers brushed the hem of her panties at the curve of her ass. "I think you miss it too."

She closed her eyes, savoring the feel of his hands on her flesh for one last moment. His palms were so big and warm, and even as a teenager he'd known just how to touch her. The way no other man had touched her since, regardless of how bad she'd wanted it to be true.

Which was why she needed to stop.

She took a deep breath.

Time to put an end to this and get to the heart of her visit. She snapped her lids open and put a hand on his arm. "You've had plenty of women warming your lap over the years. Call one of them."

"I don't want them, I want you."

"Bullshit." She pulled back. His fingers tightened on her body before they fell away. She felt the loss, the coldness of her skin where the heat of his palms had branded her. She stepped out of touching distance and put on her best poker face. The one she wore when negotiations weren't going well and she didn't want to show her hand. "You're drunk. You're lonely. And I'm available. It's the same damn story, only we're adults instead of teenagers."

The desire slid from his face. He leaned back in his chair, his expression turning once again into the smug, entitled playboy. "You were always good for an ego stroke, Penny. Always so needy and willing."

"Fuck you." She slapped him hard across the face, then reared back, stunned. Her hand tingled with the force of her blow.

He rubbed his jaw and that cruel smile curled his lips. "What? You want me to pretend it meant something?"

That was the thing about him. He'd been so damn good

at making her believe. It was why she'd given him all of her firsts to begin with. Yes, he'd ignored her existence outside in the real world, but down in that basement, he'd made her believe. She'd been young and stupid. She'd deluded herself into thinking she was special.

She'd been wrong. She'd never make the same mistake again.

No longer a shy kid, she leaned forward and looked him dead in the eye. "I don't believe a single thing that comes out of your mouth. I know you're not capable of loving anyone or anything but yourself. I know you used me. I know it didn't mean anything. I know I was just some little girl who worshipped you and you took advantage of that."

She straightened, on a roll now, releasing all the pent-up emotion she carried around with her. "But you know what? That's on you. Not me. I was honest and I was pure. I gave you my heart and you threw it in my face." She jabbed a finger in his chest. "That's on you, and you're the one who has to look at yourself in the mirror, which you obviously can't or else you wouldn't be drunk half the day."

He just stared at her, his eyes burning with what she could only define as rage. But she was past caring, and continued on, ruthless in her attack. "If it was up to me you could rot, but I'm not here for you. I'm here for them. For the family that you're hurting with your selfish self-destruction."

"Are you through?" Tone cold, his green eyes flat.

"No." Her voice snapped through the air like a whip.

His gaze never left hers as he took another long drink from the bottle. She wanted to snatch it from him and fling it across the room until it shattered, but that wasn't her decision to make.

He had to make the choice. Not her.

She felt sick but continued. She crossed her arms over her chest. "You lost your career. I'm sorry. I know football was the only thing in your life you actually cared about. It sucks. I get it. But do the math, Evan: You're thirty-three. You only really had a couple years left anyway. Football is a young man's game and you were almost past your prime."

"That's bullshit." The words exploded, vibrating through the air. "I was at the top of my game."

She hated to do this, but there was no other way. "You had three more years, tops. The average age of retirement is thirty-five. In the scheme of things you lost two to three years. It's not the end of the world."

"Get out," he spat, leaving behind no traces of the man who'd touched her.

Ruthless, she stepped forward and put her hands on the chair, bending so she was eye level with him. "Let me put this in words your football brain will understand. Stop being a pussy. Man up and get your shit together."

"Get out or I'll throw you out myself." His fingers drew so tight around the bottle she was surprised it didn't crack under the force.

She straightened. "I'll show myself to the door."

She'd said what she'd needed to. The rest was up to him.

Chapter Three

Evan woke, face planted in his couch, with the worst hangover of his life.

Everything ached. His head pounded against his skull like a jackhammer and it felt like his stomach was being eaten from the inside out by battery acid. Slowly, carefully, he sat up, his joints creaking on the way. Vision swimming, he rested his elbows on his knees, praying for a swift, sudden death. He scrubbed a hand over his jaw, before pressing his thumbs into his eye sockets, hoping to clear the cobwebs from his brain.

What in the hell happened last night? All he remembered was the bottle of whiskey, *Call of Duty*, and darkness.

A flash of memory. Of Penelope. He frowned.

Had she been here? Or had it been a dream? He still dreamed of her sometimes, but usually he dreamed of her the way she'd been back then, her glossy hair spread out over his chest, her blue eyes flirting up at him.

The image in his head this miserable morning was of her in one of her pencil skirts and a white blouse. The current version of her that looked at him with cold eyes, lips curved in distain.

Why would she come here? She never came to him. Not even when he'd been in the hospital.

He blinked gritty lids and tried to piece together the dull memories of the night before. He remembered he'd started drinking at four when Maddie had called, full of pleading tears.

He'd caught a buzz by the time James called and tried to reason with him.

He squinted. Remembering the endless hours of whiskey and gaming.

His mom called. He'd yelled and made her cry. He'd felt like shit. Worse than shit.

He'd drunk more.

The door.

Penelope. Yes, she had been there. Standing in his house, making him confront things he wanted to bury.

His encounter with her came flooding back, and for a moment he thought he was going to be sick. After all these years she'd come to him, and he'd been a total bastard. Had he really said those things to her? Touched her? Been cruel?

He rubbed his cheek. She'd slapped him and he'd deserved it. Had he really told her she was good for an ego stroke? That she hadn't meant anything to him?

Jesus, he was an asshole.

She was right; he couldn't look at himself in the mirror.

She'd been nothing but good, which is why he'd set her free that morning after the car accident that killed his father and left his sister in a coma, when he'd been out of his mind with grief. As a teenager he'd had no willpower when it came to her, and with his life in ruins and college on the horizon, he was sure there was no place for her. So he'd done the only thing he'd known would work, and broken her heart. Between his father's sudden death, his sister's life hanging on by a thread, and the cruel way he'd treated Penelope, it had been the worst day of his life.

After he'd shattered everything that had been good between them, he'd never let his guard down around her again.

She was too dangerous.

At seventeen he'd assumed she'd fade out of his life, but that never happened. She'd stuck. When he saw her he played his role and she played hers. They never discussed their past. Hell, they made sure to never be alone. But he found ways to remind her. Because he was a selfish prick, and he never wanted her to forget.

She never took it though. She always hit back. As she should. She'd hit hard last night, and he'd deserved it.

Unlike his family, who treated him with kid gloves, Penelope had laid it right on the line, confronting him with the cold, hard truth. Everything she'd said was right.

He was mourning a career that was almost over.

He was spoiled.

Entitled.

He had no idea how to go about filling the void. So like a pussy, he'd folded.

He looked around his wreck of an apartment.

His dad would be so disappointed. He'd never have let him get away with this shit.

Evan took a deep breath and picked up the phone. First things first. He pushed the button and called his mom. She answered on the second ring. "Evan, please tell me you're okay."

Her desperate, concerned voice made his chest squeeze.

He squinted at bottles, empty cups, and dirty dishes lining the coffee table and tried to clear the tightness from his throat. "I'm sorry about last night."

"It's okay," she said, her motherly tone far too forgiving.

"No, it's not." He dragged his hand through his hair, grown too long now. "I'm sorry I made you cry."

"You were upset."

"It's not a good excuse."

"We're so worried about you." Her voice cracked and he felt like the worst kind of asshole.

"Please, Mom, don't cry." How had he let it get this far?

She sniffed and he could just picture her, holding up a tissue under her lashes. He'd always hated to see her cry.

"I don't know what to do to help you," she said.

Penelope's words came back to him, that his behavior was on him, and him alone. To her, there was a right way to act and a wrong way. Unlike him, she had the strength to put her money where her mouth was. She was like Shane that way, steel spines and gritty dispositions that would not quit in the face of adversity. "There's nothing you can do. I've got to figure this out on my own."

"It's hard, as a mother. I want to fix it and make it all better."

"You can't fix my head or me, and you can't let me treat you like shit because of it." It was a start, a small one, but it would have to do.

"Language, young man," she said, reprimanding him like the good old days.

A smile ghosted his lips and it made him realize just how long it had been. "I'll find a way to pull it together."

"I just want you to be happy."

Happiness seemed too insurmountable of a goal right now, but there was one promise he could make and keep. "I won't make you cry again. Deal?"

"Deal. I love you, baby boy. Let us help you. We're your family."

His throat tightened again and he nodded. "I'll try. Love you too, Mom."

He hung up and looked around his apartment. It was a

fucking disaster. The easy thing to do was call his service
and have them take care of the place, but he wasn't going
to do that. He'd made the mess; he'd clean it up.

It was time to get his shit together. Time to make
amends.

Penelope curled up on her couch with a glass of wine
and a book in her lap. It had been a long, exhausting day.
She opened it with every intention of reading, only to
promptly zone out, thinking about Evan. She'd been busy
enough to put the scene from her mind, but now that she
finally had a chance to relax, it rushed back to last night.

She ran her hand over the printed words. Had she done
the right thing? She'd broken that unspoken barrier between
them and called him out.

There would be consequences.

Or maybe there wouldn't.

Since the morning after his father died, Evan had put a
wall between them that years had only strengthened. He'd
shut her down cruelly and absolutely, and until last night
she'd never stepped over the line.

She only hoped it was worth it, because with her visit
she'd revealed that she still cared.

That he affected her.

She trembled, remembering his hands on her thighs, his
mouth on her skin. The sound of his voice when he'd said
he missed her in his lap.

That stupid part of her had wanted nothing more than to
sink into him. But it had been the alcohol talking, not him.
Right? One brush of his mouth across her skin did not
negate his actions over all these years. The dismissive way
he treated her. The supermodels he'd flaunted in front of her.

Those actions spoke volumes, and she refused to believe the desperation in his voice or the feel of his hands

on her body. That had always been her downfall with him, believing the small moments in time instead of the big picture. She shook her head, clearing it of the destructive thoughts. It was that exact thinking that had gotten her into this mess in the first place.

She could still recall every detail of the first time she'd ever seen Evan. She'd been in kindergarten and he'd been in the second grade. She'd met Maddie in line before school and they'd been instant friends. The first time she'd gone over to Maddie's house had been a revelation.

Penelope was a late-in-life baby, born to parents who believed they'd never have children. They were older than the other parents, more tired. They loved her, but growing up had been a quiet, staid affair. The second she'd stepped into the Donovan household had been like every family comedy on television. Like everything she thought a family should be, with its chaos and mayhem. A stark contrast to her own careful family life, she'd loved being there.

Maddie and Penelope had been going up the stairs to play Barbies in her room when Shane had come barreling down the stairs, followed by Evan seconds later. She'd watched in wonder as he seemed to fly through the air and tackle Shane to the floor. The two of them broke out into a wrestling match as they fought about who-knew-what.

Mrs. Donovan had come rushing in from the kitchen to pull the two boys apart. Maddie complained Evan had pushed Penelope down, and their mom demanded he apologize. Evan had looked up at her, brown hair flopping over one eye, grinned, and uttered an insincere apology.

Penelope had looked at him and thought—I'm going to marry him one day.

A silly, childish notion.

With older parents, Penelope had spent as much time as she could at the Donovans'. When Penelope went to grade school her mom was in her early fifties. Her dad, ten years older than his wife, had been recently diagnosed with MS. Rightly so, her mother had focused on his care, and Penelope had focused on being a model child. She'd been self-sufficient, well behaved, and excelled in school. And she'd been lonely. That's where the Donovans had come in.

Maddie was the best friend a girl could ask for. Penelope had loved her spontaneous recklessness, so different from her own quiet, organized world. She used to pretend she was part of their family, and it hadn't been hard; they were warm, inviting, and didn't seem to mind that she spent far too much time there. As an added bonus Penelope had soaked up any interaction she had with Evan, and fed her puppy-dog crush.

Of course, he was one of the cool, popular kids, and she was considered a good girl in her perfect uniform, shining shoes, and glasses. Always smart, she'd been in honors classes, and while her friendship with Maddie kept her from being a total social pariah, she'd never been the kind of girl boys liked. She'd been too prim and proper. She'd never flirted or wore makeup. Had never rolled up the waistband of her uniform to get boys to notice her. She never cared either, since the only boy she'd been interested in was the one boy she couldn't have.

Evan was the king of their school. He was the best-looking, tallest, and the star football player. He'd walk through the halls and everyone wanted a piece of him. After all, it was clear he was destined for greatness. When he started getting scouted earlier than most kids, his legendary status only grew. Every girl wanted him, would fight to be with him, but he only dated cheerleaders, which Penelope was not. Other than being his kid sister's friend, Evan hadn't known she was alive.

That was, until she started meeting him in the basement. At first, they'd been completely platonic. They'd talked, played cards, laughed, and watched TV. Slowly, over time, he'd started touching her. Soft, innocent touches that would mess with her mind and body.

A brush across her knee. A fingertip down her arm. A glance over her back.

Slowly, they started sitting a little bit closer. His hand would graze her hair, and then move away. Over time he started sifting the strands through his fingers, twirling the locks, as she sat ramrod straight, terrified one wrong move would make him stop. Tension grew like a wild thing between them, until all their interactions were heavy with portent. He'd been dating the head cheerleader at the time, but Penelope hadn't cared about that. All she'd cared about was the magical time they spent in that basement, where he'd talked to her about nothing and anything and touched her like she mattered to him.

One night, they'd been watching *The Howling*. They'd been sitting close, their thighs brushing, his hand in her hair, which he seemed to spend hours stroking. She'd felt him look at her and she tilted her head up in question. His gaze dipped to her mouth and he asked, "Have you ever kissed a boy, Pen?"

Her breath had caught and she'd shaken her head. It never occurred to her to lie. She'd just turned sixteen, and most girls her age had kissed boys before, but she'd wanted it to be someone special.

Someone like Evan.

He squeezed the back of her neck, his face inching down. "I want to be the first."

And she'd let him.

The next morning at breakfast they'd said nothing to each other, and other than his flickering glance at her too-swollen lips, she'd have thought it happened only in her imagination.

The phone rang, startling her from her memory.

The ringtone indicated it was Maddie, and she picked up. "Hello?"

"Hey, you sound breathless. Did I catch you at a bad time?" Maddie asked.

Penelope cleared her throat. Slightly dismayed that, after all this time, remembering her first kiss with Evan could still make her ache. "Nope, not at all. I was settling in to read. How are you?"

"I'd be great if it wasn't for Evan," Maddie said, her voice filled with concern. "Everyone is really worried. I don't know how to get him out of his funk."

Penelope's heart sank. Maybe her visit hadn't made an impact. "I'm sorry. I wish there was something I could do."

She'd tried, but she'd failed.

Maddie sighed, the sound heavy. "We'll be in Chicago soon for the fund-raiser Shane and Cecilia are having, so maybe we can talk some sense into him then."

One of Shane's friends from high school had a daughter who had been struck down with a rare blood disorder and the medical bills were killing the family. Shane tried to pay for the treatment, but Bobby wouldn't hear of it. He had, however, agreed to a fund-raiser. Penelope knew full well Shane would match or exceed any money they raised, but it allowed Bobby to feel like he wasn't taking a handout directly from a friend who once upon a time was his financial equal. That kind of pride Shane understood, so he was pulling out all the stops. Penelope and Cecilia had planned the event, and it was sold out. The family would get everything they needed.

"I hope so," Penelope said, giving up on her book and tossing it on the coffee table. "What can I do?"

"You listening is enough," Maddie said, sniffing a little. "You're the best friend ever. I love you, Pen."

"I love you too." Other than Evan ruining her for any other man for the rest of her life, Penelope couldn't be anything but grateful for the Donovans. After she'd graduated from college her parents had moved to Florida, and while she made sure to talk to them once a week, the Donovans were more like home. And it was her duty to cheer up her best friend. "Let's talk about something fun."

Maddie laughed. "Okay, who are you bringing to the event?"

Penelope rolled her eyes. "Not this again. I'm starting to feel like a singleton from *Bridget Jones*."

"Ack! I know. I'm horrible. I don't know what's happened to me. I used to be so anti-relationship and now I'm obnoxiously trying to pair everyone off."

"Well, you've found happiness and want everyone to feel the same way."

"But still, I shouldn't foist it on you." There was a long pause over the line. "But seriously, who are you bringing?"

Penelope couldn't help but smile. "No one. Sorry."

"Sophie keeps telling me about some environmental lawyer she wants to set you up with."

Penelope snorted. "If he's so great, why doesn't she want him for herself?"

"I asked her the same question, and she claims he's more your type," Maddie said, her voice considerably lighter.

Since he wasn't a badass, troubled football player, Penelope doubted the lawyer was her type. Of course, her friends didn't know that. Her friends believed her dating preferences were sensible, successful corporate types, like her.

In theory, they were, only no matter how good a time she had with them, or how much she enjoyed talking to them, or even sex with them, they didn't hit that secret place inside her. Didn't flip that switch that turned her from composed to depraved.

Maybe a person only got that once in their lives. A person wasn't supposed to have *that* right off the bat. It set unreasonable expectations for the men who followed.

Penelope wrinkled her nose. "I'll pass on the lawyer. I'm busy with work and don't have time to date right now."

Maddie sighed. "I'm going to have to talk to that brother of mine about working you too hard."

"No, you most certainly will not. My job is my business and just because Shane is your brother, it doesn't have anything to do with you."

Penelope loved her career and was completely dedicated. Since the early days, it had always been her and Shane and that was the way she liked it. Yes, she was a bit of a workaholic, but she was the type of person who needed to stay busy.

Maddie huffed. "Oh, all right. But still, maybe you should reconsider. Sophie is positive you'll be a love match."

"I love Sophie, but every blind date she's ever set me up on has been a disaster."

"Maybe the eleventh time is the charm. You never know until you try."

"I'll think about it."

"Good," Maddie said. "I'll talk to you in a couple days."

Penelope hung up, and her mind immediately returned to Evan. He'd be at the benefit, probably with some Playboy bunny on his arm. With the memory of his hands on her body so fresh, the thought caused an unwelcome twist of a dull knife.

It wouldn't hurt to have a date.

On impulse she grabbed her iPad and Googled the environmental lawyer Sophie wanted to set her up with, clicking on the images she found. A nice-looking businessman, with brown hair and eyes. He appeared harmless, like he helped old ladies across the street on a daily basis. Hmmm . . . No, he wouldn't work at all.

But perhaps there was someone else who would.

Chapter Four

It had taken six hours, prescription-strength ibuprofen, and five garbage bags, but Evan had finally put his apartment back in order. After throwing out all the liquor in his house, he'd called his cleaning service and rescheduled their weekly visits, gotten a haircut, and shaved.

It was the most energy he'd put into a day since he'd woken up in that hospital bed.

Now, in the late afternoon sun, he huffed and puffed down the lakefront as he ran with James. An activity he hated even when he'd been in tip-top shape, but now, after no exercise in four months, he felt like his lungs were going to explode and his heart would burst.

Next to him, his brother wasn't even winded. James was probably only expending about thirty percent of his energy so Evan could keep up. It was why he'd called his middle brother in the first place. With him, Evan could humiliate himself and James would never make him feel bad about it.

James stopped running and slowed to a walk.

Evan dragged deep breaths into his lungs, fighting for air. "Why'd you stop?"

James clapped him on the back. "You really want me to answer that?"

Evan shook his head. "Pathetic, huh?"

"You've had a rough go, and haven't gotten out in months. I think we can cut you some slack." James was the practical one in the family and had a way of putting things into perspective.

Evan heaved in the lake air, willing his pounding heart to calm. He felt like shit. He'd been conditioning his body since he was in high school; how'd it go to hell in such a short time?

Of course, drowning his liver with alcohol hadn't helped.

One small step at a time, he reminded himself. All he needed to do was take one step. He didn't know how to fix his life, but he could run. He could stop getting drunk every day. Stop making his family miserable. Hopefully, the rest would come. He wheezed out, "Thanks."

James nodded. "Want to come over for dinner tonight? Gracie's experimenting, so there's bound to be something good."

Evan still wasn't sure how Gracie Roberts, baker and sex goddess, had wound up with his practical, health food fanatic brother. But she made James happy and he was more relaxed than Evan had ever seen him. Gracie adored James and wasn't shy about letting everyone know it. Ad nauseam.

As happy as Evan was for James, he wasn't sure he wanted to bear witness to their domestic bliss. "I'll take a rain check."

"Nah, you'll come. I don't want to tell Gracie no." It was an excuse. As far as Evan could tell, James had no trouble saying no to his significant other. *He* wanted Evan to come and didn't plan on taking no for an answer.

With Shane, Evan would have argued, but James asked

so little of him and always accepted him without judgment, no matter how much he fucked up. He also hadn't had a home-cooked meal in a dog's age and everything Gracie made was phenomenal. "All right."

"Good. You know how Gracie likes to feed you."

"That's because I don't complain about calories."

James laughed. "I don't complain. Much."

"It must be a real hardship for you, Jimmy. Great food, fantastic sex, and cupcakes every night. I'm crying a river here."

James's smile grew wider, but he said in a deadpan voice, "Yeah, I'm not sure how I get through the day."

They fell silent as they walked down the lakefront in the general direction of the house his brother shared with Gracie. Evan realized it was the best day he'd had in months. He no longer looked like he was living in a hostel, he'd exercised, and was going to dinner at his brother's, where Gracie would make it impossible to stay sullen. It was a start.

His mind drifted back to Penelope, as it had often during the day, and the things he'd said to her last night. He knew what he needed to do, even though he didn't want to. Not because she didn't deserve an apology, because she absolutely did, but going to her would mean talking about their past. They'd avoided that subject for so long he didn't know where it would lead.

But it didn't matter, he had to make amends.

As she'd said, it was time he manned up and started figuring out how to be a decent human being.

And, as always, that started with her.

Penelope was still in her yoga clothes when the doorbell rang. She frowned. It was too late for deliveries. Maybe it was Sophie, who sometimes liked to drop by after work. Penelope padded on bare feet through her townhome, and when she saw who was at the front door through the glass panes, she froze.

Blinked. Shook her head, then looked again. Evan.

He was the last person she'd expected to see on her front stoop. She contemplated pretending she wasn't home, but then he spotted her through the window and their gazes met.

Too late.

Heart pounding, she flipped the lock and opened the door, standing in the space she'd created so he couldn't barge in.

He wore jeans and a black T-shirt that stretched over his broad chest. He'd shaved, gotten a haircut, and his green eyes were clear instead of glassy. He looked ridiculously good.

Self-conscious in her yoga pants and minuscule top, she smoothed her hand over her ponytail and said coolly, "Evan."

His gaze flickered down her body, making her hyper-aware of him. "Can I come in?"

"Why?" Her grip tightened on the door frame. She didn't want him in her house.

A muscle tensed in his jaw. "I want to talk to you."

"We have nothing to talk about."

He took a step toward her, and in her bare feet, he towered over her five-seven. "I disagree. Now may I please come in? Or are we going to have this conversation out in the open?"

She sucked her bottom lip between her teeth, casting a glance down her block, thinking of the neighbors who might see one of Chicago's most recognizable football players standing on her doorstep. The last thing she wanted was to end up in the paper.

She sighed and stepped back, allowing him to enter, gritting her teeth as his body pressed past her. He no longer reeked of alcohol; instead he smelled crisp and clean, with a hint of spice.

She'd always loved the way he smelled. She used to nuzzle him, breathing in his scent as she burrowed into his neck. She shook the memory away and pointed. "The kitchen is down the hall."

His shoulders seemed to fill the hallway as he walked into the open living space at the back of her house that held the great room and the kitchen. He surveyed her living area, then turned to look at her. "This house looks exactly like you."

A mixture of clean lines and comfort, her home *was* a reflection of her. Soft creams, grays, and splashes of red. It hinted at modern, but she'd chosen the furniture because of its comfort. The space was efficient and neat, with an open floor plan and no separation between the living room and kitchen.

Not wanting him to get too relaxed, she walked into the kitchen area, behind the large island, with its slate counter-tops, driftwood-gray cabinets, and stainless steel appliances.

Realizing he still watched her, she said haughtily, "Since you know nothing about me you can't possibly know if that's true."

He came to a stop on the opposite side of the island, both of them facing off as they stared at each other. They were alone, with no excuses like alcohol to dull the past, and it sat between them, filling all the space.

"I know you better than you want me to," he said, his voice rich and deep, holding none of the slur from the other night.

Why, after all this time, did he keep bringing up their

past? It had been easy when she'd believed it was because he was drunk, but he was clearly sober now.

Her throat dried up and she crossed her arms over her chest. "What can I do for you, Evan?"

His gaze lingered on her lips. "I want to apologize for the other night. I was way out of line."

"Yes, you were." Her chin tilted. His presence in her house made her stomach dip in that old familiar way and she didn't like it. He needed to leave. "Is that all?"

He placed his hands on the counter and looked at her, his expression dark and intense. "This is awkward."

"It is." She might as well acknowledge it. "So let me let you off the hook. Apology accepted. You've done your duty, now you can go."

His lips twisted into a sardonic smile. "Apology accepted, but I'm not forgiven, am I?"

"Why would you need my forgiveness?" She leaned against her counter and gripped the edge. "You've never needed it before."

His green eyes met hers and his jaw hardened. "We both know you'll never forgive me. Nor should you."

She looked away, staring at the picture over her fireplace. A canvas of red and white. "I don't know what you want me to say."

"You don't have to say anything," he said, using a soft tone she hadn't heard from him in years. "I just want you to know I'm sorry."

"Thank you," she said, still refusing to look at him.

"Why'd you come?"

She cleared her throat. "I told you, I did it for them. I thought you might listen to someone who wasn't related to you."

There was a beat of silence before he continued on. "What you said, it mattered. It made a difference. I'm in a bad place, and like usual, you kicked my ass until I saw reason. So thank you."

It was the nicest thing he'd said to her in years. It made her remember how he'd been with her. Not just the heat, but how he used to be when they spent all those hours talking.

She didn't want to remember. She wanted to hold on to the ball of anger that had kept her sane. Kept her heart hard and cold.

Her throat grew tight. At least it had been worth it. She'd done the right thing. Shane and Maddie would get some much needed relief, and for that she was grateful. "You're welcome. I know football meant everything to you."

"It did."

She turned back to him. "If you try, I'm sure you can find something new to love."

"I hope so." His gaze roamed over her face, down her body, and up again. "I don't know what to do, Penelope."

He used to say she was the one person he could tell anything to. Once, she'd known all his secrets. All his fears and insecurities. She might hate him, but she didn't wish him to suffer. She took a deep breath. "That's always been your problem, believing the game was all you had."

"That's because it's true."

It wasn't true, and this wasn't the time to pacify him. He had enough people trying to placate him, and she wasn't going to be one of them. "You'll have to find a way to go on, or it will destroy you. You're thirty-three, and you have your whole life ahead of you."

He dragged a hand through his hair, and the late sun caught the hard lines of his jaw, setting off golden skin that didn't belong on a man of Irish descent. "It doesn't feel like that."

"Don't become one of those guys you hate, Evan. Romanticizing a past instead of planning a future. You'll never forgive yourself. If you want a new life, you'll have to fight for it. It's really that simple."

He glanced out the window overlooking her patio and small patch of city grass. "You always laid it right on the line. It's one of the things I like best about you."

She shrugged. Even at the height of her infatuation, she had. Enough people kissed his ass; he didn't need one more. Although she'd obviously stroked his ego in plenty of other ways. "You should probably go."

Their eyes locked. Held. Tension filled the air. He straightened. "I'm sorry."

"It's fine." One day, she didn't know when, he would have no hold on her. But today wasn't that day and she wanted him gone.

He cleared his throat. "The other night, I shouldn't have touched you."

Why wouldn't he leave? She blew out a deep breath. "It doesn't matter. It's over and done with. Let's forget it and move on."

"You always were like a drug. It's why I had to stop cold turkey." That voice, low and deep, dropping the way it had when he used to whisper in her ear, urging her to let go.

She shook her head. She had to stop thinking about that. It was bad enough when he treated her like a stranger, but now it was excruciating. "That was a long time ago. We were kids."

The intensity in his gaze pinned her to her spot. "Now that I've fallen off the wagon, all I can think about is touching you again. Tasting you."

She sucked in a breath. And here they were, the consequences of her actions staring her in the face. It was the worst thing about him, because with him, all she could think was, just once. Just one more time. If she could touch him one more time maybe she could move on.

But it was a lie.

And no matter how badly she wanted a fix, his mouth on hers wouldn't change anything. She needed to get them back to where they'd been: slightly antagonistic strangers. She steeled her spine. "I'm not fifteen anymore. I can't fix what's wrong with you."

He stalked around the counter and stopped in front of her, standing far too close, and that familiar ache built inside her. "That's not it."

"It is. I can't be your salve, Evan. Not anymore."

He searched her face, his expression creased in frustration. "I don't care what you say, I know you feel it."

She did. She felt it everywhere, like all her cells were urging her toward him. Toward home. She would not give in. "You should go."

He reached for her, and instead of moving away like she should, she remained rooted in her spot. His big hand curled around her neck, and he worked his fingers through the strands, tugging at the band holding her hair back.

Her breath increased and she licked her lips, thought about all the things she should say, and said none of them.

She didn't push him away. She would. Soon. In just one minute.

He pulled the band free and tossed it on the counter. Her hair tumbled around her shoulders.

"Jesus, this hair." He stepped closer. "It was always my downfall."

"Evan," she said, her voice coming out like a rasp. "Please."

"Please what?" He pressed against her and her whole body sprang to life. Rushing with adrenaline. He tangled his hand in her hair, the strands sliding through his fingers, so achingly familiar she had to fight to keep her eyes open.

"Please . . ." She trailed off, as her body burned up.

He rubbed a thumb over her lips. "Tell me you don't think about it. Tell me you haven't pictured every single thing I've ever done to you a million times."

Temptation was a live, hot thing burning inside her. Begging her to give in. It would be so easy to let him overtake her. They probably wouldn't even make it to the bedroom. But it was time to be strong and put an end to this madness.

She put her hand on his chest, and the muscles jumped under her touch. "I have. But you know what I remember even more? The way you took my virginity and tossed it in my face the next morning. And I sure as hell remember all the women you've paraded in front of me over the last sixteen years while you treated me like I barely existed."

God, no. Why had she said that? It was far too telling. She'd sacrificed the truth, but hit her intended mark.

His head snapped as though she'd slapped him, and the hot, desperate look in his eyes slid away. He released his hold and stepped back.

She missed him already. Body tense, she held her breath, waiting for the smug, playboy arrogance she knew so well to appear.

Instead, he ran his hand through his hair and blew out a breath. "You're right. I deserve that. I won't bother you again."

Shaken, she crossed her arms over her chest. "So, back to normal."

"That's what you want, isn't it?" His gaze searched.

No, that wasn't what she wanted. But it was what she'd get. Because it was the only emotionally healthy option, and she would not be sucked into that place where rational behavior didn't matter.

"That's what I want." Hating the nagging desire that wished he'd push. To overcome her anger until she could think of nothing but the feel of his hard body on hers. Needing to sever the ties trying to weave their way through the wall between them, she gave him her most scornful look. "You'll have to find another woman to fuck your troubles away."

His expression turned stormy, his mouth twisting. He shook his head, retreating farther. "Fine, Penny. Sorry I bothered you."

Then he turned and walked away.

A second later the door slammed, shutting the final chapter on the Evan and Penelope drama once and for all.

Chapter Five

"Do we have a deal?" Penelope asked, her gaze leveled on the man across from her, her hands folded neatly on the table.

Other than a slight shifting in his chair, Adam Hayes gave no indication she had him on the ropes. They were sitting in the Donovan Corporation's boardroom, with her people on one side, his on the other, in the final stages of the deal they'd been negotiating for months. Despite her new position, Shane had a bit of trouble giving up control. She'd had to talk him into letting her handle the project; to prove she could handle the opportunity and challenge and earn the title he'd given her. And now it was in her grasp and she was about to reap the fruits of her labor.

"Is this your final position?" Adam rolled a pen between his thumb and forefinger, as though contemplating the terms of the contract that would result in the biggest deal of the year, outside their contracts with the city, increase company revenue by ten percent, and potentially expand their reach outside Chicago.

A deal she'd found, cultivated, spent many late nights and weekends on.

Her heart fluttered, but she gave no outward sign of her excitement. She nodded. "Yes."

A thick silence fell over the table as Adam watched her with narrowed eyes. Flanked by each other's teams, there was a collective hush as Penelope sat there, unflinching.

Finally, Adam broke out into a grin. "I think we can work with this."

All the tension coiled inside her released, and she stood, holding out her hand. "Fantastic. We'll get legal working on the contracts right away."

Adam followed suit, rising and accepting her hand, which he shook vigorously. "You drive a hard bargain, Ms. Watkins."

Penelope smiled at him. "Oh, I think you're going to benefit quite nicely."

"I wouldn't be here if that wasn't the case." He extended his head in a brief nod before squeezing her fingers one last time. "I hope Donovan realizes how lucky he is."

Penelope stacked iPad and phone into a neat pile. "I'll be sure to remind him."

"Where is he? I'll remind him myself," Adam said.

Penelope had purposely scheduled this final meeting when Shane was out of the building, to ensure the ink on the deal was entirely of her own doing. She had something to prove, and when she made her points with Shane she made sure to leave no stone unturned.

Which is why she won all of their arguments.

Penelope frowned slightly. "I'm sorry, I'm afraid Shane's tied up at the mayor's office and won't be back until late this afternoon."

Adam nodded and buttoned his suit jacket. "I'll give him a call. It's been a pleasure doing business with you, although I suspect I would have gotten a better deal with Donovan."

Penelope laughed. "Yes, well, that's probably true."

Ten minutes later she texted Shane and told him they'd come to terms with Hayes.

He texted back. You pulled it off. I didn't think it could be done but I should have known better. I suppose you'll be looking for a raise.

She smiled. Of course.

Done.

She chuckled. You're so easy. I'll let you know what I'm worth.

Why am I not surprised?

Thirty seconds later he texted again. Congratulations. I'm proud of you. I owe you dinner at Alinea so we can celebrate. Name the time and place and I'll get it done.

Her heart swelled. Maybe it was silly, but Shane was like the big brother she'd never had and she wanted him to be proud. To continue to prove to him she was the smartest business decision he'd ever made.

Deal.

She had a fleeting thought to call her parents down in Florida, just for some official family support, but abandoned the idea. God bless them, they tried, but they really didn't understand what she did. They thought she was Shane's secretary and, according to her old-fashioned father, she'd wasted all that money on college when she could have gone to secretarial school and accomplished the same thing. The day she'd gone off to college, her mom had patted her on the hand and told her to learn how to type and find a good provider to take care of her. It's not that they weren't proud of her; they just came from a different generation and didn't understand her.

So she called Sophie, and when her friend picked up she said, "I did it. I closed the deal."

Sophie let out a squeal of excitement, showing all the proper enthusiasm required, and Penelope grinned like a maniac as Soph hooted and hollered and clapped into the phone.

When she'd finally calmed down, Sophie said, "It's Friday and this calls for celebration. We are going out on the town. It's time to party."

Penelope laughed. "I was hoping you'd say that."

"I know just the place, it's the hottest club, it's opening weekend, and I have an exclusive invite." As a PR executive for an entertainment company, Sophie had access to all the latest happenings around town, and club managers everywhere wanted her to show up. A couple of years ago she'd started a blog called *Chicago After Dark*, and everyone who was anyone in the city knew if you wanted to make it, you needed to land on Sophie's places-to-be list.

Unable to stop grinning, Penelope sighed. "Is this one of those places you can't go to until after eleven?"

"Of course. We'll go to dinner first," Sophie said. "I wish Maddie was in town and she could come too."

"Me too." Penelope was thrilled Maddie was happy living with her husband in the small town of Revival, but she missed her terribly. While they still saw her fairly regularly, it wasn't the same.

"We'll just have to drunk-text her all night so she doesn't feel left out." Sophie's voice was filled with maniacal glee.

Penelope laughed. "I'm sure Mitch will love that."

"He'll live. He gets her all the time, the least he can do is offer a consolation prize." Sophie huffed and Penelope could just picture her standing there tossing her long, blond hair over her shoulder in indignation. "We'll Uber so you can relax about being a designated driver. I'll pick you up at eight."

And then she was gone.

Penelope sat down in her chair, relaxed for the first time in weeks. She glanced at her calendar and saw she didn't have any meetings after four. Divine intervention if she ever saw one. She'd go to Nordstrom after work, buy a new dress and a new pair of shoes.

Tonight, she celebrated.

Why had Evan thought this was a good idea? Without alcohol to dull his brain, the music in the club was too loud, and even the VIP lounge was too crowded. A gorgeous, Victoria's Secret angel from Brazil named Rafaela Barros sat to his left and was practically trying to climb into his lap.

With waist-length, golden-brown hair, vivid hazel eyes, tanned skin and legs that went on for miles, she captured every male eye in the room, and she knew it. Once, she'd been a regular hookup and exactly the type of woman he'd always stuck with. Wild in bed. Uncomplicated. And, most important, not interested in commitment.

He'd been trying to work up some enthusiasm, but it wasn't happening. When he'd called his old teammate he'd convinced himself if he just got back on the wagon he'd be good to go.

All it would take was one hookup and he'd forget about this craziness with Penelope. Forget the way she trembled under his touch. Forget the way her electric-blue eyes seemed to peer right into him.

If he took Rafaela home he could go back to putting

Penelope in the box he'd assigned her the day he'd walked out of her life.

At least, that was the line of bullshit he kept trying to sell himself.

As Rafaela's lips brushed his ear, her long fingers curled over his thigh, and she said in her thick Brazilian accent, "I want to fuck."

"Soon." He let his gaze fall to her full, bee-stung lips. He cocked a head toward the group around the table, filled with football players, a smattering of models, and socialites. "I can't leave yet."

A lie. None of these people were his friends, and all he wanted was to go home.

Well, that wasn't true either.

All he *really* wanted was to go to Penelope's house, sit on her couch, and watch bad TV with her curled next to him. Such an impossibility, he might as well say he wanted to go fly to Mars.

He was still kicking himself for the incident at her house. He'd been a fool to touch her again. He'd known it was a mistake, but he hadn't been able to help himself. He'd broken the seal and now he was like an addict. The only way he'd kept his hands off her all these years was by never touching her in the slightest way, doing everything in his power to make sure she hated him, and never, ever being alone with her.

His plan had worked beautifully.

She clearly hated him. Although she still wanted him. No matter how hard she tried, she couldn't quite hide her reaction. Since that first night, all those years ago, they'd had powerful chemistry.

And none of the countless women he'd taken to bed had changed that.

Under the table, Rafaela's hand closed over his cock and squeezed. "Now."

He looked at her and felt nothing.

He must be out of his fucking mind. Any sane, reasonable man would jump at the chance to take her to bed. Evan had firsthand knowledge of her skills, but couldn't work up the slightest interest.

It was time to throw in the towel. As much as he wanted to get back on the horse, to go back to the person he'd been before his injury, he couldn't.

It felt like pretending.

Even before he'd been hit in the head he'd been vaguely dissatisfied with the state of his life, but then he'd had the game to distract him. Now, with nothing to fill the void, he could no longer escape the emptiness.

No matter how much he tried to talk himself into it, he didn't want to fuck Rafaela. He didn't want to party all night with a bunch of strangers. Didn't want to do anything but go home, play football, and see Penelope.

Since the last two were impossible, he settled for the only thing he could control.

He placed his hand over Rafaela's. "I'm ready to leave."

The model gave him a satisfied, pouty smile and squeezed again. She leaned over and whispered in his ear, "I've missed your big cock."

He removed her hand. "Alone."

"What?" Her brow furrowed in confusion.

"I can't do this." He looked away from her only to come face-to-face with Penelope.

She'd been haunting him for days, and for a moment he thought he'd conjured her, but the Penelope of his imagination didn't look at him with ice in her eyes and that set of her jaw. No, this Penelope was real, and she stood before him in a slim cut, off-the-shoulder black dress that hugged her lean frame, and high heels.

Their gazes locked.

Fuck. This looked all wrong.

What was she doing here? He was halfway out of his chair, mouth already open to explain, when he realized Sophie stood next to her, and he couldn't say anything to her at all.

He sat back down.

The past was a secret they'd both never shared.

Oblivious to the tension, Sophie grinned at him. "Hey, Evan, good to see you out of the house."

If he was smart, he'd slip back into this customary smug-playboy role, but he couldn't take his eyes off Penelope. "What are you doing here?"

She crossed her arms over her chest and shifted her attention across the bar.

Sophie threw her arm around Penelope. "Our girl here closed a huge, businessy-type deal, so of course I had to take her to the best hot spot in the city to celebrate."

That didn't surprise Evan; Penelope was the smartest person he knew. He didn't think there was anything she couldn't do.

All he wanted to do was explain that Rafaela meant nothing to him. That he didn't want her, had never wanted her. But he couldn't say any of that. He cleared his throat. "Congratulations."

Across from him, Darnell Jones, a running back with the Bears, craned his neck to check out the two women. Clearly they met with his satisfaction when he flashed his big, trademark smile. "You ladies want to join the party?"

Penelope flicked a glance at Evan. "No, thank you, we need to be going." She grabbed her friend's arm. "Come on, Soph."

Sophie gave her a confused glance, and nodded. "You sure? It's only twelve thirty and this is your big night."

Darnell patted his knee and leered at Penelope. "Come on over, sweet thing. Daddy will make sure to give you a proper celebration."

Evan gripped the edge of the chair and forcibly had to keep from reacting.

Penelope's gaze slid to his, flicked over Rafaela, before shaking her head. "I've been up since five."

Darnell grinned. "Might as well make it a full twenty-four hours."

Penelope gave him that fake, pleasant smile that always irritated Evan. "Thank you for the offer, but it's time to go."

Sophie's lips turned down but she nodded before shifting her attention to him. "You'll be at the benefit, right, Evan?"

His family would murder him if he wasn't. "I'll be there."

Penelope turned, dragging Sophie with her, not even bothering to say good-bye.

He watched her go, ass a steady, hurried sway, as though she couldn't get away from him fast enough. Which, in truth, she probably couldn't. Jaw clenched, he sat there, powerless to stop her, reminding him of everything wrong with his life. With him.

Rafaela gripped his jaw and dragged his attention away from Penelope's retreating form. "Is that why?"

"What?" He pried her fingers from his face and put them in her lap, and played dumb. Penelope wouldn't believe it, but this wasn't the first time a woman had questioned him about her. The last being at his brother's wedding when Penelope had caught him with the girl whose name he hadn't remembered.

Still couldn't remember.

Rafaela tilted her chin toward the departing women. "The brunette. Is she why you want to go home alone?"

God, suddenly he was just so exhausted. So fucking tired of keeping up the pretense that she meant nothing to him. Just once, he wanted to admit it to someone, even if that someone was a hot Brazilian model who meant nothing to him. He sighed, and scrubbed a hand over his jaw. "Yeah, she is."

Chapter Six

Penelope smiled at Logan Buchanan, who sat across from her at their normal lunch spot, Joe's. After years of working together, they'd moved from cordial colleagues to acquaintances, and finally to friends. Now, instead of having meetings at their office, they had long lunches that were probably only twenty-five percent business and seventy-five percent stress relief.

A former SEAL Six, Logan owned a high-tech, military-savvy investigation and security firm that did hush-hush work for the government and companies all over the world. Shane and Logan had been friends forever, after bonding over a shared misbegotten youth, and Logan's firm investigated all their top candidates.

She slipped the encrypted flash drive Logan had tossed on the table into her purse. She'd summarize the details on their top candidate for the open CFO position and report the findings to Shane and the head of HR after she got back to the office. She glanced at Logan. "Nothing alarming, I presume?"

"Just your standard, run-of-the-mill, squeaky-clean suburban husband," Logan said, putting his menu aside.

Penelope smiled. Exactly what she'd expected. "Well,

with those types you never can tell. I'm glad my instincts were spot-on."

Logan laughed. "Almost annoyingly so. He's an all-around good guy, coaches Little League, appears to love his wife, and his past employers have nothing but good things to say about him. If anything, he might be too good for you."

"What are you trying to say? We're squeaky clean." They made sure of it.

"True. But Shane's way of doing things might be hard on the guy, if you know what I mean."

Penelope did know what he meant. While Shane ran a highly ethical company, he had a blunt force about him, high standards, and was generally considered ruthless when it came to negotiations. A natural leader, he expected a lot of his executives, but being yes-men wasn't one of them. He picked strong personalities and it wasn't unheard of for staff meetings to get a bit . . . rowdy.

When she'd put together the candidates for the CFO position, part of the reason she'd selected Floyd Casella was she thought he'd be a good counterbalance to the group, but Logan's comment gave her pause. She worried her bottom lip. "Do you think he wouldn't be a good fit?"

Logan tilted his head to the side, and shrugged one broad shoulder. "You'd know better than me, but his mild manner is something to be noted. I can see where you're going with him, but he seems at odds with the rest of the group."

Contemplating, Penelope tapped her nails on the table. "People might say the same about me."

Logan scoffed, his expression turning to incredulity. "Hardly. You fit right in with that bunch."

"I do not! I'm completely mild mannered, levelheaded, and logical." She was often the only calm one in the room when things got heated, and it was her job to get them to stay on track. Floyd was her top candidate, not only because of his exemplary track record, but because she thought it would be nice to have someone else on her side to calm the waters.

"You are all those things." Logan took a sip of his iced tea, the corded muscles in his forearms flexing. "But you've also got a spine of steel, and can not only go toe to toe with any one of them, but you often win. You might not be yelling and screaming, but you don't get lost in the crowd either. You're like a hawk, staying above it all, before you sweep in for the kill."

"And you don't think Floyd is capable of that?"

Logan narrowed his blue eyes. "I have my doubts."

Penelope nodded. Logan had uncanny instincts, ones she'd learned not to ignore. She'd have to think seriously about his observations. "I'll take it under advisement and talk to Shane."

"Then my work here is done."

Penelope beamed at him. "Thank you, by the way. That might be the nicest compliment I've gotten all month."

Logan stared at her for a good ten seconds before he said, "You know, most women think a compliment is 'you look pretty today.'"

Penelope rolled her eyes. "Boring and patently untrue. Women want to be viewed as highly competent just as much as men."

Logan laughed, shaking his head. "Do you have any idea how much I wish we had chemistry?"

It was Penelope's turn to chuckle. "It is one of life's cruel ironies, isn't it? Because we are clearly perfect for each other."

"Clearly. And you've got the most killer set of legs I've ever laid eyes on."

She crumbled up her napkin and threw it at him. "Flattery will get you nowhere."

He was right. It was a damn shame. Simply put, the man was gorgeous with his dark brown hair, blue eyes, and sculpted features. He was also well over six feet, and blessed with an absolutely flawless body.

If there was one man who could rival Evan, it was Logan, but it wasn't meant to be.

When they'd first met, they'd danced around each other, and she'd wondered if it was possible she'd finally met someone who would get Evan out of her head for good.

Then, they'd gone on a date. The night turned into a series of comical disasters that quickly dashed any budding attraction they might have had.

They'd been friends ever since.

Logan waved over the waitress, who practically tripped over herself to get to him.

Penelope sighed as the girl came to a crashing, breathless halt at the table. "What can I get for you?"

"I'll take another iced tea," he said in his smooth, low tone.

Cecilia once described his voice like maple syrup sliding over a stack of pancakes, and she wasn't far off. Too bad the voice Penelope wanted to hear was a rough rasp in her ear.

She shook her head. No. She refused to think one more second about Evan, or that night at the club. She'd spent far too much time obsessing about him, and that . . . that . . . woman. She gritted her teeth at the memory. The woman with the long, golden-brown hair was clearly a model, and had been so disgustingly perfect, Penelope was doubtful they even had to Photoshop her. Her hand had been high on his thigh, stroking him like a cat.

But what really killed Penelope was the stab of betrayal she'd experienced. That swift, instinctive, forbidden thought that he belonged to her. She hated him for it, hated herself even more.

Since the morning Evan walked out of her life he'd been unwavering in his actions. He never changed, especially where supermodels were concerned.

Well, good, Penelope had done her job. She'd given him the kick in the ass he needed, and now he could trot off and bed as many girls as he wanted. He was out of the house. She'd fulfilled her purpose. She'd helped the Donovans, and that had been her only goal. Mission accomplished.

Fan-fucking-tastic.

Now they could go back to normal. She'd stayed strong the night he'd shown up at her house. She'd made sure he'd never bother her again. And when had Evan *ever* come after her? Never, that's when. Not once. She'd always come to him.

Well, except for the night his dad died, and look how that ended. With disas—

Snap. Logan's fingers flew in front of her face, startling her out of her spiraling thoughts.

She blinked. "What?"

Logan pointed to the waitress. "Are you ready to order?"

A flush heated her cheeks. Damn Evan. She straightened her spine. All right, no more thinking about him. She turned to the waitress. "Can we have a few more minutes?"

The waitress gave her a perfunctory nod before turning her attention back on Logan, biting her lower lip in a way she probably thought sexy. "Can I get you anything besides the iced tea?"

Whenever Penelope went anywhere with Logan, women practically swooned and weren't at all shy about expressing their interest right in front of her.

"I'm good, darlin'," Logan said.

The girl looked like she was going to have a good

old-fashioned attack of the vapors before she managed to get herself under control and leave to do Logan's bidding.

Penelope waved a hand in the girl's direction. "Don't you ever get tired of the fawning?"

Logan grinned and shrugged one broad shoulder. "It has its benefits."

Penelope wrinkled her nose. "Should I be insulted all these women hit on you right in front of me?"

Logan laughed. "Did you ever think maybe they wouldn't if you didn't drift off while I was talking to you? Or acted remotely interested in me?"

Penelope smirked. "Good point."

"And what exactly were you thinking about? Your expression looked like you were plotting a murder." He shuddered. "It was terrifying."

"Oh nothing," she lied. "Just something I remembered I'd forgotten to do."

"Yeah, right, you never forget anything."

Unfortunately, Logan was a little too perceptive to fall for her evasion. "I forget anything that's not in my iPad."

Except Evan. There wasn't a trace of him anywhere, yet he refused to leave her head.

Before Logan could probe any further, she placed folded hands on the table in front of her and got straight to her ulterior motive. "I had another reason for asking you here today."

He cocked a brow. "What's that?"

"I need a favor."

"Anything, you know that."

She did, which was precisely why she was coming to him. "Do you have a date for the benefit?"

"No, I haven't had time to think about it," he said, his words slow and filled with speculation.

"Would you like to go with me?"

"Why?" He gave her a once-over. "Don't you want to go with one of your normal, corporate types?"

Oh, she'd thought about it, but they didn't pack the kind of punch she was looking for. The guys she normally dated wouldn't give Evan a moment's pause. But Logan, well, that was a different story.

At least in theory.

Not that she believed Evan would be jealous. He'd seen her with other men and never showed the slightest hint of reaction. But her dates had never been men like him, and that's where Logan came into this sordid little drama of hers.

If Evan thought she was with Logan, it would prove to him she hadn't given a moment's thought to him and the supermodel, or their encounters where she'd let him touch her.

Under normal circumstances she didn't engage in game playing, but she was making an exception to the rule. Just this once. Besides, she wasn't leading Logan on, and he occasionally escorted her to corporate functions. Although, this was the first time she'd asked for something more personally related.

"With this promotion, I'm swamped, and I don't want to give anyone false hope." She said the words with a breezy lightness, before waving her hand. "I have no time to date."

Logan scrubbed a hand over his jaw. He wore a white dress shirt with the sleeves rolled up to the elbows, highlighting his lightly tanned skin. "That will save me the trouble of getting a date."

Penelope grinned. "Of course, I do realize this means you'll be spending a Saturday night sans sex, so I'll pay for your ticket to make it up to you."

Logan laughed. "Deal."

"You're the best."

Logan picked up the menu. "I aim to please."

Perfect. Penelope breathed a sigh of relief. Her plan was in motion.

At least she could knock one problem off her Evan list.

Today she'd be happy with that, and not think about all the other Evan problems she'd been trying to strike off for far too many years to count.

Evan stood, propped against his brother's large kitchen island, and tried not to get in the way. James and Gracie moved around the kitchen in synchronized motions as they prepared the last of whatever meal Gracie had planned. Evan took a sip of the red wine Gracie had slid into his hand. "Are you sure I can't do anything?"

Head whipping around, Gracie glared at him, one blonde curl flopping into her eye. "For the last time, no, you're our guest."

James rolled his eyes. "He's not a guest, he's family."

"You know what I mean." Gracie planted a hand on one cocked hip. "You're lucky I'm not kicking you out too."

Pot holder in hand, James gave his girlfriend a droll look, then shrugged. "Suit yourself, woman."

Then he dropped the pot holder on the counter, turned to Evan and said, "Let's go sit down and kick our feet up."

Gracie's eyes narrowed on James's retreating form, then she shook her head at Evan, picked up the pot holder and threw it at his brother's head. It biffed James's perfectly placed hair, glanced off his temple before falling to the floor.

Gracie yelled, "You're impossible."

Evan laughed when his brother turned to look at Gracie and said, "You're going to pay for that."

"Whatever." Gracie waved a hand through the air, a cocky, sly arrogance on her full lips.

James sat down on the couch and motioned Evan over.

He shook his head and moved to join his brother, sitting down on the leather club chair. James and Gracie were still a surprise to him, but they just worked. It was like with Gracie, James lost all that rigid control and had actually learned how to have fun. Gracie loved drama, and to Evan's surprise, James indulged her quite often.

James grabbed the remote and turned on the TV.

Evan sat back in his chair. "I don't think she's scared."

James grinned, glancing back at Gracie before saying loud enough for her to hear, "She's baiting me."

"Am not," Gracie said, leaning over to peer into the oven, her fantastic ass on full display.

"Are too," James said, and flipped through the channels. "I know what you want, and you're sure as hell going to be getting it, so you can drop the sassy act."

"We need a double oven," Gracie called out, completely changing the subject, her jean-clad hips swaying hypnotically.

She might be his brother's, but Gracie was a hard woman not to pay attention to, and Evan got distracted, unable to look away. Maddie once said she was Mary Ann and Ginger rolled into one package, and Evan couldn't deny it was a good assessment. She was the kind of woman men stopped to stare at on the street, but was so open and accessible, everyone loved her. She was a flirt, wild, carefree, and had a rack that would not quit.

Pretty much the exact opposite of any woman James had ever dated.

"You can stop looking at her ass anytime," James said, his tone amused and good-natured.

Evan ripped his gaze away and offered an apologetic smile. "Sorry."

James shrugged. "It goes with the territory."

"Do you get tired of it?" Evan asked, curious.

"Like most things in life, it has its advantages and disadvantages," James said logically. He cast another glance back at Gracie, this time with affection. "She tends to make up for the disadvantages quite enthusiastically."

Evan laughed. He bet she did. Gracie didn't have a shy bone in her body, and they'd all witnessed her devotion to James.

His mind flashed to Penelope, remembering a time when she'd looked at him with the same devotion—before he'd thrown it away. Then he remembered her cold expression on Friday night, so different from the hot, needy looks she'd given him in their youth.

He gritted his teeth as he pictured her back then. Wet, swollen lips parted as she gasped for breath, her cheeks flushed, hair splayed over his chest.

Fuck. He shook his head, shifting in his chair. He was doing it again. He could not get her out of his mind. He'd been so good, for so long, but it was like floodgates had opened and he couldn't close them. And he no longer knew if he wanted to.

That night, after the club, he'd been so tempted to go to her house. To explain. But why?

She'd made it clear she wanted nothing to do with him.

He dragged a hand through his hair. She might remember, but it didn't change that one crucial fact—she'd never forgive him for the night he'd taken her virginity and then been so cruel to her.

Nor should she.

"You okay?" James asked, ripping Evan away from his thoughts.

"What?" He forcibly relaxed into the chair. "Oh, yeah, I'm good."

James studied him, his Donovan-family green eyes narrowed behind his glasses. "Are you sure?"

"Yep," Evan said, attention locking on the television. It was like without football to occupy his mind, he'd latched on to Penelope to obsess over.

He could feel James's heavy gaze on him, but before he could probe further, Gracie called, "James, I need you."

He gave Evan one more questioning look before getting up and walking into the kitchen.

Just then the doorbell rang.

Gracie's brows furrowed. "Are we expecting anyone?"

James shook his head.

Needing something to do, Evan jumped up. "I'll get it."

"Thanks," James said.

Evan walked to the front door, opened it, and blinked. Jesus. It was Penelope.

Chapter Seven

"You!" Penelope yelled before she could stop herself. Completely unprepared for Evan standing in the doorway, taking up all the free space, stealing the air left in her lungs.

One dark brow rose. "Me."

"What are you doing here?" Shocked, she was having a hard time composing herself. Evan was the last person she wanted to see. *The last.*

Expression unreadable, he propped his shoulder against the door frame. "Unlike you, I was invited."

With those words her composure snapped back into place. He was right. She was the drop-in. Okay then, she'd do what she needed to do and get out as fast as possible. She smoothed her features into something she hoped resembled polite, and held up her file folder. "I apologize, I won't be but a minute. I have to drop these off to Gracie and I thought I'd swing by on the way home."

He wore a pair of jeans and a navy henley that molded to his broad chest. He looked far too good for comfort. She had to force her gaze to remain on his face and not roam all over his body. She remembered all too well those times she'd rested her head on his chest as he played with her until she was a hot, needy mess of ecstasy.

She pressed her lips together.

Stop. Why couldn't she stop?

She'd gotten so good at not thinking about him, but now that he'd touched her, she hadn't just taken a backward step, she'd slid all the way back down the mountain.

Their carnal, illicit past kept playing over and over again through her mind at an alarming rate. And seeing him in the flesh wasn't helping matters.

But she was an adult, and as long as she maintained her cool facade things would go back to the way they'd always been. Polite with a healthy dose of antagonism. Perfectly mature.

He *did not* know what she was thinking.

Cool, dismissive, and unaffected. Her motto. She tilted her chin. "May I come in?"

Those damn jungle-cat eyes narrowed, then he straightened and stepped back to allow her entry.

She eyed the space between him and the door. She could make it without brushing against him. "Yes, well, I'll hand these off and be on my way."

He gestured toward the hallway. "They're in the kitchen."

"Fine," she said in a tone she used for wayward union officials.

She walked through the doorway and, just as she was able to feel the heat of his body, he said, "Has anyone ever told you that you dress like a femme fatale?"

Her head snapped toward him in surprise. "Don't be ridiculous." Her voice that of a prim librarian, not a man-killer.

She dressed nothing like that. Yes, her charcoal suit was classically cut, with a pencil skirt and a wide black belt. And yes, she wore her hair sleek today, in a style reminiscent of the forties, but she looked professional, not lethal.

He said nothing, and the sound of the door clicking closed behind her was too loud in her ears.

Okay, she needed a plan. Lists helped calm her nerves. She walked down the hall and quickly started formulating one in her head.

1. Smile. She plastered a bright smile on her face.
2. Posture. She steeled her spine like her mother taught her a proper young lady should stand.
3. Explain the purpose of her visit. She clutched her folder.
4. Be brief. There's no reason to linger.
5. Exit quickly. Have an excuse at the ready.
6. Go home and drink some wine. She mentally cataloged the bottles she had on hand.
7. Do not think about Evan. She'd create another list of other things she could think about later.
8. Go to bed early. She did have an early meeting tomorrow and getting the required eight hours of proper sleep was important.

By the time she'd reached the kitchen she'd settled considerably. She'd seen Evan a million times, and would for the rest of her life. It was no big deal.

Nothing, absolutely nothing, had changed.

James and Gracie turned to look at her.

Gracie gave her a huge smile. "Well, this is a surprise."

Penelope nodded at the couple. *Step three: explain the purpose of her visit.* "I'm sorry for the interruption, but I brought over the vendor contract the venue needs for the benefit. I thought I could grab your quick signature so I can get it to them tomorrow."

Gracie wiped her hands on a towel. "You didn't have to make a special trip. You could have e-mailed them and I'd have dropped them by the office tomorrow."

Step four: be brief.

"Please, you're doing this as a favor. I don't want you inconvenienced." There, she'd explained things quite well. Penelope walked over and put the file on the counter. "I also printed you off a diagram of the space so you can figure out the best place to set up. Just let me know where you want the display and I'll make sure you get first pick."

James flicked off a pot on the stove, then turned to face her. "You're a girl after my own heart, Pen. The most organized woman on the planet."

Just what she needed to drive a man wild, organizational skills. The kind of women Evan dated probably didn't have an efficient bone in their bodies. How could they, when they hardly wore any clothes during the Chicago winters?

Stop. Not her concern. She liked her organizational skills. Being efficient was high on her priority list. Driving a man wild was not. Stay on list.

She refused to look at Evan but could feel the weight of him bearing down on her.

Penelope was about to start preparing her exit statement when Gracie planted her hands on lush hips encased in jeans, and thrust out her magnificent chest. "Hey! I'm organized."

The woman really should be illegal. She made sexy into an art form.

Penelope nibbled at her bottom lip. Not that she cared about those things. She certainly hadn't thought ill of Gracie when Evan flirted shamelessly with her. She was too practical for that.

James slid an arm around Gracie's waist. "I never said you weren't."

"It was implied." Her voice indignant and put-upon, but she curled into James.

He squeezed her. "If you say so."

Gracie's expression scrunched up, as though she wanted to argue, but then she shrugged, laughed, and whatever chaos had been about to happen, passed.

Time to exit. Penelope ignored the desire to linger, and glanced toward the front door before pointing to the documents. "I had our legal department vet the contract, just your standard disclaimers. So if you could sign on the dotted line I'll be on my way."

All of a sudden Gracie spun away from James and clapped her hands. "You should stay for dinner. We've got plenty."

Penelope couldn't help it, and her attention flew to Evan. Their gazes locked for a fraction of a second, and awareness flared between them, before she jerked away. Heart beating wildly, she chanted in her head, *exit, exit, exit* until she found her voice. "That's sweet of you, but I've got a car circling, and I don't want to intrude."

She gritted her teeth. What was wrong with her? That wasn't on her list. She'd prepared the dinner meeting excuse. But no, her brain malfunctioned and provided the lamest excuse in the history of excuses.

"Don't be silly," Gracie said. "You never intrude."

James moved to the cabinet and pulled out another plate. "You're staying and we won't take no for an answer. We have far too much food and we need you to help us eat it."

Okay, there was time to salvage the exit part of her plan. She could still claim a meeting, which was completely believable. She opened her mouth to speak the words, but instead she waved ineffectually at the door. "The car."

What. The. Hell. *Come on, Penelope, say the words, you have a meeting. Say them!* Her mind screamed but her mouth stayed stubbornly shut.

"I'll take you home," Evan said, speaking for the first time.

Oh no. She forced her jaw to remain hinged, instead of falling open the way she wanted to. This wasn't helping.

And sadly, she had no one to blame but herself, because clearly some part of her wanted to stay.

But he wasn't helping either. They had rules. Silent agreements. No being alone. Ever. Yes, James and Gracie were still there acting as a buffer, but still.

In all these years they'd managed to avoid ever being each other's rides. Tonight was not the time to change that. Especially when she could still feel his hands on her skin, his mouth skimming over her stomach.

Now she really needed an excuse.

Damn him. He knew perfectly well she had no good reason to refuse a ride home. After all, they were lifelong friends. It would look strange if she refused. But she had to try because being alone with him was not smart. Not now, they were too on edge, the past too close. She attempted to use mental telepathy to drop this, while saying in a mild tone, "That's not necessary. I don't want you to go out of your way."

He met her gaze, and if she wasn't mistaken the gleam of challenge shone in his green eyes. Dark green, panther eyes. The eyes of a predator. She cursed herself for reading that shape-shifter romance last night. Now look at her, thinking such ridiculous nonsense. "You're on the way."

She was, but she'd hoped no one would notice. She bit her bottom lip and searched for a way out.

Before she could speak, Gracie said, "Great. It's settled then."

No, wait, her mythical meeting.

James grabbed a set of silverware and put it on the plate

he'd placed on the counter. "Evan's got you. So you can call the driver."

Do not look at him. Not one little peek. She bit her lip and looked anyway.

The second their eyes met, he said, in a voice tinged with that private tone he used on her, "Yeah, Pen, I've got you."

Her pulse pounded as her stomach did a little flip of excitement.

Needing something to do, she scrounged around in her purse, even though she knew exactly where her cell was, before grabbing it from its place in her side pocket.

Okay, this wasn't a big deal. She'd had a thousand dinners with him in her lifetime. This was no different. Well, a little different since she'd be alone with him later. But she'd made her bed, now she had to lie in it. She put on a bright smile. "Let me just call Steven and let him know he can go."

Despite her normally impeccable judgment, she'd always made rash decisions where Evan was concerned. Clearly age hadn't cured her. Later, much later, when she was tucked into bed *alone*, she'd contemplate her actions.

But for now, she'd deal.

After Penelope was done with her call, Gracie shoved a glass of wine in her hand, and she was able to avoid Evan entirely as they got ready for dinner.

The second she sat down across from him, her attention locked on his, as though unable to help herself.

Her breath stalled in her chest.

He watched her, his expression intent as his gaze roamed over her face, lingered on her lips, before rising again to meet her eyes.

There was heat, far too much of it.

It forced her to be honest. As much as she wanted to blame him, she wasn't any better. Some part of her wanted to stay, and right now, that part of her was more powerful than her desire to stay the hell away from him.

Like she should.

Gracie piled a mountain of food onto her plate, pulling her from her thoughts.

Penelope blinked down at the four thick slices of beef tenderloin. "Geez, Gracie, how much do you think I can eat?"

Gracie winked at her. "It's low carb."

James laughed. "Not when combined with mashed potatoes."

Gracie put the plate down, sat in her chair before handing Penelope said bowl, and smirked. "Lobster mashed potatoes."

"Oh God, that sounds divine," Penelope said, putting a scoopful onto her plate.

She passed the bowl to Evan and their fingers tangled for a moment, shooting a jolt of electricity up her arm. His thumb brushed over her hand and she had to force herself not to jerk back.

Rid of the mashed potatoes, she concentrated on her plate. The food did look delicious. Despite living alone, she tried to cook nice meals for herself, but it wasn't always easy with her demanding schedule. Sometimes it was just easier to pick up a salad from Starbucks, along with her late-night caffeine fix, before heading to her home office to work and eat over her desk. This had been her pattern over the last couple of weeks, with the Hayes deal and the other projects heating up, and she hadn't tasted anything homemade in a dog's age.

She took a bite and her eyes practically rolled back into her head. Nothing she ever made tasted this good. The potatoes were creamy, buttery, and absolutely decadent. She took another forkful and moaned. "Wow, this is fantastic."

Gracie, whose main purpose in life seemed to be a

desire to feed people, said, "Thank you. I can't take credit for the recipe though. I convinced the chef over at Fusion 180 to give me the recipe."

Sophie had taken her to that restaurant when it first opened, but they hadn't had a chance to sample the menu staple because the chef, a dark-haired, good-looking guy in his early thirties, had created a special meal to impress Soph.

Obviously, Penelope had missed something incredible.

James scoffed, picking up his own fork. "You flirted with him and when he was tripping all over himself, went in for the kill."

Gracie waved a hand over his plate. "Where's your gratitude? You're eating the best damn mashed potatoes in all of Chicago in the privacy of your own home. And later tonight you'll do all sorts of devious things to me before you fall asleep with me naked and wrapped around you."

Penelope would not think about sex.

James scrubbed a hand over his jaw as though contemplating, before he nodded. "Good point."

Penelope looked down at her plate. They were not a good couple to be around. She could feel Evan's gaze, heavy on her, and she willed her cheeks not to flush.

Evan had done a thousand devious things to her, but she'd never slept naked with him, his arms wrapped around her. No, he'd saved that for his real girlfriends. Not her. And the one time it had happened, she'd woken to him already putting his clothes on, his expression cold and remote.

All she needed to do was remember that, and she could go on treating him like she always had.

From across the table he pulled at her. Unbidden, her gaze met his, and something flared to life.

She jerked away to stare back at her food.

This was the last time she'd put herself in this situation.

After tonight, she'd work on forgetting. She'd forgotten once, she could forget again.

She just needed to make it through this night untouched.

Because, if he touched her, she was finished.

Evan shut the car door, enclosing him inside his sports car with Penelope. Her scent seemed to fill the small space, intoxicating him with her sweetness and hint of wild.

To say dinner had been a tense affair was an understatement.

Oh, he doubted Gracie and James noticed; to them nothing appeared out of place. He and Penelope treated each other like they always did—he was the overgrown frat boy and she was his kid sister's annoying friend.

They were roles they'd been playing for years, and they were experts at it. Only now there were a million unspoken things between them. Nothing that could be discussed or hinted at in front of his brother and his girlfriend, but they still filled the air. They'd tried not to look at each other, not to linger, but it was like every time their eyes caught and held, a whole conversation passed between them.

Anger and lust. The past and the present. All the things they'd done mixed with the things they'd never dared to say.

It was quite a cocktail of emotion, and he was on edge, coiled tight, like he used to get before a big game. Only he no longer had football to release all his pent-up energy.

And he was alone with Penelope.

She stared straight ahead, her face lit by the glow of the streetlights. She licked her bottom lip in that nervous way she had, and clutched her purse.

"I'm not going to attack you," he said, and then cringed

at the gruffness in his voice. He'd meant to sound teasing, light, to put her at ease, but it came out nothing like that.

She frowned. "Of course not."

A tense awkwardness filled the air.

She pointed to the street. "Aren't you going to drive?"

He sighed and shifted into first, pulling out onto the road.

They drove in complete silence. With every block that passed, her fingers gripped her purse tighter and tighter until he thought she might rip the fabric.

Needing to break the tension, he cleared his throat. "Congratulations on your promotion. Shane told me he'd finally done right by you."

"Thank you," she said curtly, never taking her eyes off the road.

Suddenly it seemed ridiculous that he knew virtually nothing about her current life. "What is your job again?"

A beat of silence. "Chief operating officer."

This was painful.

To think, he had a reputation for being able to talk any woman out of her pants. It was almost laughable. He pulled up to a stoplight. "What's that?"

Another squeeze of her fingers on her bag. "I'm in charge of all the company's operations."

"So, after Shane, you're next in charge?"

"Pretty much."

"You deserve it."

She didn't respond.

He was about to try again, when a car full of teenage boys pulled up next to them. One pointed at the car and the next thing Evan knew, they all seemed to be hanging out their car windows, pounding on the doors and yelling, "Cool car, man!"

It broke some of the tension and Penelope whipped around, glaring at him. "Don't you get enough attention?"

Maybe it was a bit over the top, but so what? He wasn't going to apologize. "I know it's not as practical as the Prius you probably drive."

She pressed her lips together, and he wondered if she was repressing a smile, finding it bothered him that he no longer knew her facial expressions and cues like the back of his hand.

She scowled at him. "I don't drive a Prius, and even if I did, it's better than this batmobile."

His surprised laughter was like a bark. The light turned green, and instead of acting like a mature adult, he put the car in gear, gunned the engine, and shot off the line, giving the boys a show as they hooted and hollered.

Penelope glared at him and hissed, "Evan! Stop that!"

Something that had been sitting heavy on his chest since he'd taken that hit, eased. Not a lot, but a little. He laughed, and broke another one of their unspoken cardinal rules. "I miss the way you say my name, even when you're reprimanding me."

She shifted her attention to look out the window. "I don't want to talk about this."

It was better left unsaid, he knew that, but he just couldn't make himself fall in line anymore. A wall between them had been torn down that night she'd come to him, and now he didn't want to resurrect it. "You want me to pretend there's nothing between us, is that it?"

"There *is* nothing between us." She shifted in the seat before sighing. "I want it to go back to the way it was before."

"I know you do." He should want the same thing. Only he no longer bought his reasons.

They drove in silence for a good five minutes before

she said, "I didn't go there that night to rehash the past. I shouldn't have let you touch me."

"But you did let me." His fingers tightened reflexively on the steering wheel. "The floodgates are open and I don't think I can shut the door."

"Stop it," she said, her tone agitated. "Just stop. I don't want to talk about this."

They were getting close to her house, and he fully expected her to jump out of the car before he even came to a full stop, so he had to speak fast. He didn't know what was driving him; hell, he'd ignored his emotions so long he could no longer make heads or tails of them, but he knew he had to tell her at least part of the truth. "I lied that night when I said you were good for an ego stroke. And just because I've been a complete bastard to you the last fifteen years doesn't mean you didn't matter to me."

She pressed her fingers to her temples. "It's your actions that define you, not your words."

She was right, but he didn't know how to explain that in his mind he'd been doing the right thing by her. He'd been saving her. He blew out a hard breath. If she wanted actions, that's what he'd give her. "Fine, then you should know, Friday, at the club, I didn't go home with Rafaela. I slept alone."

She didn't want it to matter. It did.

The surge of happiness that came from hearing he hadn't touched the model was infuriating. She wanted to maintain some cool facade, but she couldn't seem to get it to fall into place, so she settled on anger. Through gritted teeth, she said, "I don't care about this, Evan."

He pulled to a stop and turned his head to look at her. The dark night casting him in shadows, making him look dangerous. "You're a liar."

She was. More than he could ever possibly know, but she soldiered on, toeing the party line. "Who you sleep with is not, nor will it ever be, my concern."

"That's true in theory, but not so much in practice, is it?" His voice sounded dark and rough.

Her fingers dug so tight into her bag, they hurt. She looked directly into his dark green eyes, and lied. "That may have been true at one point, but what happened between us was a long time ago. It doesn't matter now."

"Then why do you still tremble when I touch you?"

She didn't have a good reason for that, now did she? She searched her mind for a cold, plausible explanation and couldn't come up with one. In the end, she didn't have to. The light changed and he turned his attention away from her and onto the road.

Three minutes later he pulled in front of her house and before he even rolled to a stop, she had her hand on the handle. The second the car jerked to a halt, she went to open the door, only he gripped her wrist.

His touch was like an electric shock to her system. She managed to repress the gasp before jerking around to glare at him. "What?"

His hold tightened, and a muscle in his jaw clenched. "She asked about you."

The statement confused her and she relaxed fractionally back into her seat. "What are you talking about?"

Green eyes narrowed on her. "Rafaela, when I refused her, she asked if you were the reason. I said yes."

It stunned Penelope as nothing else could have. He'd admitted whatever-they-were to someone. They'd always been a secret. Always.

Evan's thumb brushed over her pounding pulse. "She guessed. In that thirty-second conversation, where we didn't even address each other, she knew. She's not even the first one."

Penelope licked her dry lips, and Evan's gaze tracked the movement.

"Kim Rossi," he said, bringing up his high school girl-friend. "She used to accuse me of sleeping with you, every other day."

She couldn't hide the shock. Back then she believed his girlfriend didn't know she existed. "She did not."

Evan leaned closer, and unable to help herself she twisted back to him.

"She did." With one hand still locked around her wrist, he slid his free hand around her neck and through her hair. "I guess technically I didn't lie, but she sure as hell knew something was going on. And you and I both know, what we were doing was more than fucking. That what we did in that basement made sex irrelevant."

She shuddered. The memories pounded through her, heating her blood, disorienting her and making her stupid. "It's in the past. It's over."

His gaze dipped to her lips. "No, it's not. If it was, things would be easy between us, instead of hard."

"It's just . . ." She searched and couldn't come up with any other reason but the truth.

"It's just that it's never really ended. You're still the woman I think about." His fingers shifted through her hair, and his voice dipped. "Tell me I'm not the one you think about when you come."

"You're not," she whispered, the words sounding every bit the lie they were.

"Liar."

They were so close now, she could feel the heat of his body, their breaths coming too fast.

"Do you think about all the things I whispered in your ear? Did to you?"

"Evan." His name on her lips came out like a plea when she'd meant for him to stop.

"Yes, just like that." His head dipped lower, closer. "That's how my name sounded before you'd start begging."

She whimpered, just like she'd done way back when.

He twisted his hand around her hair, tilting her chin up, forcing her to meet his gaze. "This is what you need to understand, Pen, what you never did get. All that power I had over you, that's exactly the power you had over me."

She shook her head, refusing to believe. "No."

"Yes. No other woman. Not back then, not now."

He released her and she had to resist the urge to chase him. To beg like she used to. But she forced herself to sit back against the door, as far away from him as possible.

"You should go," he said, his voice filled with something she couldn't decipher.

It felt like rejection, despite his words. Because that's the thing with Evan. His words never matched his actions.

At least not where she was concerned.

She moved to scurry from the car, but stopped and looked back at him. She refused to end—yet again—with him getting the last word and sending her on her way. It was time to put an end to this madness between them. Time to get back to the way things had been before. She narrowed her eyes. "I don't know what your game is, but stay away from me."

In the darkened car, he stared right back at her, his expression filled with hardness. "No."

"I mean it. No more getting me alone, no more touching me, no more anything." She waved her hand in the space between them. "Whatever is going on here stops now."

"No matter how many times you tell yourself that, Pen, I'll never believe you, and neither will you."

She wanted to scream, to deny, but what was the point? She'd already provided him with all the evidence he needed, so it was best to go on the offensive. As calmly as she could muster, she said, "Just because you can make my body respond, doesn't mean I like you. I don't like you, Evan. I haven't liked you for a very long time, and I don't see that ever changing."

He looked at her for several uncomfortable moments, the car thick with tension and anger, and everything else that swirled between them like the most dangerous of brewing storms.

Finally, he nodded. "I know that, which is why you're going inside untouched, instead of with your skirt around your waist, impaled on my cock."

Heat flooded her system, threatening to overtake her. "You just think it's that easy, don't you?"

"It is that easy. We've got years of sexual tension and frustration between us. One touch, and it's over. But it doesn't help my end game."

"I'm not a game to be played and won." They were spiraling precariously out of control. She would not give in, because the sex, the past, it didn't matter. Their differences mattered, and that's what she needed to focus on. She wasn't a model. She wasn't reckless and wild. She wanted to stay home on Friday nights and he wanted to go party. She wanted family and stability. He wanted none of those things. It was time to put an end to this, to get them back on the right track. Calmly, quietly, she said, "Our end came and went a long time ago."

"You have no idea how badly I want to prove you wrong." His gaze dropped to her mouth. "But here's the difference between you and me: I know I'm weak where you're concerned. I know we won't be able to stop. Just like I know if I take you now it will only end in disaster."

She turned her head to look out the window. "Things need to go back to the way they were, Evan."

"I don't think that's possible."

She shook her head. "You still think you have control over everything, but you don't."

He laughed, and the sound was hard and brittle. "You don't have a fucking clue what you're talking about. I don't have control over anything. Not my career, my life, and I sure as hell don't have control over you."

She wanted to argue with him, but that would take all night and she had no intention of rehashing the past. Of ripping open old wounds just so she could prove *him* wrong. "It's time to say good-bye."

Several beats of silence. "Sleep well."

Fat chance. "You too."

Then she got out of the car and walked away.

Chapter Eight

"Oh my God, Gracie, this place is gorgeous." Penelope stood in the large bakery in stunned awe. "I can't believe what you've done."

Gracie wiped her hands on a towel and grinned. "Me either. It's better than I could ever have dreamed. I can't believe we open in a couple of months."

Penelope had actually found the location for Gracie, but she couldn't get over the transformation. When she'd discovered it the storefront had high ceilings and good bones, but Gracie had designed the space so with its wide plank wood floors and vintage moldings, the bakery looked like it belonged in Paris. "You've outdone yourself."

"If my momma could see me now." Gracie wrinkled her nose. "Although, I think she'd be a bit peeved it's in Chicago instead of back in Revival."

"Are you homesick?" Penelope asked. The plan had been for James and Gracie to split time between Revival and Chicago, but lately with James's work schedule and the bakery, they'd spent more time here.

Gracie tugged off her apron and smoothed a hand over her tight jeans before tugging at her pale blue tee, which read CALIFORNIA BLONDE, and matched her blue eyes. "I miss my brother, Sam, but I know the bakery in Revival is in good hands with Harmony. In some ways, I think she's better than I am."

Penelope laughed. She'd met Harmony Jones only once, and her pale pixie features and melodious voice hid a spine of steel. "I doubt that, but it's good to have capable help."

Gracie fluffed her curls. "Ready?"

Penelope had been surprised when a couple of days after dinner, Gracie called and asked her to lunch. Although Penelope had always liked the other woman, they'd never spent much one-on-one time together.

"Yep, where do you want to go?" Penelope asked. The bakery was in the River North area of Chicago, and there were plenty of choices.

"There's that new place on Wells we can try." Gracie grabbed her jacket. "I've heard they have a pretzel burger that will give you orgasms."

Penelope laughed. "In that case, let's walk."

"Good idea." Gracie winked, grinning. "Although I'd appreciate if you didn't mention to James that I voluntarily exercised."

After an overweight childhood, James Donovan had blossomed into a swan—and exercise fanatic, something Gracie seemed to endlessly tease him about. Penelope smiled. "Your secrets are safe with me."

Gracie paused and gave her a sly look. "Right back at ya."

Penelope experienced a momentary sense of irrational alarm, but the sensation faded when Gracie brought up the upcoming benefit, and they were off, talking about plans, baked goods, and Penelope let the mild breeze and bright sun warm her face as they leisurely made their way through the Chicago streets.

* * *

Evan didn't have to look at the menu. Shane was a creature of habit and whenever they met their middle brother for lunch in Hyde Park, they always went to the same dive diner. Shane had ideas about old-school Chicago restaurants and did his best to support the small businesses whenever he could.

While they waited for James, Shane eyed Evan. "You're looking a lot better."

"I feel better." With nothing propelling him forward, it was still an effort to get out of bed some days, but he was doing it. He'd started working out again and that helped, although he'd stayed away from his former club. He didn't want to see any of his football friends. Instead he ran down the lakefront and started going to an old-school gym. If anyone recognized him, they didn't mention it, and Evan could spend an hour punching bags until he was exhausted, sweating, and unable to think about football, his failed career, Penelope, or his blank future.

"Have you called our mother?" Shane asked, before taking a sip of iced tea.

"Yes, dad," Evan said, experiencing the first stirring of irritation. He loved his brother, but out of all his siblings, his relationship with Shane was the most strained. Even as kids they'd always butted heads, with James the peacemaker between them. Time and their father dying had only made it worse, because Shane couldn't turn off his savior complex and tended to treat Evan like an overgrown child.

Not much different than Penelope, which was further salt in the wound.

Penelope and Shane were tight. Yes, there'd never been anything between them, but that didn't stop the jealousy.

Shane got to be with her, every single day.

His brother held up his hands, pulling Evan from his thoughts. "Hey, I was just asking. It's not like I'm not justified, after all. You've been in a drunken stupor for months."

"Yeah, yeah." Evan picked up the menu and pretended to study it, but anger and frustration made him add, "Just call me the family fuck-up."

"I didn't say that," Shane said.

"You didn't have to." Evan gritted his teeth, then forced his jaw to relax. It didn't matter that he'd made millions as a pro football player; he'd always be the black sheep of the family. The wild one. The one who brought Playboy bunnies to family parties, and took too many stupid risks.

A role that hadn't bothered him when football took up all his time and energy, but now felt like an albatross around his neck, made worse by the knowledge that he had only himself to blame.

"Don't twist my words. It's a simple question, and she's been worried sick about you," Shane said, his voice growing frustrated.

Evan looked toward the door, and then the clock over the fountain area. Where the hell was James? Without their middle brother as a buffer, this is what always happened with Shane.

"I called her, okay?" Evan said, flipping the page of his menu with more force than necessary. "Several times, in fact. If you'd talked to her, you'd know that."

"All right, relax." Shane studied his own menu and there was an awkward silence between them. Finally, his oldest brother cleared his throat. "The summer house in Revival is almost done, and I was thinking about having everyone go up there for a long weekend. Between all the houses, there's plenty of space."

Evan experienced a stab of loss and had to keep himself from wincing. Before, he would have had to check his schedule, but now time stretched out before him like a big question mark.

Would he ever feel that alive again? That focused and intense?

An image of Penelope flashed before him. She made him feel alive.

She also hated him. Would always hate him, despite her body's reaction.

And wasn't that just one of life's little ironies? That night in the car, he could have taken her. He could have had his fill. Fucked her until they were both mindless and satiated, and he hadn't done it. Couldn't do it. Because no matter how she responded, he couldn't forget she hated him. After all this time he still remembered the look on her face the morning after his dad died and he'd left her, and he could never be responsible for that look again.

So he'd sent her inside, and she'd left, but not before he'd witnessed the flash of anger and resentment. He knew her well enough to know she'd taken it as a rejection, as some sort of proof that he could resist her.

She was wrong.

He had too many regrets in his life. Too many bright promises unfulfilled. He didn't know what was going on between them, but he couldn't afford any more mistakes with her. He at least wanted a chance to make some sort of amends.

"Evan?" Shane's voice was a sharp snap of a whip, and Evan blinked, to find both his brothers staring at him with concern. When had James walked up?

Evan rubbed a hand over the back of his neck. "Sorry, what did you say?"

"Is everything all right?" Shane asked, his gaze narrowed in suspicion.

"Yeah, I just got distracted." Relieved James was finally

here to act as a buffer, Evan smiled. "What happened, did you get caught up by some coed?"

"Yes, as a matter of fact, one of my students needed some clarification after today's lecture," James said, sounding every bit the professor he was.

Evan raised a brow. "Was she female?"

"I don't see how that matters." James slid into the booth next to Shane and picked up his menu.

Evan and Shane looked at each other and shook their heads. At least, in this, they had solidarity.

James was clueless.

Orders placed, Penelope folded her hands and smiled at Gracie. "Thanks for inviting me to lunch, it was a pleasant surprise. It's been crazy and I could use the break."

Gracie took a piece of crusty bread from the basket and slathered it with butter. "Since I'll be spending so much time here as the bakery gets up and running, I thought it would be a good idea to get to know each other better."

"I couldn't agree more," Penelope said.

Gracie took a bite of the bread and moaned in pleasure, her eyes practically rolling into the back of her head.

Penelope usually passed on bread, especially during lunch, but decided if it was that good she'd have to break her normal rules. She snagged a piece, stared at the butter for a second, then threw caution to the wind.

It was a gorgeous day, the late spring days turning warm, and she'd run along the lake to make up for the indulgence.

Sometimes it was okay to be reckless.

Gracie swallowed another bite and put the bread on her plate. "I've decided it's time to become friends. Maddie and

Cecilia adore you, and I've always liked you even though you're such a good girl."

Penelope laughed. "Guilty as charged. I just can't help myself."

"Why do I not quite believe that?" Gracie propped her elbows on the table, her expression a touch too innocent.

The fine hairs on Penelope's neck rose. Did she . . . no . . . that was impossible. She was simply being paranoid. She shrugged one shoulder. "Wishful thinking?"

Gracie grinned.

That sensation of being on high alert didn't abate. "Ask anyone, I'm officially the most boring woman on the planet."

"Sorry, I don't believe it. Everyone knows you librarian types have the dirtiest secrets."

Penelope's heart gave a little lurch. The bread she'd been chewing turned to sawdust and she was barely able to swallow it down. No. There was no way. They'd avoided all unnecessary contact at dinner. Nobody had ever guessed. The idea alone was preposterous.

Gracie's attention darted around the restaurant, then she leaned in. "As I'm sure you've heard, minding my own business isn't really my strong suit."

The two women looked at each other, and in that moment Penelope knew Gracie had somehow figured out something was going on between Evan and her. How, Penelope had no idea, but she was sure of it. In rapid replay the night they'd had dinner at James and Gracie's played through her head, but she couldn't think of what would have given them away.

They'd acted the way they always had.

Penelope's only recourse was to lie. Wishing she still had a menu to look at, she picked at her bread. "Sorry, I don't have any secrets, let alone dirty ones. I'm just your average, everyday workaholic. I mean, I always intended to put some skeletons in the closet." She tittered and it sounded a touch too high. She smoothed out her tone. "But really, who has the time?"

Gracie flashed her most dazzling smile, holding up her hands as though in surrender. "Look, I get it, really I do. And you don't have to tell me anything, but before you continue to lie through your teeth, thinking I'm a nosy gossip, hear me out."

"Of course," Penelope said, her voice taking on the tone she used during contract negotiations when she was no longer willing to compromise and was appeasing the opposing party. "I can't wait to hear what I've got to confess. I'm one of those women who sadly never get gossiped about. So this should be fun."

"Yeah, yeah, because you're soooo boring. I get it."

"Exactly!" Penelope hoped she didn't sound defensive.

A blonde curl flopped into Gracie's eye and she tucked it behind her ear. "I've been thinking about this since that night we had dinner."

Penelope clenched her hands in her lap. Okay, this was no big deal. Gracie didn't have one stitch of proof. And who would even believe her? If she had to line up all the women in Evan's life and rate them, she'd probably be last on the list of potential bed partners.

Unaware of the chaos she was causing, Gracie continued. "I debated letting it go, and minding my own business for once, but then I started mulling it over. I've heard a lot of Donovan family gossip in the time I've known Maddie. People like to tell me their secrets because I'm so good at keeping them." She smiled again. "Since Maddie and Cecilia have this weird situation where they're married to each other's brothers, I'm the lucky recipient of all sorts of interesting tidbits of information. And let me tell you, I've heard all sorts of crazy things about those Donovan boys."

All her years in business told her to keep the protests to herself. She'd let Gracie have her say and casually dismiss the idea, the subject would change and the matter would drop.

Expression turning serious, Gracie tilted her head to the side. "You're both so good at hiding it, at first I thought it was my imagination. There are always so many people around, until that night I never noticed how it is between you. After you left, I thought about it, and it occurred to me it's because I've never seen you interact one-on-one. In fact, I've never seen you interact at all."

All she needed to do was not react. She could do that without a problem. She had years of practice. She'd just closed a multimillion-dollar deal by not reacting. This was a piece of cake. She folded her hands neatly in her lap so she wouldn't fidget. "I have no idea what you're referring to."

"I'm referring to whatever is between you and Evan."

Penelope's throat dried up. And there it was, out there in the open. She kept her voice cool. "That's crazy. Can you even imagine?"

Gracie offered a soft, understanding type of smile. "I think I only recognized it because I used to do the same thing with James. In that way I understand Evan. Like me, Evan's a natural flirt. It's kind of our default setting when dealing with the opposite sex. Since I met him, I've seen him flirt good-naturedly with every woman he comes in contact with, from Sophie to the waitress at the restaurant. He used to flirt relentlessly with me until James put the kibosh on that. That night at dinner it occurred to me, there are only two women I've never seen him flirt with— Maddie, which makes perfect sense—and you."

Penelope swallowed hard and tried to keep her expression as impassive as possible. "Evan's never been my biggest fan. Besides, I'm not really the kind of woman men flirt with."

Gracie shook her head. "That sounds good, but that's not it. It never even crossed my mind until dinner, but once I put it all together it was plain as day."

Penelope tried to play it breezy and forced a laugh that sounded as strained as she felt. "The only reason Evan even knows I'm alive is because I've been best friends with Maddie since we were six."

Gracie shrugged one shoulder. "Do you realize you guys avoid looking at each other? Avoid speaking directly to each other? When we were clearing the table, he stepped too close to you and you held your breath. Then he started away and moved around you like you were surrounded by an invisible force field. That's when I really started paying attention. I mean, when is the great Evan Donovan skittish around a woman? It happened all night, it's like you are afraid to get too close to each other."

That's because she *was* afraid. Every time they got too close another brick in the wall between them got chipped away.

She tried one more time to dissuade Gracie. "There's nothing between Evan and me."

Technically, that was the truth.

"When you think nobody is watching, you look at him the way I used to look at James."

"I . . ." Penelope trailed off.

"And then there's the way he looks at you."

Unable to help herself, Penelope leaned in.

Gracie ran a finger down the edge of her water glass. "Like he's starving. And I don't even mean sex. I mean, he looks at you like you're everything."

She couldn't speak, and didn't have to, because Gracie continued on.

"I won't force you. I know you're private and reserved,

and I would have ignored it, but I'm ninety-nine percent positive you've never told a soul, and I thought maybe you needed someone to talk to."

"Why?" She gestured helplessly, unsure what she was even asking.

Gracie shrugged. "Call it instinct, but it became crystal clear to me there's something painful between you."

No, no, no. How had this happened? She'd gone so many years without anyone being the wiser, and now Gracie had figured it out. Panic beat a wild thump in her chest.

Gracie lived with James. Had she told him?

Penelope had to find out and spoke without thinking. "Did you say anything? To James?"

Gracie's expression softened and she shook her head. "I was going to ask him, but then I figured out nobody knew. That I would have heard about it somewhere if they did." She reached across the table and touched Penelope's ice-cold fingers. "If you need a confidante, I'm a good listener. And I just have a feeling you need someone to talk to."

To Penelope's horror, her eyes welled with tears. She furiously brushed them away.

Gracie clucked her tongue. "Awww . . . you poor thing."

As hard as she tried, she couldn't choke the emotions back down, not when they'd been riding her for so long. "Please, please don't say anything to James. To Maddie. Or anyone. God, I'd die."

"I won't. You have my word."

"Nobody can ever find out. I'm supposed to be the lone female immune to him."

"You've never told anyone, have you?"

Penelope shook her head as tears ran down her cheeks. "I'm sorry. It's nothing. And there's nothing between us."

She pressed her lips together. "We do, um, have a bit of a past."

Gracie picked up a cloth napkin and held it out to Penelope. "Honey, I have a bit of a past with some guys, and I can promise you whatever is going on with Evan, that's not it. Do you want to tell me about it?"

"No!" Penelope's voice was shrill.

"All right," Gracie said softly, and smiled. "But if you need to talk, I'm here for you."

She choked on her tears, straining to get them under control and the words just tumbled out. "He was the first boy I ever kissed. The first boy that ever touched me."

Gracie nodded, a consoling curve to her lips. "He was the first boy you ever loved."

"Yes," Penelope said, looking out the window. The shock and panic at being discovered mixed with relief at finally confessing the truth. At saying the words she'd never spoken aloud. "He broke my heart."

"Oh, honey," Gracie said, her eyes creasing with concern.

Penelope sniffed, feeling suddenly ridiculous for crying about something so long in the past. She picked up her napkin and dabbed it under her lashes. "What happened between us was a long time ago. It's long over." That he'd touched her was of little consequence. "I shouldn't be telling you this. I don't want anyone to know."

"I won't tell anyone, I promise," Gracie said. "But mark my words, it's not over."

And that was what Penelope was afraid of. They'd stirred the pot, and now they couldn't seem to turn off the stove. It was only a matter of time before they bubbled over.

* * *

Evan's lunch with his brothers went smoothly until Shane asked him in that nonchalant way he had, "Have you given any thought to your plans?"

Evan stiffened and pushed his plate away. "Plans?"

Shane wrapped his hand around the dingy off-white coffee cup. "You're going to need to do something with your time. I was curious if you'd thought about it."

"Nope." Evan gritted his teeth and looked out the window onto the sidewalk, watching the people pass them by. Of course he'd thought of it, only to come up with absolutely nothing.

His future was a blank, empty space. He didn't have any idea what to do with the rest of his life. All he wanted to do was play ball.

Ironically, the more he exercised and the stronger he became, the more he missed the game that would never be within his reach again. And the worst thing was, his injury didn't affect him physically. It's not like he'd blown out his knee and it ached every time he played, reminding him he was too banged up to do any good on the field. No, he felt fine, conditioned even. It's why he took up binge drinking to begin with, and sometimes, late at night when he couldn't sleep, he wanted to return to that numb place he'd been.

Only something stopped him from sinking back into that darkness.

James rubbed the bridge of his nose under his glasses before settling them back on his face. "He has money and time, he'll figure it out."

That was his middle brother, the peacekeeper.

It was true. Technically, if he invested properly, Evan didn't have to work another day in his life. He wouldn't be surprised if that's exactly what Shane expected of him, but despite what everyone thought, Evan wasn't really cut out to be a slacker. He might have played hard off the field, but he'd worked his ass off for the game. It had been his one primary focus since the day his dad died, and he didn't have a clue where to direct his energy now that it was gone.

"I just don't think it's healthy for him to sit around," Shane said.

Evan clenched his hands. "I'm not your responsibility."

Shane's brow furrowed. "I'm just trying to help."

"Well, stop," Evan said.

"We're your family," Shane said, tone irritated. "Maybe there's something you'd be interested in at the company."

James winced and shook his head. "You just don't know when to keep your mouth shut, do you?"

Shane's brow furrowed. "What? It's a suggestion."

Evan had had enough. "I don't need your charity, Shane. It's not your responsibility to bail me out. I made fifteen million dollars last year."

James held up his hands. "I'm sure he didn't mean it like that."

"The hell he didn't," Evan said, turning a furious glare at his oldest brother. "Can't you just turn it off? Even for a second? I know you're the family savior and all, but you forget I made my own way. I owe you nothing. Now back the hell off."

Shane's expression darkened like a Chicago storm. "Why can't I ever say anything to you without you taking it the wrong way?"

"Because you can't ever say anything without being a patronizing asshole."

James's brows furrowed over his glasses. "Let's all calm down. You're both overreacting."

Shane waved a hand over Evan as though disgusted. "You've been spending your days wasted and depressed. I'm only suggesting you need a little purpose."

Evan took a deep breath and exhaled. These conversations never went well, and if he didn't put an end to it, things would degenerate further. He reached into his pocket and pulled out his money. "I've got to go."

James shook his head. "No, don't."

Evan put a hundred-dollar bill on the table, just to really hone in on the point that he wasn't even close to destitute, and got up. "I'll see you later."

Then he left.

To go sit in his fucking apartment and do nothing but stare at the wall and contemplate his empty future.

Chapter Nine

James showed up at Evan's house five hours later, a bag of takeout Chinese food in hand.

Evan wasn't in the mood to talk, and if it had been Shane he would have thrown him out, but he couldn't turn James away. He sighed. "What are you doing here?"

James raised the bag. "I thought you could use some company."

"Not particularly." Evan stood back and let him in.

James moved with that purposeful stride he had, walking into Evan's kitchen and making himself at home. He pulled out an Xbox One game from another bag he carried. "I brought the new *Grand Theft Auto*."

Evan couldn't help but smile. This is why nobody kicked Jimmy out. He always seemed to understand just what was needed. Evan moved to sit down on his couch, grabbing the remote. "I've been meaning to pick that up."

"Now you don't have to." James moved around the kitchen, the sound of clattering plates and silverware being pulled out of the cabinets. "Beer?"

Evan scoffed. "What? You don't think I'm a raving alcoholic like our brother?"

There was no response, and a minute later James sat

down and held out a plate filled with Evan's favorite, spicy shredded beef, before putting down two bottles on the table next to Evan's knees. "No, I don't. And neither does he."

Evan took the plate, not hungry. "Thanks."

They watched the action movie Evan had been mindlessly staring at before James arrived, not saying anything as they ate. When they were done, they abandoned their dinners and turned their attention to serious gaming.

An hour later Evan felt considerably more human and asked, "Where's Gracie?"

"At the bakery." James didn't take his eye off the game. "Late night construction crew."

"You're going to leave her alone with a bunch of guys?"

James laughed. "She's a grown woman, who, in case you haven't noticed, has most men eating out of the palm of her hand. She's more than capable of handling herself."

On the screen, Evan beat some guy over the head with a bat. "Good point."

"She had a late lunch with Penelope, so she's making up for some lost time after I said I was headed here."

At the sound of Penelope's name, Evan had to resist the urge to react. He clenched his jaw until it ached to keep from asking. After all these years, he should be an expert at repressing his desire for news about her, but it was a habit that refused to die, and had only become worse since the distance between them was becoming impossible to resurrect. He changed the subject. "You don't have to babysit me. I'm fine."

James paused the game and then cocked a brow at Evan. "Let's make something clear. I'm not babysitting you. Although I am not going to pretend you don't worry me."

Evan clenched his hand into a fist. "Do you know how tiring it is to have everyone constantly worrying about you?"

"Yeah, I do," James said, tone matter-of-fact. "I spent my childhood that way."

Contrite, Evan relaxed his hand. "Right."

"My only advice is stop giving them a reason, and it gets better."

Evan shook his head. "You don't think I want to?"

James shrugged. "I honestly don't know."

James wasn't supposed to take sides, but that's sure as hell what it felt like. "So you think Shane is right?"

James shook his head. "No, I think you're both wrong, and I think you're too alike for your own good."

Evan's mouth fell open. "We are nothing alike."

James laughed, and leaned back on the couch. "You are both stubborn, never know when to quit, and can't change directions once you start moving. It's why you fight. Neither of you is capable of stopping, even when you know you should. You just keep battering on, pushing your way through the argument, and thinking that will get you what you want."

Evan didn't want to think about the truth in the point his brother was making, so he turned back to the game and pushed the play button.

James sighed. "You've got to stop being angry at him for doing what comes naturally."

Evan didn't speak for a bit, but then he cleared his throat and admitted the truth, because with James he could. "It was easier before, when I had something I excelled at to compete with."

"That's what you've never understood about him, and where you *are* different." James never took his eyes off the screen. "Unlike you, he doesn't view you as competition. He doesn't want to beat you. All he wants, all he's ever wanted, is for you to be happy."

Evan shot a guy in the face. "He can't make me happy."

"No, he can't. And it eats at him. You have to remember what it was like for him. He was robbed of everything you had handed to you. While you were off at college winning football games, partying, and screwing cheerleaders, he was here working three jobs."

Evan was well aware what Shane sacrificed for him, for them all, but how long did he have to live in the shadow of it? "I know that."

"I know you do, but what you don't seem to get is his motivation. He didn't do it to lord it over you, he did it so none of us would be desolate again, and now you are, and he can't fix it and he feels like he failed you."

"I have plenty of money."

James sighed. "There's more than one type of desolation."

A sudden tightness squeezed in Evan's chest. "I'm better than I was, but it's going to take some time."

James paused the game and clapped him on the back. "I know. And that's what I told him."

Evan raised a brow. "So you're making the rounds?"

James shrugged. "Sometimes you both need a little sense talked into you."

Evan gave a sharp nod. "I'll talk to him."

"Good." James paused and toyed with his game controller for a couple of seconds. "Do you want to talk about it? What you're going to do next?"

"No." The word harsher than he intended. He blew out a breath and looked past the giant television screen to the wall beyond. Maybe he did need to talk to someone. And James, who never judged him, would be the best person. "I know I can't do nothing for the rest of my life, but the future is like a blank slate in front of me. One big dead end."

"Have you talked to your agent about offers? Maybe that will strike an interest?"

Evan cringed. "Modeling underwear for Calvin Klein is hardly a career."

James chuckled. "I guess in your thirties that gets embarrassing."

"Exactly." With his looks, Evan had had plenty of offers roll in over the years, but he'd never taken them. He just couldn't get worked up about posing in front of a camera all oiled up, or hawking razors in some cheesy television commercial.

"What about broadcasting?" James asked.

"Hell, no." Evan glared at his middle brother. That was even worse than modeling.

James held up his hands. "All right, moving on. How about coaching?"

That was one thing Evan had thought about as a maybe, something he'd thought about for the future, for that day when he retired. On his terms.

But he didn't know if he could do it. Wasn't sure he was ready to be on the sidelines of the game he loved, watching his friends and colleagues still run out onto the field while he stayed behind. How could he be a good coach, filled with resentment for the guys he was supposed to mentor and push to excel? He shook his head. "I don't think I can."

James nodded, not seeming inclined to question, which Evan appreciated. Shane would try and talk him into it because it was the logical solution for someone like him. James scrubbed a hand over his jaw. "Maybe we need to go back to basics. What did you want to be when you grew up?"

Evan raised a brow. "A football player."

James's brow furrowed. "You never had a backup plan?"

Evan picked up his beer and took a sip. "Nope."

James frowned. "Maybe we need a late-night run to clear our minds."

Running after beer and Chinese food was the last thing Evan wanted to do, but he sighed. "All right, I'll go get changed."

As Penelope waited for the elevator, she read an e-mail from her project director, Aaron, regarding the current issues report for one of their larger commercial building projects. She worried her bottom lip, scrolling through the list and making a note to set up a one-on-one meeting with him. Aaron had some issues with an alderman opposed to the development. Penelope thought it might be time to intervene but wanted to speak with him first. She tapped her task icon and started making notes on what she needed to follow up on when the elevator finally dinged.

The doors slid open and she glanced up from the tablet, already taking a step inside, only to freeze when her gaze met Evan's.

Unable to hide her surprise, she blurted, "What are you doing here?"

As there was nobody in the elevator, Evan's gaze raked over her, blatant and direct. "I came to talk to Shane."

"Why?" He was the last person she wanted to see, and her rude tone voiced her displeasure. How could she stop thinking about him if she couldn't escape him?

The doors started to slide closed. He jabbed at a button, and they sprang back open. He cocked a brow and said in a voice full of challenge, "Are you getting on?"

Heart beating far too fast, she swallowed and stepped on. She couldn't let him see her run—that would give him far too much power.

A second later she was enclosed in the small box and he stood way too close to her. His large frame took up all the available space, and she tried to ignore the heat of him.

Tension was like a vise around her throat, making her

tongue-tied. Which irritated her. She cleared her throat. "It seems I can't escape you."

She could feel him watching her, could picture his expression exactly in her mind. She stared at the floor numbers as each one lit up and then dimmed. As they made the climb to the top floor, the location of Shane's and her offices, sex filled the air, pulsing around them, making her ache.

"Maybe fate doesn't want you to escape me, Penelope." The words low and gruff.

She couldn't resist the pull and shifted her attention to him. "I doubt that."

Their gazes locked.

"Our lives are intertwined. They always have been." Without football taking up all his time, he was around more than he'd been since high school.

Penelope supposed she'd better start getting used to it. This weekend being a case in point. With the benefit on Saturday, Mitch and Maddie were coming to town, and Cecilia was already organizing a dinner that night. She just had to figure out how to distance herself. She'd done it once, she could do it again. Starting with right now. In a polite tone she asked, "Will you be at Shane and Cecilia's on Friday?"

His gaze dipped to her mouth and her breath hitched. "Yep."

Okay, so she'd see him all weekend. So what? This wasn't any different than before.

The elevator came to a halt and Penelope jerked forward. Evan's hand shot out to steady her, and his palm about seared her through her blouse. She pulled away just as the doors slid open and two women in their twenties stood there, eyes going wide when they spotted Evan.

One of them blushed and the other let out a little gasp before they entered the car.

Neither acknowledged Penelope's existence.

God help her.

There was about five seconds of silence when the girls managed to contain themselves before one poked the other in the ribs and tilted her head in Evan's direction. The brunette, clearly the bolder of the two, licked her lips and said, "Are you, like, Evan Donovan?"

Evan shrugged. "That's the rumor."

Penelope rolled her eyes.

They giggled as Penelope tried to place them. Given the floor they'd gotten on and their young ages, she suspected they were interns of some type.

The redhead beamed at Evan and fluttered her lashes. "I heard you were Mr. Donovan's brother, but I never dreamed I'd actually see you."

Penelope had developed the internship program in conjunction with some of the local universities as a way to attract women into the predominantly male world of commercial real estate. So, sadly, she had no one to blame for the fawning but herself.

Evan smiled, but didn't say anything else.

The brunette puffed out her bottom lip. "I wish I had paper to get your autograph."

Some devil took up residence inside her and Penelope said in a dry, deadpan tone, "He's on his way to Mr. Donovan's office right now. If you hurry, maybe you'll be able to catch him before he leaves." She flashed Evan a brilliant smile. "I know how much you *love* signing autographs. He adores his fans, so make sure to bring your friends."

Evan's gaze narrowed.

The redhead squeaked. "Oh my God, like, really?"

"Of course he wouldn't mind. Would you?" Penelope said sweetly, batting her lashes. "You wouldn't want to disappoint your brother's employees."

He glared at her, full of menace, but then his expression filled with calculation and Penelope knew she was about to get burned. "I don't want them to lose any valuable work time searching for me."

"We don't mind," the two girls clamored in unison, oblivious to the tension between Evan and Penelope.

"No, I wouldn't dream of it." He flashed them a smile so brilliant Penelope was surprised it didn't twinkle and blind them, before turning to her. "I know how you hate inefficiency and I don't want to be disruptive. Why don't you escort me to their desks personally?"

"I don't see how that's productive." Penelope gripped the edge of her iPad harder.

His gaze narrowed. "I'm just a dumb jock. I'll get lost."

The doors opened and the girls turned pleading eyes on hers. "Please?"

"Do you really want groups of employees traipsing up to the top floor? Where Shane works?" Evan punched the door open button and held it. "What's it going to be, Pen? I'd hate to disappoint the fans."

He'd trapped her, although she'd started it, so she supposed it was fair play. "Fine. Who do you work for?"

They rushed to tell her and a second later the doors closed and she was once again alone with Evan. Why, after it had suffered so much at his hands, did her heart continue to betray her?

She could have left well enough alone, but no, she had to engage. Because some part of her wanted to be alone with him.

Evan grinned at her. "I'll be at your office as soon as I'm done with Shane."

"You're lucky I'm nice," Penelope said.

"I don't think being nice has anything to do with it."

She squared her shoulders. "And what do you think it has something to do with?"

Evan gripped her wrist and spun her so she faced him. She glared up at him. "What?"

He jutted his chin toward the door. "Don't pretend you couldn't have gotten out of that."

She could have. So why hadn't she? She had no good excuse for her behavior. "I suppose I couldn't resist torturing you."

He pulled her close, sliding his hand around her waist. He bent low and whispered in her ear, "You've been torturing me since that first night in that basement."

The elevator shuddered to a stop and he let her go. On wobbly legs, she stepped back to an acceptable distance, and the door slid open.

She walked out and he followed, catching up to her in two strides. They didn't speak, but when she got to her office, right next to Shane's, he called out, "I'll see you soon, Penelope."

She ignored him, slamming the door behind her.

Luckily Penelope didn't have to think too much about Evan, because as soon as she sat down at her desk, Collin and Nate from accounting came calling.

Numbers, project schedules, and contract issues were far easier to manage than thinking about the game she was playing with Evan.

And she was playing a game. That much was clear by her actions in the elevator. She'd obviously lost her mind.

She'd think about it later; for now, she worked.

Thirty minutes later, her phone rang and she raced to pick it up.

Over the line, her admin spoke. "A Mr. Evan Donovan says he's supposed to see you, but he doesn't have an appointment."

Penelope took a deep breath and ignored the jump of excitement in her belly. And wasn't that just the problem.

Evan was the only time her belly jumped, her heart leapt, or nerves danced along her skin. "Give me a few minutes."

Nate, the accounting manager, closed his iPad. "I think that covers it."

She nodded and tapped a few keys on her computer, her mind already on the man outside her office. "Can you get me the revised numbers by close of business Friday?"

Collin and Nate looked at each other, as though having a silent conversation, before Collin nodded. "We can do that."

"Great." She stood. Was she rushing them out? Yes, yes, she was. She was picking up the matches and striking the flame.

She ushered them to the door and when she opened it, Evan swung around to look at her.

Nate and Collin blinked at Evan, their expressions taking on the light of excitement, but Evan didn't seem to notice. His eyes were on her.

She gestured into the empty space of her office and said coolly, "Evan."

"Penelope." His voice had always done funny things to her, and age had only increased the smooth, deep sound of her name rolling across his tongue.

The two men stared at them, and as casually as she could, she smiled. "Don't forget I want those numbers by Friday."

Nate and Collin nodded. "Will do."

They walked away and Penelope said to Evan, "Are you coming?"

Then she walked into the office and didn't look back.

A second later, he closed the door behind him with a soft *click*.

She strolled to her desk and turned toward him. "That was fast."

"I was dropping something off for my mom," he said, stopping before the chairs that separated them.

She swallowed. They were alone. Again. This time of her own doing.

He glanced around her office.

Why did he have to look so damn good? It was warm out and he wore a gray T-shirt that stretched across his broad chest and highlighted his strong arms.

"So this is where you work?" he asked.

"Yep, this is it." What happened to all the vows she'd made to herself after that night in his car? She took a deep breath. "You've been here before."

He clasped the back of the chair, his forearms flexing, highlighting all those muscles honed from years of football. "Yes, but you've always conveniently managed to not be here."

She leaned back on her desk. "I can assure you, it wasn't intentional."

When his only response was a raised brow, she pointed at the closed door. "We'd better get this over with so I can get back to work."

He stared at her for so long she had to resist the urge to fidget.

She crossed her arms. "What?"

His gaze roamed over her face before settling on her mouth. "I can't turn it off, Penelope. I'm trying, and I can't."

She swallowed hard. "You'll have to."

"How?"

"We did it before, we can do it again."

His fingers flexed on the chair, his knuckles turning white. "But I don't want to."

"What are you saying?" She held her breath, trying not to lean into his answer.

"I can't go on pretending I don't want you." His tone

was gruff, sending a tingle of warmth down her spine. "Don't pretend you don't want me too."

What was the point in denying the obvious? The tension between them wasn't going away. There was no settling back into the place they'd been all those years. "It won't change anything."

He straightened, releasing his hold on the chair. "Maybe not, but it's just a matter of time. We're like a bomb waiting to detonate."

He was right. She looked out the window. "I don't know what you want me to say."

He stepped around the chair and came to stand in front of her.

She met his gaze.

He reached for her, and her heartbeat kicked into double time as his fingers tangled in her hair. "I want you to admit I'm going to be inside you."

He would be. The air crackled with it. And she wanted him there. "We can't relive the past, Evan."

"That's not what this is about." His thumb stroked across her pounding pulse. "Tell me I'm wrong."

She couldn't. "You're not wrong."

His hand tightened on her neck, sending heat through her whole body. "Will you have dinner with me tonight?"

A date? Now? The suggestion surprised her so much she sputtered, "What? Why?"

"Because after everything we've done, I think it's time we went on a proper date."

It threw her off as nothing else could have and she said the first thing that popped into her mind. "What if someone sees us?"

A stroke down the curve of her throat. He needed to stop touching her so she could think. "So your objection is that someone might see us? Not the dinner itself?"

"My objection is everything."

"Come to dinner with me."

She shook her head. "No."

"Yes." Another slide of fingers through her hair. "You have no idea how much I want to kiss you. And someday I hope to be able to without worrying I'll end up fucking you where you stand." His attention dipped to her mouth. "But today is not that day."

Her belly dipped, and to steady herself she put a hand on his wrist, meaning to push him away. Instead she dug her nails into his skin. "Evan."

"Please, Penny."

"It will only make things more complicated."

"I know." He dipped down, skimming a path with his mouth over her jaw, and she shuddered. "Come anyway."

She didn't want to say no. She inhaled, her breath ragged. "All right."

"I'll pick you up at seven." He lifted his head and released his hold on her.

"This is stupid." So, so stupid.

"Seven o'clock," he said, his tone sure.

"I'll be ready." She wasn't ready at all, but she would be. She'd agreed. This was happening. After fifteen years, she was going on a date with Evan Donovan.

Chapter Ten

As he rang Penelope's bell, Evan had no idea what to expect from the evening. When he'd woken this morning, taking her to dinner hadn't even been on his radar screen.

He was surprised to find he was nervous.

Through the panes of glass he watched her walk down her hallway, her stride brisk and purposeful. Efficient. He couldn't help but smile. If anyone ever guessed what she hid under all the efficiency, wouldn't they be surprised.

She opened the door, ready to go in a light beige trench coat. Her hair was down in soft waves around her shoulders, just the way he liked, and her blue eyes were direct and steady on him. She nodded. "Evan."

He drank her in. Nothing about her spoke of sex or seduction, but it didn't stop him from wanting her with an intensity that bordered on insanity. He cleared his throat and tried to rid his mind of the illicit images that ran rampant. He'd vowed to take her on a proper date, to court her, and that's what he was going to do. "Are you ready?"

"Nope," she said, her voice a bit shaky. "You?"

His gaze met hers. "Not even a little bit."

The corners of her mouth lifted in the barest hint of a smile. "This is pretty awkward."

He put his hands into his pockets to keep from reaching for her. "Sad, isn't it? For two people who've known each other for almost their whole lives."

"It is sad."

He gave her a grin, hoping to lighten the mood. "I guess that's what we get for ruining a perfectly good friendship with sex."

The muscles in her neck worked as she swallowed before she cleared her throat. "I've been thinking."

"That's dangerous."

"Indeed," she said, her voice so prim and proper, he was sure it was an act. "Maybe the best strategy to deal with this current predicament is to stop making such a big deal about it."

"You have a strategy to deal with us?" Some of the tension riding him hard, eased, but he was no more relaxed.

"Of course. I'm thinking the best course of action is to focus on having a lovely evening and try and get things back on friendly ground." She looked over his left shoulder to the street below. "I need to get my purse."

What a crock of shit. "As friends?"

"Yes, well, maybe more as friendly." She tightened the belt at her waist. "We were that way once."

"We were." This was a total act, and he wasn't buying it for a second, but he'd play along. For now.

"And we can be again." She pointed to the hall. "I need to get my purse."

"I'll wait here."

"You can come in."

He could, but despite her current line of defense, they were on the verge of exploding from sexual tension, and going inside wasn't a good idea. But maybe he could work with this game she was playing. After all, he knew just how to drive her crazy, and if she wanted things out in the open, he could do that. "If you want to get back to friendly, you and I both know we can't be alone in your house."

Her breath caught on an inhale. She was just as affected by him as he was by her, no matter how composed. "We wouldn't even make it up the stairs, Pen."

She nibbled on her bottom lip and then tilted her head. "I'll get my purse."

"You do that."

She shut the door in his face, then returned thirty seconds later, purse in hand. He stepped back and she looked at his car and sighed. "You brought the batmobile."

"I know how much you like it." He put his palm on the small of her back and her muscles tensed at his touch.

Friends his ass.

"It's not very inconspicuous." She frowned at the car. "How many people drive around town in a gunmetal Lamborghini?"

He led her to the car and got her settled, then slid into the driver's seat. The purr of the engine sprang to life. "Are you afraid to be seen with me?"

She frowned, her brows furrowing as though she didn't understand the question. "I think you've got that backward."

He turned toward her and put his hand on the edge of her seat. "All right, this is item one we need to deal with."

Her eyes widened as though shocked. But he kept on going. "I was a stupid, fucking teenage boy, Penelope. You were my little sister's best friend. I was older than you. I was more experienced. And my parents thought you were a goddamn saint. You were off-limits and I wasn't supposed to take advantage of your virtue. I've done a lot of shitty things to you, and I'm more than willing to pay for them, but get this through your head: you are not in *any way* an embarrassment. I didn't hide what we did because I didn't think you were hot enough—for fucks sake, Penelope, you practically burned me alive—I hid it because I wasn't supposed to be doing it in the first place."

She blinked, then turned in her seat. "We should go."

"Fine," he said, and they didn't speak for the rest of the drive.

Twenty minutes later, the hostess took Penelope's coat and he had to clench his teeth to keep his jaw from dropping to the floor. Her dress was black, low cut enough there was no way she was wearing a bra, and slinky. It clung to her lean frame, hugged all her curves, and while it ended at her knees, it was slit up the side. When she turned around to follow the hostess to the private booth he'd requested, toward the back corner, there was no back to her dress.

She looked like sex, and if he hadn't thought her a femme fatale before, he sure as hell thought it now. People were looking at her. Men were staring. He was used to that, but this was Penelope.

She was off-limits. To everyone.

They sat down, and when the hostess left he glared at her.

Calmly she picked up her menu and raised a brow. "What's wrong?"

In an overly controlled voice, he said, "That's not exactly a friendly dress."

"It's not." She returned her attention to her menu.

"That's it? That's all you have to say for yourself?"

She shrugged one bare shoulder. "To be honest, my plan was to wear something conservative."

"Well, what the hell happened?" He hissed the words, realizing how fucking crazy they were being. Which is why he needed to have her. So he could get some control back in his life and start acting like a normal person.

She set down her menu and looked him straight in the eye. "I had it all picked out. A nice gray pantsuit with a white button-down. It's my outfit of choice when I'm undertaking tough negotiations."

Yes, that sounded quite boring and just the outfit to allow blood to get to his brain so he could think. He demanded, "And?"

She smiled, her lips a glossy red, and flicked her hair back over one shoulder, looking like sin. "Well, if you must know, I decided it would be more fun to torture you."

Penelope had no idea what possessed her to say that. Yes, every word was true, but still. She'd stood in her closet looking for the perfect outfit. She'd intended to go with something conservative and businesslike, but then she'd spotted the dress Sophie had talked her into on one of their many shopping trips, and thrown caution to the wind. She wanted him to sweat. It seemed only fair. And to her petty satisfaction, Evan's shocked expression had been worth it. She wanted to throw him off. Just like he'd thrown her off after his little speech in the car.

She gave him her sweetest smile. "Any more questions?"

When he continued to stare at her, openmouthed, she picked up her menu and pretended to read.

The waiter came up to take their drink orders. She beamed at him and said, "I'll take a mojito."

"And for you, sir?" the waiter asked.

Evan seemed to come out of his stupor. "Whiskey, neat."

The waiter nodded and walked away and Evan's gaze narrowed. "You do realize you just declared war."

"Did I?" She kept her voice cool, even as her blood pounded in her ears. Evan was a warrior, his skills honed on the gridiron battlefield. Competition burned in his cells, and here she was stoking the flames.

"Yes."

She waved a hand. "What's a little warfare between friends?"

This afternoon she'd spent a long time thinking things through. She'd always been a practical person, she was well known for her cool business head, logical brain, and analytical skills. And she'd decided to attack the problem of Evan with the same skills that made her successful at work. She'd gotten out her spreadsheet, worked through all the angles, and in the end, kept coming to the same conclusion.

There was only one way to deal with the tension that plagued all their interactions.

They needed closure.

To deal with the past and be done with it. The only way out, was through, and the more she tried to resist or deny the inevitability, the more out of control the tension became. If she cut the power supply, they'd slowly die a quiet death.

She'd decided to play it cool, employing a sort of fake-it-till-you-make-it type of strategy in order to facilitate her end game. They might end up in bed, but they'd never end up together. They were too different. When it was over, she wanted him to believe she was done, and capable of being friends with him. That she thought of him as another Donovan brother she had to put up with because of Maddie.

Evan's green-eyed gaze narrowed. "All right, what kind of game are you playing?"

"I'm not playing a game. I'm approaching this practically."

"This should be good," he said, tone clearly derisive.

She clasped her hands in front of her and fixed an impassive expression on her face. "We both agree that what we're doing isn't working, correct?"

He nodded.

"Maybe we're making this too complicated, giving it more weight than it deserves. If we're honest, and stop trying to avoid the situation, I believe we can put things back to the way they were."

"And how would you define things between us?"

"Cordial, but certainly manageable."

The waiter came back and dropped off their drinks. "Are you ready?"

Evan's attention didn't leave hers. "Give us a few minutes."

"Of course, sir." He wandered away, leaving Penelope once again alone with Evan.

"Go on," Evan said, his expression intense but unreadable.

She did, laying out her plan. "It seems to me, if we could learn to be friends, everything would be fine."

"I see, and how do you propose we do that?"

"Well"—she cleared her throat—"consider how you treat Sophie, and treat me the same way."

"There's only one problem with that."

"What's that?"

His gaze dipped to her mouth. "I don't think about Sophie naked. And I sure as hell don't have the same images of her in my head."

Penelope shrugged. "You treated me platonically for years, you can do it again."

"I could say the same for you."

She blinked. "Pardon?"

"In theory, we have years of practice treating each other platonically, so it should be easy. But it's not, is it, Pen?"

No, it certainly wasn't. Although he didn't know all these years had been an act, something she'd gotten good at over time. But now he wasn't playing by the rules they'd established. It was so much easier when he was some wild, out-of-control jock who cared about nothing but partying and football. Who treated her like she didn't exist. That was a man she could hate.

But since his injury he'd changed. Now he was more like that boy from the basement.

She sighed. "And to think, if I'd just stayed upstairs that night, none of this would have ever happened."

Expression turning quizzical, he tilted his head to the side. "What do you mean by that?"

"I mean, if I hadn't come downstairs that night, we'd never have started talking in the first place. I'd have stayed your little sister's annoying friend."

"You're wrong." The words hard, with a bit of bite. "That's what you've never understood. To me, you've never been just Maddie's friend. I've never seen you like I saw Sophie."

That didn't fit into the narrative she'd created all these years, and she needed him to fit back where she'd put him. She tried again. "But you can't deny you never would have noticed me if we hadn't started talking. It's hardly like I was on your radar."

He picked up his drink and took a long gulp, hissing out a breath as he looked past her shoulder. He put the glass down on the table. "Okay, yes, when we were kids you were Maddie's annoyingly perfect little friend. But I noticed you long before you ever came down those stairs that night. Why the hell did you think I encouraged you to stay?"

This was new information, an angle she'd never thought of before, nor wanted to contemplate. She cleared her throat. "To be nice?"

He raised a brow. "When have I ever been nice?"

He'd always been nice to her. In that basement he'd treated her like she was the most important girl in the world. She played over the stem of her water glass. "I assumed you didn't mind me because around me you could relax."

He sat forward, leaning across the table. "The first time I noticed you in a way that wasn't platonic, was your first day of high school. You walked into the house in your neatly pressed Catholic uniform, your black shoes all polished up, that white blouse buttoned to your neck. There shouldn't have been one thing sexy about you, but somehow, when I wasn't paying attention, you stopped being a kid. Your skin was flawless, your eyes the brightest blue I'd ever seen, and your hair was in a ponytail. The sun was coming in behind you, and your hair was shiny and thick and so gorgeous all I wanted was to liberate it from that tight hold you had on it and run my fingers through it."

It was the second time in less than an hour that he'd shocked her, and her throat grew tight at the words. She swallowed hard, unable to speak, which was okay because he kept on talking, making her remember the past in a whole new light.

He sat back, his strong fingers playing over the rim of his glass. "It was a weird thought and it kind of freaked me out. I was sixteen. I was supposed to be obsessed with getting into a girl's pants, not thinking about her hair. At school, before Kim Rossi, I was dating Julie . . . I can't remember her last name."

"Borkowski," she supplied for him without thinking.

He nodded. "That's right. She had this overprocessed blond hair that looked like straw, but she had gorgeous breasts and all the guys wanted her."

Penelope remembered.

He took another sip of his drink before continuing. "After that morning, every time I saw her I thought of you. I tried to ignore it, because I wasn't supposed to think of you that way, but when I touched Julie's hair all I could think about was how yours would feel. I broke up with her the second week of school."

Penelope licked her bottom lip, her throat dry. "I didn't know."

He smiled at her, and it was so reminiscent of the way he'd smiled at her all those years ago, her chest squeezed. "Why did you think I always pulled your ponytail?"

She'd forgotten. The corners of her mouth lifted. "To annoy me."

He laughed. "I wanted to touch your hair. Didn't you ever notice how I was obsessed with it? I mean, Jesus, Penny, what did you think I was doing?"

"I didn't know," she said, her voice sounding strained. Long before he'd touched her sexually he'd played with her hair. She hadn't thought about his motives; all she'd thought was she hoped he wouldn't stop. She used to live for those nights when they'd watch television, moving closer and closer. He'd rest his arm on the back of the couch and they'd be so close she could feel the heat of his body. She'd wait, breathless with anticipation, until his strong fingers finally slid over her neck to tangle in her hair. She cleared the huskiness from her throat and told him the truth. "I thought you were doing it without thinking."

His brow furrowed. "Why would you think that?"

They were already traveling down this path and maybe that's what they needed. To clear out all the misunderstanding between them so they could move on. Even though it made her ache. "Because it was a gradual thing. It never seemed intentional. It would only happen when we were fixated on some show or movie we were watching. It seemed absentminded to me. Like you weren't even aware you were doing it." She bit her bottom lip. "And you never seemed interested in touching me in any other way."

"Penelope," he said, his voice more serious than she'd heard in a long time. "Every single second I spent in that basement, touching you was the only coherent thought I had. At first, I promised myself I wouldn't touch you. You were good and innocent and I didn't want to take that away from you, and touching your hair seemed like something I could get away with."

"I didn't know. I was a kid and didn't have any experience with boys." There was a long, heavy silence and as much as she wanted to look away from him, to avoid the intensity and swell of desire and lust that filled the air, she couldn't tear herself away.

He looked at her mouth, then back into her eyes. "Obviously, I caved."

And then she saw it, the guilt lurking in the depths of his gaze. That he somehow believed he should never have touched her. It shifted her perception.

She swallowed hard. The air was humid and thick, threatening to strangle her. "I'm not sorry."

His expression flickered. "No?"

She shook her head. She had her regrets, and he'd hurt her badly, but giving herself to him wasn't one of them. "Not even a little bit."

"Why?"

Because she'd loved him, and at bare minimum at least she'd given herself to a boy she loved. She couldn't say that, but there was another truth she could tell him. "Because I was lucky."

"How's that?"

She licked her lips and his expression darkened. "I never told anyone, but I'd listen to the other girls' stories, and their experiences were so horrible. All that rough groping and awkward, sloppy kissing. They'd talk about it, wondering what they were missing and where the pleasure they were supposed to experience was, and I always felt bad for them." The heat climbed up her cheeks. "You, um, obviously weren't like that."

"Never with you." His voice dropped, turning low and intimate and it sent a shiver straight through her. "Although I seem to recall us getting plenty rough and sloppy."

"Yes." That breathless rasp was back, and an image of them filled her mind.

God, she'd never been with anyone else the way she'd been with him. With the men she'd dated, she'd always put up a wall of reserve, and no one had ever breached it. Nor had she wanted them to. Her heart had always belonged to Evan.

His fingers tightened around his glass, knuckles turning white, and she knew he was recalling some memory of the two of them. They had a thousand of them.

He cleared his throat. "It's kind of silly. I thought I was somehow preserving your virginity."

Yes, her virginity had been a technicality at that point, because God knew they were doing everything else. She smiled. "Well, we were teenagers and didn't have the clearest logic."

"I'm glad it wasn't all bad."

"Not even close."

Neither of them seemed inclined to bring up the last time, and that was fine with her. It didn't change anything; it was all the memories before that that kept her attached and wanting.

"Penelope?"

She met his gaze. "Yes."

"It was always you. I've always wanted you, even at my most terrible."

She didn't understand what they were doing, or why. "We can't go back, Evan."

"I know."

She opened her hands in a gesture of surrender. "So what are we doing?"

"I don't know, but I can't stop it. Can you?"

She shook her head. "No."

He reached across the table and took her hand. "Let's just take it slow and see what happens."

Her fingers tangled with his and she resisted the urge to close her eyes and soak up the rightness of him. She'd always loved his hands, and adulthood had only made them stronger, more capable. She had no idea where this was going, and she was positive it was stupid, but she didn't care. She couldn't go on like this. Needed to finish this somehow. She nodded. "I can do that."

More than anything he wanted to touch her. She stood there, leaning against her front door, her chin tilted, her lips slightly parted and waiting. Her coat hung open and her dress, which had driven him crazy all night, clung to her body. All he wanted was to run his hands all over her, to feel her tremble under him, to taste that mouth of hers.

But he didn't trust himself to stop.

And he wanted to give her all the things he'd never given her back in high school. Do all the things he should have done back then, now. Only he wasn't sure how to give her what she deserved and manage the sexual chemistry and tension that were ready to rage out of control with the slightest spark.

His gaze dipped to her mouth and he clenched his jaw.

Those big electric-blue eyes stared up at him, wide and slightly glassy. She used to look at him that way down in the basement. With that sort of pleading expectation. It held just as much power now as it had back then.

He flexed his fingers, fighting the urge to reach for her. "We made it."

"We did." Her teeth scraped against her lower lip and he stifled a groan.

"And you'll be at Shane's tomorrow night?"

She nodded, and then shifted her attention to his mouth, her body lifting up just a tiny bit in silent offering.

He needed to go, or he'd cave. "You need to go inside, Penelope."

"Okay." Her voice a hot little whisper that wrapped around his cock and squeezed.

Neither of them moved.

Her tongue darted out to wet her lips.

His breath increased as his chest started to burn. "Inside."

She put her hand behind her back, on the door handle. "Yes."

He needed to touch her, just once. Innocently. He stepped closer and she dragged in a sharp inhale. She was killing him.

He slid his hand around her neck, tangling his fingers in her hair.

Her pupils dilated. "Evan."

Fuck. He was so hard. All he wanted was to feel the weight of her under him. His thumb brushed her pulse beating wildly in her neck, before skimming the line of her jaw. He could give her this one thing. Put aside his primal, base desire and this one time do what was right by her. "I'll see you tomorrow night."

She nodded, and he could see the confusion etched in the corners of her eyes.

Like an idiot, he ran his thumb over her bottom lip, gliding along the wetness and the soft, plump flesh he could still recall the exact feel of, even after all these years. "Tomorrow."

Then he somehow found the strength to pull away from her. "Good night, Penelope."

She frowned, turned around and went inside.

He dragged a hand through his hair and slowly made his way back to his car, trying not to think about how everything he wanted lay right beyond that door.

Chapter Eleven

If she'd thought she didn't know how to act around Evan before, she had no idea how to act now in front of everyone. The get-together at Shane and Cecilia's was in full swing and Penelope was thrilled to see Maddie and her husband, Mitch, but she was so on edge she couldn't relax.

She had no idea what had happened last night, or why he'd left, but now she was a wreck. She kept trying to remember how she had always acted around him when everyone was around, but for the life of her couldn't get a grasp on it. She kept questioning everything. Was she looking at him too much? Not enough? What was her normal tone when she said hello? Had there been too much rasp in her voice?

She felt on display. Like everyone knew something had changed, and watched her. She hated being on display. Hated it.

Last night dinner had been . . . well . . . it had been spectacular. Like a real date, and she'd wanted him so badly, but he'd left without touching her. Despite the fact that sex practically vibrated the air.

She didn't understand anything, or him.

Now she could feel him, over on the couch, with his brothers and Mitch. Could feel the way he watched her and she willed herself not to look at him.

At some point, Cecilia had put a glass of champagne in her hand and she downed it in one big gulp.

"Whoa!" Sophie said, her expression wide with surprise. "What's gotten into you?"

Penelope jerked from her thoughts. "What?"

Sophie pointed at her empty glass. "You just slammed down an entire glass of champagne in one gulp. Is everything okay?"

"Everything's great," Penelope said, far too brightly.

Maddie and Sophie looked at each other, and then looked back at her, twin expressions of speculation.

Hey, that was her look.

"I'm good. Great." The words spoken absentmindedly as she scanned the room. God, where was the champagne? She needed more.

"You look like you need a refill," Evan said from behind her, and she nearly jumped out of her skin. For the love of God, she was never going to make it through this night.

She whirled around and glared at him. "You scared me!"

"Sorry, I thought you could use another drink." He held up the bottle.

Ugh! She wanted to punch him. Why did he have to look like that? Why did his stupid shoulders have to be so broad? His body so ridiculous? Couldn't he look horrible for her? Just once? She held up her glass. "Whatever. Stop that."

Evan raised a brow. "Being helpful?"

"Yes," she hissed.

Maddie and Sophie looked back and forth between them.

They know nothing. Absolutely nothing.

Gracie walked up, sporting a huge, knowing grin. "Everything okay here?"

"Everything is great," Penelope said, her voice sounding too high-pitched. She pressed the glass into Evan's chest. "Champagne?"

He took her wrist, steadying her as he poured. Only then did she realize her hands were shaking.

Penelope said through gritted teeth, "Thank you."

His thumb brushed over her pounding pulse. "You're welcome."

What was he doing? Why was he being so obvious?

She pulled away and found her friends all staring at her, their gazes ping-ponging back and forth between her and Evan.

He raised the bottle to the rest of the girls. "Anyone else?"

"I'll take some," Gracie said, her voice filled with suppressed laughter.

Penelope needed to get away from him. Now. Or she'd lose her mind.

Once again she drained the glass.

Evan raised a brow. "More, Pen?"

"Yes, please." She was drinking far too fast, and raising suspicions, but she didn't care. The alcohol was making her stupid, careless, but she had no intention of stopping. She was pulled too tight; in danger of seriously snapping and blowing the cover she'd worked so hard to cultivate all these years.

Evan turned to her and she lifted the flute. He tilted the bottle, but didn't pour. "Have you eaten?"

"Of course." At ten this morning when she'd choked down a slice of toast.

He steadied her hand again, and poured another glass. "Just be careful."

Oh God. Electricity shimmered along her skin where he touched her.

"All right," Maddie said, hands on her hips. "What is going on here?"

Sophie adopted a similar stance. "Yeah, you're acting weird."

Penelope jerked away, some of the bubbly liquid sloshing over the sides of the glass. "I don't know what you mean."

Maddie pointed at her. "The woman who only allows herself one drink per hour to give her body time to properly metabolize the alcohol has now had"—she peered at her watch—"three drinks in ten minutes."

"Tough day at the office." Her voice sounded like a squeak.

Sophie shot Evan the evil eye. "Did you do something to her?"

Penelope gasped in horror. "Sophie, no!"

"What could I have done to her?" Evan asked, sounding more curious than worried.

"I don't know," Sophie said, eyes narrowed, before shifting her attention to Penelope. "Did he start pulling your ponytail again?"

Gracie snorted and Penelope glared at her before shaking her head. "Don't be ridiculous."

In a totally calm, reasonable tone Evan said, "I was just being nice and getting you girls some drinks."

Maddie whipped toward her brother. "Since when?"

Evan shrugged. "Geez, Maddie, you make it sound like I'm incapable of being decent."

Maddie waved her hand in the direction of the couch. "You got up to come over here."

"So?" Evan's tone dared her to make an issue of it.

Penelope couldn't stand it one more minute and she said, "Excuse me."

She was positive they all stared after her, but she didn't look back. No, she hurried down the hall, through the kitchen and up the back staircase. She just needed a minute.

Okay, maybe thirty minutes to get under control. Once she had time to compose herself and make a list to one, explain her behavior, and two, figure out how to deal with this fiasco, she'd feel much better.

Why hadn't she thought this through? She'd had all day to strategize about tonight, but she hadn't done any of that; instead she'd obsessed on why he hadn't touched her, or kissed her, or pushed her to the ground and taken her right on her doorstep.

Now she had no idea how to act around him, and look at her, she was acting like a maniac.

She found the spare bathroom and locked herself inside, leaning against the door. She downed the last of the drink she certainly didn't need, and put the flute down on the vanity. The bathroom was lovely, with soft gray walls, white custom-made cabinets, and brushed silver metals. It would help calm her.

She closed her eyes and started to count, but her head swam.

She snapped her lids open. Bad idea. Champagne on an empty stomach was not her brightest move.

There was a knock on the door. "Penelope?"

Gracie. Thank God it wasn't anyone else.

Penelope opened the door a crack and peered out. "I'm okay."

"Let me in," Gracie said.

Penelope sighed and stood back to let her in. "I'm fine."

Gracie closed the door and held out a plate of appetizers. "You'd better eat these. I managed to hold off Maddie and Sophie, but I'm positive they'll be here any moment to check on you. Did something happen?"

Penelope took a bite of some puffed crab thing that

tasted divine. "I don't know what's wrong with me. We went to dinner last night and now I can't remember how to act."

Gracie let out a little squeal of delight. "Really now? What happened?"

She swallowed, hoping the food acted quickly because she was officially drunk. Which, in itself, was completely out of character for her. She was the designated driver. She stood quietly in the corner, watching everyone's purse while they acted all wild and crazy, then she took them home.

"Nothing," she shrieked, waving the plate as she spoke, and one of the appetizers flew, sailing across the room.

Gracie walked over and picked up the mess with a napkin. "Nothing?"

"Nope. We went to dinner, we talked, and then he walked me to the door and said good night." After their initial discussion, they'd stayed away from anything serious for the rest of the night, but the tension had been off the charts. They'd taken to long silences where their breathing kicked up and images of the past mixed with the heat of the present.

She'd been prepared for sex, ready to get it over with, and he hadn't even kissed her on the cheek. No, he'd just run his fingers through her hair, over her lips, and then he was gone.

She'd never been so confused.

She turned to Gracie. "Help me."

Gracie nodded. "Okay, what do you need?"

Even inebriated, her mind clicked away and the planning helped to soothe her. "First, I need an excuse for my behavior. Something good to tell Maddie and Sophie."

Her friends knew her too well. They knew something was up.

Gracie tapped her finger against her jaw. "Something with work?"

Penelope blinked at her. "Why would I have a problem with work?"

Gracie laughed. "Sorry, I forgot who I was dealing with."

Penelope's mind was a complete blank, filled with nothing but the truth.

There was a knock on the door and Maddie called out, "Pen, Gracie, you guys okay in there?"

Followed by Sophie's, "Open up."

In a panic, Penelope whispered, "What am I going to do?"

Gracie's brow furrowed in concentration.

"Come on, Penelope, you're worrying us," Maddie said.

"Yeah, let us in," Sophie said.

"I'm peeing," Gracie yelled. "Give me a minute."

Penelope gave her a horrified look.

Gracie waved a hand. "It was better than nothing."

Penelope sucked in great lungfuls of air. This is why she minimized her alcohol consumption. She couldn't think.

Gracie snapped her fingers. "You said you were going to the benefit with Logan Buchanan, right?"

"Right. So?" Penelope's brain refused to focus.

"Use him as an excuse," Gracie said, as though Penelope was slightly dense, which sadly wasn't far from the truth.

Her brow furrowed. "What could possibly be wrong between me and Logan?"

Gracie shook her head. "That man is gorgeous. Trust me, it's believable."

"What should I say?"

Gracie flushed the toilet and flicked on the water. "Say you developed feelings for him and you think you're going to fuck his brains out tomorrow."

Penelope put a hand on her chest. "I'd never say any such thing."

Gracie rolled her eyes. "Improvise."

"What's going on in there?" Sophie called.

"We can hear you whispering," Maddie said.

Penelope took a deep breath, plastered a smile on her face, and swung open the door. "Sorry about that. You know Gracie, she'll just drop her pants whenever."

Gracie slapped her on the shoulder. "Hey now."

Maddie crossed her arms. "What's going on?"

Sophie did the same, expression stern. "We demand answers."

Penelope pointed at the two of them. "You're the trouble-makers here, not me."

Maddie tossed her red hair over her shoulder. "Um, don't even try that. We're your best friends, we know you, what's wrong?"

Okay, before she went down the Logan road, she tried a diversion tactic. "What's wrong with having some fun?"

Sophie scoffed. "Your idea of fun is learning a new Excel formula from YouTube."

"Hey! You take that back," Penelope shouted, far too loudly. "I know how to have a good time. It's Friday."

Cecilia came up the stairs and walked briskly down the hall, looking like a polished rich girl in sleek jeans and a white flowy top. "What is going on up here?"

"Nothing." Penelope waved at them. "I went to the bathroom and they all followed me."

Maddie scowled. "Penelope's acting weird."

"I am not!"

"She is," Sophie said.

Calmly, Cecilia tilted her head. "Is everything okay, Penelope?"

She'd changed into jeans and a black top after work and

she smoothed out the wrinkles in her shirt. "I'm perfectly fine."

"The real question is, what is she hiding?" Maddie said, as if Penelope hadn't spoken.

"I'm not hiding anything." And to her horror, Penelope felt a flush crawl up her cheeks.

Sophie wagged a finger at her. "Oh my God, she's lying."

Cecilia's brows rose. "Penelope?"

Her drunkenness had only increased as the alcohol made its way into her blood. She raised her hand. "All right, all right! I'll tell you."

Her friends all looked at her, expressions filled with questions, except for Gracie's. No, Gracie wore an expression of maniacal glee.

Penelope took a deep breath and lied. "Okay, fine, if you must know, I want to sleep with Logan."

"Really now?" Maddie said.

Sophie giggled. "You little slut."

Cecilia smiled and nodded. "I can see how that would be difficult for you."

Gracie straightened from the door frame she'd been lounging against. "She's going with him to the benefit tomorrow night and she doesn't know how to tell him her feelings have changed."

All three women's expressions eased in understanding, and Penelope jumped on the Logan express with the zeal afforded any good buzz. "Now do you see why I couldn't say anything? I can't risk Shane finding out."

"What can't I find out?" Shane asked, having made his way up the stairs in all the commotion.

Penelope shrieked and pointed at him. "Get out!"

Shane's expression went wide and he cocked a grin. "Should I mention that this is my house?"

Cecilia sighed and hurried over to him, taking him by

the shoulder and trying to turn him around. "I've got this covered."

"You women are acting crazy," Shane said, gaze narrowed on his wife. "You keep going up but nobody seems to be coming down. And what can't I know, Pen?"

Oh God, no. This was a disaster. Penelope scrambled for an excuse only to say lamely, "Nothing. Nothing at all. I was . . . um . . . thinking of taking a vacation."

"What?" Shane said.

Cecilia pushed him toward the stairs. "We were just trying to tell her it's okay not to be a workaholic, but she won't listen."

"You don't actually think I'm buying this, do you?" Shane's tone was filled with amusement.

"Boundaries, Shane," Penelope said, pointing at him. "I'm having a conversation with my girlfriends, and as my boss, you're not invited."

Cecilia nodded. "I've got this. Go."

"You and I will be talking later," Shane said.

Cecilia lifted up to her tiptoes and whispered something in his ear. He pulled away, gave her a quick, hard kiss. "Deal."

A second later he was gone.

Gracie grinned and winked. "Impressive. What did you say?"

Cecilia's lips curved in a graceful smile. "I've learned, in relationships, that there's not much that can't be resolved with the promise of a blow job."

Maddie's face scrunched. "Ewwww, yuck, that's my brother."

"Oh please," Cecilia said. "I've seen the way you operate. You don't fool me."

"How would you like it if I started giving you details about Mitch?"

"Ha!" Cecilia rolled her eyes. "You stay at my house, I hear things."

Sophie shushed them. "Yeah, yeah, you're all one big inappropriate family. Let's get back to the point."

"There is no point," Penelope said, waving her hand widely in the air. "Let's go back downstairs so they don't get any more ideas."

Maddie's attention shifted back to Penelope. "Okay, here's what you do. Tomorrow at the benefit, you'll need to flirt."

Sophie jostled Maddie's shoulders and jutted her head toward Penelope. "She doesn't know how to flirt. We'll have to teach her."

"I know how to flirt," Penelope interjected.

Maddie clucked her tongue. "No, Soph's right. We'll need an emergency session."

"I don't need lessons in flirting."

They ignored her. Maddie turned to Gracie. "We'll need you, obviously. Are you available tomorrow morning?"

Penelope put her fingers into her mouth and whistled. They all stopped talking.

"Enough. I've got this." That was a lie, she had nothing, but at least they'd latched on to what they thought her problem was, and her odd behavior would be excused for at least a couple of days. "Let's go downstairs. I don't want to talk about this anymore."

Maddie snapped her fingers. "You know what you can do? You can practice on Evan."

Sophie jumped up and down. "That's a great idea. If anyone can teach you how to handle a guy like Logan, it's him."

God help her.

* * *

"I have no idea what's going on," Shane said, coming back to sit on the couch. Mitch and James had sent him upstairs to investigate why all the women had chased after Penelope, but none of them had come down.

Even though Evan knew perfectly well what was going on with Penelope, he wasn't supposed to be interested, and he'd kept quiet on the subject, contemplating silently if driving Penelope to drink was a good thing, or a bad thing.

At the moment he was choosing good.

Mitch cast a glance at the back stairs. "You want me to try?"

Shane grinned. "Your sister offered all sorts of depravity to get me to leave, so it's worth a try."

Mitch smirked, and raised a brow at James. "You want in on this?"

"I'm good." James picked up the remote and turned the channel from baseball to the History Channel. "I can get depravity whenever I want."

"Don't brag," Mitch said.

James gave him a long, steady stare from behind his glasses. "I assure you that I am not."

Before Mitch could stand, the women all tumbled down the stairs, and Penelope shot Evan an evil death glare.

Okay, maybe he should choose bad.

"Hey, Gracie," Shane said, looking at James. "Jimmy here says that you'll give him whatever he wants, whenever he wants."

Gracie tilted her head at James, a curl flopping into her eye. "Really now?"

"Does that sound like me?" James asked, his tone calm.

"Nope," Gracie said, then winked at Shane. "Even though it's true."

James didn't say anything, letting the I-told-you-so hang in the air.

Evan turned his attention on the woman who occupied all his thoughts. "Everything okay?"

Penelope frowned, and twisted her hands. She looked confused, adorable, and so goddamn hot he wanted to take her against the first available flat surface.

She rubbed her head, blew out a breath and gave him a hard stare. As though she was trying to tell him something through mental telepathy.

Sophie cleared her throat. "Um, Evan, could you help Penelope?"

Penelope gave him a look of helpless dismay.

Had she told them? That didn't sound like her. In fact, she was working damn hard trying to figure out how to act normal. "Penelope?"

She shifted on the balls of her feet and shook her head.

Sophie continued. "She needs someone to lift . . . um . . . something."

Maddie grinned at him. "Yeah, do her a solid and help her out."

"*Regular Show*!" Gracie yelled out of nowhere, snapping her fingers.

James gave her an approving nod. "Very impressive."

Evan had no idea what they were talking about and didn't care.

Penelope jerked her head toward the back door.

He had no idea what was going on, but he wasn't about to pass up an opportunity to be alone with her. With Shane and Cecilia's open floor plan and all of them so nosy, chances like this didn't come along very often.

"Sure," he said, and rose from the couch.

They stepped out onto the small deck. The late spring air was cool and mild. That perfect weather that settled in on Chicago before it turned humid and hot.

He closed the door behind him.

"Is everything okay, Pen?"

She whirled on him. "No, everything is not okay. And it's all your fault."

He decided in that moment he liked her intoxicated. She was more forthcoming and a lot less composed. He cocked his head. "I have been on my best behavior for days."

"Exactly." She jabbed a finger in his chest. "Now look what you did."

"I think the champagne is making you miss a few points in that explanation." He glanced at the house. He could clearly see the group in the living room, which meant they could see him and Penelope. He grabbed her hand. "Come with me."

"Where are we going?"

"Somewhere we don't have an audience."

He pulled her down the steps and around the side of the house. It was dark and secluded. Perfect. "Now tell me what I've done."

She blinked up at him. "You're driving me crazy."

He stepped closer to her. He should keep his distance but didn't, even though it made executing his plan much more difficult. "How?"

She craned her neck. "You know how. We're in some sort of standoff. I haven't eaten. I drank too much. I don't know how to act around you."

"Go on." He slipped his arm around her waist and she shuddered.

She leaned against the brick of the house, and he pressed close, sucking in her fresh, clean scent that cloaked all the wildness he knew lurked beneath. "Everyone got suspicious and I had to tell them something."

"And what did you tell them?" He slipped his hand around her neck, tangling his hands in that hair he could never resist.

Glassy-eyed, she looked at him and licked her lips. "You're not going to be happy."

She was there in front of him, and he had his arms around her; there wasn't a lot she could say to upset him. "Tell me anyway."

She sucked her bottom lip between her teeth and put her hands on his forearms, her fingers flexing so her nails dug slightly into his skin like a cat. "Don't say I didn't warn you."

"I'm listening."

"You know the benefit tomorrow night?"

He nodded.

"I'm, um, going with Logan."

He straightened, and a stab of possessiveness pierced his chest. His voice lost all trace of seduction. "And?"

Her lashes fluttered, and even in the dark her eyes were a startling blue, clear and direct. "And, well, they all know we're friends, and I was acting so strange. They wouldn't stop asking what was wrong and . . . well . . . I said I wanted to sleep with him."

Just the thought of her with another man made him want to punch something. He gripped her neck and growled. "Over my dead fucking body."

She took a little stuttered inhale of breath and he knew the possessiveness flipped her switch. A switch she couldn't hide from him with too much champagne rushing through her system.

She whispered, "There's more."

His fingers tightened. "What?"

She leaned her head against the brick, exposing her neck further and moaned.

"Christ, Penelope." His voice sounded guttural.

She straightened. "Sorry."

"What else?" He needed to know before he lost his train of thought.

"Maddie and Sophie thought I needed flirting techniques." She puffed out her bottom lip in a pout. "I guess they think I'm inadequate."

He couldn't help the smile that twitched at his lips. "That just shows what they know."

"I know I'm not a good flirter."

"And thank God for that." He pressed into her and his erection brushed her belly. "I don't think I could survive. Is there more?"

Her hands slid up his arms. "Yes."

"What?"

She met his gaze. "They thought you would be the perfect person to practice on."

He laughed. "Well, isn't this a lucky turn of events."

"This isn't funny, Evan."

"It is a little bit."

She frowned. "So you'll help me flirt with Logan?"

"Not in a million years." He placed his hands on either side of her head. "You're mine and nobody else can have you."

Another breathy inhale. "Don't say things like that."

"Why? When you like it so much."

"It's not true." She swallowed hard.

"Isn't it?" He gripped her thigh and lifted so she hooked onto his hip.

She rose to meet him, her head once again resting on the brick. "No."

"Your body begs to differ."

She shifted, finding that place only she fit. "Why are you torturing me this way?"

"It's torture for me too, Penelope." He leaned down close

and whispered against the shell of her ear. "You're not alone."

She twined her hands around his neck. "But you won't even kiss me."

"Do you want me to kiss you?"

"Yes," she said, and her lips brushed the line of his jaw, making him ache. "But you won't."

He lifted his head. "It's not from lack of wanting."

Her chin trembled. "That's how it feels."

Maybe it was silly, and maybe they were too far gone. But he wanted to give her all the things she deserved, which proved impossible considering she practically burned him up every time they were in the same room. He brushed his thumb over her lips. "I'm trying to give you the courtship you deserve."

Chapter Twelve

Stunned, Penelope could only stare at him, openmouthed. Maybe her champagne-addled brain was hearing things. "What?"

"You deserve better than what I gave you all those years ago. And I want the chance to make it up to you."

She blinked against the sudden swell of tears. It might be the sweetest thing he'd ever said to her, and she was at a loss for words. "Oh."

He brushed a path down her cheek. "I just can't seem to do that and touch you at the same time."

She licked her lips. "Are they mutually exclusive?"

"For me, they are." His thumb stroked the line of her jaw. "I'm like an addict with you, and now that I've fallen off the wagon, all I can think about is going on a bender."

Yes. That was the perfect description. "It's all off-kilter now."

"Once we start, we won't stop."

"I know." She met his gaze and told him the truth. "I don't want to stop, Evan."

Something pained crossed over his features. "I have

this plan about being good and chivalrous, but you're not helping."

Maybe it was the alcohol, or the dinner last night, or every second they'd been together since she went to his apartment, but his words melted her heart and healed something deep inside her. She leaned into him, trailing her mouth over the line of his jaw. "Maybe you should leave the plans to me."

He groaned and rocked into her.

She pressed back. "It's been so long."

Against the shell of her ear, he said, "I swear to God, Penelope, nobody has ever been as good as you."

She wanted so badly to believe him, and right here, right now, she did. The wounds of the past couldn't mask the chemistry that crackled and sparked between them. "Me too."

He ran his hand up her stomach and cupped her breast. "We won't be able to stop."

She arched into his touch, her mind going blank as her body took over. "We've stopped a million times."

He rolled her nipple between his thumb and forefinger. "I don't want to take you against a wall."

She let out a deep breath. She needed him to understand what he did to her. How he made her feel. And how much she needed what only he could give her right now. "I've dated plenty of chivalrous men over the years and when I was with them, do you know what I thought about? You. Everything you ever did or said to me. I don't want you nice. I don't want you careful. I want you. The way you really are. You ruined me that way and I can't go back. I don't want to."

Their gazes locked and for a fraction of a second the whole world seemed to still.

Then he grabbed her by the neck, and his mouth slammed down on hers.

It was a kiss years in the making.

Every pent-up, frustrated, angry emotion they'd ever had seemed to be poured into it.

He growled low in his throat and she answered back with a fierce, primal sound of her own. Their hands were everywhere, roaming and needy. Their tongues clashed.

She couldn't get close enough.

His fingers buried in her hair.

Her nails dug into his arms.

He pressed her against the wall, rocking hard into her.

She arched.

He surged.

It was so damn good. Everything she remembered and more. So much more.

He slanted his mouth deeper over hers and she was so desperate she tried to crawl into him. She slid her hands under his shirt and her nails raked down his back.

He grunted, and rolled his hips in the same dirty motion as his tongue.

She pulled away. "More. I need more."

"You have no idea what I want to do to you."

"Yes, I do," she said, and their lips fused together, their breathing harsh and panting in the night air. "Do it."

She got lost in the feel of his mouth. His tongue and teeth. His arms strong around her. Roaming, frantic hands. The sounds of their gasping neediness as they fought to get closer. To make up for years of wanting, greedy lust.

There was a loud clapping noise and they broke apart. Disoriented, her lungs burning, she looked around to find Gracie standing over the rails looking down at them. "I've been calling your name for a minute."

Evan stepped back and ran his hand through his hair. "Gracie, um."

She held up her hands. "Save it. Everyone is starting to wonder. You're lucky I jumped up to find you before anyone else. You need to pull it together, kids."

Questions filled Evan's expression as he shot Penelope a sideways glance.

She shrugged, still trying to catch her breath. "She kind of guessed after we had dinner at their house."

Gracie looked back over her shoulder. "You'd better get in there, they're holding dinner and getting impatient."

Evan nodded. "Give us a minute."

Gracie raised a brow. "I can't promise I'll be the one to come out here next."

"A minute," he said, his voice gruff and filled with authority.

Gracie winked. "You Donovan boys sure do have a way about you. I would have loved to have met your daddy."

"*Now*, Gracie," Evan said as though he was on the edge of his patience.

"All right, I'm going, but hurry." Gracie took her leave and Penelope turned back to Evan.

His expression was unreadable. "You told Gracie."

Someone knew besides the two of them, and Penelope wasn't sure how he'd take it. That feeling she used to get when they were teenagers and he looked right through her sat heavy in her stomach. She straightened her shoulders. "She guessed, and even when I denied it she didn't believe me."

"Good."

It surprised her. And pleased her. "You're not upset?"

"No." He hooked his finger through her belt loop. "Did you drive?"

She shook her head.

"I'll drive you home." His voice was implacable.

"I'm supposed to go home with Soph."

He crossed his arms over his chest. "Did they or did they not give you the perfect excuse to be alone with me?"

That tension eased and pooled before disappearing altogether. He wasn't going to let her slip away because they were around people who knew them. She needed this. Needed to get him out of her system. It was the only way, and it was inevitable. She understood that now. She didn't want to escape. Not anymore. "They're helpful that way."

His gaze raked over her. "You look like you've been fooling around."

"So do you."

His attention drifted to her mouth. "Two more minutes and I'd have been inside you."

She sighed. "Don't be a tease."

He shook his head. "What in the hell am I going to do with you?"

Maybe it was the champagne, or maybe it was just him, but she wanted exactly what he'd give her. Now that she'd had a taste of it again, she was like a glutton, and she didn't want to pretend otherwise. "You can run your ideas past me later tonight."

He clenched his hands into fists. "I will keep my hands to myself."

She laughed. "Good luck with that."

She flipped her hair and turned around only to be hauled back against his chest. He slid his hands into the waistband of her jeans, into her panties to stroke her wet flesh.

She gasped as he circled her clit once, twice, three times. And then he was gone. "You too, little Penny."

* * *

Dinner was his own personal version of hell.

He'd spent a thousand dinners, events, and weekends in Penelope's presence, not touching her, so technically he had plenty of practice, but it was like he'd used up all his willpower and now had nothing left to give.

Across from him she sat, with that fuck-me hair, in her tight black top and skinny jeans that made her legs look endless, all smiles and buzzed laughter, taunting him. Making him crazy.

He cursed Shane and his open floor plan where there was nowhere to drag her off to. How had he ever managed to resist her? Well, he knew how, but those reasons seemed like a lifetime ago.

He could still feel her mouth under him. Still catch her scent on the air. Could still feel their wildness. All that vibrating anticipation coiled tight and ready to explode. They'd barely spoken, barely even glanced at each other, but it filled up all the space.

It was all he could think about and he was shocked nobody noticed.

Out of the corner of his eye, he watched as she made her way into the bathroom.

He got up and refilled his wine, and Gracie followed him into the kitchen, supposedly to get her cupcakes, but he knew what she really wanted.

From the table, Shane said, "Grab the whiskey, it's on the top shelf in the pantry."

Evan went and Gracie followed him. He frowned at her. "I've got it."

She pointed to the big plastic container lining the shelf. "I'm getting the dessert." She grinned. "But now that I got you alone, we need to talk."

He rolled his eyes at who he was pretty sure would be his future sister-in-law, although James hadn't asked her yet. God only knew what his brother waited for. Probably still working on his five-year plan before he made it official. Evan pointed at the etched, frosted door of the pantry. "I can't be alone with you. You know how Jimmy is."

Gracie waved a hand. "Don't be ridiculous. Besides, I kept the door open."

Fine, she wouldn't be dissuaded, but he didn't plan on talking. He shook his head. "I'm not going to discuss her with you."

"I expected as much, but I have one thing to say." Gracie's expression got all stern and she jabbed a finger into his chest. "If you hurt her, I will gut you. Do you understand me?"

Evan narrowed his eyes, giving her the same menacing stare he used to give cornerbacks. "If I hurt her, I'll deserve it."

Gracie tilted her head and peered at him, giving him a searching look that made him uncomfortable. "You know, it's hard not to think of you as a womanizing man-whore."

Evan grabbed the bottle of whiskey from the top shelf. "Gee, thanks."

Gracie crossed her arms over her chest. "You had me convinced, but then I see how you look at her and I know it's an act. You care about her, don't you?"

"Is this any of your business?"

Gracie shrugged. "No, not really. But since I'm the only person who's smart enough to figure it out, I've appointed myself her guardian."

"Lucky me."

"I just want to be sure. After what I saw in the yard, I know you have passion, but sometimes that's not enough."

Evan relaxed. Gracie wasn't here to gossip; she cared about Penelope and wanted what was best for her. And truthfully, he was glad she had someone to talk to and watch her back. He gave Gracie a level-eyed stare and said as sincerely as possible, "It's always been her."

Gracie smiled. "You know, I actually believe that."

"That's because it's true."

Gracie grabbed her container and nodded. "Then become the man she deserves."

That's exactly what he was trying to do. "I intend to."

They exited the pantry, shutting the door behind them and returning to the table.

A second later Penelope wandered back into the kitchen, tossing her hair over her shoulder as her gaze flicked over him, then darted away. It reminded him of when she was a teenager, all those furtive glances she used to give him when she assumed he wasn't paying attention.

Back then he'd never allowed himself to linger over her or catch her gaze, fearing it would reveal too much, but he did now and their eyes caught and held.

His breath hitched in his chest. He wondered if she was still wet. Still aching for him the way he was for her. He'd find out soon enough.

She sat down, directly across from him.

He nodded at her water. "Have you recovered from the bottle of champagne you drank?"

"All better," she said, and then stretched. Her top rode high up her stomach, revealing a stretch of smooth skin. "But I could use a nap."

He hoped not, because she wasn't going to be getting any sleep.

Shane pointed to the stairs. "You can lie down if you need to."

She shook her head and yawned, although Evan thought it might be fake. "It's getting late, and tomorrow will be a crazy day with the benefit."

Sophie perked up and waggled her eyebrows. "And I'm sure an even more eventful night."

Oh, it would be, although not in the way Sophie imagined. Evan liked Logan perfectly fine, but the man would not touch Penelope.

Maddie grinned. "You'll need a lot of rest, Pen. Make sure you sleep extra late."

Mitch peered at his wife. "What are you up to?"

"Not a thing," Maddie said.

"Liar," Mitch shot back, suspicion etched in the corners of his mouth.

Penelope yawned again. "It is that time. You know I need my full eight hours."

Sophie huffed. "It's ten o'clock, but all right, I guess we can leave."

And there was Evan's cue. He shook his head. "I've got her. You go ahead and stay, Soph."

"You sure?" Sophie asked.

"We can take her home," James said.

Gracie started shaking her head. "Oh please, can't we stay? It's been a long week and I need fun."

James raised a brow. "Am I not fun?"

Gracie's bottom lip puffed out. "Of course you are, but it's been so long since I've seen Mitch and Maddie. I miss them."

James looked at Evan through his wire-rimmed glasses. "Are you sure you don't mind?"

Evan would have kissed Gracie, but his brother would punch him. Instead he rose. "I'm tired anyway, and Penelope's on my way. You guys stay."

Shane peered at him and nodded at Penelope. "Be safe, she's my most prized employee."

Penelope grinned at his oldest brother. "You just don't want to have to do any work."

Shane laughed. "You know me too well."

Evan felt irrationally irritated at Shane's closeness with Penelope. They shared something Evan didn't know anything about, and in all those years Evan had to stay away, Shane had gotten to experience everything about her life. Evan supposed his only consolation was he knew her deep, dark secrets. He looked at Penelope. "You ready?"

She rose from the chair with her customary poise. "As ready as I'll ever be."

Sophie called after them, "Don't forget to get your rest."

"Yeah," Maddie said, before giggling. "And wear that red dress Sophie talked you into the last time we went shopping."

"Good night, everyone," Penelope said, and Evan pushed her as fast as he could out the door.

On the stoop she turned and looked at him. "Was that exit as ungraceful as I think it was?"

"Do you care?" Evan asked.

Her attention fell to his mouth. "Nope."

He clenched his hand to keep from reaching for her. "You know you're not getting any sleep tonight."

"Well, I should hope not," she said, her tone all prim and proper.

He hooked his finger through her belt loop and tugged. "I'm open to discussion on the red dress."

"Evan." His name a moan as she ran her hand over his stomach. "Take me home and I'll discuss whatever you want."

He growled. "Christ, Penelope."

She just laughed and ran down the steps, that long, dark hair streaming behind her. When she got to the car, she turned and the wind whipped a lock across her cheek. She looked like the girl he used to know and this strange, mysterious woman she'd become.

Like everything he'd loved about the past, and everything he feared about the future.

She looked like sex and life.

Like something too wild to contain and too addictive to let go.

Chapter Thirteen

By the time Evan backed the batmobile into her garage, Penelope was a nervous wreck. She shouldn't be—there wasn't anything she hadn't done with him. But that was years ago.

They were different now. Changed. And despite the chemistry, and the secrets they shared, they were almost strangers to the people they'd become. The personas they'd been showing each other all these years didn't count, because in the end it was just an act, an illusion of apathy she didn't think either one of them had ever felt.

He turned off the ignition, but neither of them moved to get out of the car. He craned his head in her direction. "Nervous?"

"Yes." She bit her bottom lip. "I guess the champagne wore off."

"We don't have to do anything, you know. We could watch TV like we used to." He grinned at her. "What's your current guilty-pleasure show?"

She clasped her hands as her chest expanded. "You remember?"

He twisted and put his arm on the edge of her seat. "I remember everything about you. So what's it these days?"

That he remembered her love of pulpy trash TV filled her with a happiness that embarrassed her. She offered him a shaky smile. "I don't want to tell you."

"Come on." He picked up a lock of her hair and twirled it around his finger. "You know I'll get it out of you."

She huffed and crossed her arms over her chest, making a big show of an exasperation she didn't even come close to feeling. She couldn't believe he remembered. "*The Originals*."

His expression remained blank. "Never heard of it."

"That's because it's not on ESPN."

He tugged at the chestnut strands he still held. "Cute. What's it about?"

She smiled, relaxing a bit. "The original vampire family and their quest to conquer the witches and wolves and claim New Orleans once again for their own."

He laughed, shaking his head. "That sounds awful."

"It's not," she said with all sincerity. She loved her guilty-pleasure shows. She'd get into her sweats and stretch out on her bed with a carton of ice cream and watch with abandon, forgetting all the stress and hassles of the week. "You have to watch before you can judge it."

His gaze met hers. "Shall we watch it so I can judge properly?"

He was giving her an out. But the truth was, she didn't want it. She needed him, and would not be able to settle until she took care of this unbearable ache he created. She shook her head. "Maybe later."

"Are you sure?" He searched her expression.

Who was this Evan that was so concerned with her emotions? She tilted her head. "What happened to the guy who took what he wanted?"

He looked out the window. "He's still there, somewhat leashed at the moment."

She touched his arm, brushing her fingers over the strong cords of his muscles. "I don't want you leashed."

He returned his attention back to her. "That guy who took what he wanted caused a lot of damage, and I don't want to make those same mistakes again."

He kept saying things like that, reminding her of why she'd fallen for him in the first place. She reached for him and touched the edge of his jaw. "I won't regret it. I've never regretted anything I've done with you. Only the aftermath."

He grasped her hand and brought her fingertips to his lips. "Before we go inside, I want to tell you something. It might be hard for you to hear, and maybe it will change tonight, but I want you to know."

"All right," she said, her voice cautious as her heartbeat kicked up a notch. Did statements like that ever end well?

He didn't release his grip, and brought their clasped hands to rest on his thigh.

She didn't pull away. Considering she might have to, she wanted to feel his touch for a while longer.

He cleared his throat. "I haven't been with anyone since Shane and Cecilia's wedding."

Out of all the things she'd been expecting, this had not been it. It shocked her. She still remembered that night with vivid clarity, still remembered going home and lying in her bed, staring up at the dark ceiling, torturing herself with what he was probably doing. But why would that confession change tonight? Her brow furrowed. "All right."

"There's more. Right before the wedding, I'd been on a bit of . . ." His hand tightened on hers. "Well . . . kind of a sex bender."

She wasn't sure she wanted to hear what constituted a sex bender to an NFL player. She shook her head. "I don't need to hear this, Evan. It doesn't matter."

"It matters to me." His tone was soft.

Why was he doing this? All she wanted was to go inside and lose herself in all this heat and suppressed desire. She didn't want to talk, but one look at the set of his jaw confirmed his determination to speak whatever was on his mind. She shifted in the leather seat. "Okay."

"Even before my blow to the head, I'd been in a strange place. I was restless. It didn't matter how hard I trained, or played, it was like something was missing. I didn't understand it because in the past football had always cured my troubles. When it stopped working, I'd taken to increasingly reckless behavior, like surfing the Cyclops, and base jumping."

"I remember. Shane was worried about you." She cleared her throat. "So was I."

A small smile lifted the corners of his lips. "You and my brother, always wanting to take care of everyone and everything."

It was true. They were cut from the same cloth that way. "That's what makes us work."

He stared out the front window. The garage door was still open, and despite living on a pretty, tree-lined street, the alley was narrow and dark. Full of shadows. "I'd been hooking up with Rafaela at the time, and I was going to bring her to the wedding, but then we got in a fight and she wasn't speaking to me. A couple nights before the wedding, I was at a party, and things got out of control. I was with four or five girls that night, sometimes at the same time, I don't really remember. That night was kind of a manic, crazy haze. After I was with one of them, I passed her off to my buddies like it was nothing. Like it was totally normal to have sex with someone, then tell her to go take care of your friend."

Penelope had no idea why, now of all times, he was

telling her this. She wanted to cover her ears and scream at him to stop, but stayed quiet. Instead she pulled her hand away. When he let her go, all the warm happiness and anticipation iced over, leaving her shaken and cold.

"The girl I brought to the wedding was from that night, and you were right, I didn't remember her name. Still don't."

Finally she couldn't take it anymore, and looking stonily through the windshield said in a flat voice, "I don't want to hear this, Evan."

She couldn't stand it one more second. She didn't care how it looked. She needed out of this car. Without waiting for him to respond, she fumbled with the handle before it finally released and she jumped from the car, slamming the door. Fumbling with her purse, she found her keys and pulled them out, sliding them into the door that led into the house.

Goddamn him.

Why tonight, of all nights, did he find it necessary to play true confessions?

Before the door sprung open he came up behind her and pulled her into his arms.

"Let me go," she said, her voice filled with all the anger she was so damn tired of repressing.

"Just hear me out the rest of the way." His lips brushed her ear when he spoke and she involuntarily trembled.

She ripped away. "No! I don't want to hear about all your stupid conquests. I've had to watch them for all these years and now I have to hear about them too?" She opened the door and moved inside. She tried to slam it in his face, but he blocked her and the door slammed against the wall.

"I'm not trying to hurt you, Penelope." His voice loud now, not quite yelling but loud enough to show he was upset.

"Then why are you saying it? Right now, of all times?"

She threw her purse into the laundry room and stalked down the hall. "Do I really need to hear about your last orgy?"

"I want you to understand." Okay, now he was definitely yelling, which he had no right to. She was the wronged party here.

In the kitchen, fists clenched, she whirled on him. "Understand what? That you've fucked a lot of women?! I already know that, Evan. *Everybody* knows that. I don't need your vivid little stories as confirmation."

A muscle jumped along his jaw, as if he was attempting to contain himself. "That's not the point."

"Then what is the point? Because I really need you to get to it."

He let out a frustrated sound, then took a deep breath before slowly exhaling. When he spoke, his calm voice did nothing to reassure her. No, instead it sent coldness slithering like a snake down her spine. "I wanted you to understand my state of mind at the time so I have a chance in hell at communicating just how much seeing you that night got to me."

She stepped back and crossed her arms protectively over her chest. "What?"

He dragged a hand through his hair. "The night of Shane and Cecelia's wedding, when I saw you on the balcony and I was with that girl, I don't know, it did something to me. You just looked so . . . disappointed in me. So disgusted. And I hated it. In that moment all I wanted was for you to see me the way you used to. It took every ounce of willpower not to go after you. I wanted to break every rule we'd ever silently established. I broke away·for a bit and tried to talk to you alone, do you remember?"

At least that finally made sense. She leaned against the counter. "I remember."

"You said you were leaving and I wanted to stop you,

to insist, but your expression stopped me and I let you go. I told myself it didn't matter. That I could get any woman I wanted. That what happened between us all those years ago was just a couple of stupid kids. That *you* didn't matter."

She blinked, meeting his troubled gaze. They were only a couple of feet apart, but the distance seemed like a million miles. She exhaled. "I guess it worked."

"No, Penelope, it didn't work. That night when I took that girl home, and I had every intention of sleeping with her, in my fucked-up head it was a way to punish you. I took her home, stripped her. My head was full of you, how you looked in that purple dress, the way your hair brushed across your cheek, and all my memories of what we'd done. The girl laughed and I looked at her and something just snapped. It wasn't the face I wanted to see, and no amount of pretending could make it so. So I left, and I haven't been with anyone since."

"What? Am I supposed to be happy that you pictured me while screwing some girl whose name you can't even remember?"

He dragged his hand through his hair. "No, that's not what I'm saying."

"Am I supposed to feel sorry for you? Feel bad that having a wild sex party, and treating women like objects wasn't quite doing it for you anymore? Because it's really hard to work up any sympathy right now." God, she wanted to kill him. He'd ruined everything she'd wanted this night to be.

"Penelope," he said before blowing out a long, frustrated breath. "No, I just want you to know I thought about you. I wanted to go to you."

She tilted her chin. "If that's true, why didn't you?"

"I just—" He looked away, his fingers flexing before clenching into fists. "I didn't know how. And I sure as hell didn't know what I wanted. Then the season started, and I did what I always did and threw myself into the game. Then, after the hit, when I was in the hospital, I picked up the phone to call you a hundred times."

They were words she'd wanted him to say, but it was all wrong. It was twisted somehow, mixing with all the times they'd been teenagers and she'd silently begged him to acknowledge her. To give her some sign that the things he'd done with her in that basement weren't in her imagination. But he never had, he'd just walked off with his arm slung around Kim Rossi and didn't look back. Throat impossibly tight, she croaked out, "You never called."

A pained expression slid over his features. "What was I supposed to say, Pen? That I was a mess and needed you?"

Her shoulders slumped. He had no idea how she would have killed to hear those words. "Yes, that's exactly what you should have said."

"I couldn't."

Her heart thudded, hard and angry. "Why?"

He put his hand on his chest, as though imploring her to understand. "Think of it from my perspective. I'd treated you like shit for years, living out this fantasy of a life and practically throwing it in your face, and the second I'm told it's over I come crawling back to you. I couldn't do that. I wouldn't."

"But then I came to you."

"You did."

The sudden swell of tears filled her eyes and she turned away, putting her palms on the counter. Those two little words sinking deep into her stomach and festering like a boil of truth. She hadn't wanted to have this conversation. She'd wanted to avoid it. She'd wanted to forget the past and the future and give in to the constant temptation he invoked in her, but she could see now that wasn't possible. With Evan, she never got what she wanted. She choked back her emotions. "It's always the same song with us, isn't it?"

"What do you mean?"

"I mean, I *always* have to come to you."

"I'm sorry." His tone so somber she didn't even have to turn around to see the resignation on his face.

She brushed the wetness from her cheeks.

"Should I go?"

No, she didn't want him to go. She wanted him to fix this mess *he'd* made. But she knew he wouldn't. She didn't speak. Didn't have to. Because she knew how it worked between them, how it would always work. She came to him. He gave up.

"I'm sorry," he said, his voice soft.

Still she remained silent, waiting for what she knew would come. He didn't disappoint her. A minute later the door shut and she heard the roar of the engine.

She tried to contain the cry lodged in her throat, but it refused to stay down where it belonged and she burst into tears.

Some things never changed. This night encompassed her entire relationship with Evan.

A few hours of happiness followed by heartbreak.

Evan sat in his condo, staring out at his perfect view of the Chicago skyline, miserable and waiting. He didn't know if he was doing the right thing, but he didn't think he had any other choice in the matter.

How did he manage to fuck up everything that was important to him?

It was his fatal flaw. Unlike Shane, everything Evan touched turned to shit, despite all his advantages. And the worst part was, it was *always* his own doing.

He'd had her. He'd be with her right now, in her bed, if he'd just kept his mouth shut. But he hadn't been able to do that. No, he'd been compelled by some stupidity to be honest, to try and make her understand what she meant to him.

Only he'd done it in the worst possible way and now she hated him all over again.

It was like that last hit he'd replayed in his mind a million times since he'd woken up in that hospital bed. In slow, excruciating motion he watched himself going for the touchdown instead of taking the smart, safe path.

And now he'd made the same stupid mistake with Penelope.

He took a sip of the whiskey. At least he hadn't taken to drinking straight from the bottle again. He guessed that was some sort of perverse progress in the mess of his life.

The private penthouse phone rang. He picked it up. "Let him up, Carl."

That disembodied, banal voice. "Very well, sir."

Evan took a deep breath. Well, this was it. He was tapping out and calling in reinforcements. Maybe this wasn't his smartest decision, but he clearly didn't know what he was doing and it was time to admit defeat.

Giving up Penelope all those years ago, despite his methods, had been the right thing to do.

What he didn't know was if it was the right thing to do now. He didn't trust himself with her. How could he be good for her if all he did was make her unhappy?

There was a knock on the door and with a sigh he walked over and opened it.

James stood there, a bottle in hand. He raised a brow at the glass in Evan's hand. "You've already started."

Evan stood back and let his brother in, experiencing an uncustomary string of nerves. "Yeah. Thanks for coming."

"You're my brother, I will always come." James walked into the kitchen and pulled down two glasses. "Although I'll admit I was surprised. You're not much for talking."

He wasn't. He was making an exception for Penelope. To see if he could salvage the mess he'd made. Because if anything had come out of this, it was that he could no longer go back to the man he'd been before. He was no longer content to walk away from the carnage. He needed to fix things, even if that meant accepting that he'd never be good for her.

Evan went and sat down in the overly large club chair, remembering the night she'd come to him. He rubbed the bridge of his nose. It had taken a good hour of pensive brooding before he'd finally determined he was going to have to talk to someone, because he was making a mess of it on his own.

James, his logical, sensible, levelheaded brother, whose significant other already knew, was really the only choice.

Evan just didn't know where to start.

James put two glasses on the coffee table and sat down on the couch and poured the whiskey into the glasses. "You can start fresh."

Evan drained the rest of his current beverage, set it on the table, and picked up the other. "Thanks. Was Gracie mad I dragged you out of bed?"

James settled back in the couch, his head tilting as he took a sip. "No. Actually, she said the oddest thing."

"What was that?" Evan had some clue; after all, Gracie probably assumed he'd be busy for the rest of the night.

James pinned him with a stare, his gaze thoughtful behind his wire-rimmed glasses. "She said 'well, that's not good, you'd better go.' She didn't ask me any questions. Which isn't like her. It was almost like she already knew why you were calling."

Here was his opening. He'd never told a soul and the words stuck in his throat. Even when his dad had confronted him, he'd kept quiet and let him do all the talking. During that last conversation, he hadn't confirmed or denied, he'd just sat there in complete silence. When his dad stopped talking, Evan had gotten up and left.

He had no idea how to start or how to explain his messed-up emotions. Emotions he barely understood and didn't want to discuss, but keeping it all in was no longer an option. He'd have to figure it out as he went along. Grip tight on his glass, he said, "That's because she kind of does."

James nodded, but didn't look surprised. "And what does she already know?"

Evan peered past his brother and took a drink, shaking his head. "I don't know where to start."

"The beginning's a good place."

He exhaled and looked back at James, who studied him with the most curious expression.

Evan took another deep breath and dove in. Not quite at the beginning, but with the truth. "Well, here's the thing. I'm pretty sure I'm in love with Penelope and have been since I was seventeen years old."

James blinked, then straightened. He opened his mouth. Closed it. Shook his head. "Wait, what did you say?"

Just the act of admitting it, saying it out loud, made his head clear, so he said it again, his voice stronger now. "Our sister's best friend—you know, Penelope."

James put his drink on the coffee table. "I know who Penelope is."

Evan took another sip. "I'm not sure, because I'm not an expert or anything, but I think I'm in love with her."

To his surprise, some of the tightness in his chest eased. Maybe this is why people talked about their feelings?

James cleared his throat and sat forward, resting his

elbows on his knees and lacing his fingers. His standard thinking position. "I see. And does she have any idea?"

"Probably not." Evan thought of the look on her face when he'd been telling her about his last sexual escapade; it was the same look she'd given him the night of Shane and Cecilia's wedding. Disgusted disappointment. "Definitely not. I honestly don't know what she thinks."

"I'm sorry, I'm surprised and kind of confused. Have you ever tried to talk to her? Have you guys ever had a conversation? Like alone?" James shook his head again, as though trying to puzzle it all out. "Wait. I guess you were alone in the backyard. And now that I think back, you did seem eager to take her home. Did you try and talk to her tonight? I have to be honest, I had no idea you even knew she was alive. So you can't blame me for being shocked. You do know Shane is going to kill you if he ever finds out."

That his oldest brother was the least of his worries spoke volumes. Evan drained the rest of his glass. "Yeah, I know."

James poured him another. "He's fiercely protective of Penelope."

And he'd never consider Evan good enough for her. "I'm aware of his feelings for her."

"So you've got to think long and hard about approaching her about a potential relationship. You really need to weigh the pros and cons before you discuss anything further with her."

Evan couldn't help but laugh. "You don't understand. I've touched her more times than I can count."

James stared at him blankly. "What?"

"I was her first . . . well, everything. Her first kiss. Her first orgasm. I took her virginity."

"Penelope?" James asked, his voice full of surprise. "Our Penelope? The one we've known since she was six?

Best friends with Maddie? Works for our brother? Carries an iPad around with her and likes spreadsheets? That Penelope?"

Evan raised a brow. "I thought you said you knew who she was."

"I'm just making sure we are, in fact, talking about the same person."

"I can assure you, we are."

"And nobody knows? It's been a secret between you for over fifteen years?"

"Yes. Well, not quite. Gracie guessed." Evan took a deep breath and gulped down some more whiskey.

James's brow furrowed. "How did Gracie find out?"

Evan shrugged. "I don't know, at dinner that night she figured it out. I suppose Penelope and I looked at each other a certain way."

James's brow furrowed. "I didn't notice anything."

"I think everyone else is too close, and you grew up around us. I think the tension fades into the background. And we've had a lot of practice hiding it."

James scrubbed a hand over his face. "Okay, let's start again from the beginning."

And Evan did. He told James everything, starting with the first night, the night their dad died, the morning after. He didn't stop talking until he finished every awful detail of this evening's fiasco.

When he finally fell silent James sat back, a rather stunned expression on his face. "Yes, I can see why this is complicated."

Evan dragged a hand through his hair. "Every time I talk to her, I just end up making it worse."

James narrowed his gaze, and Evan could practically see the wheels spinning in his head. "Since Gracie, I've learned something about women, namely that they don't think the way we do."

Evan let out a scornful sound. "Tell me something I don't know, Jimmy."

James held out his hand. "No, wait, hear me out. I've learned they read into things we say, and assign a certain type of female logic to our statements. So when we say and mean X, a woman will hear X, but think we mean A, B, C, D, E, F, G, and so on. Do you see what I'm saying?"

Evan shook his head. "I don't have a fucking clue."

"Exactly," James said, as though that explained everything.

"I'm lost."

James rubbed his jaw, his brow furrowed in concentration. "Well, it's something she said there at the end, before you walked out, that's niggling at me."

"I asked her if she wanted me to go and she didn't respond."

James nodded. "Yes, well that was your first mistake, but that's not what I mean. I'm talking about right before that. What did you say she said again? The exact words."

Evan didn't know where he was going, but trudged on, as he had no concrete idea on how to fix the mess he'd made. "She said she was always the one that had to come to me."

"And then what?"

"I said I was sorry. And when she didn't speak I asked her if she wanted me to leave, and she still said nothing. So I assumed that was a yes and left."

James snapped, his expression clearing with some sort of comprehension that eluded Evan. "That's it."

Evan leaned forward, hopeful in spite of the fact that they were two guys trying to figure out the inner workings of a female mind. "What's it?"

"I'm not one hundred percent sure, but here's my guess. She tells you that she always has to be the one who makes the first move. You ask her if she wants you to leave, and when she doesn't answer you take that at face value. You took her silence literally."

"Why wouldn't I? Repeating the same thing over and over again doesn't change what happened."

James's expression turned animated, caught up in the excitement of his hypothesis. "See, Penelope's a woman, and a woman's words always have a double meaning. Her always having to come to you is like a code, and based on the rest of your discussion I'm betting the underlying meaning is that she believes you never fight for her. And being a woman, she naturally assumes that you don't fight for her because you don't care, and not because you're an insecure idiot about her. And what did you go and do?"

He'd left. Evan felt like he'd been punched in the gut as the understanding resonated deep within him. The worst possible thing he could have ever done. He blew out a hard breath. "Fuck. I think you're right."

A smile quirked at his brother's mouth. "Gracie continues to pay off."

Evan would laugh if he didn't feel like he'd been dropkicked. "Now what do I do?"

James gave him a direct, level-eyed stare, his expression turning sober. "You need to think about this, Evan. Penelope's part of our family. She's not *ever* going away. She's one of us."

"I know that."

"Are you sure this isn't about the conquest? Giving you purpose without football?"

Evan scrubbed a hand over his jaw. "If it was about that, I'd never have called you."

James nodded. "You have to understand the repercussions of this. Not only does Maddie think of Penelope as a sister, but there's Shane."

Shane. The thought of his oldest brother and their already strained relationship made his stomach knot.

"You've always lived your own life, spent more time away than the rest of us, so I'm not sure you understand the nature of Shane and Penelope's relationship," James continued, laying out all the logical, practical obstacles in Evan's way, everything he'd been avoiding while he focused on his desire for her.

Evan clenched his teeth. "I know how close they are."

James shook his head. "They are more than close; when it comes to his business, Penelope is the one person he can't live without. What if things go wrong and she decides to disentangle herself from us? From Shane?"

"She'd never leave Shane because of me."

"I don't know. I'm merely pointing out the potential consequences. You need to think it through instead of rashly acting." James sat back on the couch and sighed. "Because if you damage her relationship with Maddie or Shane, it's going to be a big deal. It's not going to be something you can just smooth over."

The words cut right through him, because James was right. If this came to light, and he messed up, his brother and sister would never forgive him. They'd choose Penelope.

That conversation with his dad, so long ago, the last real conversation they'd had, flashed in his mind.

He swallowed past the tightness in his throat. He didn't want to hurt her anymore. He wanted her to be happy. "So you think I should walk away?"

"Is that what you want?" James asked, his voice deadly serious.

Evan gave him the unvarnished truth, and even though he'd already admitted the words, the emotions strangled him. "All this time, all those other women, and none of them ever even came close to her. I can't walk away, not this time."

James nodded, his expression softening. "Then you'll need to fight for her."

"I know."

"And you understand, you can't do that and continue to keep her a secret?"

He knew what James was really saying. There would be hell to pay. Fighting for her, their relationship coming to light, would force Evan to deal with the past and his fears about himself and his future. And the truth was, she might never forgive him enough to have a real shot with her, but he couldn't let her believe she wasn't worth fighting for.

He looked unflinching into James's probing gaze. "She's worth it."

James nodded. "She is."

Evan was so grateful he'd finally let go of his own stupid ego and talked to his brother, because it wouldn't be easy, but at least he understood. He had a plan. He cleared the emotion from his throat. "Thank you."

"That's what brothers are for." James flashed a grin before his expression turned serious again. "I do have one piece of advice."

"I'll take whatever you can give me." Evan had to resist the urge to grab his jacket and go to her right now, tonight. But instinct warned him to be patient. To plan and figure out his next move instead of just letting her fall into his lap all the time.

"If you're going to go for it, go for it. Hold nothing back," James said.

"I won't." And he meant it. She was his. And he would not rest until he proved it to her.

Chapter Fourteen

In the end, Penelope couldn't wear the red dress. Instead, she settled on a strapless white number with a flared skirt and a wide black belt that tied in a bow. Which turned out to be a perfect complement to Logan's white dress shirt and black pants.

They matched. They looked good together, like a couple. She hadn't missed the wistful glances she'd received from some of the women when they walked into the benefit, located downtown overlooking the lakefront, and she found herself wishing it were true. Being with Logan would be so easy, only there was that pesky little attraction problem and the knowledge her heart belonged to another man.

One more example of life's twisted sense of humor.

Unable to keep from searching for Evan, she glanced around for perhaps the hundredth time, but he still hadn't made an appearance, even though the benefit was in full swing.

Despite his claims of celibacy, she fully expected him to show up with some fashion plate on his arm. Evan rarely went to any event alone, and she doubted tonight would be an exception.

She took a deep breath, and slowly exhaled. Eventually,

with enough time, her heart would harden and she'd go back to that place she'd been before she'd made the stupid decision to go to his condo. Back to normal. She could handle that.

Her best course of action was to accept responsibility in this current situation and stop engaging him. She'd done it before, she could do it again.

Logan jostled her elbow. "Hey, are you okay?"

She shook her head to clear it of Evan and realized she scowled, so she flashed him her most dazzling smile. "Of course, everything's great."

Concentrate on what matters, Penelope. She needed to stop pining and be grateful Logan was here and she wouldn't be forced to endure Evan and some model alone.

"You seem very distracted," Logan said, studying her with that intense scrutiny he had.

Penelope waved a hand and attempted a laugh, but it came out shaky and uncertain. She cleared her throat. "Nope, I'm just tired. It's been a long day making sure everything was ready."

Logan looked around the crowded room. "You did a great job."

"Cecilia helped. It was a joint effort. And don't forget Shane, who sponsored the whole event and made it happen."

Logan tilted her head and looked down at her with narrowed eyes. "Are you sure you're okay? You seem off."

To her horror, her throat tightened. This was why she always got eight hours of sleep; anything less and she was useless. "Yes, of course. I'm totally fine."

His expression held deep suspicion and he jutted his chin toward the balcony. "Let's get some air."

She nodded and let him lead her outside. The air was mild, warm but not hot; the breeze pleasant and not vicious like it sometimes could be by the lakefront. She breathed in deep as they walked through the crowd to the balcony's edge.

She wrapped her hands on the metal rails and stared into the night and down to the water, the waves rolling onto the shore. Focus on the good. Everything that was right. How she'd accomplished everything she'd ever wanted. Everything she'd ever promised herself, growing up in that small two-flat apartment building with her tired parents, she'd achieved.

She lived a life most of the people in their old neighborhood could never have dreamed of. Here she was, at thirty-one, an executive at one of the most prestigious companies in Chicago. Even better, she loved her job. It filled her with purpose. Challenged her. She had great friends, a fabulous house, and a killer wardrobe.

She'd gotten everything she'd ever wanted. Except for Evan. Well, that and the big, loving family she'd always envisioned when she'd had Sunday night dinners with the Donovans.

Maybe some dreams weren't meant to come true.

And that was okay. Her shoulders slumped. It was.

She had all the things that really mattered in life. Tomorrow, first thing, she'd work on putting Evan behind her. Focus on finding the right kind of man, one who would give her the family she wanted now that her career was a smashing success.

That mystery man would complement her. She wouldn't have to worry about models, or the spotlight, like she would with Evan. She wouldn't have to worry about him messing up her relationship with the people who mattered most to her. He'd slide right in, and it would be easy. Not hard like it was with Evan.

"You want to talk about it?" Logan asked, ripping her from her thoughts.

She started. God, she needed to snap out of this. She turned to face him. "I'm sorry, what?"

He smiled. "I asked you a couple of other questions, but that was the only one that got your attention."

Heat filled her cheeks and she ducked her head. It was hard to pretend she wasn't distracted when she kept drifting off during conversations. "Ack! I'm tired, that's all. I'm sorry for being horrible company."

"I believe you're tired." He reached up and brushed a thumb over her cheekbone. "Despite looking fantastic, you've got dark circles under your eyes makeup can't quite hide."

"I had a rough night's sleep." Not that tossing and turning could be called sleep. Then she'd spent the day dodging her friends—Maddie, Sophie, and Cecilia, with their flirting game-plan to lure Logan into her fictitious infatuation. The three of them were bad enough, but avoiding Gracie was the worst.

Because she knew the truth. She kept saying they needed to talk, but Penelope kept finding other things to pull her away. She wasn't ready to admit the truth yet, that she had no stories of the hot sex Gracie was expecting.

That he'd left. That she'd spent half the night crying.

That it was over before it had even begun.

And finally, that they just weren't meant to be.

Logan's hand slipped over her waist. "Hey, what's wrong?"

Penelope blinked rapidly to quell the treacherous welling of her eyes, and swallowed down the tightness in her throat, but couldn't speak. She shook her head.

Expression filling with concern, Logan pulled her close and kissed her temple. "Tell me what's wrong, and maybe we can fix it."

She wanted to pretend, but couldn't hide what was so blatantly obvious. So she stayed frozen, rigid in his embrace, afraid if she gave in for even one second, she'd start crying all over again. She managed to croak out, "It's nothing."

"Let me talk to her." That low, deep, unmistakable voice.

It must be in her imagination. She jerked up, her head swinging around as she looked into Evan's dark green eyes.

Logan frowned, stepping back but not removing his hand from Penelope's lower spine.

Evan's gaze zeroed in on where Logan touched her. "I've got her."

Shocked at his overtness, Penelope couldn't stop the gasp.

Logan studied Evan for a long, long time, before shifting his attention to her. "I see."

Penelope shook her head. "No. What? There's nothing to see." She put on her most passive expression. "What's wrong, Evan, does Shane need something?"

"No, he doesn't." Evan's gaze flicked to Logan's and he cracked a smile. "Only thing that's really stopping me from trying to rip your arm off right now is you're a black belt and will probably kick my ass."

Logan's brow rose and instead of removing his palm, he seemed to dip lower, causing Evan to grit his teeth. "Ninth-degree black belt."

Evan nodded. "I'm sure that's very impressive, and being a football player, I only know how to block and tackle. I'll concede you'll probably win."

Penelope's brain could not process what was happening. Were they discussing fighting over her? She had to be wrong. There was no way. Logan didn't feel that way about her and Evan barely acknowledged her unless they were alone.

"Probably?" Logan scoffed. "I can assure you, most definitely."

Oh God, they were. How could this be happening?

"Fair enough." Evan shrugged. "But if it's all the same to you, I'd appreciate you removing your hands from her."

The statement finally snapped Penelope out of her stupor. Cheeks burning, she hissed, "Evan, what are you doing?"

Evan looked at her. "I believe this is known as claiming what's mine."

Shock once again rolled through her and she could only gape at him. "Have you lost your mind?"

"Nope," Evan said, his voice sure and confident, his gaze steady on hers.

Logan chuckled. "Well now, isn't this an interesting turn of events."

Evan glanced pointedly to where Logan still touched her. "Hands."

Logan's palm slid away. Slowly. "Shane is not going to be happy."

What in God's name was happening here? Why was Evan acting like this? This was not how they did things. She tried to form a sentence but none of the words flying through her head made it to her mouth.

"I'm well aware of that," Evan said, before turning to her. "We need to talk."

"There's nothing to say," Penelope said, but her voice cracked, belying her emotions.

"Then you can just listen." Evan held out his hand. "Logan, good to see you again, but I'll take it from here."

Had he just dismissed Logan?

The other man shook Evan's outstretched palm, nodding. "Fair enough." He shot a sly glance at her. "If you need me, you know where to find me."

When Logan left she whirled on Evan. "What are you doing? Are you crazy? What if Logan tells everyone?"

"I don't think he will." Evan stepped into the spot Logan had vacated. "And I don't care if he does."

Anger spiked hot and fast inside her as she waved at the crowds of people inside. This was not how they did things. They were a secret. They needed to stay a secret. "So what? You're going to make me explain myself over something that happened fifteen years ago? That's over?"

He gripped her wrist and tugged, making her falter on her black heels. "It's not over."

The hope that surged made her cringe. "Yes, it is."

"No, it is not." He slid his hand around her waist.

She pushed at his chest. "What are you doing?"

"Coming for you."

Her words from last night. He'd been listening. She shook her head. "Stop this. What is wrong with you? Are you drunk again?"

"Nothing is wrong with me and I haven't had a drop of alcohol." He pulled her closer.

She darted nervous glances around the balcony and through the glass into the benefit, hyperaware that anyone watching them would know this wasn't a friendly embrace.

His chin dipped as he stared at her with such intensity she wanted to fidget. "I'm doing what I should have done all along."

Hope, the worst of all emotions because of its sheer persistence and futility. Heart hammering in her chest, her voice cracked when she spoke. "I don't know what that means."

"It means I'm going to fight for you, and I'm going to win." He slid his hand up her back and tangled his fingers in her hair. An artfully arranged, haphazard side bun with tendrils that curled over her cheekbones and framed her face. "I like your hair like this, but I like it better down."

"Stop this." But her fingers curled into his shirt. "People are going to see us."

"I don't care," he said before dipping down, mere inches away.

One lift of her toes and tilt of her head and their mouths would fuse together. She could still feel him, the memory fresh now from the night before. The hot sear of his lips. The stroke of his tongue. The rough movements of his hands over her body. When she spoke, her words were far too breathless. "Evan, enough."

"It's not enough. I want them to see. I can't woo you properly with all this sneaking around."

She could not process what was happening. She leaned back but he wouldn't let her go. "What are you saying?"

"I'm saying it's hard to seduce you from across the room if I can't look at you. I'm saying I want to touch you without having to worry about who's watching us." He plucked the pins from her hair and the waves tumbled around her shoulders, making tingles break out over her skin. "I'm saying that I'm making my intentions clear. What you want to tell them about the past is up to you. I'll stick with whatever you want to say, but from this day forward I'm done keeping you a secret. In an effort at full disclosure, I told James everything, so I'm sure he and Gracie are having a field day discussing us. But from here out, I'll sell whatever story you want, except the one that has me pretending I don't want you."

The lack of sleep, the crying, the exhaustion and crazy, roller-coaster emotions, it was all too much. She yelled, "You decided? You? Without even talking to me, you decided to out us?"

"Out you?" Maddie said.

Both Penelope and Evan whipped toward her, instinctively taking a step away from each other.

Maddie's attention darted back and forth between them. "What's going on here? Why is Evan touching you?"

Penelope stared at her best friend with a mixture of embarrassment, mortification, and horror, the world gone so silent she could hear a pin drop. And suddenly she couldn't stand it for one more second. She needed to be alone, so she could think. She let out an exasperated scream and jerked away from Evan before pinning him with a fierce glare. "You made this mess, you deal with it."

Then she turned and walked away, as fast as her too-high heels would carry her.

Evan watched as Penelope stalked through the crowd, then he turned on his sister. "Not your best timing, Mads."

Maddie's mouth opened. Closed. Then opened again. She shook her head and frowned. "What did you do? You've upset Penelope. The most unflappable woman on the planet."

Over his sister's head, he watched as Penelope stomped through the room and disappeared out of sight. Okay, she was angry. Now his sister was angry. And soon Shane would be angry.

He'd expected it and was prepared to deal with every single one of them, but Penelope was his top priority. He had to go after her and he didn't have the time to explain to Maddie.

"Evan!" his sister yelled. When he looked at her, her arms were crossed and she tapped the toe of her high-heeled sandal, looking exactly like their mother. Not that telling her that would put him in her good graces.

"I'll explain everything later, but now I need to go find Penelope."

He stepped around Maddie only for her to step in front of him and put her hand on his chest. "What have you done?"

"Nothing." Well, that wasn't true. He dragged a hand

through his hair. "Everything. It's complicated. We'll talk later."

"We'll talk now," she said in a stern voice.

Irritation and impatience pricked along his skin. He put his hand on her wrist and removed it from his chest. "I'm fourteen inches taller than you and outweigh you by over a hundred pounds. I'll pick you up and move you if I'm forced to, but I'm going after Penelope."

She blinked, rearing back to look up at him to search his expression. All of a sudden her features widened. "Oh. Oh no." She shook her head. "No, Evan, you can't have her. There are a million women waiting in line for you. Not. Her. Anyone but her."

Evan had expected this reaction as well. It still stung. If Maddie felt this way and she liked him, what would Shane say? He'd deal with it later after he went after Penny, because it was imperative he pursue her. To not let her go. To show her. Jaw tight, he said, "I'm not asking your permission."

And before Maddie could say another word, he stepped around her and headed in the direction where he'd last seen Penelope. Unable to find her among the crowd and knowing she probably wanted to be alone, he left the large room and went into the hallway.

She wasn't there.

He counted fifteen doors and exit points. He sighed. Where to find her?

He walked to the first door on his left and twisted the handle, finding it locked.

He pulled his cell from his pocket and called her. Of course she didn't answer.

He tried the next door.

And the one after that.

He went to the coat-check woman behind the counter located next to the banquet room.

Seemingly engrossed in the book she was reading, he cleared his throat. She huffed and glanced up, freezing when she saw him. He flashed her his interview, got-to-love-me smile. "Hi."

She flushed scarlet. "H-hi."

He pointed down the hallway. "Did you see a woman with dark hair, wearing a white strapless dress and a black belt, come this way?"

The woman shook her head, looking vaguely disappointed.

"All right, thanks," he said, and turned away. He tried to call Penelope again, not surprised she didn't answer.

All right then, he'd told her he was going to come for her and that's what he'd do. Even if it took him all night to do it.

He checked every door.

Every room.

The bathrooms.

The storage closet.

The stairwell.

When none of those worked, he went down one floor and started again. Methodically working his way through the hallways and cursing Shane for picking a venue that had so many stories.

He finally found her on the fourth floor down, sitting on a high-backed chair, in those little sitting areas hotels sometimes had. Eyes closed, her head rested in her open palm, that minklike hair flowing over her shoulder.

He walked over and squatted down in front of her.

She didn't open her eyes. "Go away, Evan."

He put his hands on her knees and she tensed under his touch. "I can't do that, Pen."

"Why?"

"I told you why."

Her lashes fluttered open and her blue eyes pierced right

through him. "I don't understand the first thing about what's going on here."

His fingers slipped under the hem of her dress and brushed across her soft skin. She couldn't hide the tremble. "I shouldn't have left you last night. I didn't want to leave and I was wrong." He blew out a long breath. "I know I have this reputation for being great with women, but the truth is, with you, I'm a complete idiot."

Her expression didn't change, but when she didn't pull away or speak he kept talking, deciding on brutal honesty. "I have no idea what you're thinking or what you want. It frustrates me trying to figure out the woman you've become. I can't let go. I don't *want* to let go. But the only thing I'm confident about when it comes to you is our chemistry, and how to give you multiple orgasms. I know it's not enough, but it's my only real hold on you, and I'm lost whenever I try and make us real."

She still didn't speak, but at least instead of looking resigned she looked interested, and he took it as a sign to continue. His legs were starting to burn so he stood and pointed to a chair across from her. "Can I sit?"

She nodded.

He took that as progress.

He pulled the chair close to her and sat down so their knees were touching. Once again he placed his palms on her legs and she didn't flinch away. He continued on, knowing all he could really do was be as honest as possible. "I'm sorry I hurt you by telling you about those women. I have a past, a lengthy and often seedy one, and I should have kept it to myself. All I can say is that it's my stupid way of trying to show you how, after all these years, you still get to me. You matter to me, Pen. You have always mattered. I had this plan, to show you, but obviously I'm messing it all up."

She clasped her fingers tight in her lap. "What was your plan?"

"Like I said, I wanted to court you properly. Take you out to dinner. Go to the movies. Take you to the museums I'm guessing you probably like. To prove to you that this isn't about sex. It's more than chemistry. Only I underestimated two things."

"And those are?"

The corners of his lips lifted. "I can't seem to touch you without going overboard. It's like now that the seal has been broken, every time I lay a finger on you all I can think about is pushing you down to the first available flat surface." He dragged his hand through his hair. "I mean, you don't understand. I don't think I have the patience to get you naked first. It's a little disconcerting to realize I had more control when I was seventeen than I do now."

Their gazes met, held, and clung, and the air filled with that indescribable heat they generated. She scraped her teeth against her bottom lip and cleared her throat. "And the other one?"

"I don't want to keep you a secret."

"You don't?" Her head tilted and she crossed her leg.

His hand slipped up her skirt to rest on her bare skin. He shook his head slowly. "How can I prove to you I'm serious while keeping you a secret? I can't, and I don't want to do it anymore. Even though I'm going to incur the wrath of a lot of people. Since, universally, nobody thinks I'm good enough for you."

"Do you think you're good enough for me?"

"No, I don't," he said, his voice serious. "But I want to be."

Something flickered over her features. "Do you know what I think?"

"I haven't a clue."

She squared her shoulders and Evan knew he wasn't going to like what she said. "I think this is about football. You've lost your career and now you need a new challenge to keep you interested in life. I'm conveniently it."

He put his elbows on his knees. "You're wrong. First, there's not one thing convenient about you. And second, I have thought of you and wanted you every single day we have been apart. That has nothing to do with football."

Another flash of emotion. "You left, Evan. And you never once looked back."

"I have my reasons." He looked away and took a deep breath.

"And those are?"

The time had come, and while he'd decided last night he'd tell her everything, this wasn't where he'd wanted to have the conversation. But since he was fighting for his life right now, he didn't see any other option.

He'd never told a soul, but he'd tell her, and hoped she'd understand. He looked back at her. "My dad knew about you."

Chapter Fifteen

Shocked, Penelope could only stare at him. It was the last thing she expected him to say. "How?"

Evan shrugged. "He didn't specifically say, and I couldn't ask, because asking was the same as confirming, but if I had to guess, I think he saw us together."

A million things they'd done flashed rapid-fire through her mind. She licked her lips. "In the basement?"

His gaze met hers. "Yes."

"Why do you think that? Maybe he saw us look at each other?"

He shook his head. "I don't think so. He didn't talk to me like he thought we had a crush, or were flirting. He was very serious and not happy about it."

It shouldn't matter. Patrick Donovan was dead, and they weren't teenagers anymore, but somehow it did. The expression on Evan's face, the look in his eyes, the tone of his voice, all squeezed something deep in her chest.

"What did he say?" On high alert, she straightened in her chair.

He looked past her, staring off into the distance. "He said I needed to end it. That our lives were headed in different directions. That he didn't want to see you hurt."

Penelope nodded, still not quite understanding. "You weren't hurting me."

Evan's face twisted. "Wasn't I? But that wasn't really the point he was making."

She licked her lip. "What was his point?"

He exhaled, the sound heavy. "Back then I'd already been offered full rides from three Big Ten schools, and everyone thought I had what it took to turn pro. He told me that when I went to college, I'd be exposed to a life of temptation I wouldn't be able to resist. That keeping you was unfair and cruel. That you deserved to be the star, not living in my shadow." A small smile ghosted his lips. "His words, not mine."

"But I don't understand," Penelope said, shaking her head. "We weren't together, not really. Why would he even think that?"

"That's why I think he saw us in the basement—unfiltered, the way we really were when no one was watching." He shifted his attention back to her. "And because he was my dad, I think he somehow suspected the fantasy I'd weaved in my head when I wasn't paying attention."

Her breath caught and she licked her suddenly dry lips. "What was that?"

"A future that included you."

She folded her hands to keep from reaching for him. "You never said anything that even hinted at that."

He shook his head. "I don't think I was conscious of it until he said it out loud."

She almost didn't want to ask, but they were on the path now and she couldn't stop, not until she heard the rest. "When did this all happen?"

"Two days before he died." He clasped his hands in front of him, his knuckles white. "It was the last real conversation we had."

Tears welled in her eyes and she blinked them away. "And he was mad at you?"

Evan nodded. "He told me I was selfish, that I could have any girl I wanted and I should leave you alone to have a normal life. He said because you were an only child and because your parents were older, you'd never really gotten the life you deserved. And he didn't want me to steal that away from you. He told me you needed to be with someone who would make you the center of their world."

It explained so much; all those missing puzzle pieces she'd never understood clicked into place. It was like he'd used that last conversation to mold his future, and worse, everyone in his life fed into it. And she was no exception. She brushed the tears away. "I'm sorry."

He cleared his throat and his Adam's apple bobbed as he swallowed hard. "The night he died, when I came to you, I was so fucked up in the head, Pen."

She leaned forward now, sliding her hands over his arms. "I know you were, Evan. I wasn't naive. I knew, but I wanted it to be you."

A muscle in his jaw clenched and she felt his tension under her fingers. He took a deep breath. "When we first started meeting in the basement, I promised myself I wouldn't touch you. After I broke that vow, and I knew I wasn't going to stop, I promised myself I wouldn't take your virginity. That I'd let you keep that one thing to give to the right guy. That night, I told myself I was the right guy. That my dad was wrong, that I could be all those things to you. That I'd give you what you deserved. When I went to your house, I'd convinced myself. I believed it was true. I needed to believe it. Because, in that moment, you were the only person I couldn't live without."

She'd had it wrong. So, so wrong.

He reached up and brushed a thumb across her cheek, wiping away the wetness. "After you fell asleep, I lay there watching you. All that dark hair on white sheets, the light from the street casting you in a type of glow, your face soft, your lips full and swollen because of me. I'd never seen anything more gorgeous or felt anything so right and pure. And staring down at you like that, I knew. I felt it settle deep in my bones. He was right. I know it's hard to understand, but I just knew it would play out exactly as he'd said. I couldn't do it. To take you with me would have been the most selfish thing I could ever do. So I did the only thing I could, the one thing I knew he wanted. And I let you go."

"Evan," she said on a hoarse whisper. She stood and slid into the chair he occupied, straddling him even though they were right out in the open. She tangled her hands in his hair. "I'm so sorry."

His fingers curled around her waist. "I had no other choice. I promise you, he was right. You would have hated it. So I waited for you to wake up and then I severed it, broke it so irrevocably you'd have no other choice but to hate me."

He'd been cruel that morning. It cut her so deeply she'd had no other option but to turn away. But she understood now. And maybe that's the way they had to be; there'd never be any ending on good terms with them. She leaned into him and whispered against his lips, "I forgive you."

She felt his muscles ease, lose some of that hard rigidness.

"I'm so sorry." His voice was thick and filled with regret.

She wrapped her hands around his neck. "We were kids, Evan. Just stupid kids. We didn't know."

"It was the worst day of my life."

"Mine too." She brushed her mouth over his.

He groaned, his fingers digging into the curve of her waist. "Penelope, you don't understand. We're sitting here talking about the worst shit, and it doesn't matter." He lifted his hips, yanking her down so she ground against his hard shaft. "I want you so fucking bad."

She didn't pull away, just rocked hard into him. "Then take me."

He gritted his teeth and a low growl emitted from his throat. "The party. Everyone will want answers."

"They can wait, they'll be there tomorrow." She dragged her mouth over his. "Tonight is for us."

He finally relented and his lips covered hers, and the second they did, she lost any control she'd had over the situation or him. His mouth claimed hers. His tongue swooped inside as his fingers dug hard into her.

She angled her head, granting him deeper access.

And he took it. Oh God, did he take it.

It was a hard, demanding, brutal kiss.

Raw and rough.

Dirty.

A reminder of everything they'd been and a promise of everything they'd become.

His hands were everywhere as he feasted on her and she lost herself to the sheer torturous pleasure of him.

They grew hotter.

Frantic.

Ruthless.

Until they were fighting to get closer, their mouths so fierce her lips bruised.

He growled, fisted her hair in his hand and jerked her away. They stared at each other, panting for breath.

He shook his head as though clearing it. "We need to get the hell out of here."

"Yes." She moved to capture his mouth but he yanked her back, denying her.

"Now, Penelope."

"Yes." She shuddered, her mind going fuzzy in her desire. God, she loved him when he got like this. Back then, it had both thrilled and frightened her, but now it nearly drove her insane.

"Your place or mine?"

She shook her head. "I can't wait that long."

He narrowed his gaze. "I'll get us a room."

"Good idea."

"I'm going to let go and you're going to stand up. Understood?" His hips rocked against hers, driving her mad. She pressed back, groaning when he shook his head. "I can't stand one more second of you rubbing against me."

She gave him a slow smile. "But that was always our thing."

His green eyes flashed like they burned with some sort of internal fire. "It was a limited option that at least felt like I was fucking the hell out of you."

She shivered and tried to move but he held her still. "I need it, it's been so long."

"We need to get out of here."

He released her, and true to his desires she rose and brushed a hand over her dress, breathing deep.

"You okay?"

She nodded.

He took her hand, entwining her fingers with his. Pale skin against his golden tone. She'd always loved his hands, and next to her smaller ones he looked right. Like they belonged. Tonight, she wanted to live that fantasy. She didn't want to think about anything, or anyone else. Her lashes fluttered up to him. "I don't want to stop."

"We won't."

"Do you promise?"

"Yes." He pulled her close and kissed her. A harsh press of his mouth. "Let's go."

Hands clasped tight, as though they were afraid to let go, they walked to the elevator. They got into a blessedly empty car, and he slid his hand around her waist and grinned down at her. "Everyone is going to talk."

She rose on tiptoe and trailed her mouth over his jaw. "I hope their heads don't explode."

His gaze fell on her mouth. "Right now, I don't care about them." He flicked his tongue over her bottom lip. "I have fifteen years to catch up on and all I care about is taking you in every way known to man."

She gulped as her pulse sped and hammered in her throat.

He whispered against her lips, "I'm going to do filthy things to you."

She shuddered.

"You never were a good girl that way." He nipped at her bottom lip. "The dirtier I was, the hotter you got."

She curled a hand around his neck and tugged him down, rubbing her breasts against him. "That's because you could make me do anything."

He groaned. "Anything?"

"Anything."

Evan was going to lose his fucking mind. He took a deep breath. He'd have her soon enough. He would not take her in an elevator. He would at least make it to a bed. "You know there are cameras in here."

Her blue eyes flashed and a healthy flush slashed across her cheekbones. She glanced around. "I didn't think about that."

"If it wasn't the first time, I wouldn't care."

She let out a little gasp and the elevator came to a stop. Thank God. That sound was almost his undoing.

He took her hand and dragged her across the lobby to the front desk. He took out his wallet and said to the middle-aged woman in her neatly pressed hotel uniform, "Give me the penthouse suite."

"That's not necessary." Penelope squeezed his fingers.

The clerk glanced at Evan, her gaze going wide, before darting to Penelope.

"The penthouse." His tone indicating he didn't expect any further discussion.

The clerk tapped into her computer before clearing her throat. "Sir, that's four thousand dollars a night."

Beside him, Penelope stiffened and started shaking her head.

Evan pulled out his American Express black card. "Your point?"

Penelope elbowed him in the ribs. "Evan. This is ridiculous."

Evan ignored her and handed the card over. "I'll want late checkout."

"Not a problem, sir." The woman began typing.

Penelope glared at him. "This isn't necessary."

Evan slid a hand around her waist and gave the clerk a smile. "I assume there's a private elevator."

"Of course, Mr. Donovan."

Good. He didn't want to risk running into anyone from the benefit. Not because he cared—he'd be dealing with them soon enough—but he didn't want one more thing to get in the way of taking her.

As soon as he had the key in hand, he took Penelope by the elbow and led her as fast as he could to the elevator. The door opened immediately and they stepped inside. He inserted the key card and the doors closed.

And the second they did, he was on her.

He couldn't get close enough.

It was like some feral beast had taken residence inside him and wouldn't let go. He tangled his hand in her hair, twining it until he fisted it and jerked, forcing her more open.

He'd had ideas of taking it slow. Of teasing and tormenting her until she begged, but that was going to have to come later. Much, much later.

He pushed her against the wall, kicking her feet wide apart and inserting his thigh between her legs. She moaned against his mouth, moving to stand on tiptoes and rocking against him.

He cupped her breast, and frustrated by the fabric, yanked her strapless top down, exposing her to him. When his thumbs brushed over her hard nipples she keened, kissing him harder.

Behind him the door opened into the suite. And he meant to stop. Meant to pull away but couldn't. Just as he was working up his motivation, she gripped his shirt in her hands like she was going to rip it off, and consumed his mouth like she was starving.

On a low growl he devoured her. Unable to get control of his hard, bruising kiss.

He lost track of everything. Consumed by her mouth, her tongue. The slide of her hair, her breasts, and the relentless arch and roll of her body as they fought to get closer.

Reason tried to rise to the surface, chanting in his head that he needed to get her to a bed. He went to maneuver her, only to get distracted when her nails raked down his arms, and the next thing he knew he slammed her against the wall again.

Her hands were everywhere, driving him crazy, making it impossible for him to think straight. He could think—if she'd just stop. He grasped her wrists and jerked them over her head, immobilizing her questing fingers.

Between hard, dirty kisses that were more erotic than

any sex he'd had since her, he managed to pant out, "This is going to be a fucking disaster."

She licked at his mouth, rolled her hips and gasped out, "More. Now. Take me."

Get her to the bed. He must take her on a bed. He moved them a couple more inches, letting her wrists go before skimming his lips down her throat. When he got to her jugular, he felt the pounding of her pulse against his tongue, and he bit her. Hard enough to leave a mark.

She cried out, arching into him. She gripped his shirt and tore at it. "Skin to skin."

Bed. He pulled away, but instead of moving her, he pulled his shirt, still buttoned, over his head and dropped the article of clothing to the floor.

He managed to get her a couple more inches to the bedroom door, but then his bare chest touched hers and he let out a vicious curse. It was a shock to the system.

Her head fell back. "Oh God, Evan."

His name on her lips. In that sweet, wild rasp.

"I'm sorry." He stumbled them both into the room and they tumbled to the floor. "Too fast."

"Now. Goddamn it, now." She bowed off the floor, reaching for him.

He slid her dress up those endless fucking legs, until it pooled at her waist and he stripped her of her panties. He gritted his teeth as he slid his finger against her slick flesh and brushed over her clit.

She rocked her hips up, moaning.

He looked at her then, her cheeks flushed, mouth swollen and wet, hair fanning out over the carpet, eager and abandoned. He pushed a finger inside her and she was hot and tight and wet.

For him.

She ran her hands up his arms, and her lids fluttered open. "Please, I can't wait anymore."

Something broke inside him and he just lost it. Everything became a frantic, rushed, crazy mess.

He fumbled for his buckle, and she reached for him, straining under him. He pushed down his boxer briefs and the second his aching cock strained free he impaled her.

He wanted to slow down.

Wanted to savor that he was finally, after all these years, inside her.

But, as impossible as it was to believe, it was better than he remembered, like a hot, wet vise several sizes too small, squeezing him so tight he lost his mind.

She arched up, raking her nails over his back.

He sank into her again and again, mindless and animalistic in his insatiable lust for her.

He kissed her, his tongue rolling over hers in rhythm to their questing bodies. Her fingers dug into him and he slammed hard into her, their bodies moving across the floor as they tried to get closer.

Harder.

Faster.

He pulled away and growled into her ear. "I can't fuck you hard enough."

"I know. More." She wrapped her legs around him, bringing him in deeper.

Her muscles rippled around his cock and he couldn't take it any longer. He wrapped his fingers around her throat, and thrust hard and high, while he whispered in her ear, "You're mine."

"Yes."

Another deep thrust. "Always have been."

And another. "Always will be."

"Yes." She rocked up into him, faster, more urgent, and he knew she was close. He tightened his hold, like he knew she liked it, and she came around him, crying out, ripping his own orgasm from him as he followed her into mind-numbing oblivion. Lost in a pleasure only she could bring him. Wringing every last sensation from her before he finally collapsed on top of her.

He didn't know how much time passed as they lay there, hearts hammering away, shuddering and panting, but eventually her pulse slowed under his touch.

He raised his head and stroked a lock of hair from her cheek.

Her lashes fluttered open.

He shook his head. "I told you it would be a disaster."

She laughed. Well, giggled really, a Penelope rarity.

"I kept meaning to get you to a bed."

"Where is the bed?" She looked around, catching sight of the mammoth king-size bed filled with about a thousand pillows. "Well, we made it to the vicinity."

"I didn't think we'd make it out of the elevator." He dragged a hand through his hair. "I didn't even get you naked."

"You almost did. So that counts." She trailed a finger over the line of his jaw. "I think it's rather befitting, don't you? After all the endless hours we spent on the floor."

"We were teenagers."

"Yeah, so?"

"I was supposed to be showing you I've matured."

She gave him a sly smirk. "Actually, back then you took a lot more time."

His brows slammed together. "You little brat."

He pinched her, then tickled her ribs. She screamed and twisted under him, pushing his hands away as she moved against him in the most delicious of ways.

"It's your fault," he said, wiggling his fingers into her waist, where she was most vulnerable.

"Evan! Stop!" She gasped for breath as she laughed.

"No way." He licked at her neck. "Tell me how good it was."

She squealed and, unable to push him away, her fingers started their own path down his stomach. "It was the best."

Their bodies slid together and they went still. Their eyes met and heat filled the space between them. His desire and longing for her stirred, renewing with such intensity it took his breath away. He touched her cheek. "It's not enough."

Her hands trailed over his back and he shuddered. "It's not."

"Maybe we can make it to bed this time."

"I don't think I care."

He groaned and pulled out of her, sitting back on his haunches only to freeze. *What had he done?* His heart kicked up a notch in his chest.

She blinked at him. "What's wrong?"

He dragged his hand through his hair. "I didn't wear a condom."

Chapter Sixteen

Well, wasn't this just the ultimate afterglow buzzkill.

As blindsided as he looked, Penelope sat up, shaking her head. "I didn't even think of it."

How could she have not thought about it? She was the most organized person on the planet. She had spreadsheets for her spreadsheets. She kept lists. Multiple-part lists with bullet points. She never forgot anything.

So how could she forget *this*, of all things?

"Fuck." He blew out a hard, angry breath, ripping her from her thoughts. "I'm sorry. Goddamn it. How could I not think about it?"

"It's not your fault, Evan. We both should have thought about it. We are both to blame."

Their eyes met.

She read the regret in his expression and hated it. After all this time, and now this happened? "It will be okay."

"Are you on birth control?" Evan asked, sitting back on his haunches.

She shook her head. She never took unnecessary medication if she could help it and didn't like the pill because of how it messed with her hormones. It hadn't mattered in the past, because she'd always made her partners use protection. "I'm not."

He scrubbed a hand over his face. "I don't even have a good excuse. It never even crossed my mind. In my whole life, I've never forgotten to wear a condom. Ever."

She nodded. "I haven't either. I guess we got carried away."

"I'm so sorry, Pen. This was the last thing I wanted."

Okay. She needed to pull it together. She took a deep breath. There was only one way to handle this. Practically. "I have an app on my phone that tracks my period. I'm pretty sure it's the wrong time."

He nodded. "All right."

She rose as gracefully as she could off the floor, yanking her top over her breasts while the skirt of her dress pooled at her knees. He followed suit, pulling up his pants and zipper but discarding the belt.

So they were dressed. Next step, figure out when she might have last ovulated. All she needed to do was take this next step, then go on to the next one.

She picked up the small purse she'd dropped in the elevator and took out her phone, only to sigh when she looked at the display.

"What's wrong?"

"I have about fifteen missed calls and just as many texts." She wanted to scream. All she wanted was one night without being bombarded with reality. Was that too much to ask?

Evan looked at his cell. "I'm about the same."

She gritted her teeth and scrolled through her apps until she found what she was looking for. She squinted at the calendar filled with the little dots, and worried her bottom lip. "I think it's okay. It's not impossible, but it's not that likely."

"So that's good then, right?" Evan cleared his throat,

looking distinctly uncomfortable. "I mean, I know it's not foolproof, but we're Catholic . . . Isn't this kind of our way?"

Penelope's head snapped up and a smile ghosted her lips. "Your parents had four kids."

He shrugged. "I'm sure we must have been planned."

She raised her brow. "Your parents never planned anything."

"I know for a fact they planned Maddie. My mom wanted a girl."

"Fine, we know one of you was planned. Should we call her up and ask her about the rest?"

He scrubbed a hand over his jaw. "Probably not a good idea."

"Probably not." Okay, next step. It sat like a lump of coal in her belly, but she wouldn't avoid it. She was not an avoider. She handled her problems head-on. No matter what. All she needed to do was be pragmatic about it. Women did it every day. She put her phone on the table and squared her shoulders. "There's only one real option here if we want to ensure complete protection. I'll take the morning-after pill."

He studied her for a long time before saying slowly, "Is that safe?"

"I don't know, I think so, but I'll have to Google it." So that's what she did. She sat on the chair, picked her cell back up, and opened the Internet app. She read about ten different pages of consistent information until she felt sure she had the facts. The research calmed her enough to think. This would be okay. It was a solution. She looked up to find Evan sitting in the chair across from her, watching her with a strange expression on his face, but she didn't ask about it. She just recited what she'd learned as dispassionately as possible. "From everything I read, it's ninety-five percent effective if taken in the first twenty-four hours and it's generally safe for all women with some minor side effects."

His jaw hardened. "What are the side effects?"

She clicked the side effects link. "Nausea, abdominal pain, fatigue, headache, menstrual changes." She shrugged, scrolling through the rest of the list. "Annoyances, really."

A muscle jumped in his cheek. "And nothing more dangerous?"

She shook her head. "It doesn't seem like it."

"I don't like the idea of you suffering at all because of my stupid mistake."

"It's both of our mistake. I could have stopped you at any time, and I didn't." They'd gotten carried away and forgot. She'd forgotten. She was organized, but she was still human; it had been an error. She cleared her throat. "It seems like the best option."

He nodded. "That's what it seems like."

Awkwardness permeated the air, making her feel cold and alone.

All that heat. All that desire. Gone. It squeezed her chest and made her throat tight.

Far too brightly, she smiled. "Great, then it's settled."

She needed a second to herself, and she stood, turning toward the bathroom, only to have him snag her wrist and pull her back around. He stepped close and slid his arms around her. His bare chest and warm skin felt like heaven and she wanted nothing more than to sink into him, but remained rigid in his embrace.

"I'm sorry," he said, his voice soft.

"Me too."

He ran a finger down her jaw and lifted her chin. He brushed his mouth over hers. "Nothing's ever easy for us, is it?"

Tears stung at the back of her throat, and only then did she realize how upset she was. She shook her head.

He sank his fingers into her hair. "All I wanted was one night where I didn't have to think about anything, or anyone, but you."

"Me too," she said, her voice sounding like a croak.

His expression darkened, his eyes flashing emerald. "Is there anything I can do to make it okay?"

"I don't know." She blinked, and wetness tracked down her cheek. "I just want to go back to how we were in the elevator. Reality is already banging on the door. Is it wrong that I want to ignore it?"

It was so unlike her. She was the responsible one. The designated driver. The one who dealt with problems head-on and refused to look the other way. But she was so tired. And she'd wanted him for so long.

She wanted a night off. Was that too much to ask?

"No, I feel the same way." He smiled, and wiped the tears away. "Why don't we do this? It's a perfect night, and we've got a huge balcony that overlooks the entire city. I'll order room service and champagne and we'll sit outside and relax and talk, and let ourselves get naturally back on track."

Actually, that sounded just about perfect. "Yes, that's a good plan."

The corners of his mouth lifted. "I have my moments. I mean, not over there on the floor or anything, but right now."

She smiled. Maybe they could salvage this night after all.

An hour later, maybe a bit drunk on champagne, Penelope laughed as he told a story about a locker room incident from his rookie year. The sound of her laughter floating through the night air eased his mind a little. Maybe this mistake wouldn't once again ruin everything between them.

Stretched out on a double chaise longue, they lay under the stars with the whole city in front of them, and talked.

Talked like they used to, but everything was new and undiscovered. They put away who'd they'd been in the past, all those years of silence, and learned each other now.

It was nice. Unexpected. A happy consequence of their rash behavior. The more they talked, the more she seemed to relax, and Evan drank her in.

Feet bare, long legs stretched out, one knee bent, her white dress rode high on her thighs. Dark chestnut hair a tangled mess, it tumbled over her shoulders and she was so gorgeous he couldn't stop staring at her.

She sighed, a contented, happy sound that made Evan's chest squeeze.

"What was that for?" He brushed a curved finger over her bare arm. Now that he could touch her, he took every opportunity to do so, even though he kept himself from getting too carried away. It was like they'd made some silent pact to learn each other and he wasn't going to ruin that.

She smiled and waved her glass of champagne over the vista of the city. "Growing up, did you ever in a million years think we'd end up here?"

They'd grown up in a working-class neighborhood on the South Side, with streets lined with identical bungalows and apartment buildings, the confines of their lives locked into a ten-block radius of their community.

Most of the people they'd gone to high school with still lived there, working their trade jobs, living paycheck to paycheck as construction workers, firemen, cops, and electricians. Most of the guys he'd hung out with in high school were still friends; they played cards on Friday night, drank at the neighborhood bar on Saturdays, and went to each other's Sunday barbecues.

He shook his head. "Nope. Back then, every guy I knew wanted to play pro ball. That's what we talked about. The dream. Even though schools were scouting me, it was still impossible to really imagine."

She rested her head on the cushioned pillow. "Do you ever talk to any of your old friends?"

Evan shook his head. "I tried to keep in touch, those first couple of years, but I don't know, they couldn't forget I was living their fantasy, and I couldn't forget I was no longer one of them. Eventually, I stopped trying." He laughed. "My mom said she got an invite in the mail for me, a fifteen-year reunion at Lucky's." The local watering hole.

Penelope pushed her hair off her cheek. "I haven't heard that name in forever. Are you going to go?"

He furrowed his brow. "I doubt it. Especially now."

Penelope shrugged one bare shoulder. "You think the only reason they'd want to see you is if you're a football star?"

"Maybe they'd be happy now that I've fallen." His stomach tightened at the reminder that part of his life was over. That he didn't know who or what he was anymore without the game.

"Hmmm . . . ," she said, the sounds purring in her throat. "Maybe they'll surprise you."

"Maybe."

"I think you should go."

He tried to envision walking into Lucky's. Seeing all his old friends, making small talk, and then he realized that in his mental picture Penelope stood next to him, and it didn't sound so bad. "I'll make you a deal. I'll go, but only if you come with me."

Her expression widened, as though he'd surprised her. "Really?"

"Really."

Slowly, she nodded. "All right. This should be interesting."

He laughed. "That's one way to put it."

They fell silent, and he rested his head on the cushion, looking up at the stars. Penelope rose onto one elbow, propping her head against her open palm, watching him.

He met her gaze. "What?"

"Have you thought about it?" In the glow of the soft lights, her expression was a bit wary. "What you're going to do now?"

He wasn't sure he wanted to talk about it, but she wanted to know, so he'd tell her. "Since the hit, I've thought of little else."

"And? Have you come up with anything?"

He shook his head. "I can't get over missing it. Nothing else holds any appeal."

She smiled. "I'm going to tell you something I've never told anyone, but you can't laugh, and you *cannot* let it go to your already too-big head."

That caught his attention. He shifted more fully to face her. "I promise."

An actual blush spread over her cheeks. "You know, last year you did that fantasy camp for underprivileged kids."

Unsure where she was going, he nodded. "I remember."

She looked away and shrugged one shoulder. "Well, I went to it and watched you."

Shocked, he blinked. "You did not."

"I did."

"Penelope, I would have spotted you."

"Well, you didn't."

* * *

Penelope couldn't believe she was telling him this, but here she was confessing her dirty little secret. She never thought she'd tell him in a million years, but it was something he needed to hear. Something that would help him see himself in a different light.

Or at least that was her hope.

She covered her face with one hand and shook her head. "Oh my God, this is so embarrassing."

He pulled her hand away. "Tell me."

She hadn't known why she'd done it, or what had possessed her. It had been a rare impulsive move. "If you remember, you gave tickets to Shane, but the camp was during his honeymoon, so he couldn't go."

Evan nodded. "I remember."

"Well, I went into work that Saturday to catch up on some things and I had to go into Shane's office." She sighed, unable to believe she was humiliating herself in this way. But here she was, and there was no turning back. "The tickets were lying on his desk. And, I don't know, I got this impulse."

Evan laughed, and when she scowled at him, he covered it with a loud, fake cough.

"Anyway, I decided to go."

"How did I not see you? It was invite only, so it's not like the place was packed."

Okay, now came the really crazy part. Evan had always been the one person who brought out her spontaneous, crazy, throw-caution-to-the-wind side. A flush spread out over her chest. She cleared her throat. "Well, um, I went to a shop in Bucktown and bought a wig."

He burst out laughing. "You did not."

"I did." It was out there now, she might as well own it. She gave him a sly smirk. "I was a pixie blonde that day. I wore jeans, a giant Ditka jersey, and aviator sunglasses. You'd never have guessed it was me."

Still laughing, he shook his head. "I actually think I remember you."

She punched him in the arm. "You do not."

"Do too." He grinned at her. "I thought you had a hot ass."

It was her turn to shake her head. "You're the worst."

His expression turned sly. "Do you still have the wig?"

"It's in a box in my closet." She waved her hand. "Way, way in the back."

His gaze dipped to her mouth. "Will you wear it for me sometime?"

She plopped back onto her back as the warm night air blew over her. "Not the point of this story, Evan."

He traced a path down her arm. "And what's the point?"

She looked at him. "You were great with those kids. Teaching them. Coaching them."

He had been, and she'd watched, enraptured, as they'd crowded around him, eager to listen to every word he spoke.

His expression clouded and he shrugged. "I don't know if I can."

"All I'm trying to say is that coaching is an option, one you'd be good at."

"I'll think about it."

"Good." He wasn't ready, but at least she'd planted the seed. It was enough, and she wanted to return to the light mood. "So now you know, and if you ever mention this again there will be serious consequences."

"Yes, Miss Watkins." He grinned at her and scrubbed a hand over his jaw. "Since I can tell you hated telling me this very blackmail-worthy story, I think it's only fair I reciprocate."

The hairs on the back of her neck tingled, and she looked at him, brow raised. "Yes?"

"You're not going to be happy."

She'd have worried, but his expression was too filled with amusement. "I'm listening."

He took her hand. "Do you remember when we all spent that weekend at Maddie's and you were dating that accountant?"

"Yes," she said very slowly. Bill was a lovely man whom she'd wanted to love but couldn't. She narrowed her eyes. "You brought some Calvin Klein model."

He nodded. "That's the weekend. We all stayed over Saturday night."

"I remember."

He shrugged. "I fed him double shots of vodka all night."

"You did what?!" She sat up, spinning around to look at him.

In a completely calm voice, he said, "The guy was drinking screwdrivers. Screwdrivers, Penelope. I mean, it might as well been an Appletini. You couldn't sleep with a guy like that. So I kept feeding him doubles, hoping he'd pass out and wouldn't touch you."

Penelope stared at him openmouthed. He had. He'd passed out in the middle of the bed and couldn't be moved. She'd gone and slept with Sophie.

She wanted to be mad. Should be mad. But she couldn't deny it gave her a perverse pleasure. She climbed on top of him, straddled his thighs, and straightened until her spine was ruler straight. She gave him her most stern expression and plastered her hands on her hips. "You're telling me that you intoxicated my date, then went and slept with a model?"

"Nope." Evan slid his hands onto her hips. "When I told her I was staying up with my brothers, she told me she was taking an Ambien."

"And that's the only reason?"

"I wouldn't have touched her anyway." He squeezed. "If

I couldn't sleep with you I liked the idea of both of us sleeping alone."

"I can't believe you."

"I didn't want him touching you."

She shook her head. "You certainly got your wish."

He grinned. "I'm not even sorry."

"You're the worst."

He ran his hands up her sides. "I am."

"You need to pay." And she knew exactly how. Not that it was much of a punishment. She just knew what she wanted. It had been a long time, but she still remembered the taste of him, still remembered his fullness in her mouth, the expression on his face. And she wanted it. She leaned in close, ready to shrug off the civility between them. She trailed her lips along his jaw and his grasp on her tightened. She traced a path to his ear and when she got there whispered, "I should be really mad at you."

A low sound vibrated from his throat. "You should."

"I should make you suffer." She followed the sound, licking down his neck and slithering on top of him. "But I want to taste you."

"Christ, Penelope." He gripped her hips, and rocked up. "I don't think I can take it."

"Please." The word a purr, and when he groaned she couldn't help the surge of empowerment. She slid down his legs, her mouth trailing down his chest. She flicked her tongue over his flat nipple and he cursed, tangling his hand in her hair and holding her firm while she scraped her teeth over him.

Breath coming fast, he said, "You'll be the death of me."

An insatiable hunger swept over her, and she fumbled with the button and pulled down the zipper on his pants.

He ground out in a strangled voice, "Penny, trust me, this isn't a good idea."

"I think it's a fine idea." She met his dark gaze as she

encircled his shaft, squeezing the way she knew he liked. Long ago he'd taught her exactly how to please him and she hadn't forgotten. Her grip firm, she stroked up, twisting over the head of his erection.

His hips jerked and his head fell back as he fisted her hair. "God, you drive me so crazy."

She slithered farther down his body. Still stroking him with a firm grasp, she leaned down and licked the slit where moisture had already pooled, before covering the head and sucking him deep into her mouth. He mumbled something unintelligible and she took it as a compliment, and hummed in appreciation in a way she knew would vibrate down his shaft.

He moaned. She slid down the length of him and he filled her, stretched her lips, and she took him in as deep as she could before slowly sliding up the length of him, her tongue swirling a path.

"Stop," he said, his voice so hoarse it cracked. He released his grip on her hair, sending waves tumbling over her shoulders.

She looked up at him, expression a silent question.

His features were almost pained, the skin pulled tight over his sharp cheekbones. "Let me look at you."

She licked her lips, nodding.

His gaze roamed all over her, as though drinking her in, as though he couldn't believe she was here in front of him. He tucked a lock of hair behind her ear. "You are, by far, the most gorgeous woman I've ever laid eyes on."

The man had been with supermodels, and she opened her mouth, unable to stop the protest forming on her lips.

He shook his head. "Yes, Penelope, you are. All this time, right here, right now, is what I thought about. Everything else paled in comparison."

The words. The sincerity and desire ringing in his voice

filled her chest. She couldn't help it, her throat locked up and her eyes brightened.

His thumb brushed over her cheek before he twined his fingers around her neck and pulled her up. Their lips met and it was like being sucked into a storm. The mad, crazy rush of the elevator overtaking them once again.

Their mouths fused.

Their tongues met.

The kiss turned rough, and greedy. She clutched at his shoulders. Desperate to get closer. His hard cock brushed the inside of her thigh as she straddled him, and she shifted, until she sank into that spot only he seemed to fit. He groaned and his fingers sought the zipper of her dress. When it was finally undone, he said, "I'm going to at least get you naked."

Then the fabric was whisked over her head and was gone.

Their mouths met before the fabric even hit the floor. Nipples aching, she pressed her breasts against his chest, rubbing against him like she was in heat. He growled, reached between them and plucked the hard bud, rolling it between his thumb and forefinger.

He tore his mouth away, and her head fell back as his lips sucked her nipple into his mouth. His tongue teased, swirled, before his teeth nipped and pulled.

Lust and need roared inside her and she clasped his head, pressing him closer as she cried out. Through panting breath she said, "I-I can't wait."

A low, animalistic sound emanated from the back of his throat. "Someday I will get you into a bed."

Then he took her. And she didn't think of anything but him, and them, for the rest of the night.

Chapter Seventeen

Curled into the thick, fluffy hotel robe, Penelope stretched out on the chaise longue and squinted into the bright sun. Last night had exceeded even her wildest fantasies. They'd been insatiable, unable to get enough of each other. She'd lost track of how many orgasms she'd had. He'd taken her in every conceivable way and in every conceivable place. On the couch, against the wall, on the floor, in the bathroom, her hands splayed on the mirror, in the shower. Their movements rushed and frantic, as though if they weren't connected somehow they'd be ripped apart.

Deep into the night, they'd finally made it to the bed and some of their urgency melted away. Their touches turned long and slow, their mouths fusing for languorous, exploratory kisses. They couldn't stop touching, and when they'd fallen asleep they'd stayed together, limbs locked, arms intertwined, bodies pressed together.

It had been the best night of her life. She was sore and bruised, her skin marked and tight, her mouth so swollen there wasn't a person alive who wouldn't know what they'd been doing.

She stared out at the skyline, a crystal blue, the weather warm and mild.

It was a perfect day to follow a perfect night.

But reality refused to be delayed any longer.

They still had to go to his mom's later this afternoon.

And Evan was out buying the morning-after pill.

She took a long, deep breath. It made perfect sense to take the pill. It was logical, pragmatic, and perfectly safe. This niggling would go away as soon as she swallowed them down.

Behind her the door to the penthouse opened and Evan came through. Penelope took a sip of coffee and waited for him to come outside. He was dressed in his clothes from the night before, and he looked rumpled and wrinkled and so damn beautiful it almost hurt to look at him.

He sat down on the edge of the lounger facing her before dumping the contents onto the space between them. A box with the words Plan B on the label, and a box of condoms.

Evan's expression was chagrined. "I got quite the look from the pharmacy tech."

She laughed. "I can imagine."

She stared at the box, with its bright purple and green, springtime colors. Happy, cheerful colors to distract you from the inevitable. She bit her lower lip and tried to ignore the knot in her stomach. She was just nervous.

Evan cleared his throat. "It said to take it within twenty-four hours to be most effective, right?"

She nodded.

"So, you could technically wait? Until later?"

She instantly relaxed, and the sense of relief frightened her. Of course she wanted to take the pill. There wasn't even a question. Yes, the odds were against pregnancy, but any chance was an unacceptable risk. She was a responsible person. She didn't play with chance if she could help it.

She looked at the box again. She could wait. She looked

at Evan, who watched her with such intensity she didn't know what to make of it.

The decision was made, but it didn't hurt to wait on the off chance it made her feel sick. Nausea was the most common side effect and did she really want to waste the rest of their time in this fantastic hotel room, ill? No, she didn't. She had plenty of time to take it. "I can wait."

His expression cleared. "So we wait?"

She nodded. "We wait."

Evan scooped the contents into the bag and dropped it to the patio floor.

Out of sight, out of mind.

He pointed at her phone sitting next to her on the table. "How many messages have you gotten?"

A smile lifted the corners of her lips. "About a hundred."

He sighed. "Yeah, me too. Have you read them?"

She shook her head. "Not yet. I guess I'm not ready to deal with them."

He dragged his hand through his hair. "I suppose we'll have to soon enough."

"I know." She took another sip of coffee and stared off into the distance.

"Are you upset I outed us?"

"I'm not sure upset is the right word." She pressed her lips together. "I would have liked to have a plan. Been prepared. Had explanations ready for Maddie and Shane."

Evan rubbed a finger down her arm. "I hadn't thought of that. You deserved a grand gesture, and that's what I was going for. And I'm not going to hide how I feel about you anymore. To anyone. Regardless of the consequences."

All this time, that's all she'd ever wanted, but now it thrust her into a spotlight that made her uncomfortable. She liked being on the sidelines, liked being the person behind the scenes. Unlike Evan, who was always the center of attention.

She took a deep breath and slowly exhaled. "Those consequences affect me too."

He nodded. "I know. In my mind, a public declaration seemed like the only thing you'd believe."

It was the last thing she'd ever expected. That thing she'd always secretly pined for but never believed he'd do. "You're probably right."

"Does it bother you that they're not going to be happy about this?"

She looked back at him and could tell by his expression it bothered him plenty. "I don't know. I wish I didn't have to explain, especially when I have no idea what to say."

"I'd love to say we don't have to explain anything but, as we both know, that would be a lie. And I know it's on me. I mean, would your parents even know who I am?"

She laughed. "Probably. But they wouldn't question it or, God forbid, ask for details. Besides, they're off in Florida and with my dad wheelchair-bound, they won't be coming to Chicago anytime soon to check on me."

"We've always been your family." It wasn't a question.

"I suppose that's true."

"I don't want to do anything to ruin that." His expression turned serious. "We can create your plan now, before we go to the party later."

Surprised, she blinked. "Really?"

A smile quirked his lips. "Let's tackle the biggest issue first. Shane will clearly be the worst. He's not going to be happy."

She twined her fingers with his and he squeezed, holding fast and tight and strong. "He won't be."

"Do you think it will affect your working relationship?"

The concern etched into his features touched her. She'd been living with his coolness, distance, and cocky attitude for so long she'd almost forgotten he could be like this. Thoughtful. Considerate.

She blew out a long breath. "I don't think so, but I don't know. When I first started working for him we had a long talk about boundaries, and he tries to respect them. But sometimes it's hard to separate when we work together so closely. The last time we had a serious issue was when Maddie ran off to Revival. I didn't know where she was because she wouldn't tell me, but I refused to let him talk to her when she called. We also fought about him using Logan to find where she was, and I lost that battle. We were both stubborn in our positions, but it didn't impact our working relationship. Of course, we were always talking about Maddie, not you. So I don't know what he'll say."

He squeezed her hand again. "I'll take the fall for it. All right?"

"What do you mean?"

"I'll take the blame. He's already going to be pissed as hell at me, so just let me take the brunt of it when we get there."

"I've been dealing with your brother for a long time. We'll see how it goes."

There was a hard glint in Evan's gaze. "I created this mess and I will deal with it. And that's final."

She knew how complicated his relationship with Shane was and hated she would be another source of contention between them. "I don't want you using me to hash out your issues with your brother."

He shook his head. "I'm not, I'm taking responsibility."

She believed he thought that, but she'd also had years of watching the two brothers interact, and Evan sometimes seemed determined to take Shane's protectiveness the wrong way. Just like Shane seemed determined to treat Evan like he was still a college kid. They were strong-willed and hardheaded and it would play out regardless of what she said, so she opted for levity. She raised her brows. "Final, huh?"

His features relaxed and he cocked his head. "Too much?"

She opened her thumb and forefinger an inch apart. "Just a bit."

"I just don't want you to have to deal with it, Pen."

She tugged at his wrist, and he scooted closer to her. "That's unrealistic. I'm going to have to deal with it, same as you."

His brow furrowed. "But you shouldn't have to."

This was new for him, this desire to take responsibility. "You have to understand, my relationship with Maddie and Shane is not an extension of you. It's separate, completely apart from you."

His gaze met hers. "I just want to take the brunt of the backlash."

"Evan. We're both responsible and we'll deal with it together."

He sighed and wrapped his fingers around her neck, his fingers shifting through the strands like he'd been doing for what felt like a million years. "Someday I'd like to be a positive influence on your life. Is that too much to ask?"

She smiled, moving closer. "You have your uses."

His attention shifted to her lips. "Do you have any idea how obscene your mouth looks right now?"

She shook her head.

"It's swollen and red and looks like sex." He trailed over her neck and collarbone, pausing at the V of her robe. "Are you naked under here?"

"Yes."

Gaze hot, he met her eyes. "Are you sore?"

"Yes," she said, her voice a whisper.

He bent down and brushed his lips over hers. "Should I just lick you to orgasm then?"

She curled her hand around his neck and tugged him close. "That's certainly a start."

Later that afternoon, Penelope once again stared at the morning-after box. Although this time, instead of sitting on a gorgeous terrace overlooking the city, she was in her kitchen.

The time had come to take it.

Evan walked into her kitchen and his gaze narrowed on the box, then shifted to her. "Are you okay?"

She nodded, swallowing past the lump in her throat. "I should probably take it now."

"Technically you still have time."

She did. It was the best, most logical solution to rectify their mistake. But staring at that box she knew the truth.

She didn't want to.

Based on timing alone, the chances of her actually being pregnant were incredibly small. This was just an extra precaution.

An extra precaution she didn't want to take.

She looked at the package. She wanted to play the odds.

It's not like she'd actually get pregnant. The timing was off.

The thought was crazy. Insane. Not like her at all.

But with Evan she'd never taken the rational path. She always followed her heart. And in her heart she did not want to take those pills.

"Pen?" At the sound of Evan's voice, she tore her attention away from the box.

He stood there, dressed in an evergreen T-shirt that matched his eyes and a pair of faded jeans that molded to his powerful body like a second skin. The corners of his mouth dipped. "Are you okay?"

She couldn't tell him. God, he was an athlete. Women

probably tried to trap him into pregnancy every day of the week. She took a deep breath. "I should take the pill."

His expression clouded. "I'm sorry you have to."

They hadn't used protection all night. He'd come inside her over and over again. He'd known the risks as well as she had, but they had been operating under the assumption that she'd take the pill. She cleared her throat. "We're both at fault. I didn't think about it any more than you did."

He studied her for several long beats. "We'll use condoms from now on."

No more reckless behavior for her. She nodded sharply. "Yes."

He walked around the kitchen island to stand next to her, running his large palm over her back in a slow circle. "You don't want to take it, do you?"

That she'd been so obvious had her spine snapping ruler straight. "Of course I do. It's the smart, practical thing to do and I'm a smart, practical person. It fixes the mistake and the problem is resolved. I mean, God, could you even imagine?"

She picked up the package and, jaw clenched, she started ripping into it. "I've got to take it now, so I'll have time to take the second pill in twelve hours."

He didn't say anything but she felt his heavy, watchful stare. She didn't want him to know. She pulled out the pills encased on a cardboard flat. With shaking fingers she pushed the pill from the package and it fell into her open palm.

She picked up the glass of water, determined to stop procrastinating. To stop letting these crazy thoughts distract her.

Evan grabbed her wrist. "Penelope."

She blinked at him and the moment her eyes met his, her throat closed over.

He shook his head. "I don't want you to take it."

"What? Why? Of course I need to take it. We have to be smart about this." Her heart hammered; he wanted the same thing she did.

"When have we ever been smart?" he asked, his tone low and soothing.

"But—" she began, but he cut her off.

"You don't want to take it. *I* don't want you to take it. So don't, and we'll see what happens. Nature can decide for us."

Hope and fear and everything in between beat wildly in her chest. "That's insane."

"It is," he said, and a smile curved his lips. "Maybe we've always been insane and it's just time we acknowledge it."

It was a safe risk. Considering how regular she was. At least she could assure him of that. "I'm not going to be pregnant. It's the wrong time."

He shrugged. "If you are or you're not, we'll deal with it. But I don't want you to take that pill. And I haven't wanted you to since you brought it up last night."

She swallowed hard, the pill still in her palm like an unwanted weight. "Why didn't you say anything?"

"I was trying to be a good feminist."

She choked out a laugh. "What?"

"You know, a woman's right to choose and all that. But this morning when you were willing to put it off, I grew more hopeful." He leaned in close. "Don't take it, Pen."

Her lashes lifted, and her breath stuttered. "And if I am? Pregnant, I mean."

"Then you are."

She wanted to ask more what-ifs but didn't. Her fingers tightened on the white pill. "It's irresponsible."

"Yeah, it is. But we're not teenagers anymore. We're adults, we have money and resources."

She bit her lip. "Are you sure?"

He released her wrist, then curled his hand around her neck. He brushed his lips over hers. "I've never been so sure of anything in my life."

The knot of tension, sitting tight in her stomach, unraveled. "You're right, I don't want to take it."

"I know." His tongue licked her bottom lip. "Throw it away."

She did. She just opened her palm over the kitchen sink and they watched it bounce along the edge of the stainless steel then disappear down the drain. She waited for the rush of panic that should envelop her at any moment, but it didn't come. All she felt was happy.

She looked back at Evan and he grinned at her and pulled her belt loop. "Hmmm . . . How should we celebrate?"

She laughed. The man was insatiable. "Aren't you tired yet?"

His hand slid around her waist. "Nope. I have fifteen years to make up for."

She arched a brow. "And you're trying to make them up in one day?"

His gaze dipped to her lips. "Are you saying no?"

"Have I ever said no to you?"

"I think we have time for one more round before we have to get ready to go to the party from hell." He lifted her to the counter, and she wrapped her legs around his waist.

She kissed him, sucking in all that heat and strength, unable to get enough of his mouth on hers. Her tongue swirled over his and he moaned, pulling back long enough to whisper against her lips, "Condom."

"One more time won't matter." She'd clearly gone crazy and she didn't even care. Just this once she would throw caution to the wind. She licked into his mouth and his grip on her hips tightened to the point of pain. "I want to feel you come inside me one more time."

"Christ, Penelope." He ripped her top off, throwing it to the floor. And his T-shirt quickly followed suit.

She'd gone off the deep end. That was the only reasonable explanation. But then his skin pressed against hers, and she vowed to think about it all later. Much, much later.

Chapter Eighteen

Evan pulled his truck into a parking spot, a half a block down from his mom's bungalow. He pushed off the ignition switch and turned toward Penelope. "Ready?"

She shook her head. "Nope."

"It's pretty ridiculous, don't you think?" Evan took her hand. "It kind of feels like we're kids on our first date."

"It does." She tucked her hair behind her ear. "Being late isn't our brightest idea."

He smiled, hoping to ease her nerves. "I'm afraid that one's on you."

She sighed. "I know."

Right before they were ready to leave, she'd dropped to her knees, right there on the kitchen floor, and he was only a mere mortal. He'd ended up taking her on the floor from behind, hard and rough, her body squeezing him like a vise, wringing every last bit of pleasure from him until he'd practically seen stars.

She was all put together again, looking polished and sophisticated in a blue, flowy sleeveless top that matched her eyes. Her dark hair was smooth and shiny, cascading over her shoulders. There wasn't a trace of the wildness she reserved just for him, but she still wore the evidence of him.

Her mouth was still red and swollen, the color on her cheeks high, and there were faint marks he'd left on her neck. It pleased him, far more than was comfortable.

He squeezed her hand. "We just have to rip off the Band-Aid and get it over with."

She looked at him, blinked, then looked away, brow furrowed.

He tugged her wrist. "Hey, what's wrong?"

Her lashes fluttered and her fingers twitched. She shook her head. "Nothing."

He gripped her chin. "You don't think I know you well enough to know there's something you're not saying?" He released her and ran a finger down her arm. "Tell me."

She shook her head again. "It's just, I don't know what to say when they ask me."

"Tell them the truth." He was done hiding her. Done hiding how he felt about her.

"But . . ." Her voice dropped to a whisper. "What is the truth?"

Then he got it, understood what was so clear in his mind wasn't as clear in hers. "I guess we haven't really talked about it."

"No, we haven't."

He wanted to just lay it on the line, but that was too reminiscent of their past, when he'd held all the power in their relationship. He curled his hand around her neck and pulled her close, brushing his lips over hers, soft and gentle. Not letting himself get sucked into her mouth and the way she felt under his touch. "I want it all, Pen. I want us. I want the chance to fight for you the way I should have a long time ago. And I want the chance to be the man you deserve. If you'll have me."

Her blue eyes turned bright and she blinked. "This isn't because of football?"

He shook his head. "No. That's what I was trying to tell you the other night, only I screwed it all up. This, you, us— it's been on my mind since the night of Shane and Cecilia's wedding. What I didn't say the other night, what I should have said, was I did come to you; I just couldn't get out of the car. You were on my mind far before I lost football. In fact, I don't think you ever left."

She swallowed hard. "And if it doesn't work?"

His heart skipped a beat at the thought of losing her. "Do you think that's a possibility?"

She looked away. "I don't know. This isn't something we've ever done. We have no idea how we'll function out there in the real world, not confined to four walls, illicit passion, and unlimited privacy."

As always, she had a point, even if he didn't like it. "If it doesn't work, at least we'll know we tried, that we did something."

When she didn't speak he rubbed her arm with the crook of his finger. "All I know is, all these years, you've overshadowed every relationship I've ever had. Can you honestly tell me it hasn't been the same for you?"

She sucked in a breath. "No."

An ego-driven, entirely inappropriate satisfaction filled his chest, but he pushed it aside. "You know what I want from you, where I stand—so tell me, Penelope, where do you stand?"

He wanted the choice to be hers. She deserved that after all the years he'd kept her hidden away.

She expelled the breath she seemed to be holding and clutched her hands in her lap. "I think we need closure, and how else can we get that if we don't try and see what happens?"

It wasn't exactly an undying declaration of love, but it was a step forward. "And what do you think we should tell everyone?"

She glanced at his childhood home located on the south side of Chicago, the windows lit up by bright light. "That we're trying this out, and we'd appreciate if they'd respect our privacy."

He laughed. "Have you met my family?"

The corners of her mouth lifted in a smile. "It's worth a shot."

"That it is." He leaned over and kissed her, long and slow. Filled with heat and promise and all the things they still hadn't said to each other. When he pulled away, he said, "Just remember, one day this will be normal to them and we'll be off their radar."

"We just have to make it through this one night."

"Exactly."

And together, they climbed out of the truck. He took her hand and put on his game face, ready to get this disaster over with.

When they reached the front door she tugged away from him and he let her, knowing she was nervous and one of the ways she compensated for nerves was with extreme composure. But he wouldn't leave her side, and whether she liked it or not, he'd do most of the talking. Take most of the heat.

He opened the front door, and they were all there sitting in the living room. Sophie, Mitch and Maddie, Shane, his mom, and Great-Aunt Cathy, all stopped what they were doing and turned to face them. Well, at least they beat James and Gracie.

Several long moments of extended silence passed where nobody seemed to move or even breathe.

But then Great-Aunt Cathy clucked her tongue. "It's about time you got here, boy. Do you know how long we've been waiting for supper? I'm an old lady with blood sugar issues."

"Sorry about that, Auntie," Evan said, shutting the door and pressing a palm on the small of Penelope's back. "Gracie and James aren't here."

Aunt Cathy huffed and sat back on the sofa, arms crossed. "They had the decency to call and tell us to go on without them."

"I didn't think of it." Evan had been preoccupied with other things.

An awkward hush fell over the room.

Shane's eyes narrowed on Evan, his jaw set in that hard, stubborn line. Cecilia, Evan's sweet, perfect sister-in-law, patted her husband's leg, and when he looked at her she shook her head.

His head tilted and she raised a brow and they seemed to have some sort of silent conversation that left Shane shrugging.

Evan's mom shifted her gaze from him to Penelope, then back to him. "We're having pizza."

Everyone else just stared at them, and Penelope shifted on the balls of her feet. Evan nodded. "Sounds good."

His mom glanced pointedly at Penelope. "That's nice of you to give Penny a ride."

Mitch laughed. Maddie shot him a death glare.

Sophie just kind of looked stunned.

Next to him, Penelope cleared her throat. "My car is in the shop."

With that Shane scoffed. Cecilia dug her heel into the

top of his shoe until he yelped and yelled, "Ouch, would you settle down, woman?"

"Me? You're telling me to settle down?" She pointed at her chest, looking regal and sophisticated, entirely befitting of Chicago royalty. "You'd better not even start with me. You are on my list."

Shane rolled his eyes. "I'm always on your list."

"Because you go out of your way to drive me crazy," she said, her voice refined and haughty.

Shane slanted a glance at his wife, then leaned over and whispered something in her ear that made a healthy flush settle over Cecilia's cheeks and a wide grin break out over her lips.

Evan realized his mother was attempting to give them a polite out. A way to take the heat off. He looked down at Penelope, who looked up at him, her expression a mixture of pleading, hope, and exasperation.

He decided not to prolong the inevitable and he shrugged at her.

She sighed and shrugged back.

He turned to his family and said, "Penelope's car is fine. I drove Penelope here because I wanted to, not to do her a favor or be nice. I'll probably be driving her to all family parties from now on. So you'd best get used to it and move on. This isn't open to discussion."

Next to him, Penelope shook her head and rubbed her temples.

Shane opened his mouth to say something, but before he could get any words out the front door slammed open and Gracie flew into the room like a mini tornado, followed by a more subdued James.

Gracie pushed passed Evan and Penelope, held out her hand and screamed, "We're getting married!"

James smiled, shook his head and shoved his hands into his pockets.

All the focus that had been on Evan and Penelope shifted. Everyone started talking at once and there was a mad rush from the couch and chairs as they stormed James and Gracie. Gracie flashed the ring and jumped up and down, clearly on cloud nine.

Penelope grinned up at Evan. "James was always my favorite Donovan."

He laughed and they went over to congratulate the happy couple. When he got there, he clapped his middle brother on the back with one hand, and took Penelope's with the other. "Congratulations, it's about time. Leave it to you to land the great Gracie Roberts."

Behind his wire-framed glasses, James slanted a glance at his fiancée, basking in all the oohs and aahs over her ring, and smiled. "Piece of cake." He turned a pointed look at Penelope, who was paying elaborate attention to the bride-to-be while her fingers remained tight in Evan's. "You seemed to fare all right in the end."

Evan nodded. "I managed to figure it out."

"You're welcome, by the way," James said, grinning. "You owe me one."

Evan gave Penelope a little squeeze and she squeezed back. "That I do."

The pressure was off, at least for now.

Maddie and Sophie ambushed Penelope when she stepped out of the bathroom. Maddie stood there, her arms crossed. "You've avoided us long enough."

Sophie stood in an identical posture, nodding furiously. "You've got some serious explaining to do."

Penelope straightened, lengthening her spine until she towered over her much shorter friends. "Isn't that my line?"

"Not this time," Maddie said, grabbing her by the elbow.

Sophie flanked her, and the two of them pushed her into the deserted kitchen at the back of the house.

Maddie whirled on her. "Evan? Are you serious? Evan?!?"

Penelope tried to remind herself her friends had no idea of her past with the Donovan-family bad boy. But this wasn't the time to explain everything. She rested against the countertop and tried to look as casual as she could. "What's wrong with Evan?"

Maddie's expression turned dumbfounded. "He brought a Playboy bunny to my aunt and uncle's anniversary party."

Yes, he had. Penelope recalled every detail of trying to ignore them. She waved a hand. "That was a long time ago."

Maddie opened her mouth to speak, but Sophie held up a hand to stop her. "Maybe you're not the best person to have this discussion, since Evan is your brother."

Maddie cocked a hip. "By all means, talk some sense into her."

Sophie nodded and eyed Penelope. "Look, I get it. Evan is, like, smoking hot."

"Ewww," Maddie said.

Sophie shushed her and returned her attention to Penelope. "Anyway. Since I'm not *his sister*, I understand. Not only is he gorgeous but he's got that whole dangerous, bad-boy thing going on, and maybe you're just tired of walking the straight and narrow. But you're not a casual sex kind of girl, and Evan is definitely a casual sex kind of guy. We don't want you to get hurt."

It was Maddie's turn to nod. "I mean, don't get me wrong, I love him to pieces, but he's not the kind of guy you take home to your mother."

"There are better guys to take a walk on the wild side with," Sophie said.

"Ones who aren't as much of a risk," Maddie continued.

They'd clearly talked about the situation and made all the correct decisions for her while she was off having nonstop sex with Evan.

Sophie sighed. "Unfortunately, we've known you too long. We know your dirty little secret."

"Which is?" she asked, still stalling for time. Unsure how to explain to her friends she had real, actual dirty little secrets they had no idea about.

Sophie glanced around, as though about to confess something torrid. "That you're as pure as the driven snow, completely monogamous, loyal, and faithful."

Maddie gave a little humph. "Everything Evan is not."

"What's going on in here?" Evan stood in the door frame, his broad shoulders propped against the wood molding.

Her heart skipped a beat, then gave a hard little thump. Was it bad that she was this happy to see him? She smiled. "They were recapping your man-whoring ways, in case I'd forgotten."

He nodded, his gaze intent on hers. "I see."

Sophie and Maddie watched them with hawk eyes, as though they were ready to swoop down and rescue Penelope at a moment's notice.

He raised a brow. "And what else did they say?"

She shrugged. "That I'm pure and virginal."

He laughed. "Are you now?"

The smile tugged at her lips, but she worked to keep it contained. "I am."

"And I'm the big bad wolf?" he asked, his gaze dipping down to her lips before returning to her eyes.

"They're worried you're going to hurt me, since I'm the faithful one."

Maddie seemed unable to keep quiet one second longer and slammed her hands on her hips. "There are plenty of other women. You need to leave Penelope alone."

"Yeah, Evan," Sophie said, her voice stern and entirely unlike her. "She needs a man who will love her the way she deserves."

Evan's shoulders stiffened and he jutted his chin toward Penelope. "Did you happen to mention you're the one woman I've always been faithful to?"

Maddie let out a little yelp. "It's only been a day, Evan!"

"Yeah," Sophie said. "That's hardly an accomplishment."

Penelope ignored them and said to Evan, "I hadn't gotten that far. I was letting them unwind a bit first."

"You always did have more patience than me." The tone of his voice turning low and unmistakably intimate. "Most of the time."

An image of last night, sheets tangled at their waists, the room dark and quiet except for the heavy sounds of their harsh breath. Him moving inside her, his hips a slow grind against hers that drove her crazy. Their bodies slick with sweat.

And her whispered pleas in his ear, begging him to go faster, take her harder.

"I have more discipline than you." Penelope's words came out a husky rasp.

"I don't like what's going on here," Maddie said, breaking the spell.

Sophie didn't speak, just looked back and forth between Evan and Penelope.

"I'm not going to hurt her, Mads," Evan said.

"Please don't," Maddie said, her voice distressed.

Penelope realized her best friend was truly upset, and

worried. All she saw was her rule-following friend hooking up with her notorious brother. She didn't know the past. Or how it was between them. She straightened from the counter and walked over to Maddie, and slid an arm around her friend's small shoulders. "I promise I'm okay."

"Just don't get hurt," Maddie said, "He's used to women who . . . well, that are okay with casual."

Penelope looked at Evan over Maddie's head. He watched his sister, his expression resigned and almost pained. And she realized he was ready to take the fall for this. Ready to let them all believe the worst of him because that's the side he was used to showing to his family and didn't know how to turn it off. But he didn't have football to escape to anymore, he had nowhere left to run. And Penelope couldn't take one more second of him being the bad guy.

She sighed and turned toward Maddie. "It's not casual."

Maddie's brow furrowed and she clasped her hands. "That's the problem, Pen. That's what you think."

"She's right," Evan said, his voice thick. "Casual is the last word I'd used to describe her."

Maddie searched her brother's expression. "But you don't stay with anyone longer than a month."

Evan's gaze met Penelope's and she read the question in his expression and nodded. She was going to tell them anyway. It was just a matter of time before the past came out.

Evan returned his attention to Maddie. "That's because they didn't compare to Penelope."

"What?" Maddie's eyes widened with surprise.

"Since high school, I've always measured other women against her."

Penelope's chest gave a little squeeze at the words. All this time, all these years later, he was finally saying everything she'd wanted to hear.

Sophie's brows knitted together. "I don't understand. Are you saying you've been carrying on since high school?"

"Not exactly." Penelope cleared her throat. "But things weren't entirely innocent."

Evan laughed and she scowled at him.

Maddie rubbed her temples. "What does this all mean?"

Penelope struggled to find the words, unable to articulate what it all meant or exactly what she was doing.

In the end, Evan came to her rescue. "It means nothing will change for you. Penelope will still be your best friend, she'll still come to the house for dinner, but instead of coming by herself, she'll come with me. And leave with me. We have a lot of history most of you aren't aware of, and it's time we deal with it and see what happens."

Maddie's chin tilted and she sniffed. "How mature of you."

Evan smiled. "I can be mature sometimes."

Sophie flipped her blond hair and shook her head at Penelope. "I can't believe it. You slut."

Penelope burst out laughing, and the tension broke. This is why she loved her friends.

While Evan stood by, the three of them came together in a group hug and, huddled together, Sophie said, "I expect details."

"Oh God, please no." Maddie's voice was pleading before she sighed. "You know, *someday* I'd like to be able to share details with someone."

Penelope grinned and squeezed her friends. "You share details all the time."

"But you can't share them back," Maddie said.

"You know I've never been much of a sharer," Penelope said.

"Well, get over it. I will be calling to hear every last one." Sophie bumped her hip into Maddie. "Don't worry, you've still got me and you're officially out of brothers, so we can swap as many details as you want."

They pulled apart and Maddie turned to her brother, who watched them all with an amused expression. "If anything happens to her, I'll never forgive you."

Evan looked at Penelope, his gaze intent. "It won't."

It was a promise. And she believed him.

Only time would tell if it was one he could keep.

Chapter Nineteen

Evan threw the trash bag in one of the garbage cans lining the alley, thankful for a few minutes of escape from all the togetherness. He loved his family, but without football taking so much of his time, there was no longer a buffer. No longer something he could escape to when they started to overwhelm him.

Jimmy had always considered himself the odd man out, but Evan didn't see that at all. James belonged. He was the rock. The voice of reason in the chaos. The family anchor that steadied the rest of them. Evan was the outsider.

Since he'd left for college, he'd spent far more time away than with them. He was the visitor. All these years he'd let them see what he'd wanted them to see, and now he was paying the price.

Not that he didn't love them, because he did; after his injury they were the only ones he'd let in. But they wore on him too, in a way they never seemed to wear on each other. They were always so together. Dinners, and getaways, and trips to Revival, and holidays, it never ended. They were a group. Sophie and Penelope were a part of that group.

He was the one that needed to work his way in.

It was Penelope they were concerned about. And they'd

make him prove his worth. It was only a matter of when and for how long.

All things considered, the night was going as well as could be expected, but Evan couldn't wait for it to end. For the most part, everyone was playing it cool and pretty much ignoring the elephant in the room, and he and Penelope kept a reasonable distance from each other.

But he wanted to touch her, to establish the easy intimacy he witnessed between his brothers and sister and their significant others, but he understood that took time. And despite how she was in private, she liked her reserve in public, and he didn't want to take that away from her.

He walked through the gate and down the narrow path next to the garage, only to slow when he saw Shane on the bottom step of the deck, arms crossed, doing his best imposing stare.

Evan took a deep breath. His time of reckoning had finally come.

Shane leaned against the railing. "I've been coached on handling this calmly."

Evan cocked a brow. "And how's that going for you?"

"Not that great."

Evan decided to go on the offensive. "Can't we just handle this like brothers? And not like you're my surrogate father?"

A muscle in Shane's cheek jumped. "I'm not sure I know the difference."

Of course, that was the problem. Had always been the problem between him and Shane. Their lines were blurred by the past, their father's death, and the role Shane had been forced into when he'd been too young.

Evan blew out a breath. "I care about her."

"Do you?" Shane asked, his voice hard.

"Yeah, I do."

"Are you sure this isn't about getting your ego stroked?"

Anger sliced sharply through him and he had to fight to keep his voice calm. "I can go out and get my ego stroked by hundreds of women."

"Exactly. So why don't you go screw around with someone who doesn't mean anything to the rest of us?"

Evan's hands curled into fists. "Because she's not fucking interchangeable."

"That's bullshit. She's hardly your type, she's not a model, and she has two brain cells to rub together, and you're going to do nothing but hurt her."

Evan opened his mouth to argue, but stopped himself. Shane wasn't in the mood to have his mind changed, and everyone knew there was no stopping him once he'd decided. It was one of the traits that made him so successful. Unfortunately, it made him stubborn as hell, and nothing Evan said right now would change what he believed. So there was no point in trying. He walked up the steps until he was eye level with Shane, and said through gritted teeth, "I don't need to justify myself to you."

"The hell you don't. Penelope is like a sister to me," Shane said, his voice growing loud. "Not only that, but she's my most valued employee; when things go south, then what's going to happen?"

"It's not going to go south."

Shane grimaced. "Please, be realistic. Have you ever stayed with anyone for more than a month? What's going to happen to her when you grow bored and you take off to go base jumping or some such shit?"

"I'm not going to get bored."

Shane shook his head. "What? Do you actually think you have a future? Do you even know the concept of commitment? You're nothing alike. She needs someone who will treat her the way she deserves."

Evan's temper started to boil, threatening to consume him, but to what purpose? Nothing he said or did at this point would make a difference. If he flew off the handle, he'd just reinforce Shane's perception that he was wild and impetuous. He wouldn't rise to the bait. Evan walked past him. "I'm done with this conversation."

Shane grabbed his arm. "I'm not going to let you hurt her. I don't know what you did to her, but she's not like you, she's not used to the games you play. She's good, and kind, and you're going to break her heart and I'll have to pick up the pieces."

"Fuck you, Shane." Evan pulled his arm away. "You don't know the first thing about it, or her."

"The hell I don't. While you were off playing football, I'm the one who gave her a job and worked with her every day. You barely even know her. And I don't want you using her to get your life back together only so you can dump her when your head's back on straight."

Rage filled Evan, making his vision hazy. He turned toward his brother. "You've already got it all worked out, don't you? And you know what, go ahead and think whatever crap you want about me, but don't underestimate Penelope. Do you understand me?"

Surprise flickered over Shane's features. He opened his mouth to speak, but Evan had already turned away and walked into the house. He stopped dead in his tracks at the sight of Penelope and Cecilia standing in the kitchen. A second later, Shane followed him in and froze.

The four of them all stared at each other, nobody saying anything.

Finally, Cecilia looked at her husband and sighed. "You couldn't mind your own business, could you?"

Penelope's expression stayed completely blank, and remote.

Shane jutted out his chin. "You knew that was never going to happen."

Evan walked over to Penelope and took her elbow, but she stayed rigid, her mouth pursed in a flat line as she looked at Shane.

"What?" Shane said, his shoulders tightening as he straightened. "Someone had to speak the truth."

Cecilia shook her head. "Oh, Shane."

Penelope shifted her attention to Evan. "I think I'm ready to go."

She was upset. Shane had pretty much just spewed her worst fears about him, and Evan had no idea what she must be thinking. Alone they could talk and he could begin the process of convincing her again. He squeezed her elbow. "All right."

She narrowed her gaze on Shane and anger sparked in her blue eyes. "I have to finish my PowerPoint on my three-point system for fixing your life."

Shane took a step toward her. "Pen."

Penelope held up her hand. "I think you've said more than enough."

Cecilia turned a concerned gaze on Penelope. "I'm sorry."

"Why are you apologizing?" Shane said, his tone aggressive and edged with defensiveness.

"Because somebody has to," Cecilia hissed. "Now will you please just shut up before you make everything even worse?"

"I'm protecting her," Shane yelled, and something inside Evan snapped.

He stepped forward and pushed Shane's shoulder with a brutal force. "That's not your job anymore, got it?"

Only an inch shorter than Evan, Shane didn't even budge, and his gaze turned mean. "You can't even take care of yourself, how in the hell are you going to take care of her?"

Cecilia closed her eyes and rubbed at her temples.

Everyone who had been sitting in the living room stampeded into the kitchen as Evan and Shane squared off.

Evan should stop, get back under control, but it was impossible, because deep down he knew the truth. Shane was right. He hadn't even protected Penelope from pregnancy. He unleashed all his anger, all his frustrating, impotent rage. "You don't know shit."

Full of aggression, Shane jutted his jaw. "I'm not going to stand by and watch you hurt her."

"I'm not going to hurt her."

His mother whistled. "Boys! That's enough."

But they were past listening.

"Somebody needs to look out for her, and that person is me," Shane yelled.

A fierce, visceral possession clouded what was left of the rational part of Evan's brain. "She's mine, back the fuck off."

He shoved Shane, who shoved him right back.

In the recesses of his mind, Evan knew this was the worst way to handle things but he couldn't stop.

He pushed Shane again.

Shane knocked him in the shoulder. "I'll back off when you start rolling out of bed every day before noon."

Evan gritted his teeth as they stood toe to toe, both breathing hard, ready to come to blows. Waiting for that one little move that would make all hell break loose. He yelled, "You love it, don't you, that I lost my career, just so you can lord it over me."

His mother clapped her hands. "Boys! Stop this, this instant!"

"Stop," Maddie said, her voice pleading. "James, do something."

"I'll love it when you get your shit together and stop fucking around with Penelope." Shane shoved Evan.

His mind went numb, adrenaline pumped furiously through his blood. He curled his hand and cocked his fist. Like lightning, he swung, only to be stopped from the satisfying contact when his wrist met with an immovable object.

He swung around and James stood there, a weary expression on his face. "Let me go, Jimmy."

"It's enough." James released him, but before Evan could get in a swing, James stepped between them, placing an open palm on their chests. "If you want to hit him, you'll have to go through me. Remember, despite your differences you're still brothers."

Evan glared at Shane.

Shane glared right back.

James, who had a long history of dealing with his brothers' aggression, stayed firmly between them. "Evan, you must understand that you have a bit of a past when it comes to women, and Penelope is important to Shane."

Some of his adrenaline began to wear off. "It's not like that."

James turned to Shane. "You've got to stop treating him like he's the family fuck-up."

Shane's expression fell and his shoulders slumped. "That's not what I meant."

James nodded. "You two never mean half of what you say to each other. I understand you're upset, but calm down and think about this. Work it out. We're family."

"I just want what's best for her," Shane said.

"Well, so do I." Evan vowed that someday, someone would believe him.

Aunt Cathy clucked her tongue. "Did either of you boneheads realize the girl you're fighting over left?"

Evan jerked out of his anger and aggression and spun around and yelled, "Goddamn it!"

Without a backward glance he ran into the living room

to find it empty. Everyone else ran after him, and he spun on his heel and ran upstairs, searching bedrooms and bathrooms only to find them empty. He pounded down the stairs while everyone stood watching him, but paid them no mind as he raced outside and peered up and down the street.

But he was too late. She was gone.

Maybe it was childish of her to slip away, but she didn't care. Not even a little bit.

She hated being the center of attention and she'd just been so embarrassed. She was furious at Evan for causing that mess.

But she was even more furious at Shane. Didn't he understand how humiliating it was to listen to him yell in front of God and everyone that Evan would get bored with her? That she wasn't exciting enough to keep his interest? That the only thing she was good for was fixing him so he could move on to the type of woman he was meant to be with?

That conversation between Evan and Shane had highlighted everything that was wrong with her life. Everything wrong with even contemplating a relationship with Evan. They'd cemented all those doubts niggling insistently in the back of her head, forcing her to confront things she didn't want to think about. It revealed all her worst, secret fears she'd tried so hard to hide.

It's not that she didn't know her worth. Because she absolutely did. She was smart and capable. She was successful and accomplished.

But she wasn't like Evan.

She wasn't larger than life. She didn't do drama and scenes and magazine spreads. She didn't make waves.

How was a future possible when they were so different?

And eventually, he had to realize he'd be better off with someone like him.

It wasn't self-esteem; it was practicality.

She slid farther under her throw, curling up on her couch while she waited.

Evan would come for her—of that much she was certain—and he wouldn't be long. She'd been lucky. She'd jogged down to the busy street two blocks away and hailed a cab almost immediately. But he couldn't be far behind.

For now, she just sat and stewed in her public humiliation.

When the doorbell rang, she was tempted to ignore it, but what purpose did that serve? She got up to open the door. The second she did he stormed in, turning on her, his expression filled with an anger that surprised her.

"What the fuck was that all about, Penelope?" His voice loud, filling her hallway and practically vibrating off the walls.

Her head snapped back. She'd been expecting contrite, apologetic even, but he was mad. Like really mad. In a calm tone she said, "What do you mean?"

"Why did you leave like that?"

She crossed her arms protectively over her chest. "Isn't that obvious?"

"No, it is not." He pointed a finger at her. "I'm trying to present a united front and you go and take off on me."

Anger and irritation spiked hot in her blood and too late she remembered Evan made her volatile. She didn't like volatile. It was one of the things she used to remind herself when she'd get angsty over him. She batted his hand away. "Oh please, that little scene had nothing to do with me. That was about you and Shane. All I did was provide the bone."

He shook his head. "That's bullshit. I was doing it for you."

"No, you weren't. You were doing it for you."

"How can you even say that?"

Her reasons for leaving snapped into place like the crack of a whip, deflating her anger and leaving her sad. She looked at the trendy, chunky watch on her wrist. "You're fifteen minutes behind me, Evan. So, let me ask you, how long did it take you to realize I was gone?"

"I'm sorry." He dragged his hands through his hair and his shoulders slumped. "I'm not very good at this relationship stuff."

"Relationship?" Her tone was soft, conveying none of the emotions storming away inside her. "It's been fourteen hours and it's already a disaster."

"It's an adjustment."

What was the point of all this? His methods might have been all wrong, but there was truth to what Shane said. They weren't meant to be together. It was never going to work between them. Why avoid the inevitable conclusion? The words stuck in her throat but she pushed them out. "Maybe we just have to come to the realization that sex is all we have in common."

The green of his irises turned flat and cold as he stared at her through hard, narrowed eyes. "One little hiccup and you're ready to call it quits?"

The *no* vibrated in her skull and she looked away, holding her breath as she waited for him to just leave. The silence was suspended between them as a thick, heavy tension, filling up all the free space in the tiny hallway where they stood.

This is how things always went. No matter their passion, they couldn't sustain.

A few hours of happiness followed by heartache. It was always the same story.

Her stomach clenched and she stared at the picture she'd hung in the parlor, of her, Maddie, and Sophie at a party. They looked young and happy. She steeled her spine, waiting for him to leave so she could be alone.

"No."

His voice was so sharp, she jerked her attention back to him. "What?"

He shook his head. "No. You almost had me convinced, but I'm not fucking falling for it."

"I have no idea what you're talking about." Some sort of survival instinct had her stepping back and she hit the wall, with nowhere left to run.

He stepped toward her, grabbed her wrists, raised them over her head as he pressed his body into hers. "You're right. That was about Shane and me. But it's also about you and me. I'm not going to let you push me away, Penelope. You talk a very good game, but it's not going to work this time. I'm on to you."

All the air caught in her lungs, then expelled with a *whoosh*. "I'm not playing a game. I'm being realistic."

Face close, he met her gaze. "You don't think I know what Shane said pushed every button you have? That he vocalized every one of your fears? That deep down, just like him, you're waiting for me to walk away?"

Her heart started to pound against her ribs and a kind of panic swept over her. The words resonated deep inside her, shaking her to the core, forcing her to confront the truth.

She was. Where Evan was concerned, she was still vulnerable. Still blindly in love with him.

When he hurt her, she'd be crushed, so she kept trying to make the decision for him, only he wouldn't fall into his expected role.

Her throat closed up tight and she croaked out, "Let me go."

"No." The word absolute. "I will not let you go."

"Please, Evan." Her voice a soft plea.

He squeezed her wrists. "All those years ago, I hurt you

and I was cruel. But I was just a dumb, messed-up kid, Pen. My father had just died, my sister was in a coma, and in my fucked-up way I thought I was doing the right thing by you. It's not an excuse. It's only an explanation."

"I don't blame you." God, all she wanted was to get away from him so she could compose herself. So she could push all this away.

"The hell you don't. You do, and you're right to blame me." He manacled her wrists with one hand, and slid his finger around her too-tight throat with his other. "But I'm not going to walk away."

The tears welled in her eyes and no matter how hard she fought it, they wouldn't be contained. "Yes, you will."

"You're wrong. I don't expect you to believe me, but every time I stay, you'll believe a little more. You can't push me away." His thumb swept up and brushed the wet tracks from her cheek. "And there's more between us than just sex."

She started to tremble, she wanted him so damn much and she was so scared. He could crush her. And now everyone knew, and when it ended, she'd lose her makeshift family too. Not them physically, because they'd never walk away, but their respect. They'd look at her with pity before they lowered their gazes. Behind her back they'd whisper they'd known, but she hadn't listened.

It would never be the same again.

He leaned down and brushed his mouth over hers. "Someday you'll trust me. Believe in me. All I can do is prove it to you every day that this is worth sticking out."

At the next brush of his lips, she responded with all the urgent, desperate desire she kept locked away.

He pulled away and shook his head. "Don't kiss me like that."

"Like what?" Her voice choked.

"Like you think it's the last time." He softened the next brush of his lips. "It's not the last time, Penelope."

"Okay." Tonight, if he wouldn't walk away, she didn't have the strength to do it for him. She leaned her head against the wall, tilting her chin in an invitation.

His thumb brushed over her lower lip. "I want you so damn bad."

"I want you too." Her lashes drifted closed as she waited.

His grip on her wrists tightened. "Let's go watch TV."

Her lids snapped open. "TV?"

He nodded. "We can watch your show, so I can properly make fun of it."

"But . . ." Her gaze darted toward the stairs leading to her bedroom.

"Later." Another brush of his lips over hers. "Now I show you this isn't about sex."

Lying next to her on the couch, Evan rested his open palm on Penelope's stomach. Her eyes were closed, her dark hair fanned out, her chest an even rise and fall. Sometime during their third episode of *The Originals*, which was just as campy and horrible as he thought it would be, she'd drifted off and he'd contented himself watching her sleep.

None of them, even her, believed him. They were all waiting for him to bail, and sadly, he couldn't blame them. He couldn't blame his sister. Or Shane.

And he sure as hell couldn't blame Penelope.

All people had to go on was his behavior, and the evidence was stacked against him.

Her dark lashes swept over her cheeks. Asleep, she lost her air of utter competence, the efficient set of her jaw. She looked vulnerable. Breakable. Which she was. Deep down where nobody knew to look.

And it was his fault.

How could he have known all those years ago that the harsh words meant to drive them apart would have such a lasting effect? Would come back to haunt him.

He had to figure out a way to prove it to her. To convince her she wasn't just convenient; but other than time, what could he do?

He took a deep breath. He supposed he could start by figuring out what the hell he wanted to do with his life. Because everyone was right, he might be rich, but he had no purpose, and when it came right down to it, he wasn't raised that way. Each day, stretched endlessly before him, wasn't healthy for his psyche. He'd gotten back to conditioning his body, but his mind needed something to chew on too.

Maybe if he started showing some signs of stability it would start to convince her.

He knew what he had to do. What he'd been avoiding thinking about since questions about his future had started to plague him. He had zero interest in modeling or doing commercials. He didn't want to do broadcasting. He couldn't stand the thought of going and sitting behind a desk every day.

He knew and loved only one thing in this life. And it was the one thing he was truly good at. What Penelope had said about him and those kids at the fantasy camp was right. He had loved it, been good at it. Coaching had been his plan for that date far off in the future when his playing days were over.

Those days had come faster than he'd anticipated, and he still missed playing too much for comfort, but if he wanted people to see him as an adult, and for Penelope to see him as someone with staying power, he'd have to man up and start living the future, today.

All that stopped him was ego and an unwillingness to see himself as anything other than a football player. But he had to put all that aside.

First thing in the morning he'd start making calls.

He couldn't play anymore, but he still loved the game. He didn't have to give it up; he just had to transform his contribution. He'd never won a Super Bowl as a player, but maybe someday, he'd win one as a coach.

He couldn't keep holding on to the career he'd lost, or all the things he had left to accomplish. They weren't undone—they were merely different. He'd had his time, and now he had to make peace with the fact that it was over.

It was time to become the kind of man his father would be proud of.

That someday, Penelope could believe in.

Chapter Twenty

The following morning, Shane didn't waste any time. He was at her office door before Penelope even powered up her computer. He was dressed in dark gray slacks and a white button-down, his sleeves rolled up indicating he was ready to get down to serious business. His powerful forearms flexed as he shut the door behind him and motioned to the chair across from her, on the opposite side of the desk. "May I?"

She flipped open her iPad cover and pulled up her task list for the day. "You're the boss."

He grimaced, and ran a hand through his hair. "I'm in that much trouble, am I? It's never good when you call me the boss."

He sat down on the chair and she scrolled through the app, jotting down a few notes as she went.

"Are you just going to ignore me?"

She didn't look up. "What would you like me to say?"

The chair creaked as though he shifted around. "Go ahead and yell at me. Fight it out. But you know I can't stand the silent treatment."

She finally glanced up and folded her hands neatly in

front of her. "You know why I'm mad. The question is, are you sorry?"

He crossed one ankle over his knee and sat back in the chair. "I'll tell you the same thing I told Cecilia. I'm not going to apologize for looking out for you. You're like a sister to me, and I don't want you to get hurt. I love my brother, but he's hard on women. I'm protective of you. I care about you. And I believe you deserve better than what he can offer. I can't be sorry for that."

Asking Shane not to guard what he considered his responsibility to keep safe was tantamount to asking him not to breathe. That also wasn't the point. "So then you don't know why I'm mad."

Green eyes, so similar to the eyes of the man she could never forget and was fast realizing she didn't want to, narrowed on her. "Why don't you fill me in?"

Her knuckles turned white where her hands were clasped. "You didn't even ask me, Shane. Nor did you ask Evan. You assumed you understood and charged in on your white horse without any factual evidence that I need, or desire, a rescue."

"I have years of evidence. I know Evan's type, and you're not it. I've seen the men you date. You and Evan don't match."

His words were an irritant, scratching along her skin, but she remained calm. "You don't get it. To quote you, you don't know shit about it. Forget Evan for a second. You know me, know how I am, what I think, how I operate. You know I'm smart, capable, and better equipped than anyone to run my life. Yet, instead of talking to me, bothering to ask a single question, you concoct some story in your head and make me the victim. Too stupid and blinded by the great Evan Donovan to remember how to rub together those two brain cells you claim I have."

"I'm sorry. I didn't think about it like that, and it's not

what I meant, I . . ." He trailed off and the strain in his voice chipped away the tiniest bit of her anger. "He only dates supermodels."

It stung. Shane had no idea how he dug the knife into old wounds, but she refused to let that dissuade her from her point. "And tell me, Shane, did you by chance ask Evan what his intentions were?"

His gaze slid away. "No."

"Let me ask you another question. Has he ever misled you about his feelings for a woman?"

A shake of his head.

"And yet, you don't think it's possible, in this case, that he might actually have feelings for me. Because, oh, I don't know, you think I'm not hot enough for him?"

Shane's attention snapped back to her. "What? No! I don't think anything like that. You're twisting my words."

"I'm merely pointing out you've made me up into some sort of infatuated little girl too blinded by your brother's reputation to think rationally or make my own decisions, and I won't stand for it." She stood up, not bothering to disguise the hurt and anger in her tone. "I deserve better from *him*? No, I deserve better *from you.*"

"Penelope—"

She held up her hand and forced her voice into something that resembled calm. "If you'll excuse me, I have a conference call in a few minutes."

Shane blew out a deep breath. "Cecilia warned me, but I wouldn't listen."

She crossed her arms over her chest. "Your wife's a smart woman. Don't make that mistake again."

He opened his mouth to speak, but her admin came over the line. "I've dialed in, and they're waiting for you to start."

He stood and shoved his hands into his pockets. "I thought you were lying about the call."

"I never lie about business. Or anything else." She squared her shoulders. "I'm too practical to make up stories."

"We'll talk about this later."

She tilted her chin in the air. "I'm in meetings all day."

His gaze narrowed. "Fine, after work then. Since this is personal it's better anyway."

She wanted to push back the snide remark, but couldn't. She smirked. "Evan hasn't dumped me for a Victoria's Secret model yet, so he's picking me up at six."

A muscle jumped in his jaw, and with jerky movements he picked up her iPad from the desk and started pressing the screen. Several moments later he handed it back to her. "I'm on your calendar at five thirty. I'll see you then."

Then he turned and walked out of her office, leaving her to deal with her day in some semblance of peace.

After a long, grueling workout Evan spent the entire morning on the phone talking to his agent, the new head coach of his former team, and the offensive coordinator. After a crap season, this was a rebuilding year, which was in his favor. When he'd concocted his plan, his biggest worry was that if he was serious about coaching, he'd potentially have to move. And that wasn't an option, considering Penelope worked here in Chicago.

Thankfully, he'd always had an excellent relationship with the offensive coordinator, Bill Laughton, and he was a local boy, something that was always appreciated in Chicago. After a lot of discussion, he was scheduled to go in for a meeting at the end of the week to discuss the open wide-receiver coaching position.

With the plans for a career under way, he picked up the phone and dialed his mother. Time to play clean-up. Again.

When she picked up, he said, "Hi, Mom, I wanted to

apologize. I didn't mean to ruin Maddie's last night before she went home, or the news of James and Gracie's engagement."

The silence that stretched over the line was so long, Evan checked to make sure they hadn't gotten disconnected. "Mom?"

There was a *ping* in the background. "Apology accepted."

He wasn't ready to share his plans yet, with anyone, but he wanted his long-suffering mother to know he was well on the way to getting his shit together. "I want you to know that I'm better. I know I scared you for a while, but I'm getting stronger every day."

"And is this because of Penelope?" Her voice was curious, and a bit sly.

He sat forward on his couch and picked up a coaster, spinning it like a top on his coffee table. "She's part of it, but I can assure you I'm not playing with her emotions."

"I don't think that."

"You don't?"

"No, I do not."

Well, at least there was one person who didn't think he was such a prick he'd start up with Penelope for sport. "Thank you."

His mom cleared her throat. "Your father . . . he, um, mentioned once he'd seen the two of you . . . in the basement."

It shouldn't surprise him—his parents' marriage had been strong, loving, and open—but the news still did. At least he had confirmation that his dad had probably gotten quite the eyeful. They'd been deep into the clandestine relationship at that time and there wasn't much they weren't doing. He blew out a breath. "He was pretty mad at me."

"He spared me the details."

Evan laughed.

"But it worries me—"

Evan cut her off. "I promise I only have Penny's best interests at heart."

"That's not what I was going to say." She sighed, long and heavy. "I think he was wrong, to tell you to stop. I understood his reasons, and I don't know if things would have worked out between you, but maybe you'd think differently about yourself if he hadn't said those things to you."

"Mom, I feel fine about myself. I'm okay. Yes, I had a rough go and life threw me a curveball—but in the grand scheme of things, I know I'm about as lucky as a person can get."

"Oh, my sweet boy," she said, her voice cracking a bit. "I'm not talking about things, I'm talking about how you believe that football is all you have to offer, when that's not true."

It's what Penelope had said, but he didn't buy it. "I don't think that, Mom. I'm fine. I promise."

There was another beat of silence. "At least I know Penelope will take good care of you."

The statement sent a jolt of irrational anger through him and he pressed his lips together to keep from saying anything stupid and impulsive that would result in another apology phone call to his mother. Through a clenched jaw he said, "She's not going to take care of me. *I'm* going to take care of *her*."

"Evan."

"Yes, Mom?"

"I believe you."

"Thank you." At least he had one person on his side.

"You need to make up with your brother." She got that tone in her voice she'd use back when they were kids and in trouble.

"I will."

"Promise me, or I'll tell Aunt Cathy you'll fix the Beast."

"That's playing dirty." Evan shuddered. Aunt Cathy

had an old yellow Buick that took up about three lanes of traffic and was her pride and joy.

"I want your word."

He sighed as though he was put-upon, but the truth was he had every intention of having it out with Shane. "Fine, I promise."

"Good," she said, sounding oh-so-pleased.

"Good-bye, Mom."

After they disconnected he called his sister.

When she picked up, her tone was not friendly. "Yeah?"

"I know you're mad at me, but I'm calling to apologize."

"Did Penelope forgive you?"

"Of course she did." She hadn't really been mad at him. She'd been afraid. But he had no intention of sharing that with Maddie.

"She did? Just like that?"

"Yeah, she did."

"Why?"

Evan dropped the coaster and toyed with the Xbox controller on his coffee table. "She's mad at Shane, not me."

There was about thirty seconds of silence before Maddie tsked into the phone. "You couldn't have picked Sophie, huh?"

He laughed, shaking his head. "You'd have been okay with Soph?"

"Yeah, actually, I would have."

"And why's that?" The thought of being with Sophie was so preposterous it bordered on ridiculous. She was cute as hell, sexy and fun, and had more energy than she knew what to do with, but he'd never once had a sexual thought about her. No, his focus had always been on Penelope.

"Because she's Sophie, she'd be able to get over you. I know Penelope better than anyone. She hides it under all that polish and reserve and she's so damn capable nobody ever thinks to question it, but at the end of the day, she just wants to belong someplace. She was so lonely growing up and we're her someplace. I don't want her to lose that."

"Mads," he said, his tone as deadly serious as he could make it, "I'm going to tell you something I haven't even told her, and I'm only telling you this because I know how important she is to you and I want you to understand. But you can't tell her, okay?"

"Okay." The word was delivered slow and suspicious.

"I love her. I have loved her since I was seventeen years old. A long time ago, I hurt her and now I've got to pay for it, but I'm not going to let it happen again. If it ends, it will be because she left me, not the other way around. Do you understand?"

Maddie didn't speak for a long, long time, but when she did, her voice was considerably softer. "Yes, I think I do. I have one question."

"What's that?"

"Why haven't you told her?"

"Because she's not ready to believe me."

"And are you working to fix that?"

"Besides football, it's the only thing I ever worked this hard at."

"Good, because that's what Penelope deserves. Somebody who will work for her."

"And that's what I'm going to give her." If it went down, it wouldn't be from lack of trying.

After he hung up with his sister, there was only one thing left to clean up, but he wasn't going to do it over the phone.

No, he'd be dealing with Shane in person.

Everyone wanted Evan to man up, and that's exactly what he was going to do.

* * *

Evan was supposed to pick up Penelope at six, so he went to his brother's office at five fifteen, hoping that at the end of the day Shane wouldn't be tied up in one of his endless meetings. He was in luck; when he got there Shane's door was open and he sat behind his massive desk. He wore a white dress shirt with his sleeves rolled up to the elbows and no tie.

Evan knocked on the door frame and Shane looked up, his expression widening in surprise. Evan gestured to the chair. "Can I come in?"

Shane glanced at his watch. "I'm supposed to talk to Penelope in a few minutes. She's . . . um . . . pretty mad at me."

Evan nodded, came in and shut the door behind him. "I don't think she'll mind. She probably doesn't want to talk to you anyway."

Shane rubbed his jaw. "She doesn't."

Evan sat down in the chair across from his oldest brother and awkwardness settled between them. Determined to be adult, he sighed. "Can we stop all this? Aren't you tired of it?"

Shane narrowed his gaze. "Yeah, I am. Despite my best intentions I always turn into a raging asshole around you."

Evan laughed and some of his tension seeped away. "I just want us to be brothers. Like we are with James."

"I don't know why I ride you so hard. I don't mean to." Shane sat back in his chair and he shook his head. "I think, out of all of us, you just seem like you've had it easy. Everything has always fallen into your lap. And, maybe, in a twisted way, after your injury I felt it was my responsibility to toughen you up. I'm sorry I took it too far."

Evan had never really thought about it like that. How it must have looked to Shane, busting his ass while Evan went off to Ohio State to do nothing but play football. In high school there'd still been some perspective, and he'd had his family to keep him grounded, but once he'd gotten to college, he'd been treated like a god.

There was truth in what Shane said; everything Evan wanted had, to some extent, fallen into his lap because he'd been blessed with an innate talent that no amount of training or playing could make up for. Yes, he'd honed his skills, worked his ass off, sweated, hurt, and played hard—but none of that would have mattered if he hadn't been gifted. And he'd had nothing to do with that. He'd just hit the genetic jackpot.

Maybe it was time to show his brother some respect, instead of acting like a defensive kid. "I guess I never said thank you."

Shane scoffed, running a hand through his hair. "You have nothing to thank me for. You were the one person who never cost me anything. You had a free ride and you've always done your own thing. You don't owe me anything."

Evan grinned. "It kind of eats at you, doesn't it?"

Shane laughed and shrugged. "Maybe just a little."

"Well, if it makes you feel better, I had the freedom to do that because of you. I know that and appreciate all that you've done, even if I never say it." Evan sat forward, putting his elbows on his knees. They'd cleared the air on their history enough for now, and it was time to address the elephant in the room. "I understand how it looks, with Penelope, but I'll tell you the same thing I told our sister this afternoon. She matters and I'm going to do whatever it takes to make her happy."

Shane blew out a breath and looked out his window for a few moments before returning his attention to Evan. "She's important to me. We went through it all together. She's really the only one who knows how lean and tough all those years at the beginning were. She stuck by me, didn't make a big deal if I had to short her paycheck to pay a contractor. She is the one person in this company who is indispensable to me. Anyone else can leave, but her."

Evan nodded, maybe for the first time really grasping Penelope's importance to the empire his brother had built.

A smile lifted the corners of Shane's mouth. "Did you know she had to force me to hire her?"

"No," Evan said, sitting forward to learn more about that time in her life that had nothing to do with him.

Shane laughed. "She was relentless. I think I told her no about twenty times."

"How'd she convince you?"

"I'd been working out of this hole-in-the wall trailer I'd drag with me to every site, and the guys had been busting their asses to make schedule, so I took them to lunch. While I was gone, she picked the lock, broke in, and when I got back she'd organized the entire office. It was small, but it was spotless, everything was filed, and she'd had all the invoices I needed to sign neatly stacked on my desk with little color-coded flags."

"That sounds like her."

Shane looked off in the distance over Evan's shoulder. "Anyway, she acted as though I'd been expecting her, explained some system for the colored paper, and then handed me a stack of messages. I hired her on the spot and she's by far the best business decision I ever made. To me, she's family. And, as I reminded Cecilia last night during our blow-out argument, I did have a hell of a fight with Mitch when I found him with Maddie that first time. I'm protective of the women in my life, and maybe I went about it all wrong, but I only had Penelope's best interests at heart. I don't want to see her hurt."

Evan sighed and sat back in his chair. "I understand. And I get that I've been with a lot of women, but Penelope's the only woman who has ever mattered to me. You and I, we're not that much different when it comes to her.

I can only promise you she's as indispensable to me as she is to you."

Shane shook his head. "How is that even possible?"

"When we were teenagers we used to meet down in the basement." Evan cocked a brow. "And you remember what used to go on down there."

Shane's eyes went wide. "Oh really?"

"Really." Evan went on to explain the barest details of their relationship, as well as the last conversation with their dad, and to his surprise Shane just listened. He didn't interrupt, didn't look disapproving.

He just nodded, and when Evan was done talking, he said, "That's one I never saw coming."

"Yeah, well, you can thank her for pulling me out of the deepest parts of my depression."

"Oh?"

He nodded. "She came to me."

Shane smiled. "How exactly did she do it?"

Evan grinned back at his brother. "She slapped me across the face and called me a pussy."

Shane roared with laughter, shaking his head. "Yeah, that would do it."

Evan glanced at his phone. "It's about that time."

"I have one question."

Evan raised a brow. "Yeah?"

"How are you doing? Without football?"

Evan shrugged. "It's not easy. Especially when I still feel like I can play. But I'm taking steps to move on and I'm sure it will get better as time goes on."

"Just as long as you're okay."

"You know, I think I am."

Shane nodded and stood, and Evan followed suit. Shane gave him a sideways glance. "For the record, I don't think you're a fuck-up."

"Glad to hear it."

Shane jutted his chin toward the door. "I'll walk you to her office."

"Does that mean I have your blessing?"

Shane gave him a long look, then nodded. "You're my brother. I'm never going to stand in the way of what makes you happy. But, Penelope doesn't have any brothers looking out for her, so if you make her cry, I'm going to have to treat you the same way we'd treat Mitch if he made Maddie cry. Fair enough?"

That's the kind of statement that would normally rub him the wrong way, but the conversation had the intended effect and eased the tension between them considerably. And it was fair. Penelope deserved someone who cared about her with such ferocity. Evan could live with that. "Fair enough. But since we're making ourselves clear, I'll say this one last thing and then we can put this subject to bed. I owe you for taking care of her for all these years. But I've got it from here."

Shane grinned. "Yeah, I think you do."

Chapter Twenty-One

Evan and Shane stood in her office doorway, one dark, the other blond, both big and beautiful. Matching green eyes stared at her, and she raised a brow. "Everything okay? I don't have to call security, do I?"

Shane chuckled, looking calm and relaxed. "I think we're good."

She shifted her attention to Evan. He nodded. "We're good."

"You boys made up?"

Shane stepped inside her office and slid his hands into his pockets. "I still owe you an apology."

"You do." She kept her voice implacable. She wasn't quite ready to forgive yet.

"I was wrong," he said, sounding contrite.

"Yes, you were."

He flashed his most charming grin and she couldn't help but thaw a bit. "You'll have to find it in your heart to forgive me. I'm not rational when it comes to your well-being."

Full of questions, she darted a quick glance at Evan, who just shrugged at her. "He's an idiot, but he means well."

Shane turned and punched Evan in the arm. They were

more relaxed than she'd seen them in a long time, and for that she couldn't help but be happy. At least there was one good thing that came out of this mess, and for that, she was thankful.

She looked at Shane. "I'm still mad at you."

"I know," he said.

She picked up a pen and clicked the top. "I want you to stop treating him like he's a frat boy who can't keep his dick in his pants."

"Done."

The corners of Evan's mouth tilted and she read the amusement in his eyes.

"And I don't want to hear about the endless parade of supermodels anymore."

"That's fair." Shane's lips twisted into a smile that matched Evan's, and standing there together, they were quite the picture of seeping testosterone and charm.

She never could stay mad at Shane long, even when he deserved it, and while her anger started to thaw, she could still have a little fun. "You still owe me dinner at Alinea for the Hayes contract."

"I haven't forgotten," Shane said.

"Evan will come too, and since it will be your treat, I can promise you he'll have very expensive taste in alcohol that evening."

Shane jerked his head toward Evan. "He's a millionaire."

"So are you," she shot back.

"Fine," Shane said, giving a good show of being put-upon, but she knew the truth.

He wanted her forgiveness, and knew she was giving it to him.

She gave Evan a sly glance. "Well, isn't he agreeable? What else should we rake him over the coals for?"

Evan's gaze flickered over her mouth. "I could do without hearing the story about how he took the rap for me so

I wouldn't get kicked off the football team when I pulled the fire alarm back in ninth grade."

She nodded. "Sounds fair."

Shane sighed.

Evan scrubbed a hand over his jaw. "I think you deserve a raise."

She let out an excited little gasp. "I think that's a fantastic idea."

"Fine. Five percent," Shane said.

She crossed her arms. "Twenty."

"Ten," Shane countered.

"Fifteen. And that's my final offer." She studied her nails.

"Oh, all right. You're a bloodthirsty one."

Evan laughed, his amusement clear in the rich, hearty sound.

Shane scrubbed a hand over his jaw and said to Evan, "It's all fun and games now, but just remember how ruthless she can be when it's turned on you."

Evan shrugged and a wicked grin spread over his lips. "I've got her under control."

Penelope snapped up, dropped the pen, and slammed her hands on her hips. "What did you just say?"

Shane patted Evan on the back. "That's my cue. You're on your own. And may God have mercy on your soul."

With that, he took his leave, closing the door behind him.

With slow, deliberate steps she walked around the desk and leaned against the edge. "Under control, huh?"

"Too much?" Evan walked toward her and the air shifted.

"I'd say so," she said, her voice already lowering and going husky. "But I know how important it is for you to be tough in front of your brother."

Today, with him standing in front of her with that expression on his face, she believed in them. And that's what she wanted to hold on to.

"I'm not interested in him." Evan's gaze traveled the

length of her body, all the way to the tips of her high-heeled black pumps. "Have I mentioned I like the way you dress?"

Today she wore a black shirtwaist dress that buttoned down the front, had a wide matching belt, and ended at her knees. It was slim cut and accented her long frame and blue eyes.

She put her hands on the desk, and it caused her back to arch, just a bit. Just enough to attract his notice. "You have."

It worked; he lingered on the swell of her breasts, before stepping toward her. "I never can figure out how you manage to cover yourself so appropriately and look so goddamn gorgeous."

Heartbeat kicking up a notch, her breath caught and when she spoke her voice was far too husky. "Do you think compliments will win you any favors?"

"I hope so." He was close now. Close enough she could feel the heat of his body. He slid his hands on the desk, forcing him to lean down and her face to tilt up to his. "I haven't touched you in twelve hours."

No, he hadn't. She licked her dry lips.

His head dropped and his lips grazed over her neck, sending gooseflesh down her arms. He whispered, "I've had this reoccurring fantasy."

"What's that?" Her voice was low and full of smoke.

His teeth scraped over her skin. "I've always wanted to corrupt you in your office. Fuck you across your desk. On the floor." He raised his gaze to her windows. "Against the glass."

Her blood pounded in her veins as her skin grew tight. She could see right into the office across the way. "The buildings are too close." She glanced at her unlocked door. "And someone might come in."

"Exactly." He pressed his open mouth to the curve of

her throat, his tongue licking over her. "That's what gets you so excited."

She might be hyperventilating, but she managed to croak out, "It doesn't excite me." She didn't know why she was protesting when the evidence spoke so loudly to the contrary. Maybe it was precisely because it was exactly the kind of thing most people would think she was too proper for. The kind of thing Evan knew better.

His fingers hooked at the edge of her belt. "Let's just see about that, shall we?"

She shook her head, but arched her back in invitation. With him, she wanted to be wild, wanted to shrug off all her properness, to act with abandon.

He straightened and unhooked the clasp of her belt before looking into her eyes. "It's like you knew what I'd be doing to you when you picked this outfit."

Maybe she had. She bit her lip. "I'm at work, we should stop."

The objection only magnified her excitement.

He released the belt and it dropped to the desk with a loud *thump*. "I don't think so." His hands roamed over her hips and the curve of her waist. "Tell me I'm not going to find you wet."

She couldn't, because he would. Her nipples were pulled tight, and in less than a minute flat he'd managed to set her body on fire. That was Evan, taking her from proper Catholic girl to depraved, since the dawn of time.

He popped the first button, and then the next.

And she did nothing to stop him. This was exactly the kind of thing she'd only do with Evan. The kind of thing she'd missed doing for years. The kind of thing a relationship with a man like Evan was designed for.

Outside her office there were voices, and everything inside her stilled.

Evan laughed, and it was pure sin. "Perfect."

Her gaze trained on the door, her breath coming in short, hard pants. "Evan, someone might come in."

He leaned down and rasped into her ear, "I am going to fuck the hell out of you. I'll take you rough and I'm not going to be quiet about it."

She whimpered, unable to speak. A type of panic-filled excitement and arousal mixed like a powerful cocktail and beat a steady path through her blood. He popped the next button; she let him.

In fact, she wished he'd rip it off. Because with him, she always gave in to her base desires. It's how he got her in the first place.

And why she couldn't give him up.

"I'm going to be inside you, and they're going to be right outside." His deft fingers moved over the buttons on her dress, opening them as though he had some sort of divine intervention on his side. "Are you going to be able to be quiet? Or am I going to have to put my hand over your mouth?"

She gasped, lifting her hips at a vivid memory of them on the floor, his hand clamped over her mouth as she screamed against his palm, coming so hard she lost all reason.

Another evil, knowing laugh. "Oh yes, I remember."

"Evan," she whispered, her body restless and impatient.

He spread the fabric of her dress and his gaze raked down her body. "Tell me this isn't the underwear of a woman who knows she's going to be engaged in immoral acts."

"I don't know what you mean," she lied. The black lace bra and panty set was sheer, provocative, and she had thought about him this morning when she put it on, as he lay stretched out on her bed, asleep. The sunlight cast him in a golden glow, his tanned skin a stark contrast to her white sheets.

There was a flurry of talking outside the door, obviously someone carrying on a hallway conversation, startling her from her thoughts. She tensed, but somehow grew unbearably more excited.

"Excellent." He smoothed a path down her legs. "Spread those thighs for me."

This was so not like her. She didn't do things like this. Which is what she loved about him. And she was so damn hot. So damn wet.

He squeezed her thigh and it sent a shock wave through her. With a darted glance at the door, she slowly spread, planting her high-heeled shoes on either side of his feet.

His expression was full of heat. Full of danger. He ran his finger over her panties, right where she wanted him the most. "They're right outside, Penelope."

Her head fell back, her spine arched, and she urged him closer.

He reached up and undid the pins in her hair, dropping them to her desk as her hair spilled free. He stepped between her legs, jerking her forward.

She let out a low, needy sound that came from the back of her throat and it seemed to echo her desperateness through the room.

"This fucking hair." His voice a low growl as he fisted it in his hands.

The sounds from the hallway grew closer and she squirmed against him. He held her tighter.

And then his mouth was on hers. His lips rough. His kiss was raw and dirty, sending desire crashing at warp speed through her entire body. She lifted her hips, instinctively seeking his hard cock where she needed him most, and he rocked into her, sending a container of pens flying.

The sound too loud in a space filled with nothing but the low hum of her computer, their hard breath, and their mouths that couldn't seem to get close enough.

He released her lips, bending down to suck at her neck, his tongue dragging over her pounding pulse. He trailed over her shoulder, nipped at her collarbone before skimming the curve of her breast. He licked her nipple through the lace, then pulled it deep into his mouth.

She cried out. And with one hand still bracing herself on the desk, she dragged the other through his hair and tugged him closer. His teeth scraped over the distended peak and sharp, exquisite pleasure raced along her skin. "Oh . . . God."

His mouth and teeth still tugging at her breast, he slipped his hand between her legs and into her panties, to circle her clit. She was so slick it was almost embarrassing.

He vibrated his approval against her skin, and plunged first one, and then another finger inside. Hips rising, she moved insistently against his hand. Not caring how she was acting. Not caring about the people outside. Just needing something harder than his fingers could deliver.

Needing him.

"Evan. God, Evan." Something crashed to the floor.

The voices were louder now and it should have cooled her blood, but it didn't.

He lifted his head and looked deep into her eyes. "Tell me what you want."

She yanked at his arms, unmovable under his strength. "You." She arched up in invitation.

"No." He put one hand on his belt. "Tell me what you *really* want. How you want it."

Dazed, she blinked at him, unsure of what he asked.

He traced his thumb over her swollen bottom lip. "Open that prim little mouth of yours and tell me what you need."

Understanding dawned and her breath was a rapid rise and fall in her chest. She leaned back and met his hot, feral gaze. "Fuck me."

He slowly undid his belt as his attention shifted to her mouth. "I'm listening."

The voices were a constant murmur now, and she looked at the door. "I want you to take me while they stand outside."

He slid his zipper down, parting his jeans that dipped low on his hips. "Are you going to scream for me when you come?"

Another arch of her body in invitation. "Don't I always?"

He took her mouth in a brutal kiss, and when he let her go she swayed. His lips skimmed down her jaw, pausing at her ear. "I'm going to fuck you loud and dirty."

With those words she lost all sense of reason. A low, needy sound vibrated from her throat and she grabbed for his jeans and yanked them down. He pushed the contents of her desk aside, sending items to the floor with a loud clatter before pushing her down with a press of his palm.

Crazy now, past caring or thinking, she hooked her leg over his hip. Desperate for him.

He looked down at her, shaking his head. "I love you like this. All panting and desperate."

"Now." Was that voice even hers? Filled with rasp and smoke and heat.

He tugged her panties down her legs, tossed them to the floor, reached into his pocket and took out a condom. He ripped it with his teeth, made quick work rolling it down his shaft, before filling her with one powerful thrust.

She arched off the desk and let out a gasp.

He rocked into her, circling his hips and she ground back, in a rhythm they'd perfected long ago, but was now all the better. Because he filled her, completely. He set a slow, grinding pace that had her moaning and mindless. It was just as he promised, loud, dirty, and he played her body like it was made for him, managing to bring her to the edge of orgasm without sending her tumbling over.

His hands on either side of her head, he bent low. "Look at me."

Her lashes fluttered open and their gazes locked together.

"Mine." His voice a low growl.

"Yes." Her hand slid around his neck, wanting him close, needing to touch him.

"I know your secrets."

Sweat broke out along her spine as he angled his hips, his pelvis rubbing against her clit.

Beyond reason, the words fell from her lips. "Harder. More. Please."

"Christ." His hips started to move faster. Deeper and more punishing.

He hit a spot that had her keening perilously out of control. "Mark me. I need it."

He banged his fist on the table. "You're killing me."

"More," she gasped out. Another thrust she rose to meet.

"You need to be marked." A low, primal growl that set all her own primitive desires.

"Yes." Claimed. Fucked. Taken. Marked. And any other possession he could grant her.

He set a dirty pace that took her breath away.

Climbing faster and higher than before, she moaned. "So good."

He bent down, covering her. "That's right, Pen, it's so fucking good. Nothing feels as good as your tight, wet pussy squeezing my cock."

She whimpered, the orgasm building inside her picking up velocity and strength.

"Let me hear you," he urged, his lips skimming down

her neck. He shifted and hit a spot so good it ripped a short scream from her throat. "Let everyone hear you."

He bit her and she cried out.

He groaned. Fucked her harder. Deeper.

Unable to control the stream of sounds coming from her any longer, he covered her mouth with his hand. "Go ahead and scream. It just makes me harder to watch you struggle."

And that was it. She tumbled right off the edge of the cliff, coming so hard she thought she might pass out as she climaxed and pulsed crazily around him as he drove into her again and again and she loved every single second of it. Loved every second of him.

Still trembling, he cursed and thrust into her once more in a vicious motion as he came, pumping hard inside her.

He collapsed on top of her as they fought to get control of their breathing and quell her shaking muscles, spent body, and overactive mind.

When they'd finally calmed, and her pulse no longer felt like it was going to pound out of her neck, he gave her a soft kiss. "We're a mess."

She smiled and brushed a lock of hair off his forehead with trembling fingers. She loved him. She'd never stopped loving him. He was it for her. It terrified her. "We are."

Another brush of his lips. "But I know you're the kind of girl who's prepared for anything, so I'm guessing you have a roll of paper towels, hand wipes, and various other cleaning supplies on hand."

Boneless and satisfied, her muscles like Jell-O, a surprise giggle slipped from her throat. "You know me too well."

He straightened and pulled out, then slowly ran the tip of his finger over her belly.

She flushed. "I, um, went a little crazy there at the end."

"I go a little crazy every time I'm inside you." His voice an intimate rumble.

She propped herself up on her elbows and looked down. Clothes a mess, her dress open, she looked wanton.

Exactly right.

Chapter Twenty-Two

Life had been perfect. Too perfect. She'd had ten days of absolute bliss. Ten days of Evan. Ten days of falling deeper and deeper in love with him. And now she was paying the price for all that obnoxious happiness with the day from hell.

This morning she'd overslept and things had gone downhill from there. She'd had to forgo her early morning yoga class, which put her in a bad mood. Then, because Evan was sleeping in her bed, she'd had to rush around her bedroom while trying to be quiet. At one point, as she was eating a piece of toast while trying to put on her shoes, she'd looked at him sprawled out on the mattress, resting peacefully, and wanted to chuck one of her heels at his head.

She'd left for work officially crabby.

The day had gone downhill from there.

There was a contract dispute with the city.

One of their largest projects was behind schedule and over budget.

She and Shane had had words about one of the project directors.

Every meeting she'd had was filled with problems.

She'd barely had time to breathe or think, let alone eat. Her mood had gone from crabby to downright bitchy. Shane was on the warpath.

Everyone was tense.

Shane called an emergency meeting at five o'clock, where they'd been ever since. Now two hours later, Penelope rubbed her aching temples. "Let's take fifteen minutes."

Shane, his sleeves rolled up to the elbows, nodded. "Fine, but we're not leaving until we have answers."

Penelope envisioned fifteen stifled groans. She jumped up and ran to the bathroom before her bladder exploded.

Two minutes later she stood in the stall, her hands clenched into fists at her sides.

She'd gotten her period.

She tugged her suit jacket. Great. Fantastic.

She was relieved. So, so relieved. At least she believed it was relief sitting heavy in her chest. Of course it was relief, what else could it be?

A baby was the last thing on earth she needed.

Her throat tightened and the sting of tears threatened. All the muscles in her face tightened.

Oh no!

Those were not tears. She would not cry.

She had nothing to cry about. She was happy. Thrilled.

This was PMS, plain and simple. She didn't want a baby. God, she couldn't even imagine. Look at her, it was seven and she was still at work. When would she even see a baby? And then there was Evan; yeah, things were good between them for now, but that was bound to change once the sex wore off. Once they settled into real life and the newness of being able to touch each other lost its luster.

Because the sex was ridiculous and destined to fade. To lessen in its intensity. They'd get this all worked out of their systems, he'd get bored, and then what? Did she really want to be a single mother?

See, her period was the best thing that had happened to her all day.

She should be celebrating.

A little sob slipped from her lips and she viciously shoved it back down.

She would not cry.

She was happy.

Crisis averted.

She started counting all the reasons she was lucky to not be pregnant.

All the logical, pragmatic, sensible reasons.

When she was under control, and she'd properly shoved whatever emotional outburst she'd been about to have back where it came from, she smoothed down her clothes, washed her hands, and returned to work.

Never to think about this again.

At nine, Penelope walked in looking exhausted and strained. Evan put down the computer and sat up, making room for her on the couch. "Tough day at the office?"

She kicked off her shoes and left them in the middle of the floor in a haphazard heap instead of lined up on the stairs like she normally did. "Something like that."

She stripped off her suit jacket, threw it on the chair, and crawled onto the couch. "How was your day?"

It had been a good day, a great day. He'd had four interviews with key members of the coaching and front office staffs, and later the offensive coordinator called him and told him he was currently the front-runner for the job. He had a meeting with the head coach and GM at the end of the week and he was one step closer to securing his future.

He hadn't told anyone, and planned to keep it to himself unless he got an offer. If things didn't pan out, he'd have to sit down and talk to Penelope about options, but he'd cross that bridge when he came to it.

He tugged her wrist and pulled her so her head rested on his lap. "Better than yours, from the looks of it. Want to talk about it?"

"No." She closed her eyes and he began pulling pins from her hair. "What did you do today?"

"I tried to cook you dinner."

"I'm sorry I'm so late," she said, her voice already heavy and sleepy.

He stroked her hair off her cheek. "Don't be. All you missed was the disaster."

A smile flirted over her lips. "No good?"

He dropped the pins on the end table and shifted his fingers through the thick strands. "The guy on YouTube made it look so easy."

"They always do." She yawned. "I just need to rest."

"I'll try not to wake you during the night." He did that sometimes. Wake up from dreams where he was racing down the field, his blood pumping with adrenaline that had no outlet, a warm, sweet Penelope curled against him. Naked. He'd seduce her awake, then take her with a ferocity that bordered on violent, until they both fell back into an exhausted sleep. He ran a palm down her rib cage.

She tensed, all her muscles tightening under his touch. With her eyes still closed she said, "Probably for the best. I got my period today."

The sharp stab of disappointment that sliced through him surprised him. It wasn't like he'd actually expected her to be pregnant; in fact, he'd tried not to think too much about the day they'd dropped those pills down the sink. He'd assumed the avoidance stemmed from not wanting to think about the panic he'd probably experience if she was. Now he knew the truth. He hadn't wanted to think about it because deep down there was a part of him that wanted to get caught. Wanted her to have no excuse but to stay with him.

He had no idea what to say or how she felt, so he said the first thing that popped into his head. "I'm sorry."

Her lids snapped open. "Why? This is a good thing."

His fingers played down her body, sliding over the silk of her white blouse and fabric of her gray skirt. If that was true, why was she coiled tight? "There's not a little part of you that's disappointed?"

She sat up as though she'd been catapulted off his lap. "Of course not. That's the last thing I wanted. God, can you even imagine?"

Instinct warned him to tread lightly. She was like a skittish colt—or at least what he imagined a skittish colt would act like. One sudden move would send her running. He expelled a breath. "Yeah, actually I kind of can."

Her brows slammed together. "Don't be insane."

Everything about her was on edge. Her shoulders were at her ears, her expression too fierce, her voice too high, her eyes too bright. He reached for her and said softly, "Penelope."

She reared back before he could touch her. "It's fine, Evan. Don't talk crazy."

"I'm not saying it's not for the best. I'm only suggesting that it's okay to be a little disappointed."

"I am *not* disappointed," she shrieked, and sprang up from the couch and swiped her shoes from the floor. "I'm going to bed. Maybe you should see yourself out."

And with that, she stomped up the stairs and a second later a door slammed.

Well, shit. Now what?

Penelope locked the door of the bathroom, grabbed a towel and slid to the floor. What had she done? She'd acted crazy and emotional, and she'd revealed far too much. Evan wasn't stupid, and he was far too in tune with her moods, and her deepest and most intimate thoughts. God, this was humiliating. The last thing she wanted was Evan believing she was all upset because she wasn't going to live out some tabloid dream of being the NFL bad boy's baby momma.

Besides, she was not disappointed.

Again, she repeated her list of all the reasons it was great she wasn't pregnant.

Then she buried her face in the fluffy white towel and the tears that had threatened all day burst forth, and she started to sob. Cry in a way she hadn't cried since that night Evan deserted her. She hated it. Hated every second of the disappointment she had no right to feel crushing her chest. But she couldn't stop it. Couldn't get it under control. No matter how much she tried, the tears would not relent.

There was a knock on the door.

She raised her head and yelled, "Go away, Evan."

She just needed him to go away. To leave her alone. To give her five seconds to breathe and regain her composure.

"No. I can't do that, Penelope."

She cursed, and buried her head again to stifle the noise of the sob tearing from her throat. Why couldn't she get him to go? "I want you to leave. I want to be alone."

There was noise against the door, and when Evan spoke his voice was more at her level. "No, you don't. You don't want me to see you upset. There's a difference."

"I'm not upset!" She ferociously wiped the tears from her cheeks.

There was a moment of silence. "Then why are you crying?"

She leaned her head against the door. "Please, just go. I've had a really bad day and I want to go to sleep."

"I can't force you to talk, but I'm not leaving you."

She needed that other Evan right now. The one who bailed when things got tough. The one who brought home Playboy bunnies and played Xbox and got drunk all day. He'd leave. He wouldn't even look back. Where was that guy?

Because she couldn't handle one more second of mature, understanding Evan.

When the flow of tears finally ebbed, she took a deep breath, got up and washed her face with ice-cold water. She put drops in her eyes, smoothed moisturizer over her skin, brushed her teeth and hair, and slipped into a night-gown she'd had hanging on a hook behind the door.

Next time she looked in the mirror there was no evidence of her emotional outburst other than the heavy ache sitting in the center of her chest. She opened the door and Evan sat on the bed, elbows on his knees, wearing a cautious expression.

Throat swelling, she didn't trust herself to speak. Instead she walked around to her side of the bed and climbed in, pulling the covers up to her chin, turning on her side.

There was a deep sigh from Evan before he got up.

She held her breath and waited for him to leave, caught between relief she'd be alone and fear he'd walk out and never come back. He had to be wondering what had become of the sane, rational woman he knew.

When she heard the pull of his belt, she let out a low hiss of air as another tear slipped out of the corner of her eye to fall onto her pillow.

There was more rustling of fabric and then a *thud* on the floor. A second later the bed creaked as he climbed in.

She tensed.

He slipped his arm around her and pulled her close, kissing her temple.

The strength of his body felt so good against her

back, safe and warm. Settled against her he just fit, fit like nobody else.

She relaxed and he squeezed her tight. Here in the dark, where he couldn't read her face, she could let herself need him.

He whispered into her ear, "I wanted to get caught too, Pen."

She burrowed deeper into him, his cock brushing the curve of her ass. She didn't want to think, all she wanted was to get lost in him. She pressed back, tilting her hips.

He shuddered and his mouth fell to her neck. He kissed the skin there, lips open, tongue sliding along her skin.

It was like lighting a match and tossing it into lighter fluid, and the flames engulfed her. She craned her neck, tilted her chin, and that was all the invitation he needed for his mouth to claim hers.

It started out as a soft, gentle kiss, but it was like something snapped between them.

Everything was hungry. A raw, ravaging desire that would not be satiated. Their mouths a frantic, consuming meld as their tongues met.

She twisted, facing him, and his hand slid into her hair, gripping her tight and holding her still for his onslaught.

And he was brutal. Hard. Demanding. Filled with unleashed passion.

Perfect. Just what she needed, to forget. She moaned and her nails dug into his shoulders. She shifted, throwing her leg over his hip. Pressing closer. Closer.

His hands sought to gain entry under her nightgown, but the fabric was twisted and prevented access. He squeezed her through the cloth. With him, it was never enough. He could never claim her enough.

He growled, reached for the straps of silk at her shoulders and yanked them until her breasts spilled free. He cupped them, rubbed his thumbs over the peaks as he kissed her.

He rolled her nipples, finding that sweet spot between pleasure and pain that drove her crazy, and she cried out. He lifted his head and slid down, capturing her nipple with his lips. He licked and sucked until she was writhing and gasping his name.

He lifted his head. "What do you want?"

"You." God, that was all she wanted. All she needed in this moment.

He laved the hard buds, lapping and nipping and pinching until they were red and she was rocking against him. Her hands a frantic pull and drag over his skin. "My period."

He lifted his head and covered her lips before saying, "I don't give a fuck about your period."

He might not, but she did. She shook her head. "We can't."

He growled, took her hips and flipped her to her back, before rolling against her. "Fine. We'll do this old-school."

He shimmied his hips, then positioned her so her blue panties were flush against his cotton-covered erection. He squeezed her ass.

"Evan," she said, her voice hoarse. She pressed her forehead against his and began that slow, ancient grind against him.

They'd had plenty of practice and they knew just what they were doing. Their hips moved in circles, retreating and coming together in hard little surges. His cock thrust against her clit. And despite not being inside her, she wanted him so bad it wouldn't take long.

He moaned, and moved his hands to her questing hips, helping her so they rocked hard together. Her head fell back and her breasts bounced and he dug his fingers into her ass hard enough to leave bruises. It was just what she needed and she moaned out. "Oh God."

He increased the pace.

And she met him, stroke for stroke, pounding against him, working her hips. Sweat slicked down her spine and beaded at her temples, and when the first swell of her climax threatened she pushed it away, not wanting it to end.

When they were like this, crazy and full of that relentless desire that drove them, nothing else mattered. There was no thinking. No future or past. There was just now.

"Fuck. Right there." He played with her nipple, rubbing over the hard peak in circles.

"Yes," she said, her hips moving faster and faster.

He growled. A low, primal sound of satisfaction. He gripped her hips. "I'm going to come all over you."

That one image was all it took to push her over the edge. She cried out, moving faster and faster until she came in a wild rush that sent her over the edge. Her nails raked down his back as the orgasm crashed through her in hard, ruthless waves of pure ecstasy.

He reared up, pulled out his cock, and aimed, his hand flying as all his muscles bunched up tight. He came all over her breasts in hard jerks and angry splashes that landed on her neck and nipples as he decorated her skin.

Panting for breath, they just stared at each other, their eyes dazed and wide. His chest heaved and he dragged a finger over the wetness, then painted her full, swollen lips. He shook his head. "Fucking gorgeous."

Her tongue flicked out and licked over his finger and he groaned.

She whispered, "Do it again."

"You're going to be the death of me." He traced a slippery spot over her nipple and something hot shivered through her. "I like you marked."

She nodded.

His eyes met hers. "And you like being marked."

She licked him from her lips. "I do."

As the aftershocks wore off, and the mad rush of desire calmed, the sadness she couldn't seem to shake rolled over her.

She didn't want to be sad. Didn't want to feel like she'd just lost something important. She wanted to go back to looking at everything rationally.

She didn't want to mourn for a mythical baby she had no right to.

She ran a hand through Evan's hair. "I'm sorry. I had a bad day and I took it out on you."

"We should talk." Even in the darkness she could see the concern on his face.

"Can't we just rest? I'm so tired."

"All right." He brushed her cheek. "I'll get a washcloth so I can clean you up."

He rose from the bed, his golden, muscled body beautiful in the moonlight. How had this happened? How was he even in her bed? Sleeping with her every night.

Making her need him. Love him. Want things.

She turned to stare up at the ceiling. She wanted to be sane, normal Penny again.

Chapter Twenty-Three

To say the week had been tense was an understatement. It was like Penelope just shut down and Evan had no idea what to do about it. Of course he had no actual relationship skills, having spent the last twenty years screwing around and then taking off when the woman started to expect anything. He'd tried to talk to her, but she kept insisting she was fine. And hell, even he knew a woman saying she was fine was not a good sign.

He was convinced she was upset about not being pregnant, but she refused to discuss it. Again, saying she was fine. In fact, she'd gone as far as making a doctor's appointment to get on birth control to prevent any other unfortunate accidents.

Her words.

He'd supported her, and logically it was the right move, since sex seemed to be the only thing they had actually figured out, but it didn't change the instinct that warned him everything was about to go to shit.

Evan hoped the long weekend in Revival with their friends and family would put things back on track, but only time would tell.

After miles and miles of Illinois cornfields, abandoned

farms, and silence, Evan finally couldn't take it any longer. He blew out a breath. "Are you ever going to tell me what's wrong?"

"Nothing is wrong." She stared out the window, her shoulders tightening.

Frustration turned to anger and he snapped. "You know, this is never going to work out if you won't fucking talk to me."

Still not facing him, she took in a shuddery breath. "Then maybe it won't work out."

"That's all you have to say?"

"What would you like me to say?"

"Yell at me. Hell, throw things. Break something. Tell me you hate me. But this silence, this wall between us . . ." He swallowed hard.

"It feels like before." She delivered the words quietly, with no real inflection.

Yes, that's exactly what it felt like. That last morning between them when everything had been broken and over. And that was just fucking unacceptable. He glanced in the rearview mirror, then swerved to the side of the road, slamming on the brakes.

That got her attention and she gasped, grabbing the dashboard before whirling to glare at him. "What the hell do you think you're doing?"

He just stopped. Stopped trying to figure her out, stopped trying to figure out what she wanted him to say or do. Stopped trying to prove anything to her. Stopped waiting until that magical day when she believed him, because more and more it was looking like that wasn't going to come. He shifted in his seat and faced her. "Are you ever going to stop trying to push me away?"

Her already brilliant blue eyes brightened until they were electric, but she didn't say anything.

He just gave in to his darkest fears because he didn't

know what else to do. He clutched the steering wheel. "You're never going to believe me, are you? I broke what we had too well, and now I can't fix it. You're never going to trust me with anything but your body, are you?"

She clutched at her seat belt. "I don't know if I can."

He shook his head. "And I don't know how to prove something to you that you can't see, that you can't calculate in one of your spreadsheets. I have no idea what you're thinking, or how you feel, and I don't know how to force you to tell me. I can't block and tackle my way out of this. It's like that last hit that did me in. I knew it would be bad, I knew I probably wouldn't make it, and I still went for the touchdown. So that's all I can do with you. I'm going to go for the touchdown, Pen. I'll either win the game or go down in a blaze, but at least I'm not taking the easy way out."

The cords in her neck worked as she swallowed and clenched her hands in her lap. "What are you saying?"

He shifted to face her more fully, then he cupped her jaw and forced her to at least meet his gaze. When her eyes met his, the tears were bright and one slipped down her cheek and he brushed it away. "I love you, Penelope. I have loved you since I was seventeen years old and I will love you when I'm ninety-five. You are, and will be, the only girl I ever love. On the side of the road in the middle of nowhere isn't where I wanted to tell you. I had some grand gesture in mind. One that somehow would allow you to seep inside me and see how I feel about you. That would convince you."

He let her chin go and stroked a path down her throat, loving how she shuddered under his touch. "Tell me how to make you believe."

She said nothing, and other than the tears spilling down her cheeks, he had no idea what was going on in that mind of hers. He waited. Then she buried her face in her hands and started to sob.

Unbuckling her seat belt, he gathered her up close, cradling her in his arms as she shook. He kissed the top of her head and rubbed her back in slow circles as he murmured what he hoped were soothing noises.

When she finally settled he lifted her chin with the crook of his finger. "I belong to you. I always have and always will." Her attention skirted away, but that didn't deter him. "You can't get rid of me."

She pressed a finger to her lips.

She didn't speak, and he didn't push. Everything about them was too raw, so he let her settle back into her seat. When she looked out the window again he sighed and pulled back onto the road. They drove in silence for fifteen minutes before she spoke. "Evan?"

"Yes?"

She didn't turn to face him, just continued to stare out into the cornfields. "I love you too."

He took her hand and brought it to his lips.

At least it was something.

They'd made the drive to Revival but the long, scenic roads did nothing to clear her mind. Evan had left her alone in the guest room at Maddie and Mitch's house to take a call, and now she was alone with her thoughts.

She touched the windowpanes that looked out over Maddie's backyard. It was green and lush, filled with weeping willows and large oak trees. There were wildflowers, hydrangea bushes, and roses scattered through the yard, and beyond the trees lay the glimmer of a river running a lazy path.

It was the most idyllic place Penelope had ever seen. Peaceful and serene.

Later this afternoon they'd head down for a swim. There would be laughter, music, and alcohol. It would be like stepping into another time. Her muscles would relax, the sun would warm her skin, and they'd all catch a little buzz. And maybe, just maybe, this god-awful feeling would go away.

She pressed her forehead to the glass and closed her eyes.

Evan loved her.

The only boy she'd ever wanted since she was six years old had just told her he loved her, and she couldn't get rid of the heavy feeling in her chest. It was like a lead weight had settled on her sternum and refused to budge.

Everything he'd said in that car had been right.

She didn't believe. Not the way she should. She didn't trust him.

But it was more than that; she didn't trust herself. Not where he was concerned.

Ever since she'd gotten her period she'd had to come face-to-face with the truth. She was scared, and she wanted to keep him.

Being pregnant had guaranteed that.

She hated herself for the thought. It was wrong. But true. She wanted to keep him so badly it had become twisted in her brain. How could she admit that to him? To anyone? She just had to figure out how to get over that feeling of loss on her own.

The door opened and she lifted her head, opening her eyes when it clicked shut. Evan came up behind her and put his arms around her waist. He kissed her temple. "You okay?"

"Yes." Although her voice held the barest of tremors. She'd lost it in the car. She didn't know what came over her, but it was like a dam had broken and her emotions were one big giant swinging pendulum. "Was everything okay on the phone?"

"It's all good." His hold tightened around her waist, and despite her unsettledness a surge of desire pulsed through her.

No matter what, she couldn't keep from wanting him. Needing him. And maybe that was the problem.

Evan was the one thing she couldn't put into a neat little box. Nothing about him or them was contained, and for a woman who thrived on organization and order, it was uncomfortable.

But he was trying so hard, and what she needed right now was so unfair, she had to start somewhere. She had to let him in, at least a little. That much she could do.

"I'm sorry. I don't know what to say," she admitted.

He let her go and tugged her toward the bed. When her knees hit the mattress he pushed her down before running a hand down her legs to take off first one shoe, and then the other. Then he climbed onto the bed with her and laid a palm over the flat of her stomach, propping his head on his other hand.

He looked down at her, his green eyes intent, his features so gorgeous she wanted to reach up and trace the lines of his bones to make sure he was real. Flesh and blood.

Mortal like she was.

She didn't know how to stop seeing him as the boy she'd idolized. The one who held all the power, and her heart, in his big hands.

He slid his thigh along her leg, leaned down and brushed a kiss over her lips. "I'm sorry things are never easy with us."

Her throat grew tight. "You're right. I don't believe."

He nodded. "I know."

She swallowed hard, hoping against hope to quell the tears. "I thought . . . when all this craziness began . . . that it was just a matter of getting it out of our systems."

His hand smoothed over her belly. "That's never going to happen."

"It's hard." She bit her lip. "I have all these years of watching you pretend to not care about me. Parading one beautiful woman after another in front of me. In all that time you never even hinted. You never even glanced in my direction. It was like after that night, what we'd done was a figment of my imagination. *That's* the evidence I have. This, now, is the dream."

His expression clouded, turning as dark as a storm cloud. "I played my part too well, and now I have to pay the price. I told you when this started I'd pay, and I will, because you're worth it, whatever the cost."

"But it's not fair."

He shrugged. "Life's not always fair. I can deal with that, I just don't want you to shut me out."

"I'll try."

They fell silent for a while, just lay on the bed, their bodies close, their breathing moving in time, perfectly synchronized.

She didn't care what he said, she couldn't keep doing this to him. To herself. It wasn't healthy, and she'd always been proud of how she handled life. She either needed to believe, or she needed to let him go.

It was really that simple.

There was a soft knock and Maddie called through the door, "We're all going down by the river. Are you coming?"

They looked at each other and Penelope called back, "We'll be right down."

"Good, 'cause he's had you long enough. I need my girlfriend, Evan."

He laughed and shook his head. "In a minute."

Evan ran a hand through his hair and she moved to get up, but before she rose, he placed a palm on her stomach, immobilizing her. "Before we go, let me ask you something."

Brow raised, she looked at him.

"You were a good actor too. We've fooled a lot of people over the years, including your best friends. You never hinted either. But it was all a lie, wasn't it? Hidden away, beyond all that efficiency and control and dismissal, you still wanted me. Right?"

There was no use in pretending otherwise. "Yes."

He leaned down and kissed her, a soft, deep kiss that filled her with a hope and promise that made her want to cry. Then he pulled away and trailed a finger over her jaw. "Isn't it possible that if you felt all that for me and managed to hide it, that the same could be true for me?"

She blinked. Was it? She didn't know.

But she wanted to believe.

Chapter Twenty-Four

Evan left Penelope to catch up with the girls while he met the guys down by the river. Blankets were already stretched out on the grass, speakers blared classic rock, and drinks had already been passed. It felt almost like high school, although back then they'd spent their time in the woods of a forest preserve. He grabbed a beer from the cooler and sat down on one of the beach chairs next to Shane and Mitch before twisting off the cap and throwing it into the makeshift garbage. Opposite them, James and Mitch's best friend, Sheriff Charlie Radcliffe, were involved in some sort of intense discussion about forensic evidence.

If things with Penelope weren't so precarious, life would be pretty close to perfect. He'd never play football again, but he would be a wide receiver coach, and he actually felt pretty damn good about it. Penelope had been right that night she'd come to him; football was a young man's game, and in that world he'd been almost past his prime. Yes, he could have played for a couple more years, but the truth he hadn't wanted to face was that that part of his career had been coming to an end. Life had a way of taking decisions out of your hands, but he was starting to come to peace with it.

He'd still get to be part of the game he loved and in the city he loved, close to his family.

And Penelope. If she let him in. Right now that seemed a big if. There was something wrong, something she wasn't telling him, and he had some ideas of what it might be but hadn't puzzled it all out yet.

Shane cocked a brow. "How's it going?"

"Pretty good." Evan flipped his sunglasses over his eyes and stretched out his legs. It was hot and humid, but the sun felt good on his skin. He nodded at Mitch. "You taking care of my sister?"

A huge grin spread over Mitch's face. "Always."

"Good. How's life over in small-town prosecution?"

Mitch shrugged. "Fairly boring but sane. I'm thinking of making a move to the state attorney's office."

Shane scrubbed a hand over his jaw. "Come back to Chicago and work for me. You're there all the time anyway."

Mitch grew up in Chicago and had been a big-time criminal defense lawyer but, after a fall from grace, moved to Revival and never left. Every once in a while Shane liked to suggest Mitch come work for him, but Evan suspected it was all in good fun.

Mitch shook his head and gave Shane a no-fucking-way glare. "Not in a million years."

Shane grinned. "Everyone thinks I'm so hard to work for, but look at Penelope. She manages to survive quite nicely." He took a slug of beer before shifting his attention to Evan. "And speaking of our girl, how is she doing?"

"My girl," Evan corrected before flashing his brother a grin. Things were better between them and they were both trying to let go of the past and focus on being brothers. "Does Cecilia know you're this possessive over Penelope?"

Shane laughed. "Yeah, she's learned to live with it. Although you sleeping with her helps considerably."

"Glad to help you out," Evan said, his voice wry.

Shane moved in his chair. "But seriously, is everything okay? She seems stressed, which isn't at all like her. I tried to talk to her, but she basically stonewalled me."

Evan made sure to keep totally still, to not tense his muscles at all. "She's fine."

Shane looked at him for a long time before taking another swallow of beer. "All right."

Before there were any more questions, James's head shot up and his brow furrowed. "Woman, where are your clothes?"

Evan turned in the direction of James's dark scowl and about choked on his beer. Gracie strolled down the path in the most minuscule excuse for a bathing suit that was ever invented. The bikini was the same color blue as her eyes and it somehow managed to support her overflowing breasts while still being skimpy.

"Oh no," Shane said under his breath. "I swear she lives to get him all riled up."

Mitch chuckled. "Gracie? No, never."

"Doesn't sound like her at all," Evan agreed.

All three of them shifted their chairs to watch the show.

Gracie beamed, her hair up in a ponytail, tendrils curling around her face. She waved, her new diamond ring flashing in the sun. "I assume everyone's ready for a good time."

James narrowed his eyes. "I believe a question is on the table, Grace."

Grace. That was new.

She winked at Shane, Mitch, and Evan before waving a hand over her spectacular body. The woman belonged in a *Playboy* spread, no question about it. "What? This old thing?"

His brother's jaw turned hard. "Are you trying to get me worked up?"

She laughed, low and seductive. "What was your first clue, honey?"

James closed his eyes and took a deep breath. "I will not give in. I will not give in."

Gracie shrugged and lay down on the blanket right in front of James. "Suit yourself. I'll just rub this oil all over." Then she proceeded to do just that, really slathering it on with elaborate care.

Evan watched, amused at this woman who'd captured his brother's heart and made him crazy in the best possible way. Much like with Penelope, it was a match nobody saw coming, but it was clear the two were perfect for each other, balancing each other out and making them stronger as individuals.

It's what he wanted to be for Penelope, but he was pretty sure he was failing. The key to her heart a mystery to him.

James ran a finger over the curve of Gracie's breast. "You missed a spot."

She grinned and arched into his touch. "Do you mind?"

James's gaze flicked over her. "You can manage. I know you have plenty of practice touching yourself."

Gracie slicked an unnecessary amount of oil onto her stomach. "Careful, or everyone might think you can't satisfy me."

He laughed, as if the idea was completely preposterous, which Evan was pretty sure was probably true. "Or maybe they all know you can't resist putting on a good show."

Charlie chuckled in that low, lazy way that revealed the last hints of his Southern roots. "He's got you there."

"You just shut up," she said with a glower before pouting

at James. "Shouldn't you be jealous? He's, like, staring right at me."

Once upon a time Gracie and Charlie had a friends-with-benefits relationship that ended about the second she met James, although it had taken a good long time for the two most stubborn people on the planet to admit they were attracted to each other.

James glanced at Charlie, sighed, and said in a deadpan voice, "I've gotten used to him."

"You are no fun, Professor."

"Too bad you're stuck with me."

Gracie huffed and adjusted her bikini top. "It's quite the hardship."

James pinched her and she let out a yelp. "I should drag you to the garage apartment and teach you a lesson, but I'd hate to ruin your fun."

Evan had no idea what James did to Gracie in that apartment, but he'd heard screaming more than once and he guessed it wasn't from torture, with the way she sucked in her breath.

She licked her lips. "Promise?"

James traced a path over her oil-slicked belly. "Promise. This bathing suit is already on the list. Do your worst, baby girl."

Gracie shuddered, and after that seemed to miraculously settle down, making Evan wonder if that's what she'd been after all along.

Ten minutes later the rest of the girls came down the path. His sister and Sophie wore their swimsuits, but only Penelope looked all proper in her cover-up. A black number that zipped from her neck, all the way to her knees. Her hair was in a ponytail and her skin was free of makeup. She looked a lot less pinched than when he'd left her, and he was grateful his sister and Sophie had obviously done the trick.

And jealous, because he wanted it to be him.

Shane looked around them. "Where's Ce-ce?"

Maddie waved toward the house. "She had to take a call, she'll be here."

Penelope glanced at him and offered a small smile before shifting her attention to the water. "Is it nice?"

"Cold, but nice," Mitch said, reaching up to Maddie's arm, before rubbing a hand over her stomach. "Everything okay?"

Maddie grinned and pushed his hand away. "Everything is fine."

Penelope still stared out at the water. "I'll warm up first." She walked over to the cooler. "Anyone want anything?"

Maddie sat down next to Mitch and Sophie plopped down on the blanket as Penelope fetched cans and bottles from the cooler. After handing out drinks, Penelope looked around, her brow furrowing as she chewed her bottom lip. Her gaze fluttered toward him before looking away.

He silently willed her to come to him, but he supposed old habits die hard, because she sat down next to Sophie. A second later she pulled her sunglasses from the top of her head and covered her eyes.

Evan stifled his sigh.

Sophie perched up on her elbows. "Pass me the sunscreen, Pen." Penelope picked up a bottle of Coppertone and passed it to her friend, who frowned. "Aren't you hot?"

Penelope shrugged. "I'm okay."

Sophie squirted a big blob of lotion on her hand and passed it to Penelope. "Stay awhile. Relax. Get some sun."

Penelope glanced up at the afternoon sky. "I could use a little color."

"Exactly," Sophie said.

Penelope unzipped her cover-up and tossed it to the grass down by her bare feet. She wore a black bikini, with gold circles on either side of her hip and between her breasts that held the suit together.

Evan immediately wanted to cover her back up, suddenly sympathizing with James.

Maddie whistled. "Damn, girl. That is a hot suit."

Damn indeed.

"That's enough out of you," Penelope said.

Charlie rubbed his jaw and gave her a long, appreciative once-over. "New suit, Pen?"

Evan shifted in his seat and his fingers tightened reflexively on his beer.

Next to him, Shane mumbled under his breath, "Easy there."

Penelope refused to look at Evan but did turn to glare at Sophie. "Why do I let you talk me into these things?"

Sophie laughed before adjusting the white bottoms she wore. She raised her oversized Chanel sunglasses and propped them on the top of her head. "Because you know I'm right and always pick out the best things." She tossed a sly glance at Evan. "Didn't I do good?"

"Helpful as always, Soph." Evan's gaze raked down Penelope's body. Gracie wasn't the only one working on a payment plan.

Maddie curled up next to Mitch and turned her attention to Evan. "So, what's new with you?"

All eyes shifted to him.

Well, he supposed now was as good a time as any to share the news. When he'd first gotten off the phone he'd thought he'd wait until after the weekend, but there was no real reason to keep quiet. Everyone was here, and at least this way everyone could stop worrying about his future and what he was going to do about it.

Evan cleared his throat. "I got offered a job with the Bears."

Shane grinned and clapped him on the back. "Really? Good for you. Doing what?"

"Wide receiver coach." Evan shrugged. "It's a start."

Maddie clapped, and jumped up to hug him. "Oh my God, that's fantastic! Congratulations!" She whirled to Penelope. "I can't believe you didn't tell me."

In that second Evan realized his mistake.

Penelope's head tilted, her beautiful mouth pursed in surprise. She opened her hands in a gesture of surrender. "What can I say, it was a surprise."

Evan experienced a sudden sinking in the pit of his stomach.

"I thought you didn't want to coach," Shane said.

Evan drained the rest of his beer. "I changed my mind."

Shane's expression filled with pleasure and he called out to James, "Did you hear that, Jimmy? You're going to have to start watching football again."

James flashed him a grin, then nodded. "Never had any doubts at all."

Evan had, about a great many things. Including the stupid decision to spontaneously announce a job offer Penelope knew nothing about.

One look at her distant expression, tight shoulders, and silence told him everything he needed to know.

Things had just gone from bad to worse.

The afternoon passed in a lazy way that reminded Penelope of the summers they'd spent in high school wasting the day at Oak Street Beach, only better. It was small, intimate, and she was doing a good imitation of someone having a good time. The strawberry margaritas Gracie made were strong, delicious, and Penelope had just the right amount of buzz.

It was hot, sticky, and humid. The air smelled like earth, water, and summer. The day worked its magic and all the tension drained away from all her muscles.

Too bad she was furious.

And hurt.

Evan never even told her he was looking for a job. As far as she'd known, he'd been spending his days playing Xbox and working out at the gym. Because she loved him, she was happy for him; he deserved to find something he loved that he could spend his time on and be successful at.

That wasn't what she was mad about. She was mad because he'd never even told her and it just seemed like one more example of everything that was wrong between them. One more piece of evidence stacked against them that proved they couldn't make this transition into the real world.

She took a deep breath. Now wasn't the time. Now she needed to focus on her friends. And squeezing whatever fun she could find out of this day.

She sat on the dock with her two best girls, their toes in the water as they watched the boys in the river, frolicking around like puppies. Somewhere along the way, Mitch and Maddie had put a floating dock closer to the river's center and the guys were doing backflips into the river, trying to out-trick each other. She watched Evan. Water streamed off his golden skin, practically glittering in the sun. With his body, honed to perfection, his hair slicked back, and dark sunglasses on, he looked like one of those high-fashion magazine ads. His swim trunks rode so low they showed the cut of his hips she'd licked too many times to count.

He said he was hers. Said that he loved her. So why

hadn't he told her about this huge important thing in his life? Wasn't that what couples were supposed to do?

She blew out a long breath and took a sip of her drink, which Gracie had put in a stainless-steel travel mug so it wouldn't get warm. As the slushy strawberry liquid had slid down her dry throat, she wanted to thank Gracie, but she'd disappeared with James about an hour ago and hadn't returned.

Sophie sighed and looked up at the sky. "Man, this is the life."

"Yeah, it is." Maddie flung her arms around Sophie and Penelope. "I'm so glad you're here. I love when you guys visit."

Penelope squeezed back. "Me too."

And she was glad. She just needed to forget everything else and enjoy it.

Charlie climbed out of the river and sluiced water from his dark hair. Sophie whistled. "Damn, that man is one fine piece of ass."

Maddie laughed. "He is a work of art."

"Can't disagree with you there," Penelope said, because the Revival sheriff was the very definition of a fine piece of ass.

Sophie shot her a sly glance. "Even though you're officially dating an Adonis?"

Evan climbed out of the water too, standing next to Charlie, and the two of them made quite a sight. Penelope smiled. "I'm not dead."

Sophie exchanged a glance with Maddie. "But you are taken."

Penelope shrugged.

Maddie gave a frustrated little growl. "You're the most aggravating woman on the planet. Why won't you spill?"

She'd never been one to talk about the details of her love

life, even when they hadn't included Evan. "What would you like me to say?"

"What's going on with you two?" Maddie asked.

All Penelope's tumultuous emotions spun through her head at lightning speed. How she loved him more than she could even admit. The look on his face as he'd told her he loved her.

Was she supposed to say she mourned a pregnancy she hadn't even believed she'd wanted? Or that she ached for the kind of family they all took for granted?

She couldn't confess her fury that he'd started a career and hadn't even told her about it. His family was ecstatic and relieved. They'd never understand her hurt, nor would she subject them to it.

She dragged her foot through the water, closing her eyes as it cooled her off. She didn't want to think about that now. Those problems belonged in Chicago and not here, on this perfect day in this perfect spot.

"We're . . . taking things slow," she said, her voice careful.

Sophie snorted. "Isn't she just a blabbermouth?"

Maddie sighed. "She's already been drinking too."

Wanting to change the subject, Penelope said to Soph, "What about you? You haven't dated anyone."

Sophie shrugged. "I have so. I just haven't dated anyone noteworthy. And believe me, if I start dating an NFL pro-bowler, I sure as hell wouldn't be able to shut up about it."

Penelope tilted her chin toward Charlie. "I'm sure he'd be game for a hookup."

Maddie nodded in eager agreement. "I'm positive he would be."

Sophie sucked through her straw. "Nah, then I'd have to be awkward every time I saw him."

"I don't know about that," Maddie said. "Friends with

benefits seems to be his MO, and he's still friends with all his hookups."

Sophie wrinkled her nose. "Not interested. Besides, the guy doesn't know I'm alive."

"I highly doubt that." Penelope slurped the last of her drink through a straw and the loud noise filled the air. Maybe if she drank enough she could forget how miserable she was. "I'm empty. I'll get more."

Sophie handed over her cup, and Penelope looked at Maddie. "Hey, where's your drink?"

Maddie waved a hand. "Oh, I forgot it."

Sophie leaned back and looked Maddie up and down. "Wait a minute. You haven't had a drink all day."

Maddie's face flushed and her gaze darted away toward her husband. "I have so."

Penelope's stomach gave an uncomfortable little drop.

Sophie shook her head vigorously, her hammered-gold earrings glinting in the sun. "No, you haven't. You've pretended to drink."

Maddie bit her bottom lip. "No, I've drank, I swear."

Penelope's chest squeezed and her heart started to pound fast against her ribs.

Sophie gasped and pointed an accusatory finger at Maddie. "Oh my God, you're pregnant!"

"Shhhhhh!" Maddie glanced around. "I knew I wouldn't be able to pull it off with you guys. Please, don't say anything. We're going to tell everyone tonight at dinner."

Sophie squealed and clapped her hands. "Did you hear that, Pen? Our little girl is knocked up!"

Penelope felt the crush of something horrible settle inside her. It was ugly and wrong. It twisted in her belly, and for a second she thought she'd throw up. Sudden tears sprang to her eyes, and she blinked them away, thankful she wore oversized sunglasses. She put on her best and brightest smile and sat back down on the dock. "This is the best news I've heard in forever," she said enthusiastically.

"Thanks, guys," Maddie said, and gave a little sniff.

"Well, I'm furious you didn't tell us sooner," Sophie said with feigned indignation.

"I wanted to tell you in person. We were going to say something the weekend of the benefit, but then James and Gracie got engaged and I couldn't steal their thunder, so here we are. I'm officially fourteen weeks today. I've been to the doctor, had the first ultrasound, and the little bean was swimming away, healthy and strong. I can't wait to show you guys the picture. It's so cute!"

Sophie sniffed. "We're going to be aunts!"

"You are!" Maddie laughed, the sound happy and full of excitement.

With that one statement, everything that had been plaguing Penelope, everything that had been eating at her, rushed through her like a freight train. But she had to ignore all that, all the violent emotions storming through her, all the sadness and loneliness clogging her chest, and focus on her friend. Her *best* friend, whom she loved and adored and was thankful for every day. Maddie deserved all the happiness and excitement she'd worked so hard for; she deserved the very best. Penelope would give her no less.

Heart breaking, she put on her most brilliant smile. "I call baby shower plans."

Sophie waved a hand and huffed. "You can have them. I call impractical baby gifts."

Penelope beamed at Maddie. "I'll make sure you get all the practical things you actually need but aren't exciting."

Sophie laughed. "And I'll make sure the baby has the most kick-ass pair of shoes I can find."

Maddie threw her arms around Sophie and Penelope. "I love you guys!"

Penelope squeezed back, and ignored the loss and petty jealousy deep inside. They were thoughts and feelings she had no right to.

She'd put those in a box and focus on her friend.

Chapter Twenty-Five

Evan walked in and closed the bedroom door, ready to have it out with her. He'd made a mistake. Fine, he'd deal with that. Sooner rather than later.

Penelope sat on the bed, rubbing lotion over her long legs now brushed with color from the sun.

"I'm sorry. I should have told you first." He sat back in the winged-back chair in the bedroom. "I didn't think about it."

"It doesn't matter." Her voice was flat, her dark hair falling over one shoulder. "Congratulations, by the way. You've got it all worked out."

"You're angry."

"I'm fine." Clipped, hard words.

Aggravation was like an itch on the inside of his skin that he couldn't scratch, and he blew out a hard breath. "I'm not going to keep begging you to talk to me, Penelope."

Her head whipped up and she snapped, "Who asked you to? In fact, quit asking, it's annoying."

He shook his head. "How can I quit asking? Won't that give you the proof you're looking for? The evidence that I don't give a shit about you?"

He wanted to stop this, but she wouldn't goddamn talk

to him and it wasn't in his nature to keep coddling her like this. He'd tried that route and all it did was make everything worse, and he wasn't going to do it anymore.

She narrowed her eyes. "Everything is fine. Perfect."

"Whatever." He looked out the window at his sister's yard with a sick sense of resignation. "I should have told you first when I started talking to them, but I wanted to surprise you."

"Mission accomplished. Consider me surprised."

He folded his hands and tried to hold on to a rapidly fraying temper. "It was part of my plan to prove to you I could get my life together. I got the call when we got here and Maddie asked and, well, I don't know, I was excited and wanted to share the good news. I should have told you first."

She lifted the other leg and began massaging lotion into her skin. "You could have told me when we were talking on the bed."

"I could have."

"So why didn't you?"

His gaze slid away. "I don't know . . . it didn't seem like the right time."

She didn't look at him, but said in a voice so calm it sent a chill through him, "You keep talking about how you want to build this life with me, but it's just lip service. You don't want to build a life *with* me. You want to build a life for yourself and take me along for the ride when it suits you."

"That's unfair, Penelope." His tone a barely controlled force.

She finally looked at him, and when she did her eyes were cold and flat. "Is it? You planned a whole career, something so important to you, and didn't even think to discuss it."

"That is bullshit!" he yelled, so loud everyone in the

house must have heard. "Don't twist this to suit this story you keep trying to sell yourself in your head."

"I'm not, I'm stating a fact."

"You're stating a fear. And you're not any fucking better than I am."

"I'm not, I'm just more honest."

"What a load of shit. You're not honest. You're afraid. I screwed up. I admit it. I'm here, dealing with it, which is a hell of a lot more than I can say for you."

Her jaw worked as she looked out the window. "I can't do this right now."

"Tough. We're doing it."

She sat there in a white tank top and shorts, looking tanned and beautiful, and so remote he didn't know how to reach her. "I need to think. Figure things out."

"What do you need to figure out?"

She took a deep breath and exhaled slowly. "I can't keep looking for a way to keep you. I can't keep pretending your family belongs to me. It's wrong."

That last missing piece of the puzzle clicked into place and a cold, sick dread filled him. She was going to leave him, and there was absolutely nothing he could do about it. "My family does belong to you."

"But they don't. I only want them to."

He met her gaze and could see in her eyes she was already gone. He had two choices—he could either give up, or he could go down with a fight. Unfortunately, fighting would mean delivering some tough love, and that would hurt her. But he had nothing left to lose. He blew out a breath and hoped for the best. "Yeah, you're right."

Her expression twisted in a sad sort of satisfaction, and Evan wanted to go to her, but didn't. Because they had to be able to be real with each other. To stick it out through the tough battles.

Before she could say anything, he continued. "When

we were kids, way before there was anything between us, I overheard my parents talking about you. They were actually fighting about Maddie. My mom liked to compare Maddie and you, and Maddie felt she always came up short. I was young, and I only caught bits and pieces of the conversation, but I remember my dad saying the only reason you were so good was because your parents didn't pay attention to you. That you didn't rebel like Maddie because you didn't have the same love and safety she did."

Under the rosy glow of the sun, Penelope's face drained of color.

"We all kind of knew that you were always around because you didn't really have a family. That while your parents loved you, they didn't know what to do with you, and we had no problem being your surrogate family. That night my dad talked to me, that was exactly his point. He wanted you to go out there into the world and find yourself, without me or any of us blocking your way."

Jaw tight, she clasped her hands. "I see."

"No, you don't see. You didn't do any of that, did you?"

She shook her head and looked out the window. "No, the first thing I did was talk Shane into hiring me, even though he didn't want to."

"And you never got over me."

"No." She lowered her head, as though she was ashamed. "Maddie's pregnant. She's going to tell everyone tonight, so don't ruin her surprise."

The news hit him like he'd been sucker punched. She was dying inside, but she wouldn't let him in to help her. He got up and walked over to her, kneeling on the floor and taking her hands. "Pen, it's not crazy. What you're feeling. We didn't say it, but we both know that when you washed those pills down the drain, a part of us wanted to be caught."

Despite the sun her fingers were cold in his hands. She

tried to pull away but he wouldn't let her. "Can't you see, Evan? What better way to make sure you can't leave, than to tie you to me forever?"

"Then I'm just as guilty as you are. You don't think I want that tie?"

She blinked, shaking her head. "I don't know."

"Penelope, look at me." His voice sharp enough to have her lifting her head. "I have never, in all my life, forgotten to wear a condom. Even if she told me she was on fifteen kinds of birth control, I still wore one. I sure as hell don't think it was a coincidence that you were the one."

She twisted, trying to get up, but he wouldn't let go. "It doesn't make my actions any better. Or change the fact that I didn't take that pill for ulterior motives."

"Who cares?"

She snapped back. "I care."

"You're twisting that morning in your head to suit what you want to believe. We wanted the same thing, and we made the decision together. If I'd wanted you to take that pill, you would have, even though it upset you." She opened her mouth to speak, but he cut her off. "If *you* wanted to take that pill, I wouldn't have stopped you even though it upset me. And do you know why we want that tie so badly, Pen?"

She bit her lower lip.

"Because we wanted something that would make it impossible for us to be torn apart. What you don't seem to be able to get through your thick skull is that I want the same thing."

She stared out the window, looking lost and confused, so he went on.

"I know you want some sort of proof, but I don't know how to convince you of something so intangible. But you're not wrong for never wanting to leave us. Because deep down you're just a girl who loves her family and wants to be close to them. We're your family. Not by blood, and thank God for that, but because we love you and you're important to us. Because you make our lives better. You just have to believe. The way Maddie believes you can solve any problem. Or how Shane thinks you're the smartest person on the planet and is so possessive of you it actually kind of annoys me. And the way I believed the night my dad died that you were the only person on this earth who could make the pain go away. The way I believe you are the only woman I will ever love. You just have to believe in return."

Her expression twisted, and her eyes brightened as she stood in a sudden *whoosh*. "I—I need to think. Please, just leave me alone."

He rose from the floor, met her eyes and nodded. There was nothing else he could say. No words that would make her believe. "All right. I'm not going to chase after you, no matter how much I want to. If we get through this, I will knock down, drag out, never-go-to-bed-angry fight with you, but I can't do this for you, Penelope. I can't tackle you to the ground and force you to believe in me. In us. You know what I want, the rest is up to you."

For the first time in Penelope's life she put her needs before the needs of others. Her whole life she'd kept quiet, stayed in the background, never causing a scene or any drama, but today she couldn't do it. She could not put on a happy face for one more second, so she left. She just slipped from the house, leaving everything behind, and started walking. She didn't know where she was going, or why, but she walked down the drive, and when she got to the highway she picked a direction and kept on going.

And true to his word, Evan didn't follow her. Only this

time, instead of it being because he'd given up on her, it was because she'd given up on herself.

Evan was right.

Every single thing he'd said had been dead-on. She kept waiting for some magical moment that would convince her he loved her like he said. That all her worry would disappear, her heart would open, and she could depend on him. But it never came. No matter what he said, no matter what he did, she kept waiting. Waiting for the boy who had ignored her in the hallways while he walked hand in hand with his real girlfriend. The boy who had said those horrible things to her so long ago. She kept waiting for the guy he'd been all these years ago to show back up. The man she despised but still wanted, despite her best intentions.

That was the man she believed in.

But there'd been no trace of the frat boy persona that had taunted her all those years as she'd watched him from afar. Not so long ago she'd asked him to man up, and by God, he had listened to her. Now he was all man. Mature, emotionally astute, and so damn certain it made her want to scream. They'd switched roles. He had it all together and she was the mess.

She hated it. But the harder she tried to keep it together, to hold it all in, the more out of control she spun.

She was the rational one, not him. That's what she depended on. It defined her worldview. She was not emotional. She was the one who held it together and calmed everything down while everyone else freaked out. That's what made her comfortable. And that's where she knew she fit.

In her mind, even though she'd never allowed herself to realize it, she was the sidekick.

She was the bridesmaid.

The aunt.

The hand of the king.

The best friend.

The designated driver.

She was the glue that held all the pieces together, who disappeared into the background.

She *was not* the heroine.

He kept thrusting her into that role, but that's just not who she was.

She started to cry, and just kept on walking.

Chapter Twenty-Six

Evan sat with his brothers on Shane's back porch, trying his best to hold it together. He hadn't said anything to anyone, because he honestly didn't know what to say, and sure as hell didn't need one more person telling him how he screwed up.

All he could do was wait it out and hope Penelope came to her senses.

And even though everyone would blame him, deep down he knew he'd done the right thing. It about killed him, but he couldn't force her to believe. He'd fight to the ends of the earth for her, but it meant nothing if she kept waiting for him to bail.

All he wanted to do was drown his sorrows in a bottle of whiskey, but he'd stuck to iced tea, wanting a clear head if she came back to talk.

The back door banged open and Maddie flew out, her red hair flying, her cheeks flushed. When she saw him she came to a crashing halt and pointed at him. "What did you do?"

James and Shane both shifted their attention to him, their expressions filled with questions.

Well, so much for keeping this quiet.

He gave his sister a level stare. "I didn't do anything."

"Then where is Penelope?" Maddie demanded, her voice loud.

For one sickening moment Evan thought she'd somehow packed up and left for good, but that was impossible. He'd made sure he'd taken the keys. If she left, she'd be forced to confront him. He dragged a hand through his hair. "I don't know, Mads."

"Did you hurt her? I swear to God, Evan, if you hurt her I will tear you limb from limb," Maddie yelled.

Cecilia came out from the house, a frown on her face. "What's going on?"

Shane shook his head and turned to Evan.

Evan held his breath, waiting for the accusations to start, and felt that old stirring of defensiveness.

Maddie's eyes welled with tears. "Where is Penelope? She wouldn't just leave. That's not like her at all. What did you do to her?"

Evan opened his mouth to speak but Shane said, "Geez, Maddie, give the guy a chance to explain before you jump all over him."

Shane coming to his defense startled him so much he lost track of what he was going to say.

Maddie planted her hands on her hips. "Did you cheat on her?"

Anger spiked hot in his blood. "Christ, Maddie, of course I didn't cheat on her."

Shane's brow furrowed. "He wouldn't do that."

James's gaze narrowed behind his glasses at their baby sister, who was clearly in a temper. "You're overreacting."

The support disoriented him, throwing him off his game. He'd been prepared to stand alone, but here his brothers appeared to be on his side.

"I am not!" Maddie screamed. "I want to know what my

brother did to my best friend. I knew this was a mistake. I should have stopped you the night of the benefit."

Evan blew out a breath and tried to remember that his sister was pregnant, and that this outburst was probably hormone-related. "If you wanted to stop Penelope from falling into my evil clutches, you'd have to go back a lot longer than the benefit."

"Don't be logical with me!" She stomped her foot.

Mitch came into the porch, followed by Sophie. He gave his wife a wary glance. "Maddie, what are you doing?"

"Trying to find out where Penelope went," she said with a little sniff.

Mitch sighed. "I told you this was none of your business."

"You stay out of it." She whirled on him. "You . . . you . . . jerk. You don't know anything about it."

Mitch pinched the bridge of his nose. "I know enough to know the guy is head over heels and would probably cut off his own limbs before he'd hurt her."

"You don't know that," Maddie said. She turned to Evan. "I love you, but you have a horrible track record."

"Madeline, that's enough," Mitch said. "You're not even giving him a chance to talk."

Sophie glanced at Evan and then bit her lip. "I've got to side with Mitch here. It's pretty obvious he loves her."

Maddie's brow furrowed. "Why do you think that?"

Sophie waved a hand over in Evan's direction. "Because it's written all over him. Hell, Maddie, he can barely take his eyes off her. You're just not paying attention."

Maddie frowned and turned to him. "Then where is she?"

"I don't know," Evan admitted. "Yes, she's upset, but I can't help her, Maddie, even though I want to."

"What does that mean?" Maddie hugged herself and Mitch came behind her and gathered her up.

All eyes turned to Evan and he sighed. "You do know this is none of your business."

They all just stared at him.

This was family. They meddled and fought, but in the end they stood by each other.

He shrugged and looked away. "Unfortunately, Maddie isn't the only one who doesn't believe. And no matter how hard I try, I can't convince her otherwise. You know how she is. She wants some sort of proof and I don't know how to give her evidence of something intangible."

"You can't," Cecilia said, coming up and patting him on the shoulder before going to Shane.

"I know that." He gazed out into the yard. "She has to believe on her own. I can't do it for her. She wanted to be by herself, and I let her go, not because I don't love her, but because I do."

The tension seemed to seep from Maddie and she said, "I'm sorry."

"Me too." His chest squeezed. "If you have another suggestion, I'm open, but right now she's determined to break away from me, and honestly, I don't know what else to do. Unfortunately, I tend to screw up grand gestures, so I'm out of ideas."

James looked down at his phone and said, "She's at Sam's."

Evan frowned. How had she made her way to Gracie's brother's dive bar? She had to have walked at least five miles on the highway. He clenched his glass of iced tea. "His bar?"

James nodded and held up his phone. "Gracie texted."

He moved to stand. "I'll go get her."

Sophie held up a hand. "Let me. That girl needs some tough love and you Donovans are way too soft on her. I'll get her."

Maddie pulled from Mitch's arms. "I'll come too."

Sophie shook her head. "No, let me talk to her." She turned to Evan. "Keep the faith. I'll bring her back."

Evan could only hope. He'd always thought football was the one thing he couldn't live without, but he knew now that was wrong. It was Penelope.

Penelope watched with deep suspicion as Sam poured her a shot from a bottle of Scotch. She wrinkled her nose. "I don't like Scotch."

Sam smiled. His blue eyes, which matched his sister's, twinkled. "Trust me. I keep this on hand for you Donovans."

She scowled. "Don't you have any champagne?"

He laughed. "Honey, this is Revival."

"So, no?" Now that she'd decided to give herself permission to give in to her emotions, she was in full disgruntled mode.

"No."

Penelope took the glass. "I'm not a Donovan."

Sam shrugged. "You couldn't tell it by me."

She eyed the brown liquid, already knowing she wouldn't like it, but since Sam insisted, she picked it up and downed it in one fast gulp. It burned going down and hit her stomach at warp speed, sending a pleasant warmth through her belly. She coughed. "That's horrible."

Sam held up the bottle. "Another?"

She nodded.

He poured.

She downed another.

He filled the glass again. "You want to talk about it?"

"I'm not much of a talker."

Sam put the bottle down on the bar and rested his hands on the counter. "So, do you want to talk about it?"

Between the sun and her empty stomach, the alcohol

went straight to her head. She gave Sam a long once-over. Blond, with high cheekbones, a strong jaw, and a lean, long body, the man was quite nice to look at. She put her chin on her hand. "You're really good-looking."

He grinned. "You're evading."

"Where's your girlfriend?"

"Where's your boyfriend?" Sam shot back.

At the thought of Evan her heart gave a little lurch and she picked up the glass and downed the shot. She didn't want to think about her own stupid problems. She needed another life to focus on and it might as well be Sam's. There wasn't anyone else around. "Do you like anyone?"

Sam chuckled and poured her another shot. "Why? You want to pass her a note for me?"

Penelope waved a hand between the two of them. "We never talk. I think we should."

He scrubbed a hand over his stubbled jaw. "See, that's the problem with us. We both want to listen, kind of makes for a hard conversation."

Her head swam and she nodded with utter seriousness. "That's true. I leave the drama to *them*." She swept a hand toward the door. "They like it and they're so much better at it than I am."

Sam narrowed his gaze. "Makes sense."

She pointed to her chest. "I'm the logical one, you know."

"I've heard," he said, his voice full of amusement.

"You must know what I mean, you grew up with Gracie. Now there's a woman who knows how to cause a scene."

Sam held up the bottle. "Should I give you another one?"

"Yes, please." Penelope tilted her head. "Do you ever get tired of it?"

"Of letting them take center stage?"

She nodded, somehow not surprised Sam knew exactly

what she was talking about. She'd heard a rumor from Cecilia once that he had some sort of sixth sense. Ridiculous, really, but right now she believed it.

See, she could believe in ESP, so why couldn't she believe in Evan?

He shrugged. "Not particularly. I've never been one who likes attention. And too much drama grates on my nerves. But more important, somebody has to be the calm one, and I like to be that person."

Penelope sipped the drink this time, and somewhere along the way, it had switched from horrible to delicious. "James used to be on our side, but Gracie converted him."

Sam's lips quirked in the beginnings of a smile. "Oh, I don't know about that. He supports her, and understands her, and he sure as hell loves her, and I'd never tell anyone this but—" He cut off, grimacing and darting a quick glance around the bar as though someone might be lurking in the shadows.

Penelope looked around too, then leaned in. She liked secrets. As long as they weren't hers.

He leaned in conspiratorially. "Gracie would kill me if she ever heard me say this, but I know you're the kind of person who keeps her mouth shut."

With vigor, she nodded, and her head about floated off her body. "I am."

"James indulges her because he understands what she needs, but make no mistake, he has her firmly under control, and he's the only person I know who settles my sister."

Penelope nibbled on her bottom lip. "I guess I never thought of it like that."

"People like them, they need people like us. It's a balance."

"But what do we get in return?"

"Don't you know?"

Did she? Her mind was fuzzy, but somewhere the answer

to that question niggled in the corners of her brain, but it wouldn't quite crystallize. She shook her head.

He grabbed a towel and started wiping down the bar. "You can't think of one thing you get from Evan?"

Evan. She sighed. "I've been in love with him since I was six years old. I worshipped him, you know? He was everything a boy should be, totally out of my reach."

"Apparently not that far, from what I understand."

She shook her head. "But that's just the thing, I've always been in the background and Evan's not a background kind of guy. We don't match. He's supposed to be with someone fantastic and otherworldly."

Sam smiled. "Oh, I don't know. I think he's ended up with someone pretty fantastic."

Penelope rolled her eyes. "Okay, dad. Forget the pep talk, you know what I mean. Guys like Evan don't end up with the librarian."

He shrugged. "Apparently they do."

"Does this sound totally stupid?" Her brain wasn't functioning properly.

"Nope, not at all."

"It feels stupid. Cowardly. I've wanted him for almost my whole life, but I've always seen him as some impossible, unrealistic desire, and now I'm scared. I tell myself I want to believe him, seize the day and all that nonsense, but that's just not in my nature."

Sam nodded as though all this made perfect sense, and she was glad it did to him because it was a muddled mess to her. He threw the towel back onto the workspace below the bar. "You're a businesswoman; in the end, it all comes down to risk versus reward, doesn't it?"

"True."

"So, ask yourself the question. Is Evan worth it? Does the reward outweigh the risk?"

"Everything inside me says yes, but what if he doesn't love me enough?"

"Oh, I'd say he loves you more than enough."

"How do you know?" Her heart started to pound.

"I just do."

Before she could think anymore, the door blew open and Penelope whipped around, hoping it was Evan, only to be crushed with disappointment to find Sophie standing there.

"You're not Evan," she said, then burst into tears.

Sophie sighed and walked over and gathered Penelope up in her arms. "At least I know you're not entirely an idiot."

"Not entirely," she wailed. She tried to pull herself together but couldn't. She was just all logic-ed out.

Sophie patted her on the back. "There, there. I've been waiting for this for years. So this is what we're going to do. We're going to enjoy our first breakdown over a boy, then you're going to pick yourself up, stop being an idiot, and go make up with that poor man you're torturing. I mean, geez, Penelope, I always knew you were a ballbuster, but this is going too far."

The Scotch turned on her, swinging her emotions all over the place. Sobbing, Penelope hiccupped. "H-he's t-t-tortured?"

Sophie rolled her eyes. "Of course he is, he loves you. I mean, he said you didn't believe him, so tell me, what's it going to take to talk some sense into you? Do I need to slap you?"

Sam rubbed his jaw. "That could get interesting."

Penelope laughed, then burst into tears again.

"See, this is what you get when you don't talk to anyone," Sophie said, handing her a napkin. "You get all sorts of fucked-up thoughts and nobody knows you've gone straight off the deep end into crazy, so they can't talk you out of them."

"I'm supposed to be immune," Penelope wailed, wobbled and fell off the bar stool, landing in a heap on the floor.

Sophie sighed down at her, shaking her head. "When they fall, they fall hard."

Sam laughed, leaning over the bar. "You need help there?"

"I've got her." Sophie grabbed Penelope's arm and yanked her up from the floor. "Up you go."

Penelope stumbled, then held out her hands. "I'm okay."

Sophie cocked a brow at Sam. "How much did you give her?"

Sam eyed Penelope. "I thought she needed a good meltdown."

"Well done," Sophie said, helping Penelope back onto the stool. She turned to Sam. "Would you mind excusing us for a moment? I think we need some girl time that will need to be vaulted forever."

Sam grinned. "Sure. I have some paperwork to do, just give me a call if anyone wanders in."

"Deal."

Sam took his leave and Sophie glared at her. "All right, let's hear it. What happened? 'Cause you've been dodging me for weeks, and that's never a good sign. So spill, and don't leave anything out."

Penelope meant to regain some composure but she cried out, "I'm not pregnant."

Sophie blinked before her eyes went wide with shock. "Okay, honey, you're going to have to start this story before that."

And Penelope did. In between sobbing, hiccups, blowing

her nose, and about five hundred tissues, she told Sophie every single detail of her Evan saga.

Every. Single. Detail.

The dirty parts. The sad parts. The humiliating parts. And every other part in between.

She spilled all her secrets, leaving no stone unturned.

Through it all Sophie nodded, sighed, oohed and aahed, and even shed a few tears of her own when Penelope told her about that night she'd lost her virginity.

They talked for three hours. People came and left. Sam wandered in and out, an unobtrusive shadow who took care of their every need without asking.

When she was through, Sophie nodded and said, "Okay, first things first. One, from this day forward you are not allowed to keep secrets like this. You've been carrying this around for a million years and if I'd known I would have set you straight a long time ago. Two, if you want the guy's babies, have them. He's clearly amenable. Three, what is your problem? Are you going to throw away the love of a lifetime because of some stupid issues you have?"

Penelope blinked, her head snapping back.

"I'm going to tell you something and I trust you will never repeat it. But do you honestly think you were the only friend of Maddie's that had a crush on Evan Donovan?"

"Ummm . . ." The alcohol had made her a bit dim-witted. "Yes?"

Sophie waved a hand. "Please. Every single girl who ever went over to Maddie's house had a crush on him, including me. But you're the only one he ever touched."

"You don't like Evan."

"Well, sure, not now, but as a boy-crazed teenager I did. Only he never gave me the time of day. He never paid attention to me like he did to you."

"Evan never paid attention to me. Everyone knows that."

Sophie shook her head. "You have so much to learn

about men. Um, yes, he did. He used to look at you all the time. And pull your ponytail. And tease you. I was soooo jealous. If I had any idea he was taking you down to the in- famous Donovan basement and violating you, well, we probably wouldn't be friends today."

"I didn't know."

Sophie let out a screech. "Why do you think Kim Rossi hated you so much?"

"I didn't know she hated me until Evan told me."

"I'm ninety percent sure she was actively plotting your murder."

Penelope wiped the tears away. "I don't know why this matters."

"I'm trying to give you that proof you're looking for. Evan has *always* had a thing for you. He's never treated you the way he treated other women. And it's so obvious after watching him that he loves you, Pen. I'd kill for a guy to look at me that way."

Penelope's breath caught. "What way?"

Sophie sighed, her expression softening. "Like you're everything he never knew he always wanted. Like he hasn't eaten in a month and you're a medium-rare steak. Like his whole world is better because you're in it."

"Evan looks at me that way?"

"Yes!" Sophie smiled. "You're just too busy thinking about spreadsheets to pay attention."

Sophie was right, she was so busy trying not to pay at- tention to Evan for fear someone would guess her deepest secret, that she never got to witness what was so clear to her friend. Penelope reached out and squeezed her friend's hand. "Thank you."

"You're welcome."

Penelope ran her finger over the ridge of her glass. "You really think I should have his babies?"

Sophie laughed. "I really do."

The heavy weight that had been plaguing her for weeks lifted and her heart expanded and her eyes welled with tears. And just like that, after all the fight and struggle, she gave up the ghost of the past, that fateful night so long ago when they were just kids and too stupid to know what they meant to each other. She loved Evan and he loved her. She deserved that life with him, and was brave enough to take it.

She was ready.

Chapter Twenty-Seven

"Evan." A soft whisper through his restless sleep. He shot awake, blinking into the darkness. He had no idea when he'd drifted off, but he'd felt like he'd been waiting for an eternity.

Penelope stood over the bed, the moonlight streaming over her, casting her dark hair in its eerie glow.

"You came back," he said, his voice hoarse with sleep.

She nodded. "I'm ready to believe."

He rolled over on his back. "You are?"

She climbed on top of him, straddling him. "I love you so much."

Relief, swift and powerful, swept through him. He placed his palms on her bare skin, resisting the urge to turn her over and just drive into her. "I love you too, Penelope."

She leaned down, that hair that had been driving him crazy for as long as he could remember forming a curtain around his face. "I'm sorry, I was wrong. I've been running scared and I can only promise I'll make it up to you."

"I don't blame you. You're right—" She cut him off by brushing a kiss over his lips. She tasted like alcohol and her. "Are you drunk?"

"Not as much as I was. But enough to see how stupid I

was being." Her voice was soft in the darkness. "I want you to know, it wasn't you. It was just hard for me to believe I landed the boy of my dreams. It was doubt in myself, not you."

He trailed a path down her cheeks. "You're the girl of my dreams too, you know?"

"I do," she said, and he didn't catch even a hint of doubt in her eyes.

"You believe?"

"I do."

There was a new love and trust shining in her eyes and finally, after all these years, he relaxed. He was back where he'd been meant to be all along.

She leaned down. "From this day forward, the past stays where it belongs, in the past. You're absolved of the sins committed by a seventeen-year-old boy who had lost his father. I should have forgiven you a long time ago."

"I'm still sorry I hurt you."

She scraped her teeth over his jaw, then sat up and swept off her tee and dropped it to the floor. "I'm sorry I hurt you too." She leaned down and kissed him, her mouth hot and hungry on his.

He growled and flipped her over. "I need you so much, Penelope."

"I need you too." She lifted her hips and he slid her shorts and panties down her legs. She pulled him back down and kissed him like she was starving. "I just want you."

He'd had this plan in his head, of how he'd woo and convince her, how he'd make it all up to her, but nothing between them happened the right way. And the truth was he needed to secure their future right now. He released her mouth. "Will you marry me?"

Her questing hands stilled. "You want to marry me?"

"I'd marry you right this second if it was legally possible. If I didn't think you secretly wanted a big wedding, I'd whisk you off to Vegas and marry you in the first chapel we happened across."

A smile flirted over her lips. "Why do you think I want a big wedding?"

He laughed. "Because I know you. And I know there's this part of you that wants to have all eyes on you, even if it's only temporary."

Her expression turned curious. "Why would you think that?"

He chuckled. "You don't think I've noticed how hot you get at the idea of being watched?"

She burst out laughing and covered her eyes. "You're the worst."

He pinched her. "I believe we have a question on the table."

"Yes, I will marry you." She pulled him close.

"We'll get a ring as soon as we get back to Chicago."

"All right." She gave him the most seductive, most satisfied grin he'd ever seen. "I knew it."

"Knew what?"

"The first time I laid eyes on you, I knew I was going to marry you."

He laughed. "You were six."

"I know." She clutched at his back, her nails raking down his skin. "Take me."

He rocked against her. "How do you want it?"

She moaned and then opened her eyes to meet his gaze. "Mark me."

He'd been marking her since that first time so many years ago, and he had no intention of stopping now. "Always."

"Make me yours."

He slid a hand around her neck and gripped her throat. "You are mine. You always have been and you always will be."

She pressed her hips into his. "And don't you ever forget it."

"Not in a million years."

Penelope walked through the little local bar, Lucky's, on her way from the restroom to Evan, nodding and stopping to say hello to the people she recognized. It was Evan's reunion, but she ended up knowing more people than she realized.

It had only been a month since that night in Revival, but things were moving at lightning speed. Evan had put his condo up for sale, had started his job, and couldn't be happier with his new career choice.

It turned out Evan's fears were unfounded and he'd taken to coaching like a duck to water. The job filled him with a renewed purpose, and with the gleam in his eyes when he watched game tapes, she didn't doubt that he'd be a head coach someday. Hopefully here in Chicago, but they'd determined that night in Revival that they would do everything together, no matter what, and they'd cross that bridge when they came to it.

Everyone was thrilled they were getting married, and Maddie tried to convince Evan to wait until after she had the baby, but Evan said he'd been waiting for fifteen years, and he refused to wait any longer.

He'd given Penelope six months to plan the wedding, which wasn't as difficult as she'd thought once she started throwing Evan's name around. Turns out being a future NFL wife had some perks, and Penelope wasn't above using them to her advantage.

They'd had a long talk about their pregnancy scare and she'd confessed all her mixed-up emotions about that time. And even though kids were high on the list, they decided after all the time they'd spent apart, they wanted to be married awhile before they tried.

It felt right.

So here she was, at Evan's reunion, rocking the red dress she wore, a slinky number courtesy of Sophie. She looked damn good, if she did say so herself. Of course Evan had taken one look at her, started shaking his head, and ordered her to change.

She refused.

They fought. They fucked. She won.

As she made her way through the room she noticed the eyes of the men on her, skimming over her body in appreciation, only to stall when they saw her engagement ring, and she couldn't help her tiny smile.

The ring had been a compromise. She'd picked the setting, a diamond infinity band, but Evan picked the stone—and what a stone it was. It was huge, and so brilliant she was in danger of blinding people, as her friends frequently complained. Shane had taken one look at it and grinned at his brother. "I guess you didn't want to take any chances."

Evan had winked at her. "Nope."

She bemoaned the size and Evan, God bless him, pretended to believe her. He was even kind enough not to mention all the times he caught her gazing at it with astonished awe.

She'd never been one for flash, and she gave pretense to the modesty she was known for, but honestly, it was the most kick-ass ring ever.

She spotted Evan talking to a short, curvy woman with long, curly hair, and even from the back, Penelope knew who it was immediately.

The infamous Kim Rossi.

Evan's head lifted as though he sensed Penelope on the air and he smiled in that way he reserved just for her.

She squared her shoulders and walked over to them.

Kim turned, her eyes going wide at the sight of Penelope.

As she sidled up to Evan, she prepared herself for the woman to say something scathing, but to her surprise the woman grinned and pointed at Evan. "For the love of God, man, will you *finally* admit it?"

Evan's arm slid around Penelope and he shrugged, chagrined. "All right, I admit it."

Penelope looked back and forth between them. "Admit what?"

Kim held out her hand and offered Penelope a warm smile. "Hi, I'm Kim Taldeski. I don't think we ever met, but I did hate you from afar."

Penelope laughed and shook the other woman's hand. "Penelope Watkins, and yes, I remember you. I believe the animosity may have been mutual."

A man walked over to them, a beefy, teddy bear of a guy who looked at Kim like she hung the moon. She grabbed his arm and beamed at him. "This is my husband, Hal."

They all exchanged greetings and Kim pointed at Evan and Penelope. "Evan was my high school boyfriend, but he was secretly in love with Penelope, so, you know, it didn't really work out that well."

Evan chuckled and squeezed Penelope's waist. "Sorry about that. Unfortunately, I'm guilty as charged."

Kim waved. "Please, we were kids. Besides, you dumping me was the best thing that ever happened to me."

Hal and Kim looked at each other and their love was a palpable thing. Hal shrugged. "I met her the summer after senior year and haven't let her out of my sight since."

Evan nodded. "Sounds like a smart man."

Kim smiled at Penelope. "So, Evan tells me congratulations are in order."

It was Penelope's turn to beam. "Yes, thank you."

Kim picked up Penelope's hand. "Damn, girl, now that's a ring."

Penelope's cheeks heated, caught between embarrassment and the urge to gush over its sheer awesomeness. "Thanks. He picked it out."

Evan rubbed a hand over her back. "And she pretends it annoys her."

"Nice," Hal said, clearly not really all that interested. He turned to Evan. "So I heard you took a job with the Bears."

Evan nodded. "As the wide receiver coach."

"What do you think their chances are this year?"

And then they were off, talking football, Super Bowls, passing patterns, and a bunch of other things that Penelope didn't know about but made Evan extremely happy.

Kim ginned at her. "Men and their football."

"Isn't that the truth."

Kim looked her up and down, but the maliciousness of the past was gone and there was nothing but friendly curiosity shining in Kim's pretty face. "You're even more beautiful than I remembered."

"Thank you, you too," Penelope said, and meant it. Kim had a kind of warmth that had eluded her in high school.

The other woman laughed and waved her away. "Oh please, you always were a sweetie. There's not a woman in the room who can hold a candle to you. Evan did always have great taste in women."

Penelope grinned, and touched the other woman's arm. "I agree."

Kim tucked a lock of hair behind her ear. "So I have to apologize about something. You remember that time when your clothes were stolen from the locker room and you had to wear your gym uniform the rest of the day? That was me. And, well, I might have messed with you some other ways too."

Penelope smiled. "Well, in fairness, I was after your boyfriend."

Kim shook her head. "True, but he was yours to take. I knew, you know. Sure, I hated you for it, but I knew it was you all along, and I'm not the least bit surprised you're getting married."

Penelope was over the past and just wanted to leave it where it belonged and focus on the future. "It doesn't matter anymore. Let's just put the past behind us."

"Deal."

Penelope smiled warmly, finding she quite liked the adult version of Kim Rossi. "Would you and Hal like to come over for dinner next week?"

"That would be fun. I'll need a sitter for the kids, but we'd love to." Kim put a hand on Penelope's arm. "And see, everything worked out just the way it was supposed to."

Penelope looked over at Evan, his face animated as he talked about the game he loved. The game that had both pulled them apart and pushed them back together again. "Yeah, I think it did."

He caught her watching him and immediately turned back to her, sliding his arm around her waist. "Everything okay?"

"Everything is perfect." And it was. She had her dream boy. But even better, she had her dream man. Her first and last love. After all this time, they'd come full circle and were as good as new.